EAGLE'S GUARD

For the Bier Clan

Let the adventure begin!

Lindsey

EAGLE'S GUARD

Book 1 of the Eagle Rider Saga

LINDSEY
STIRLING

Cookies and Oxygen
PUBLISHING

Text copyright © 2017 Lindsey Stirling

Illustrations copyright © 2017 Iain Stirling

Lindsey Stirling asserts the moral right to be identified as the author of this work.

First published as an ebook by
Cookies and Oxygen Publishing in 2017

This paperback edition published in Great Britain by
Lindsey Stirling and Cookies and Oxygen Publishing in 2017

ISBN 978-1-912403-01-1 (Paperback Edition)
ISBN 978-1-912403-00-4 (ebook Edition)

Printed and bound in the UK by Book Printer

Cover design by Iain Stirling

Cookies and Oxygen Publishing
www.cookiesandoxygen.co.uk

For Iain, fellow creator,
And for Mum and Dad

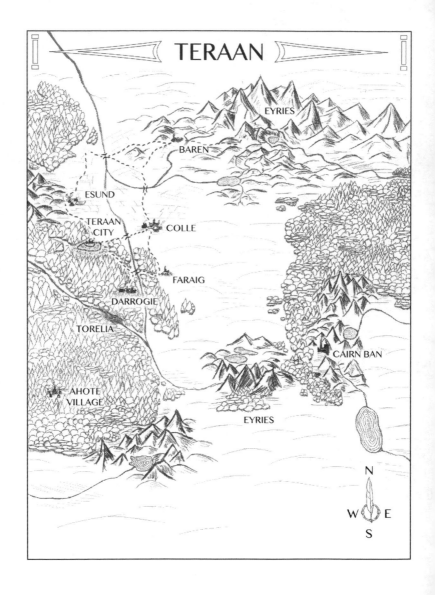

RUNES

Ailm (Elm) the seer, insight, the changeling

Beith (Silver Birch) the healer

Coll (Hazel) wisdom

Dair (Oak) strength

Eadha (Aspen) the wind, patience, the river

Fearn (Alder) the shield, the warrior, secrecy

Gort (Ivy) the troth, the faithful, the binder

Uath (Hawthorn) dread

Iogh (Yew) longevity, the resilient

Luis (Rowan) the protector

Muin (Vine) the listener

Nuin (Ash) the spear

Onn (Gorse) the bond, the joiner, the craftsman

Peith (Mountain Birch) the thunderbolt, the swift

Ruis (Elder) music, the dancer

Suil (Willow) the prophet, the woeful, water

Teine (Pine) fire

Ur (Heather) the renewer

1. A Burning Building

With his fingertips, Aiden sketched a shape in the air. Lines of light appeared in the wake of his fingers and remained shimmering before him, a circle with a line struck through it. It was the magical rune of Ailm, the seer. He enclosed the rune between finger and thumb and looked through. It focused his gaze and the distant Silver Eagle jumped into view. The edge of each feather, the curve of its talons and the sharpness of its beak became clear. Silver feathers rippled in the wind, wings spread wide, casting a shadow across the sun.

Aiden reached up, almost forgetting the great distance. As if it saw him the Silver Eagle swooped low, its eyes a flash of light. A Rider sat upon its back. Aiden squinted yet saw nothing but the silhouette of a person. The Eagle turned and gave an echoing call. Aiden's heart thumped with a sudden certainty. The Eagle wanted *him* to go with it. He was *meant* to go with it.

He stepped to follow but something held him. The Eagle flew further away and he tried to twist free. There was a quiet thump as his blanket slid to the ground and he curled his toes against the cold. He squeezed his eyes shut, but it was too late. Pale light shone through his eyelids and his mother's soft humming drifted up through the floorboards. He sat up, rubbing his face. A dull ache filled his chest, where moments before it had barely contained the wild beating of his heart. He shook his head and threw the rest of his blanket aside, walking quickly to the window.

Aiden opened the shutters with a creak, letting grey light seep into the room. He lifted a foot onto the windowsill and balanced there, one hand resting gently against the wooden frame above. His younger brother Andor shifted in his bed but did not wake. Aiden stood, ducking his head out of the window so that his face was almost pressed flat against the outside wall. Then he jumped, fingers catching the cool slates of the roof, toes finding familiar grooves in the stonework. He lifted himself onto the roof.

Aiden shivered in the dawn air as he scrambled over the slates. After a short way he laid himself down, leaning his head back. He wished he was back in his dream.

A bird wheeled above him and Aiden reached out a hand to sketch Ailm, the seer, in the air. Light shimmered behind his fingers, just as it had in his dream. He caught the rune in his hand and looked through, focusing on the bird. Black raven's wings flapped back at him. Aiden sighed. The Silver Eagle, and its Rider, remained nothing but a dream.

Aiden let the rune fade and sat up. It seemed that no matter how much he wanted it, there was no escaping the real world. He looked out across Teraan City. Shadows fled the rising sun, racing across cobbled streets to hide in the alleyways or under the boughs of trees. Dew glistened in the gardens and dampened the earthen path that wound its way behind the houses.

The rhythmic thud of footsteps echoed along the street, followed by a patrol of the King's soldiers on their dawn rounds. Aiden leaned forward watching as they passed, heads held high in their gleaming leather armour, the King's crest, the winged crown encircling a tree, etched into their round shields. Black cloaks billowed out behind them, tiny runes for strength and protection sewn in silver thread along the edges of the cloth. Some of the cloaks were no doubt his father's handiwork.

And would one day be his. Aiden slumped back onto the roof. Just a few months more and he would no longer be an apprentice but a cloakmaker. He tried to tell himself that there was nothing wrong with being a cloakmaker, but he could not shake the dream of the Silver Eagle. He wanted more.

Across the City, a sea of slate roofs spread before him, broken up by the jagged tops of trees and the cobbled canyons of streets. At its heart stood the tall stone buildings of the Restricted Zone and behind them a glimpse of the pink sandstone of the Palace. Aiden imagined an Eagle Rider, one of the great guardians of Teraan, taking flight from one of those turrets, soaring across the horizon to battle with a wild magic creature in a whirlwind of runes. His gaze swept with it across the City, past the great outer Wall and the houses beyond, to where the fringes of the City were consumed by the ever-whispering branches of the deep forest.

A lightness grew in his chest. What adventures awaited him out there? But Aiden stopped himself. His father was waiting for him.

Slowly, Aiden shuffled across the roof and sank to his stomach, lowering his feet and dropping down to the wooden ledge of his windowsill. He slipped inside the room and grimaced. Andor was gone and if his little brother was down before him then his father was certainly not going to be happy. Aiden threw on a change of clothes and took the stairs to the kitchen. The warm smell of oats filled the air and his mother, Kari, looked up from stirring the pot, her cheeks rosy in the glow of the fire. Aiden grabbed a few mouthfuls as he sped past, his mother raising her eyebrows at him.

Aiden slipped through the door into the workshop. Light shone in through the big window at the back and danced across the myriad of colours of cloaks and cloth hanging along the walls. The shop at the front of the room was empty, but behind the big wooden counter Aiden's father, Brokk, stood at one of the smaller worktops.

A cloak surrounded by spools of thread and frayed offcuts covered the surface before him and his nimble hands pushed a needle and thread through the earthy-red material. Andor leaned in next to him, his green eyes fixed on their father's work.

"Sometimes Aiden," said his father, not lifting his head, "it amazes me that your twelve year old brother still makes it down to work before you. And you're the one who's almost finished his apprenticeship."

"I'm sorry," said Aiden, stepping forward to stand by the worktop. "It was only a few minutes."

"I'm not annoyed *because* you are late," said Brokk, tying off his thread before looking up. "I'm annoyed at *why* you are late."

Aiden set his mouth in a hard line and said nothing. Why today?

"You spend too much time up on that roof," said Brokk. "You'll be eighteen soon. How can I trust you to be your own man and take on more work in the shop, when I can't even trust you to get through a simple day's work without being distracted by magic?"

"Why do the runes have to be a distraction?" said Aiden. "We use them in our work, don't we?"

Brokk drew in a slow, careful breath as he reached for a new spool. "Yes. We sew runes of thread into cloaks to give added strength or protection, but what you do is entirely different. You draw runes with light in the air. You're calling directly upon the wild magic when you do that. That's dangerous Aiden. Wizards train for years before mastering the art. If you got it wrong there's no knowing what might happen to you. I don't want you to wake up blind one morning… or worse."

Aiden shook his head, his jaw tight. "That's not how it works Dad. Using the runes *makes* it safe. They harness the wild magic so that it *can't* go wrong."

Brokk lifted his head. "I'm just worried you won't know where the line between the two is. You can't deny that magic has got you in trouble more than once in the past."

Aiden looked down. Maybe it had, but not for a long time. "I'll be careful, alright Dad? And I won't let it get in the way of work."

Brokk folded his arms, his brow furrowed. With a slow shake of his head his expression softened. He reached out an arm to pat Aiden on the shoulder. "Let's put it behind us son. Now come, I have a job for you."

Aiden followed his father over to the other workbench where jars of coloured powders were stacked neatly in rows. He sat heavily on the stool and avoided looking at his father as he set him the task of mixing dyes for a hunting cloak. The fine art of getting the colours just right, so that the wearer would be almost impossible to see in the woods, was one of the few skills Aiden had yet to learn before his apprenticeship was over. Yet why bother when a simple rune, drawn correctly with the right thought behind it, could do all that and more? Aiden clenched his fists, releasing them slowly. He would learn because that was what was expected of him, but he wished that just once his father would recognise his talent with the runes and let him actually use it.

Brokk left the brothers to their work, moving to the front of the shop to prop open the door. He stayed there, taking a seat on the far side of the big counter that split the room, a complex piece of sewing in his hands. Aiden dragged his eyes back to the dyes in front of him and tapped tiny amounts of the powders into a small bowl in front of him. He absently moved a spoon around the mixture tracing the shapes of feathers, his mind drifting back to the slow swoop of the Silver Eagle.

"When are you going to teach me another rune?" Andor whispered.

Aiden sat up straighter and glanced over at their father, but his greying head did not lift from his sewing.

"Didn't you hear Dad?" Aiden whispered back. "If he's not happy about me using runes, he'll be even less happy about me teaching you."

"But you can't stop now," said Andor, reaching across the workbench towards him. "You've only taught me three. There's eighteen. And Dad's not going to teach me any for work till I'm older."

Aiden frowned at Andor and then glanced away. His brother reminded him too much of himself, and not just in appearance. His curiosity would be the ruin of him. "Maybe another day," said Aiden.

Andor frowned. "When you were my age you'd already learnt all eighteen. Why do I have to wait?"

Aiden folded his arms. "If you want to teach yourself like I did, then feel free."

Silence fell between them and their mother's humming drifted through from the kitchen. Andor scowled, drawing back to his own worktop. Aiden watched him for a minute, trying not to smile at the deepening furrow between his brother's green eyes. Maybe Andor would be different. Maybe he had more control over his curiosity. After all, if their places had been reversed, Aiden would not have been sulking about having to wait to learn, he would have been teaching himself. And he had, so that by the time he was nine he knew all the runes and by the time he was twelve he could use them all well.

Aiden turned back to his bench, trying to block out everything but the dyes in front of him. What was he trying to accomplish? Camouflage. Nothing more, nothing less. He added water to his first mixing, watching the colours run together into a muddy brown. It did not look quite right, but he took a scrap of cloth and dunked it in anyway. He wrung it out and laid it to dry. What did it need? Ailm, the changeling, his mind whispered. Or Onn, the craftsman.

He pushed the thoughts away. It needed more green.

For the next few hours Aiden tried all sorts of combinations and created more variations of brown than he thought possible. But he could not get it right. And it did not help that silver tipped feathers tinged the edge of his vision.

Footsteps padded across the floor. "Not quite Aiden," came his father's voice.

Aiden looked up, but Brokk was already speaking to Andor. One of the travelling markets was in town. It did not surprise Aiden that his brother was going and not him. For a moment he felt a stab of regret. Then the tension in his shoulders began to ease. With his father gone he could take a relaxed lunch break and get his head straight. Maybe then the afternoon would go better.

The front door swung closed behind Brokk and Andor with a quiet thud. Aiden paused, then was on his feet, grabbing some food, up the stairs to the window ledge and climbing back up to the roof.

Aiden slumped down onto the slate roof and breathed in the warm pine-scented air. The patter of footsteps on the cobbles mixed with the gleeful cries of children playing. He wished he could be so free, but he would have to make do with these fleeting moments on the roof. He stretched out, letting the tension dissipate from his limbs, feeling the warmth of the slates soaking into him. His eyes flickered, lazily watching people as they walked by below. He was tempted to sleep, but suddenly his eyes went wide, dragging his body upright.

It was a girl. And she had vanished right before his eyes.

Or had she?

Aiden saw her a little way down the street, her steps bringing her closer to his house. She was hooded in a green cloak, a deep purple scarf wrapped over her nose and mouth. The long ends of her reddish-brown hair escaped around her shoulders. She stepped nimbly through the crowds as if some unseen force created a path for her. Then, as suddenly as she had appeared, she disappeared again.

Aiden sat up straighter, thoughts of sleep banished from his mind. He strained his eyes to catch a glimpse of the girl. Had no one else noticed her vanish? It seemed not, for those in the street carried on as if nothing extraordinary had just occurred.

Leaning forward, Aiden's fingers traced the shape of Ailm, the seer. He brought the shimmering rune up to his face and peered down at the street. Where was she? Maybe he had imagined the whole thing?

Aiden lowered his hand, but just before he let the rune fade to nothing he caught the green flash of her hood. She emerged from his uncle's bakery across the street with a hot pastry in hand. Aiden focused on her hooded head and gasped. Her cloak was like nothing he had ever seen before. It was speckled with the runes of Fearn, the shield, Iogh, the resilient, and Luis, the protector. And not runes like his father would sew. These were real runes, drawn with light.

No wonder she had been able to vanish with magic like that in her cloak. But where could she have acquired such a cloak? What sort of a person needed a cloak to make them invisible? Who was this girl?

Aiden scrambled across the roof and jumped into the branches of the pine tree in his back garden, swinging himself down to the ground. He slipped through the passage at the side of his house and walked casually out onto the street. Without Ailm he could not see the girl at first, but he found that as he concentrated she slowly came into view, eating her pastry in the corner of an alley. The runes in her cloak were not meant for true invisibility then, just clever concealment, otherwise he would never have seen her without the magic.

Aiden crossed the street and stepped through the doorway

into the thick, sweet smell of the baker's. He blinked as his eyes adjusted after the brightness of the street. Behind the counter stood Branwyn, his cousin, a small, wiry figure with long dark hair pulled back from her face. Aiden smiled.

"Hi Branwyn," he said, leaning over the counter. He glanced around, checking that no one else could hear. "I need your help."

"What for?" she replied, her blue eyes sparkling as she dusted floury hands on her apron and leaned in conspiratorially.

"There was a girl in here a minute ago and her cloak was covered in magic. And I don't mean a few runes sewn around the edges. I mean it was covered in real runes. Enough to make her disappear. Don't you find that strange?"

"Aiden, you think everything is strange," she replied.

Grinning, Aiden leaned in closer. "Yes, but this is stranger than usual Bran. That girl is hiding something."

Branwyn wrinkled her nose. "How do I help you?"

"What do you know about her?"

Branwyn shrugged. "She's been here a few times before. Always has good money, but then so does everyone. I don't know what you want me to say. I never noticed any magic."

Of course not, Aiden thought. He had only seen the runes on her cloak by using runes himself. Branwyn had no such skill. He met Branwyn's eyes. "Come with me. We'll follow her, uncover her secrets."

Branwyn laughed and shook her head. "Don't be ridiculous Aiden. I have work to do and I'll bet you do too."

"It's fine," said Aiden. "This is what lunch breaks are for."

"Well I've had my lunch already," said Branwyn.

Aiden gave her a mock frown. "You're no fun anymore Branwyn. We used to sneak off all the time exploring the City and tracking down runes, following around people who were much less strange than this girl."

She just laughed at him again. "We can't spend all our days having adventures. Sometimes we have to live in the real world."

"Well, enjoy your afternoon in the real world," said Aiden, giving her a big grin. "I'm going for an adventure."

With that he left the bakery, screwing up his eyes against the sudden brightness. He ran a hand through his unruly brown hair and glanced to the place where the girl had been sitting. She was gone. But as Aiden focused on the empty spot she came into view. It was only the magic in the cloak bouncing his attention elsewhere. He looked away quickly, hoping he had not caught her attention, and watched her slyly from the corner of his eye.

The girl stood, tucking her scarf close around her neck. She looked both ways along the street before stepping out into the crowd, threading her way between two carts stacked with vegetables. Aiden walked after her, straining his neck to see her above the sacks of potatoes. If he lost sight of her just once he might never be able to find her again.

She continued on, dodging a group of children as they chased each other in and out of the alleys. Aiden stumbled as one of the young boys ran right under his feet. He looked up quickly, ignoring the boy's angry chatter. Where was she? How could he have lost her already?

He saw Halfdan, the blacksmith, step out of his doorway, his face sooty and red, a pair of tongs, tips still glowing, in his hand. Halfdan waved and Aiden smiled at the man who had taught him Teine, the rune for fire. The blacksmith's cat jumped down from the window ledge, trotting after something. He twined himself around someone's ankles and the person reached out a hand from under a green cloak to rub his ears. Aiden laughed. His eyes may have lost her, but the cat was not to be fooled.

The girl stroked the cat for a few seconds longer before continuing along the street. She reached its end and took a left.

Aiden followed. The street broadened and the girl moved swiftly and gracefully, flitting among the people like she was made of nothing but air. Aiden hastened his steps but was caught behind a cart laden with timber, the smell of freshly hewn branches filling his nose. He pushed his way past, muttering apologies at the shouts that followed him. Aiden fixed his eyes on the green hood ahead.

"Watch it," cried a man, an armful of books and papers swirling into the air.

"Sorry," said Aiden, ducking past and hurrying on before he could be made to help pick them up. He lifted his head, brows creased. He had taken his eyes off the girl.

He scanned the street. He had just passed the weathered stone buildings of the old barracks. Where would she be going? Lots of retired soldiers lived in this area but there were plenty of other people too. And too many of them seemed to be on the street. Aiden craned his neck. He wanted to use Ailm, the seer, but his father's words rang in his mind. People were wary of the runes unless they were being used by a trained wizard or soldier. He narrowed his eyes, almost willing the rune to work without actually drawing it.

And then he saw her.

She was much further away, almost rounding the next corner, but she turned aside, her green hood disappearing through the door of a tall sandy-coloured building. Aiden ran after her. One building's length away he slowed. What was he going to do when he got there? He stepped closer...

An ear-splitting crack rent the air. The building erupted sending shards of stone in all directions and a rush of hot air knocked Aiden to the ground.

The street filled with a cloud of dust billowing upwards in a swirling storm of grey that blocked out the sun. Aiden's ears were left ringing and for a few seconds he clutched his head before the screams and cries began to filter through. His fingers shook as he rubbed dust from his eyes. All around people struggled to their feet, clutching at each other or brushing dust from their clothes, wide-eyed confusion on their faces. Moaning sounded from amidst the stone debris strewn across the street and someone cradled their arm to their chest, blood trickling between their fingers.

Aiden pulled himself to his feet, ignoring the sore places where he was bound to have bruises later. The acrid taste of smoke caught the back of his throat and he brought a hand up to cover his mouth and nose. He could hear others coughing nearby. Somewhere a voice called out for the Eagle Riders.

To Aiden's right the bare shell of the tall sandstone building loomed through the haze. Its front wall was almost completely blown away, baring the building's interior to the street and leaving the wooden floors sagging at a dangerous tilt. Already fire burnt in the ruins, licking its way skywards. Soon the whole building would be alight.

Aiden knew it was dangerous to stay, but something held him. Maybe, just maybe, the girl was still alive. His eyes strained to see through the filthy air, stinging as the smoke bit at them. On the third floor Aiden could barely make out the limp shape of a body. Was it her? Was she still alive? Yes! With shaking arms she rolled onto her side, sitting up and coughing. Runes flashed on a cloak of green.

The building groaned and shuddered. Flames crackled around the foot of the building, spitting sparks into the air as it devoured the furniture, tongues reaching for the wooden boards of the stairs. Distantly Aiden heard the heavy rattle of soldiers running. Would they make it before the fire took over? Even then, Aiden doubted it would be enough. They needed the Eagle Riders. It would take powerful magic to stop the fire and maybe more to save the people within. Aiden clenched his fists and looked to the empty sky.

They were not going to make it in time.

Aiden ran into the burning building. Flames billowed around him, the heat singeing his skin as he jumped through. He felt like he was going to be sick, but for some reason he could not abandon the girl. She was his responsibility.

He ran across the floor, climbing through heaps of rubble. Smoke stung his eyes, sending tears dripping down his face. He choked, his mouth almost too dry to breathe. The stairs stood ahead, floorboards splintered by falling stone, the banisters edged with soot. He took the first steps on his tiptoes. Chunks of wood dropped from the ceiling above, trailing fire. A floorboard snapped beneath his foot, swallowing his ankle. Aiden grabbed the banister, crying out as the heat seared through his hand. He gritted his teeth and pulled himself up, taking the steps two at a time until he reached the third floor.

The girl knelt near the open face of the building, hunched over the body of an older woman sprawled on the floor beside her. She shook the woman by her shoulders and brushed the hair and dust from her face. Aiden rushed to their side. The girl looked up, eyes wide, blue and bright with tears. Her hood had fallen down to reveal her long, reddish-brown hair, tangled and dirt-stained by the explosion.

"She won't wake," she said, her voice cracking. She wiped her cheek and Aiden wondered how she could look beautiful even with the layer of grime across her elegant face.

"Can you move?" said Aiden.

She pushed herself onto her feet, wincing as she almost lost her footing. Her gaze dropped to the woman. "She needs you more," she said, her hands balling into fists. Her face was turned from him, her shoulders tensed. How could she be so brave?

"I'll be back for you," said Aiden. The fire was not so high yet. He would have time. She gave a tiny nod.

Aiden lifted the woman onto his shoulders, silently thanking his father for the hours spent lifting heavy reams of cloth. The woman stirred but did not awaken. Aiden moved quickly towards the stairs, sweat mixing with the dirt on his face. Dark smoke poured up the stairwell and he coughed, pulling up the collar of his shirt to cover his mouth. He started down the stairs, the crackle of flames growing louder. The building groaned again and gave a violent spasm. Aiden swayed to the side, straining against the weight of the woman. He righted himself and hastened on, the black tendrils of smoke becoming flickering reds and oranges as he descended.

A few feet from the ground Aiden pulled back. The bottom steps were gone. For a moment he stood frozen. The fire cracked to his right, spitting sparks, the air scorching his face. Aiden jumped. He landed heavily, staggering forward and twisting his body before both he and the woman fell into the flames. A few more steps and then he burst through the jagged gap of the doorway into the arms of a person. He could not get his eyes to focus, but he felt the weight of the woman lifted from his shoulders.

Aiden turned, shielding his eyes against the glare of the blaze. The image of the girl burned in his mind stronger than the fire. He had promised to go back for her.

A soldier of the City Guard caught his arm. "It's too dangerous boy. I'm sorry, but whoever's still in there is as good as dead."

"No!" Aiden shook free of the man's grasp. She would die if he did not go back.

Once more Aiden jumped through the flames. Ahead fire consumed the wooden boards of the stairs, glowing brilliant shades of red and white, threatening to crumble more of the steps to ash. The heat seared his skin through his clothes. It felt like the very air was being sucked from his lungs. He drew Peith, the swift, a zig-zag of light and threw the rune at his feet. He ran and leapt with all his might, urging Peith to carry him over the void where the bottom steps had been, the fire leaping after him.

Aiden's feet landed solidly, the step splintering underneath him. Using both hands and feet he propelled himself forward taking three steps at once, the speed of Peith coursing through his limbs. Wood crumbled beneath his feet, flaking away in clouds of ash as the fire licked at his heels.

He passed the second floor, a tremor racing up behind him, cracking the already charred and weakened wood. Aiden pushed himself faster, muscles burning. Something snapped and jerked him to the side. Then the stairs dropped from underneath him.

Aiden jumped, reaching out with both hands as the speed of Peith carried him on. The floor above loomed closer and his arms caught the edge. He screamed as he slid back. His fingers clawed at the floor, finally snagging on a groove in the wood. He jerked to a halt, his body dangling over an abyss.

With a cry Aiden hauled himself up and crawled away from the edge. He looked down at his shaking hands. If he had missed… If he had fallen… He turned his head, swaying as dizziness washed over him.

"You came back," whispered the girl.

Aiden got to his feet and took a few shaky steps towards her. They were not safe yet. Not by a long way. The way out was gone.

He grabbed the girl's hand and pulled her to her feet. He drew Dair, strength, and placed it in her open palm, watching as the slanting line and wide zig-zag of the rune spread its golden light through her body. She pulled back from him, fixing him with an unwavering stare. Whether she was angry or afraid or just plain surprised, Aiden could not tell. "Can you walk now?" he said.

She took a hesitant step and nodded, glancing down at her leg.

The floor shuddered. A splintering crack ripped through the building. Aiden staggered forwards, catching the girl's flailing arm before she tumbled backwards. He held her tight, a wave of dizziness washing over him. They were going to die. To jump down would kill them both instantly. To wait would be to succumb to the fire. He looked at the girl and saw the same thoughts reflected in her eyes. No. He forced the thoughts away. He was not going to give up.

A glimpse of silver caught his eye and Aiden saw what he had not noticed before. The stairs continued up.

With the girl's hand clasped firmly in his, Aiden pulled her towards the stairs. Below them part of the floor cracked and broke off, crashing down through the flames. The girl stumbled, crying out and grasping her leg. Aiden pulled her back to her feet, dragging her onto the stairs as flames devoured another floorboard. He put her arm around his shoulders and half lifted her up the steps. Flames caught below them, racing up the dry wood, trying to devour them.

At the top they crossed the room to the nearest window which was somehow still intact, the glass shining with the heat. Aiden cast around for something, anything, that would clear their path before the fire reached them. He grabbed a chair and swung it, smashing the glass. The roar from below grew louder, as if the fire was straining to catch them. Aiden climbed onto the windowsill. Vague shouts rose up from the ground, but he refused to look down. The girl leaned out after him and watched as he pulled himself onto the roof. He rolled onto his stomach, reaching back down.

"Take my hands," Aiden shouted.

She hesitated, then firmly pressed her lips together and climbed onto the windowsill, reaching up to grab his hands. Her grip was strong as she pulled herself up beside him. Together they crawled up the steep slope of slate to the top of the roof and stood looking out. A gaping smoke-filled chasm lay between them and the next building. There was nowhere else to go. They had outrun the fire into a dead end. All that remained was for the flames to eat them up with the rest of its prize.

A mighty crash sounded and the whole world seemed to tremble. Aiden took the girl's hand in his, her touch cool after the heat of the fire. Their eyes met and for a moment Aiden could almost forget that he was about to die. The blue of her eyes was like a cloudless sky, her hair like autumn leaves swirling in the wind. Her grip tightened on his.

"It's a good view from up here," said Aiden, forcing a smile to his lips.

Her mouth twitched and if the circumstances had not been so dire he imagined she might have smiled back. "Yes," she said. "If it wasn't for the smoke."

The roof shifted beneath their feet and they fell against each other. Aiden caught hold of her, refusing to let her fall even at the last.

Then the building collapsed.

2. A Tale of Fire and Magic

The building juddered and dropped suddenly, Aiden's stomach lurching into his mouth. The girl tightened her arms around him, as if somehow, together, they might live. Her whole body trembled, her head of tawny hair buried in his chest. Aiden wrapped his arms tight around her, unable to stop the shaking in his own limbs. Slates slipped away beneath their feet. These were the last seconds of his life. His throat tightened at the thought of his family waiting for his return that would never come.

Stone cracked and wood splintered, the roof splitting apart beneath them. They fell down amidst the rubble. Acrid smoke billowed up, scaring Aiden's lungs and blurring his vision. He longed to see the sky just one last time. He did the only thing he knew and frantically sketched a rune in the air. The curved lines of Eadha, the wind, swirled around them with a thunderous roar, sweeping aside wood and stone and lifting them out of the reach of the flames.

For a second they rose up from the building, Aiden casting rubble aside with the current of Eadha. He reached for the sky, but he was tired, so very tired. His eyes streamed and flickered. As if from a great distance away he felt the solid glow of the rune slip from his fingers. They floated for a moment and then they were falling once more, back down through the rubble, past the stairs they had so frantically climbed.

The cry of an Eagle pierced the flames and a shadow swooped, breaking through the clouds of smoke. A twisting rope dropped down into the maelstrom, flashing past Aiden's face. With a speed that surprised himself, he grabbed the rope, still clinging to the girl with his other arm. They jerked to a halt, swinging over the void that had once been the third floor. A horrible tearing ripped through Aiden's shoulder as he took their weight. He cried out but somehow held on to both the rope and the girl.

The walls dropped around them and Aiden flinched back from falling rubble. Flames leapt towards them, but they rose skywards, away from the crackling heat until blue horizon broke through. Aiden closed his eyes, gritted his teeth and tried not to think of the pain or the height as the Eagle carried them away.

Aiden's feet hit solid ground and his eyes jolted open. He tried to stand, but his legs buckled beneath him and he collapsed sideways onto the cobbles, the girl rolling limply out of his grasp. His other hand still fiercely gripped the rope, a dull throb pulsing along his arm. People he did not know crowded around them. He ignored their meaningless babble, blinking through smokey tears to focus on the girl. He was alive, but was she?

She lay on the cobbles, her cloak tangled around her body. Her eyes were closed, her face pressed to the ground, almost peaceful. Aiden's throat tightened. Then he saw her chest rise with the tiniest of breaths. Aiden let his head roll back. She was alive.

Soldiers pushed through the crowd, hands reaching down to lift her up and carry her away. Aiden opened his mouth, trying to speak. What was her name? Who was she? But a violent cough racked his body and he rolled onto his front, pain spiking along his arm. His mouth tasted like ash.

Someone stepped into his vision. From his position on the ground all Aiden could see was a pair of boots, well-worn but still slightly ornate. He squinted up at the man who occupied the boots.

He had a weathered face with wind-worn cheeks, yet his armour was intricately made and even Brokk would have envied the fine blue cloak on his back. A few paces behind him, oddly out of place in the middle of the street, was a Great Eagle, golden feathers shining through the grey air. He was an Eagle Rider.

The Rider dropped to a crouch next to him. "Are you hurt?"

Aiden put a hand to his left shoulder, the ache sharpening as he acknowledged it. He tried to sit up but winced as his raw and blistered hands touched the ground. Dizziness washed over him.

The Rider helped him up and held him steady.

"Thank you," Aiden rasped. "You…" He bowed his head. "You saved my life."

"And you saved two others," said the Rider with a smile.

Aiden opened his mouth to speak, but he did not know what to say.

"Here, drink this," said the Rider, lifting a bottle to his lips.

The cool water burst down his throat and Aiden gulped at it until he choked. The Rider beckoned someone over, taking a wet cloth and a bundle of fabric from them. Then he took Aiden's hands and began to dab away the sticky blood. Aiden gritted his teeth and tried not to flinch.

"You've done extremely well today," said the Rider. "What's your name?"

"Aiden Brokksson," said Aiden. It was unfathomable that this man of legend had saved his life and was even speaking to him. Over the Rider's shoulder he caught a glimpse of the Eagle watching the street, yellow eyes blinking slowly above the sharp hooked beak.

"What brought you to this fateful street?" the Rider asked.

Aiden winced as the Rider spread a salve over his hand. "I was just passing through." He had no intention of revealing his real purpose. It all seemed so foolish now.

Other Eagle Riders now circled the blaze throwing down runes of Suil, water, and Eadha, the river. The curving lines of the runes arced over the building, shimmering like rainbows in the mist, then bursting into rain as they fell. Aiden's eyes widened and his skin tingled as if the air around him was filled by the power of the runes.

"How did you know there were people in there?" the Rider asked.

Aiden's mind went blank momentarily. "I… I just saw her go in."

The Rider nodded slowly. The building rumbled and a cloud of dust billowed out as another section of wall collapsed. Aiden flinched. He had been inside that only minutes before. The Eagle Riders flying above threw down more runes dampening the flames and smoke.

"Why did the building explode?" said Aiden, turning sharply to the Eagle Rider.

The Rider looked at him, head tilted slightly back as if to see him better. "I don't know." He leaned in then, knotting the last bandage around a cut on Aiden's arm, before laying a hand gently on his uninjured shoulder. "You'll live."

The Rider turned back to his Eagle. "Wait," Aiden called after him. "What about the girl and the woman? Will they be alright?"

The Eagle Rider smiled over his shoulder. "Because of you, I think so."

"Who were they?" said Aiden, but his words were drowned by another rumble from the building. The Rider ran the last few steps to his Eagle before swinging himself nimbly onto its back. The Eagle's wings flexed, muscles bunching as it lifted itself into the air. Aiden's heart leapt with it. All the stories he had heard as a boy could not match the awe of seeing an Eagle Rider with his own eyes.

A foot scuffed behind him and Aiden dragged his eyes from the sight. A young soldier stood there. "I'm to see you home," he said.

Aiden nodded, letting his eyes close briefly before standing and following the soldier away from the burning building. His feet dragged like deadweights beneath him. What had just happened? He fingered the bandage on his arm, following it up to the tattered and blackened threads of his shirt. How had he even survived?

"Aiden!"

A familiar head of thick brown hair pushed through the crowd towards him. Aiden wearily waved before turning to the soldier. "I'll be fine from here."

The soldier nodded and began to retrace his steps.

Branwyn burst upon him, breathless. "Aiden, I'm so glad I found you." Her face danced as she spoke. "I tried to find you after I heard the explosion, but your Mum said you hadn't come back after lunch." She stopped and frowned, looking him up and down. "Aiden, you stink and you look like a mess." She took his arm and inspected his bandaged hands and various other injuries, causing Aiden to flinch. "Did the girl do this?"

"No. That was the explosion."

Branwyn's mouth dropped open and she stared at him, eyebrows raised. "You mean…"

Aiden started his slow walk along the street again. Everything was too much effort. He just wanted to be home. Branwyn ran a few steps to catch up with him. She put an arm round his waist and he gratefully leant on her shoulders.

"You look terrible," she whispered. "And you sound awful too."

"I've been through fire," said Aiden, laughing. He coughed as smoke caught in his throat. It still felt like his lungs were full of ash.

"So what happened?" said Branwyn, watching him intently. Aiden gave her a sideways smile. She scowled at him. "Come on. Tell me."

"Well, after I left you I followed the girl to a house near the old barracks. I never found out what she was doing. The building exploded almost as soon as she went inside."

Branwyn's hand tightened on his waist. "Is that how you got injured?"

Aiden shook his head. "The blast only knocked me over. I got these," he gestured to his bandages and charred shirt, "when I went in to get her out."

"You did what?" said Branwyn, gawking at him.

"No one else was doing anything to help," said Aiden. He wondered if he should mention the other woman he had saved too, but Branwyn's awed gaze was already making him uncomfortable. "By the time I got to her the fire was really bad and we had to go up to the roof. Honestly I thought we were going to die. There was nowhere else to go." Aiden gave an involuntary shudder, as he remembered that moment of hopelessness when he thought there would be no escape. He could still feel the rumbling under his feet and the blackness of the air as the smoke enveloped them.

"But how did you get out?" said Branwyn, a frown creasing her brow.

"An Eagle Rider saved us," said Aiden.

"An Eagle Rider!" said Branwyn, eyes widening. "What was he like?"

Aiden smiled at the memory. "Really he was just a man, but he felt like so much more. And he was kind. He bandaged me up. Anyone could have done that, but he did it."

"And the Eagle?" said Branwyn.

"Magnificent," said Aiden, remembering the brief glimpse of the sleek golden feathers, the curved beak and the hard, glinting eyes. "Just like you would have imagined from all the old stories."

"Wow," Branwyn whispered. "I wish I had been there to see that."

Aiden smiled again, knowing that he would never forget his

encounter with the Eagle and its Rider. It was the same sense of longing and excitement that he felt when he dreamed of the Silver Eagle. Aiden looked to the sky, expecting to see a Great Eagle, but there was nothing but hazy blue tinged with smoke.

"So tell me about the girl," said Branwyn, giving Aiden a playful smile. "What was she like?"

"There's not much to say," said Aiden with a small shrug. "It's not like we had much chance to chat."

"No?" said Branwyn, turning her face to him, one eyebrow raised. "You must have found out something."

"She was brave," said Aiden. And beautiful, he thought, turning away to hide the tug of a smile around his mouth. Branwyn would only tease him.

"Oh, *brave*," said Branwyn, poking him in the side and smiling up at him.

Aiden frowned. She was going to tease him anyway.

"And what was her name?"

Aiden frowned. "I don't know."

"Didn't you ask her?" said Branwyn, giving him that smile again.

"I didn't get a chance," said Aiden. "By the time we were safe she was unconscious. Her injuries were much worse than mine and the soldiers took her away so quickly.

Branwyn was silent for a moment. "It sounds like you were lucky."

Aiden nodded.

"Do you know what caused the explosion?" Branwyn asked, her voice quieter now.

"I don't know," said Aiden, frowning again. "I asked the Eagle Rider, but he never really answered my question." And why would he? He was no one special.

They turned onto their home street, the shadows lengthening around them. Branwyn walked Aiden right up to his door before removing her arm from his waist. Aiden smiled gratefully at her. "Thanks Bran."

She returned his smile and turned to make the short walk across the street to her own home. Aiden reached out to push the door open, then stopped, turning back to Branwyn.

"I'm sorry about this morning," he called over to her. "It wasn't fair to ask you to come when you were working."

Branwyn looked back at him. "It's alright," she said, smiling. "I did want to come, it's just my father would have been annoyed and… oh you know."

Aiden nodded, grimacing. "I've got my own father to face now."

"Good luck," said Branwyn, laughing.

Aiden gathered his thoughts and opened the door to his house. His father was sitting by the counter, a slim silhouette in the candlelight, waiting for him. He stood up quickly as the door swung open, a sharp frown on his face. But almost instantly Brokk's expression changed, his step faltering. He reached out towards Aiden, taking him gently by the shoulders.

"What on earth happened son?"

Aiden sighed. He wondered where to begin and what even to say. Should he tell his father he had been chasing a girl? Should he tell his father why? Brokk would not want to hear that runes were involved. But if he did not mention the runes, his father would think him a fool for getting into such a mess over a mere girl. And if he did not mention either, how could he explain his actions?

A gasp sounded from the kitchen doorway and Aiden's mother rushed over to him, her fingers brushing over his tattered and blackened clothes and hovering over his bandaged arm. Her eyes met his.

"I'm fine Mum."

Kari shook her head. "No you're not. Now come through and sit down."

His mother led him through to the kitchen and sat him down at the table. Aiden sunk into a seat, gratefully lifting his weight from his tired feet. Andor looked up at his arrival, his mouth dropping open. Brokk followed them through, standing over the table.

"So where have you been Aiden?" said Brokk.

"I didn't mean to be so long," said Aiden. He looked down at his red raw hands under the table feeling the blood pulse under his skin. It had been easy to tell Branwyn the whole truth, but why could it not be easy now?

Brokk folded his arms. "You disappeared for most of the afternoon and now you come home looking like… like this."

Aiden pressed his lips together. He could not—no would not—lie to his family. No matter how much they might hate the truth. He looked up. "I saw something when I stopped for lunch. It was a girl in the street and she wore a cloak covered in runes. So many runes for secrecy that people hardly even saw her…"

"I should have known it would be magic," Brokk said, shaking his head. "It's always magic that gets you into trouble."

"Who said I was in any trouble?" said Aiden, raising his voice in return. Why did his father always jump to conclusions? Why did he even bother trying to tell him the truth?

Kari put a hand on her husband's arm. "Let him finish his story Brokk."

Brokk frowned but fell silent.

Aiden scowled at him. "I was curious so I followed the girl further into the City. But the house she went into exploded." He paused, his skin prickling at the memory of the fire, the girl's scared blue eyes looking up at him. "I went in to rescue her," he said quietly.

His family stared at him, utterly silent. No one moved.

"Did you save her?" Andor asked, biting the tips of his fingers.

"She wasn't the only one there," said Aiden. "There was an older woman, who was unconscious, so I had to help her first. By the time

I went back for the girl, we were trapped. An Eagle Rider saved us both."

Andor's eyes grew wide. "You met an Eagle Rider," he said in wonderment.

Aiden nodded, half smiling.

Brokk took a step closer to Aiden so that he was looking into his eyes. "Believe me son, it was a brave thing you did, going after that girl." Brokk nodded. "But it was also a reckless thing. You can't just go running off chasing runes and putting yourself in danger. You're not a wizard or an Eagle Rider. You have duties here."

Aiden's throat tightened. Even after the whole story, all his father seemed to care about was work and responsibilities.

"It wasn't magic that caused any of this..." said Aiden quietly, leaving the rest of his sentence unsaid. He did not have the heart to tell his father that it was a dream of the Silver Eagle that had taken him up to the roof. A dream of adventure. Of something more than cloakmaking.

"Aiden you were almost killed today," said Brokk, throwing his arms out wildly.

Kari put a calming hand on his arm. "Enough Brokk. He's had a hard day. And your son saved two people's lives. Just be proud of him."

"I am proud," said Brokk, gazing at Aiden, his eyes shining. "I'm just afraid that one of these days he's going to get himself killed because of magic. It was bad enough when you were only nine and I had to come and get you from the Restricted Zone. You were all bruised and blackened from the runes they had thrown at you. And I thought then, I never want to see my son like that again."

Aiden looked up at his father and wished he did not have to put him through this pain. But magic had saved him today. It was the runes that had given him the speed to outrun the fire. It was the runes that had bought him and the girl those extra few seconds before the Eagle Rider arrived. He had tried to ignore the dreams of the Silver Eagle. He had tried to focus on his work. But after today how could he go back to that life when he knew, with a deep certainty, that something more was possible?

3. In the Ruins

Aiden writhed under his blankets and then suddenly froze. His eyes flicked open and slowly focused on the wooden rafters above his head. No flames scorched the walls. No smoke poured up through the floorboards. Only the four familiar walls, the battered brown chest, and Andor's bed against the next wall. Andor still slept, his body rising and falling gently with each breath.

Pale light shone through cracks in the wooden shutters. Aiden listened for any other noises, but there were none. It was still early. He closed his eyes again. It was the second night since the fire and the second night that the dreams had plagued him.

With a groan, Aiden sat up, every muscle in his body protesting the movement. He shivered a little as he left the heat of his blankets, but was grateful for the cool touch of the air on his fiery skin. A sheen of sweat plastered his forehead, as if there really had been a fire in his room during the night. He flexed his fingers, wincing as the skin of his palms tugged at the movement. The burns were healing but not fast enough for his liking. He swung his legs out of bed and gingerly pulled a clean shirt over his head. He paused, pressing his hand into his shoulder and biting down the pain. It was swollen to almost twice its normal size.

Standing slowly, he finished dressing and walked quietly to the window, easing open the shutters. The grey light of pre-dawn swept into the room and he leaned out over the windowsill. The garden was swathed in shadow and above him the roof lay inviting, calling him up to his usual perch. He dropped his head. It would be stupid to try.

Andor rolled over and squinted at his brother through sleepy eyes. "What are you doing Aiden?"

"Wishing I was up there," said Aiden, turning to face his brother.

Andor rubbed his eyes. "Can't you use runes to help?"

Aiden shook his head and touched his shoulder. "I think it would still hurt."

Andor frowned, laying his head back on his pillow and shutting his eyes.

Aiden gave a small smile. He walked slowly from the room and downstairs to the darkened kitchen. He stoked the dying embers of the fire causing a spark to jump. He dropped the poker and stepped back suddenly. Was that how the fire had started, with someone simply causing sparks to fly, or had someone meant for it to happen? Aiden rubbed his brow and turned, taking the back door out to the garden. He sat down on the wooden bench below the workshop window, dew seeping into his trousers. Why would someone want to cause a fire?

He leaned his head back against the wall. Why would someone wear a cloak of runes? Who was the girl? And what was she doing there? He closed his eyes and pictured her tousled red-brown hair and tear-stained blue eyes. If he had not been on the roof that lunchtime, he would never have seen her. If he had not dreamed of the Silver Eagle the night before, he would never have been on the roof. And she would be dead.

The door clicked and Aiden's eyes sprang open. His father stepped out to throw away a bowl of old dyeing water. The water splashed into a muddy puddle on the ground. Brokk turned and jumped at the sight of Aiden, a short laugh escaping his lips.

"You're up early son."

Aiden shrugged. "I'm always up early."

"Surely not this early?" said Brokk, raising his eyebrows.

"I was awake anyway," said Aiden.

Brokk frowned. "Did you dream about it again?"

Aiden nodded.

"Give it time," said Brokk, taking a step towards him. "It will get easier."

The dreams, yes, thought Aiden, but would the not knowing just keep eating away at him?

"Come on in," said Brokk. "Your Mum's put on the porridge."

Aiden followed his father inside. The cosy glow of the fire danced across the familiar stones of the kitchen walls. Kari dropped the wooden spoon in the pot hanging over the fire and came to place her hands on either side of his shoulders.

"How are you feeling?" she said, looking into his eyes.

"Fine," said Aiden.

"That shoulder's still swollen," said his mother, pressing her fingers to it.

"And sore," said Aiden, shrugging out of her grasp. A dull throb was already emanating from the core of his muscles.

"How are the hands?" said Brokk, peering over Kari's shoulder.

Aiden spread his hands palm up, skin stinging as it pulled against half healed blisters.

Brokk winced. "You won't be working with those for a few more days yet."

Kari spooned some porridge into a bowl and clunked it onto the oaken tabletop. Aiden slipped onto the bench to eat, his father taking the seat next to him. Aiden shuffled, trying to find a comfortable position, but he felt trapped. It was like his father was trying to keep him from getting into any more trouble.

A knocking sounded from the workshop and the front door

creaked open and closed. "Hello," came Branwyn's voice. A second later she appeared in the kitchen doorway, two cloth-wrapped bundles in her arms. "I've brought some bread."

"This is a lovely surprise," said Brokk standing and taking the bundles from Branwyn, their warm aroma drifting across the room.

Aiden slipped out of his seat before his father could trap him again. He sidled over to Branwyn and bent his head to whisper in her ear. "I don't think I can stand another day like yesterday. Stuck inside with nothing to do except get fussed over by my Mum." He gave Branwyn a pained look.

She bit her lip, trying to disguise a smile. "Why do you think I'm here?" she whispered.

Aiden's face lit up.

Branwyn turned to his parents and put her most charming smile on her face. Aiden hid a grin behind his hand.

"I've come to take Aiden off your hands for a day," she said, tucking a loose strand of dark hair behind her ear.

Kari turned to Aiden, her forehead creasing. "Are you sure you are rested enough Aiden?"

Aiden nodded. "I'm fine Mum. It will do me good to get out."

Brokk folded his arms, his eyebrow raised. "Just take care, especially if you're thinking of investigating that burnt building. We know what you're like."

Aiden dropped his eyes. His father knew him too well.

"You're not thinking of going back there?" said Kari, her voice sharpening.

Aiden glanced between his mother and father. "I have to go back," he said quietly, meeting his mother's wide eyes, willing her to understand. "I need to know what happened there. You don't know what it was like. What it's like now."

Branwyn cut in. "Don't worry Aunt Kari," she said. "I'll keep him out of trouble."

"Well, be careful," said Kari, gently squeezing his arm.

"And Aiden," said Brokk. "Don't spend too long there. That place has caused you enough trouble already."

Aiden nodded and followed Branwyn outside to the bustle of the street. Pattering footsteps and the babble of voices filled the air around them. Branwyn darted ahead, past a man leading a pair of horses. Aiden grimaced and waited for them to pass. On the far side of the road Branwyn waited, her eyes crinkled with laughter.

"Feeling a bit stiff?"

Aiden frowned. "I'm just taking it easy today."

She laughed and linked her arm through his making Aiden wince as she tugged at his sore shoulder. They walked together to the end of their street before turning onto King's Avenue. Carts stacked high with flour or vegetables from the northern farmlands trundled on towards the Palace, while empty ones headed back through the City and beyond the Wall. They kept to the edges of the street, weaving past merchants setting up stalls for the day.

"How did you manage to get out of work?" Aiden asked Branwyn as they walked.

Branwyn smiled. "I told my father that you needed my help."

"And he just let you go?" said Aiden.

Branwyn laughed. "Unlike you, I don't have a reputation for getting into trouble."

Aiden could not help but smile back at her.

The pair continued along King's Avenue until they saw the long old buildings that had once served as barracks to the City. They were just houses now, but many old soldiers still chose to live there. A short way past them the street where the burning building had stood was now blocked by a wooden barricade guarded by two soldiers. Aiden pulled Branwyn to a halt and pointed.

"Is it down there?" she whispered.

Aiden nodded. "We need to find a way past." The barricade was simple, a ramshackle fence really, but with the soldiers standing there they could not get by without being seen. He let his eyes wander along the street. It was not unlike his own, the ground cobbled and lined with rows of stone houses sitting above shops or workshops, deserted since the fire. The spiky tops of evergreens in the lane behind peeked above the roofs. If only he could climb, it would be easy to scale a tree and scramble onto the roofs.

Branwyn gripped his arm. "There's no one guarding the lane. Once we're round the corner all we have to do is sneak through a garden."

"Of course," said Aiden, they would not need to climb anything at all. He made his way across the main thoroughfare, leading Branwyn into the shade of wooded lane behind the houses. The noise of the street faded away.

They followed the lane until it felt like they were far enough from the soldiers. The houses here had darkened windows, their chimneys bare of smoke. Deserted. Aiden tugged at Branwyn's sleeve. He snuck across the garden, leading her through the gap between the houses. Just before emerging onto the street, he stopped, Branwyn almost running into his back. Aiden frowned at her and then tentatively peered out onto the street. The soldiers were just visible, but they were too busy looking outwards to notice them.

"Come on," he said to Branwyn, pulling her out from hiding.

Aiden led the way a little further along the street. A fine layer of ash covered the cobbles, sticking to their boots as they walked. Blackened stonework had been pulled into piles of rubble on either side of the road. The dry air caught in his throat and he almost expected to see the fire still raging, but only the smell of scorched air remained. The street was cold, crumbling and silent, as if the emptiness of the ruined building was spreading. Aiden tugged his cloak closer. He had come so close to death.

"Are you alright?" said Branwyn, coming alongside him.

He shrugged. "It's just memories. I almost died here."

Branwyn squeezed his arm.

"Let's look around," said Aiden.

They approached the ruins. The blackened walls stood ragged, only the back wall still standing as high as the roof had once been. Jagged spikes of wooden beams hung from their slots, a few ashy floorboards still clinging to them. Part of the interior wall survived, splitting the ruins into two rooms buried under stacks of rubble, though in a few places the ground was clear as if someone had already been there trying to create some semblance of order.

Aiden stepped through the skeleton of the doorway, moving to his right to follow the path he would have taken to the stairs. Branwyn moved behind him into the other room. Subconsciously he drew Ailm, the seer, and brought the shimmering rune up to his eye. It showed him nothing but the charred and cracked stones and crumbling remains of floorboards. What else had he expected to see? He kicked a stone. It skittered across the ground pulling others with it until a whole heap came rushing down around his feet. Aiden jumped aside, losing control of Ailm.

What was he really looking for amongst the rubble? The reason he had survived? The reason he had almost died? Something to prove it had not just been a freak accident? He climbed further through the rubble, drawing Ailm again and holding it between his forefinger and thumb. He picked through the stones, tossing some aside with his free hand. He flipped a piece of wood over with his foot. It had been part of a chair, part of someone's life. He stopped, feeling suddenly like an intruder in someone else's sorrow.

Aiden lowered the rune from his eye, but just before he let it fade completely it caught a brilliant light shimmering softly amongst the stones like a star. It could only be one thing: the afterglow of magic. And by its brightness something very powerful must have been cast here. Aiden's pulse quickened and he stepped towards the light.

It came from a piece of rubble still half buried. Aiden bent down to extract it, ignoring the uncomfortable stretch of his muscles and the pinpricks of pain in his fingertips as he dragged the stone out. It was about the size of his hand. One of its faces was flat, while the others were rough and irregular as if they had been cracked in the fire. Aiden looked at it through Ailm and gasped. The stone was full of runes, so bright he could hardly believe they had already fulfilled their purpose. There was Teine, fire, and Peith, the thunderbolt, Nuin, the spear, and Uath, dread. This was it. This had caused the explosion.

Footsteps sounded behind him. "I've found something Bran," he said.

Before he could stand, something cold slid along the side of his neck. He jerked his head away, but stopped, dead still, as he caught sight of a blade.

"Who are you and what are you doing here?" said a voice that was definitely not Branwyn's.

Aiden let Ailm fade into the air and tried to still his racing heartbeat. He clutched the stone tighter, its rough edges biting into his raw palms. He would use it as a weapon if he had to.

"Answer me," said the voice again. A man's voice, with the ring of authority.

"My name is Aiden Brokksson," said Aiden through a clenched jaw, his neck taut with the strain of keeping still.

"Aiden Brokksson?" said the voice, rising with a hint of surprise.

The cold sword tip fell from Aiden's neck and he let out the breath he had been inadvertently holding. He stood up slowly and turned around to take in a tall young man only a few years older than himself, with brown eyes narrowed into a frown. He was dressed in hardened leather armour, a sword held comfortably in his hand. A long midnight blue cloak hung from his shoulders and a blue band embroidered with a golden feather was tied around his arm. An Eagle Rider, thought Aiden. But no, where was the Eagle?

"You're the one who saved them, aren't you?" said the man.

His face reminded him of someone. "Do I know you?" said Aiden.

"No," he said, shifting his grip on his sword. "But my father told me about you. It was quite something, the way you rescued those people. The way you used the runes... only Eagle Riders and wizards are that good."

Aiden shifted uncomfortably. Was it accusation or admiration in the man's voice?

"What are you doing here?" said the man, raising his sword ever so slightly.

"Why should I tell you?" said Aiden, gripping the rock in his hand tighter, wondering how quick the man would be if he attacked.

A bemused smile crossed the man's face. "I'm not the one who sneaked in past the guards."

Aiden said nothing.

The man smiled again and lifted his head up high. "I am Tristan Arthursson of the Feather Guard. My father is Captain Arthur of the Eagle Riders. Are you sure you don't want to tell me what you're doing here?"

That was who Tristan reminded him of. The Eagle Rider who had rescued him from the fire.

Branwyn appeared through the ruins, a small noise of shifting rubble trickling through the air. She froze at the sight of them. Tristan spun around, jumping to the side and lifting his sword in one sleek motion to face both Aiden and Branwyn at the same time. Branwyn flinched and drew into herself, but she did not make a sound.

Aiden took a step closer to Branwyn. "Don't hurt her," said

Aiden.

"So this is Bran," said Tristan, raising an eyebrow.

"My name is Branwyn Aransdottir," said Branwyn, lifting her chin and stepping up next to Aiden.

Tristan pointed the sword at her. "Then maybe *you* will tell me what you're doing here? Or do I have to call the guards?"

Branwyn took a step into Aiden's side and he felt the tremor running up her arm. Her eyes were wide, but her lips were pressed firmly together, silently promising him to say nothing.

"Branwyn's not got anything to do with this," said Aiden. "I came because I wanted to see the building again. I almost died and I want to know why."

Tristan's eyes flicked between them before he slowly lowered his sword. "And have you found anything?" He nodded to the stone Aiden still held.

Aiden looked at the stone too. Should he trust Tristan with what he had found or would it only get them into more trouble? He held out the rock, it might be the only way to find out more. "It's covered in runes. Teine, Peith, Nuin, Uath."

"Fire, the thunderbolt, the spear, dread," Tristan mused, taking the stone from him and turning it over in his hands. "How did you find it? Did you use Ailm?" he asked.

Aiden tensed. It felt wrong telling a stranger that he could use magic but then Tristan already knew he could. He nodded hesitantly. "The runes on the stone have a strong afterglow."

Tristan nodded, drawing Ailm, the seer, in the air for himself. It flickered and was not as bright as Aiden would have drawn. Tristan squinted through the circle of the rune. "I can see the afterglow, but not the individual runes." He looked up. "That must have taken some skill."

Aiden shifted on his feet but said nothing.

Tristan stepped back and sheathed his sword. "Thanks for the stone," he said. "Now if I were you, I'd get out of here before *someone* alerts the guards." He turned and began to walk out from the ruins.

"Wait," said Aiden, calling after him.

Tristan stopped

"Do you know what this place was?" said Aiden, pointing to the ruins.

"A house," said Tristan, with a shrug of his shoulders. "Belonging to the old woman you saved."

Aiden frowned. "But why did it explode?"

Tristan held the rock aloft, smiling. "Because someone put runes into this rock."

"I know that," said Aiden, clenching his jaw. "But why bother?"

"Didn't you see it?" said Tristan. He stepped back through the rubble and came to a place where the wall was still mostly intact. He pointed to a black mark that had been scraped with charcoal onto the stone. It looked like a crown but upside down. Aiden wondered why he had not noticed it before. "That's a Brathadair symbol," said Tristan.

"Brathadair?" said Branwyn, stepping up beside them. "Wasn't it the Brathadair who killed the Queen all those years ago?" She looked to Tristan, a frown creasing her brow.

"They did," said Tristan, regarding her calmly. "And they've barely done a thing since... until now."

"So why are they back?" Aiden mused. And why had they targeted this house? Who was the old woman that the Brathadair wanted her dead?

"I wish I knew," said Tristan. "But for now, you should get out of here before I change my mind about letting you go."

"I have one last question," said Aiden.

Tristan raised an eyebrow.

"The girl I saved. Do you know who she was?"

Tristan shrugged. "Probably just a servant girl. And lucky that

49

you were there to rescue her."

Aiden nodded, dropping his head. Was that all? He felt sure there was more to her. Maybe he should tell Tristan about the girl's cloak. Maybe she was the one who had set off the explosion. But the image of her amidst the flames, her tear-filled blue eyes wide with fear, jumped to his mind. No. It had not been her. Mentioning the cloak would only cast suspicion on her and Aiden was not going to betray her.

"You have five minutes," said Tristan, drawing him back to the present. He nodded once to them, turning away and leaving them standing alone in the ruins.

4. Sign of the Brathadair

Branwyn watched Tristan disappear down the street, shivering in the silence he left behind. She wrapped her arms around herself, her skin prickling at the thought of the symbol on the wall behind her. An inverted crown. Her father had once told her about the Brathadair, said they were traitors of the worst kind. Now their sign sat proud in the midst of destruction.

Aiden still stared at it, but she could not bring herself to turn around. Looking at those smeared black lines again would somehow make it more real. Her stomach rolled and she suddenly felt sick. She reached out a hand to Aiden. "We should go," she whispered, her eyes flicking down the street.

Aiden did not move so she tugged on his sleeve. "Aiden. Tristan's going to send the guards." It was not the only reason she wanted to leave, nor even the most urgent, but she doubted any other excuse would make Aiden move.

At last Aiden turned away and they left the silent emptiness of the ruins behind them. Branwyn calmed as they darted back into the shadows of the alleyway and through the garden to the wooded lane behind the houses. As they drew near the noisy cobbles of King's Avenue she rushed out into the bustle of colour and movement.

Branwyn moved seamlessly into the crowds, stopping after a few paces. Aiden was gone. She looked back and saw him walking slowly along the edge of the street, rubbing his shoulder, his neck stretched to keep her in sight. Guilt spiked her chest. She pushed back through the crowd to his side. "Are you alright?"

Aiden nodded, giving his shoulder one last rub.

Branwyn frowned. "I don't believe you. Maybe we should head home."

"No." Aiden shook his head. "We should make the most of our day out."

"Alright then," said Branwyn raising her eyebrows. She never quite understood why Aiden could not be content at home. "How about we go someplace we've not been in a while?"

"Where are you thinking?" said Aiden.

Branwyn rubbed her chin. "How about the tower? It used to be your favourite, but we've not been there in years. Plus it doesn't involve climbing so you won't hurt yourself any further."

"Alright then *Mum*," said Aiden, rolling his eyes at her.

"Come on," she said. "I've got some bread and cheese. We can eat while we walk."

The pair made their way south along King's Avenue, through the rings of streets and houses that formed the City, chewing on the soft brown loaf and nutty cheese. Branwyn scraped back the hair that blew into her face. She tried to let the sunlight warm her skin, but the chill of the ruins seemed to cling to her. Beside her Aiden walked silently, his eyes glazed as if his mind was elsewhere entirely.

"Did you find what you were looking for? In the ruins I mean," Branwyn said.

Aiden blinked, shrugging his shoulders. "Sort of. I'm not really sure what I was looking for."

"If you ask me, we've just found more questions," said Branwyn. She twisted a piece of bread in her hands. "Who exactly are the Brathadair? I thought they didn't exist anymore."

Aiden shrugged. "All I know is that they assassinated the Queen ten years ago. And they can't be all gone. Not if they're putting their mark to burning buildings."

Branwyn frowned. It was not the answer she had wanted to hear.

Ahead the crowds grew thicker as the road narrowed to pass under the arch of Teraan City's outer Wall. The old stone fortification towered over thirty feet high, a mighty barrier encircling the City, or at least most of it. No wars had been fought in Branwyn's lifetime and houses were beginning to spread out onto the plains beyond and into the fringes of the deep forest.

Branwyn and Aiden approached the Wall where heavy oaken doors sat open under the archway. Two of the City Guard stood silently watching those who passed through and Branwyn spied two more soldiers through the thin window of the gatehouse. They made their way the few feet under the arch, their footsteps echoing off the walls.

"Remember the time we got shut out because we didn't get back through before dark?" said Branwyn, as they re-emerged into the sunlight on the far side of the Wall.

"Yes," said Aiden, laughing. "Your Dad was not happy with me, although I seem to remember it was actually your fault we were late. You were chasing a cat or something."

"It was a dog," said Branwyn sheepishly. "But what I still can't believe is that the soldiers wouldn't let us through the gate. I don't even know why they still close the gates at night. It's not like there's really any danger."

Aiden shrugged. "Tradition? And there's always the chance that a Wulver or a Cu-Sidhe will sneak in and attack."

"No one sees Wulvers or Cu-Sidhe anymore," said Branwyn, wrinkling her nose. "Not even the hunters who go properly out into the forest."

"No, I suppose you don't really see them so much anymore," said Aiden.

"You're sad about that, aren't you?" said Branwyn, tugging his arm.

Aiden grinned at her. "Well, sometimes I think a bit more excitement round here would be nice."

Branwyn raised her eyebrows. "Be careful what you wish for."

"Don't worry," said Aiden, his eyes crinkling with laughter. "I've had quite enough excitement to last me for a while."

Branwyn smiled back, but somehow it felt forced. Why could she not believe that one adventure would be enough for Aiden? He was always looking round the next corner, searching for something he did not even know he was searching for. He could not even spend two days at home without getting restless. Branwyn was glad to think of her own home waiting for her at the end of the day, with its familiar smells of bread and the warm heat of the ovens. That was her life and she could not imagine anything else.

Not far from the Wall, Branwyn and Aiden turned from the main road and headed out amongst the low cottages with thatched roofs. Grass covered the lanes and Branwyn had to push past bushes that spilled out from the gardens. The broken head of a rickety stone tower jutted out from above the roofs and treetops. It was a watchtower, a remnant of the old days from before the sprawl of houses and maybe even from before the Wall, when men had warred not only with men but also with the wild magic creatures of the land. The old towers were destroyed long ago, but somehow this one had survived, the last of its kind, forgotten and crumbling, overrun with creeping plants and mice.

At the base of the tower Aiden pulled back the thick bushes and Branwyn clambered past and in through a low window, eyes squinting in the gloom. She crossed the floor, a musty smell rising from the ground as dust swirled around her feet. She took the worn steps of the stone stairway and spiralled upwards, following the beam of light that streamed in from above. Aiden followed her up. At the top she emerged onto the open platform, the wind whipping sideways and blowing her skirt around her legs.

A smile spread across Branwyn's face as she leaned her elbows on the parapet and surveyed the City. It was too long since she had been up high. Tiny people scurried about below and Branwyn drew in her shoulders against the vastness of the world. The rosy walls of the Palace peeked out from behind the circle of the Restricted Zone and from within the shape of an Eagle Rider rose into the sky.

"Look," she said, pointing. "Maybe it's the Eagle Rider you met."

Aiden lifted his head and watched it, his eyes faraway, as if he was there with the Eagle and not right beside her. He drew a rune in the air, trails of light following his fingers. He brought it up to his eye.

"Well?" said Branwyn.

"It's not the Captain," said Aiden. "It's a woman."

"Let me see," said Branwyn, pulling his hand with the rune down to her eye level. She peered through, squirming a little as sparks of runelight tingled over her hand. Aiden pulled the rune bigger so that it made a window big enough for them both to look through. The Eagle soared, barely moving its golden wings. Kneeling on its back, with her feet tucked into a leather harness that sat just between the wings, was the Rider. Her face was wrapped in a scarf against the wind, but her short curly hair blew free behind her.

"I wonder where she's going," said Aiden.

"It's mid-afternoon," said Branwyn. "It's probably just the usual patrol."

Aiden pushed her lightly. "You have to be so logical don't you."

Branwyn folded her arms. "Well we can't all be dreamers."

"What's life without a bit of adventure?" said Aiden, grinning.

Branwyn pulled back from the rune. It was amazing what the runes could do, but they always made her feel just a little bit jumpy, especially since she could barely control them. How did Aiden do it so easily? She rubbed her arms, trying to rid herself of goosebumps.

Branwyn turned back to the City, looking out north beyond the Palace to the green-brown haze of the plains and fields where farmers grew wheat, barley, and oats, and kept flocks of sheep, goats, and cattle. She had never been there and she tried to imagine the smell of the grass and the sounds of the sheep, but all she heard was the whinny and clop of a horse's hooves in the street below. The ever-present sounds of muffled voices and the rumble of cartwheels floated by, softened on the wind. Branwyn tucked her fingers under her arms to warm them.

"Time to go?" said Aiden.

Branwyn nodded. "It's getting cold up here."

Aiden laughed. "It's not that bad."

Branwyn wrinkled her nose. "I'm used to working near an oven all day."

They made their way back down the darkened stairway and out into the City, ambling the streets in the rough direction of home. They passed a few places where they used to play: a stand of old oak trees, stepping stones across a stream, alleyways criss-crossed with hanging sheets. Branwyn felt like she was ten years old again.

It was late in the afternoon before they arrived back on their home street. Branwyn yawned as they approached the house. "We used to be able to run these streets all day."

"Speak for yourself," said Aiden. "I still could if I wasn't injured."

Branwyn raised her eyebrows. "Really? I'd like to see that when you're better."

"You think I won't?" said Aiden, throwing his arms out wide.

Branwyn smiled. "I think you'd do anything if someone

challenged you. Like the time that kid dared you to jump from the roof of his house onto a moving cart."

Aiden laughed, pushing open the door to his house.

"What are you two laughing about?" said her Uncle Brokk, laying down the cloak he was working on and rising from his stool.

"Branwyn was just reminding me about the time I jumped onto a moving cart," said Aiden.

Brokk smiled. "I seem to remember you jumped *through* a cart, and I had to pay for it."

A smile spread across Branwyn's face as Aiden looked sheepishly at the floor.

The door to the kitchen burst open and Andor bounded through. "Aiden's back. And Branwyn," he shouted. He bounced around their feet. "What did you do today?"

Brokk shooed Andor back and Branwyn followed her uncle and cousins into the kitchen. A cosy glow lit up the fireplace and her Aunt Kari stood up from the loom in the corner, tucking the loose threads away and flexing her fingers. Aiden drew up an old wooden chair and sank into it, closing his eyes and leaning his head back. Kari smiled at Branwyn and laid a gentle hand on Aiden's shoulder. Branwyn slipped onto the bench behind the big wooden table, swinging her legs beneath her, glad to be off her feet.

"Where did you go?" said Andor, poking Aiden in the side.

Aiden flapped his arm at him.

"Hey," said Kari, putting an arm between them. "Your brother's injured."

"We've just been at the old tower," said Aiden, holding up his hands.

"Is that it?" said Andor, frowning.

Branwyn bit back a laugh. Aiden was forever teasing his brother.

Aiden relented. "We also went back to the burnt out building, to try and find out what happened."

"I hope you didn't put yourselves in any danger," said Kari a frown forming on her face.

"The fire was all out. It was quite safe," said Branwyn. The words rolled off her tongue before her mind could disagree. She forced a smile to her lips. In the fun of the afternoon she had almost forgotten the charcoal sign scraped on the wall, but now the memory of it came back with a shiver that ran through her entire body.

Kari relaxed and comfortably folded her arms.

Andor perched himself on the end of the bench and fixed his eyes on his brother. "What did you find?"

Aiden sat forward in his chair. "Well, we met Tristan Arthursson of the Feather Guard..."

Branwyn closed her eyes and pictured the scene as Aiden described it. He skipped over the part where Tristan's sword was pointed in her face, but she remembered too well the heart-racing terror of that moment. It had been alright though and after that Tristan had been... well, kind. She could think of no better way to explain it. Not how she had imagined a soldier at all. Would she even call him handsome? Branwyn stopped herself. That was silly thinking. She would probably never see him again.

"The Brathadair?" said Brokk, the sharpness in his voice bringing Branwyn's attention back. Aiden must have told them about the symbol. "It's a long time since I heard that name."

Branwyn shifted uneasily. "Uncle, is it true that they were the ones that killed the Queen?" she said.

Brokk nodded. "Yes, that was them. Though it was ten years ago now. You'd have only been seven. I'm surprised you remember."

"I thought the Brathadair were dealt with all those years ago," said Kari, wringing her hands.

"It's possible some escaped capture," Brokk mused.

Branwyn swallowed. She had thought her aunt and uncle

would discount the notion of the Brathadair's return as ridiculous. But they had not.

"But who are the Brathadair?" said Aiden. "What do they want?"

Brokk sat down on the bench beside Branwyn. He looked intently at the table for a moment, as if gathering his thoughts, and then began.

"The Brathadair began around one hundred years ago, in the time of King Cormac, the grandfather of our present King Brandr. At that time Cormac was at war with a dark wizard called Sorcier."

"No, no," said Kari. "You need to start with Sorcier and Ectan. You're getting the story all confused."

Branwyn frowned. She had heard of Sorcier before. He was a nightmarish character in children's stories, used to scare them from playing around with wild magic. She had never thought he was a real person.

"Alright," said Brokk, shaking his head. "Let's start with King Ectan, Cormac's father. As you know the royal family is forbidden from using magic so Ectan, like every other King, had a wizard as one of his close advisors. That wizard was called Sorcier. But although Ectan was forbidden from using magic, he was extremely interested in it. Together he and Sorcier sought out many magical objects and experimented with the use of runes. People say that it was at this time that Sorcier taught himself to use wild magic. By the time anyone found out, he had already learnt to do many things that no one else had before."

"But why didn't it affect him?" said Branwyn, thinking of all the stories she had heard of people attempting to use wild magic and ending up losing an arm or a leg, or going blind or mad, or even dying.

"He must have had magic in his blood," said Aiden.

"What does that mean?" said Andor, his eyes wide.

"He means he must have come from a family of wizards," said Brokk. "Those born with the skill for magic. They have a greater tolerance for it."

"Yes, he was born into a wizard family," said Aiden, "but what I mean is that it's not impossible for a human to use wild magic." Branwyn wrinkled her brow. She had not heard Aiden speak like this before. He continued, his eyes bright. "In small amounts it can be done and the more you use it, the better you get."

"You can't use wild magic without it changing you," said Brokk, drawing his fingers into a closed fist.

Branwyn folded her arms closely across her chest. Brokk was right. Wild magic was dangerous. What Aiden was saying was almost too crazy to believe and yet he spoke with such surety. She had always known Aiden was good with runes but to know such things. He sounded like a wizard.

"I'm not saying it doesn't change you," said Aiden, looking down. "But you can build up a strength for it by using it a little at a time. It's almost like it gets into your blood, like wild magic creatures."

Brokk's knuckles grew white, but before he could speak Branwyn leaned in. "You're not saying that humans can use magic like, say an Eagle or a Kelpie or a Cat-Sidhe?"

"No he's not," said Brokk, shaking his head firmly. "The ancient creatures of Teraan, the Eagles, the Fae, the River Folk and the Tree Spirits…"

"And the Kelpies, the Wulvers, the Cat-Sidhe and the Cu-Sidhe," Andor added.

"All the Sidhe," said Brokk, raising a reproachful eyebrow at Andor, "can use wild magic without consequence. But it's different for humans. We can't control wild magic, so it becomes warped and things go wrong. Sometimes it causes injuries or deformities. Sometimes it does things to people's minds."

Branwyn put a hand to her mouth. What if Aiden was using wild magic? What if it changed him?

"Don't worry Bran," said Andor, reaching across the table to her. "That's what the runes are for. They let you control wild magic so that stuff doesn't happen."

She gave a small smile. Andor spoke with a youthful innocence, but it was true. And Aiden only ever used the runes.

"The runes can still be dangerous," Brokk cut in, giving both his sons a long stare.

"Not if you know how to use them properly," said Aiden, meeting his father's gaze.

"And you do? You've been trained?" said Brokk.

Aiden opened his mouth to speak, his eyes narrowing. Branwyn bit her lip. This was why she never heard Aiden speak of magic. It always ended in an argument.

"Come," said Kari, her voice almost strained in its brightness. "Let's get back to the story."

Brokk pressed his fingertips together and smiled at his wife. "So whether or not Ectan knew about Sorcier's activities, the King did nothing to stop him. He encouraged it and treated Sorcier more like a son than his true son Cormac. It was when Ectan died suddenly that the real trouble started, for there was a rumour that he had made Sorcier his heir rather than Cormac.

"Of course, Sorcier was a wizard so he was forbidden from being King because of his skill with magic, but there were still many who supported him rather than Cormac. War broke out and those who sided with Sorcier became known as the Brathadair, which means traitors. Luckily for Cormac, he had the Eagle Riders. The Eagles could use wild magic and that, along with the unparalleled skills of their Riders with the runes, was enough to defeat Sorcier and his Brathadair."

"But what are the Brathadair doing now?" said Branwyn,

pursing her lips.

"They want their revenge on the royal family and the Eagle Riders," said Brokk. "A lot of the Brathadair were magic users and, after Sorcier's defeat, Cormac hunted them down and killed them and their families. Since then, the survivors have been causing trouble for the royal family and the Eagle Riders. Assassinating the Queen was just one of their exploits. They say that one day Sorcier will return to claim his Kingdom and they are only paving the way."

Branwyn shuddered. "But that's silly. Sorcier's dead."

"Of course," said Brokk, smiling. "It's just nonsense. History turning into legend."

"You should all still be careful though," said Kari. "Even if Sorcier is long dead you don't want to be getting mixed up with the Brathadair. And you certainly don't want the King thinking you are involved with them."

Branwyn shook her head firmly. She would have no problems with staying away from the Brathadair. She stood to leave. The low golden sun was catching the tops of the trees outside the window. It had grown late without her realising and her parents were probably waiting for her to come home.

"Thank you for the story Uncle Brokk," she said, heading for the door.

"You're welcome," said Brokk. "Send my love to that sister of mine."

Branwyn smiled and waved to the others. As she slipped out the door she caught sight of Aiden, sitting motionless on his chair. She had no intention of investigating the Brathadair, but she could not be so sure about her cousin. As she crossed the street to her own house she hoped that Aiden would know to leave well enough alone.

5. Summoned

That night the burning building plagued Aiden's dreams again. The flames caught him, sucking the air from his lungs, singeing his skin. He blinked furiously through the smoke. Suddenly his vision cleared. The girl stood before him. Her tawny hair floated around her head, her lips parted as if trying to call out to him. Aiden frowned. There was charcoal on her forehead, the smeared lines of the Brathadair symbol. The smoke darkened and the flames burned black. There was a man in the fire reaching out a hand, clawing his way towards him. An aching chill burned through his body. Sorcier.

Aiden sat up. He winced as half-healed hands pressed down on the blankets. Mid-morning sun streamed in through the window and the soft sounds of voices and footsteps from the street soothed him. It was just a dream.

He got up and dressed quickly, before taking the stairs to the kitchen. His mother sat at her loom in the corner, weaving threads into a deep green cloth. She looked round and smiled warmly at his arrival.

"How are you feeling today?" she asked.

"Not too bad," said Aiden, though he was surprised to have slept so long. Gingerly he stretched his shoulder, but he smiled to find it felt looser than the day before. Not quite normal again but getting closer. If only he could dream of the Silver Eagle once more, instead of fire.

"Good," said Kari, turning back to her weaving. "I think there's a bit of porridge left over the fire if you're hungry."

Aiden helped himself to the last scrapings of porridge and took his bowl out the back of the house. He sat under the window of the workshop, looking out on the earthen lane at the end of their small garden. No one passed by under the boughs of the trees and, for a while, he daydreamed of Eagles and Riders, trying to push the fire from his mind.

The muffled creak of the front door sounded through the wall. A chair scraped the floor as Brokk quickly got to his feet. Aiden stood and peered in through the window. Two shadows filed in through the doorway, momentarily blocking out the light with their bulky armour and shields. Aiden ducked down. What were soldiers doing at his house? They must know that he had been back at the building and that he had used magic there. Did they think he was Brathadair?

Aiden drew Muin, the listener, a sleek curved line crossed by the tight curve of another. For a moment he held the rune in the air, undecided. Then with a slight shake of his head he brought the rune up to his ear.

"We are looking for Aiden Brokksson," said the first soldier, the words a sharp command.

"He is my son," said Brokk, slowly and clearly. "What do you want with him?"

"The King has summoned him to the Palace," the soldier replied.

"What is it about?" said Brokk, his voice quickening. "Is he in any trouble?"

Silence. Aiden desperately wanted to look in through the window, but at the same time he did not want to be seen. What were the soldiers doing? Should the silence worry him?

"He would do well not to keep the King waiting," said the

soldier, his voice clipped.

"Andor, fetch your brother," Brokk said quietly.

Aiden quickly dropped the rune and tried to sit casually on the bench, as if he had heard nothing. But he had heard and the only reasons he could think for the soldiers being there were not good. He licked his lips nervously. What would they do to him if they thought he was somehow involved with the Brathadair? He would be locked away for sure and probably for a very long time. The back door opened and Aiden jumped.

Andor's face peeked out. "There's soldiers here to see you," he said in a small voice.

Aiden nodded and stood, following his brother back into the house. Kari came through from the kitchen, giving Aiden's arm a gentle squeeze. Aiden stepped before the two soldiers, trying to keep his face expressionless. The soldiers stared at him intently and his shoulders tensed. It felt like they were pulling all his thoughts apart.

"You are Aiden Brokksson," said the soldier in charge.

Aiden gave a small curt nod.

"Come with us," said the soldier, without any further explanation.

Aiden did not know what to say, so he did not say anything. In the corner of his eye his parents tensed and a worried look passed between them. Aiden hesitated, his feet like lead weights. He glanced at his father.

"Now," said the soldier, taking a half step forwards.

Aiden nodded, trying to pull his fractured thoughts together.

"Will you not give him a moment to change into something smarter?" said Kari, stepping into the space between Aiden and the soldiers.

"He will be fine as he is," said the soldier firmly. His partner already stood by the door, holding it open.

Aiden's mother turned to him and gave him a quick hug. She

whispered "good luck" in his ear as she stepped back.

Before he knew it, Aiden had said goodbye and was leaving the shop behind. A few steps down the street he turned to look back. There were his parents, familiar and safe, standing in the doorway of the shop he had known his whole life. The sun shone on their faces and Aiden's heart tugged back to them. It felt like he was leaving them behind. One of the soldiers coughed and nodded his head forwards. Aiden took one last glance behind and then followed them onwards.

From his house they made their way to King's Avenue. Yesterday this great long street had been Aiden's friend, taking him out past the Wall and bringing him back to old places and fond memories. Today it led inwards, to the heart of the City where the towers of the Palace loomed over the Restricted Zone. Every step brought it closer, twisting Aiden's gut between fear and anticipation. The last time he had entered the Restricted Zone he had been nine years old and uninvited.

They neared the walls of the Restricted Zone and the two soldiers drew to a halt outside the solid wooden doors. A part of Aiden still doubted the doors would open for him but they did, creaking slowly outwards. The soldiers set off again, but Aiden hesitated. There was a strange sense of finality, as if by walking through those gates nothing would ever be the same again. He glanced once over his shoulder. Then putting one foot in front of the other he followed the soldiers through the gates. The gates closed behind him with a resounding thud. There would be no going back now.

In spite of the circumstances Aiden's mouth twitched into a smile. The same thrill he had felt when sneaking in all those years ago tingled in his fingertips. Nowhere to hide. That had been his first thought then and it was the same now. Yet that had only made it more fun.

The cobbled streets rang with the ordered beat of soldiers marching. The grey buildings stood tall like stern statues, their walls bare in the absence of trees. It seemed as though nothing had changed, though as he looked up the roofs did not seem quite so high as they once had. He smiled. He was a bit taller than he had been then.

They followed the road through the buildings and barracks that housed the City's soldiers and officials. Streets angled away on both sides, leading to stables and armouries. The clang of metal upon metal echoed along a street from a nearby forge or maybe from the training grounds. The sound rang distantly in his memory. He pictured the men and women in the training grounds, lined up on the dusty earth, hidden from general view by the walls of the arena. They had all stuck their swords point first in the ground before them and waited. Their captain, a small, but solid man with some magical skill, drew a rune in the air. It was *the* rune, Uath, dread; the rune no one had been willing to show him.

For a second Aiden smiled at the memory. Then he remembered. He had drawn the crossed lines of Uath and was so shocked by the sudden cold and darkness that overcame him, he had slipped down the roof of the arena. He had scrabbled and caught himself, but everyone had seen him.

After that his memories of the Restricted Zone were a twisting blur of grey stone and cobbles as he raced wildly to escape. And then that stunning bolt of Peith, the thunderbolt, had brought him down. His nine year old self might have sneaked in, but he had also been caught and neither the soldiers nor his father had looked kindly on him.

Aiden looked up and saw the Palace gates standing tall at the end of the road. The sun caught the weathered wood, casting soft shadows that brought to life the exquisite carvings of Eagles and interlace that adorned the entryway. On either side it was flanked by the smooth red sandstone of the Palace wall. There stood the one place even he would not dare to enter unasked.

It was then that he noticed the compliment of six soldiers guarding the gate. They were attired in deep brown leather armour and dark red cloaks. Their eyes scanned the streets with an alert and uneasy gaze.

At the gate, Aiden's escort spoke briefly to one of the sentries who left his post to come and inspect him.

"Anything to hide?" the guard asked gruffly.

Aiden shook his head somewhat nervously. The guard beckoned him closer, patting down his arms and legs just to be sure. He nodded, almost disappointedly, when he found nothing and gave a signal to the others at the gate.

Slowly the beautiful doors swung inwards and Aiden caught his first tantalising glimpse of the Palace. It stood ahead, carved from warm pinkish sandstone, rising up three floors high. Arched windows and doorways glinted in the sun, as if gilded in silver. The battlements of its three towers reached into the sky, a flag rippling in the breeze at the highest point.

The true extent of the Palace was hidden amongst thick gardens. The inside of the boundary wall was shrouded by trees, thick with new spring leaves, their roots covered by a tangle of bushes. There were trees in this forest that Aiden could not even begin to name. Beyond the trees sat a great lawn, bordered by flashes of red and orange and purple flowers. To one side of the path there was a fountain bubbling away, the sun sparkling off the water, and to the other Aiden saw a strange archway, covered in vines. It was somehow more wildly beautiful than Aiden had ever imagined. Everyone in the City could see the tops of the towers, but only a privileged few got to walk through the King's garden.

Aiden jumped as the wooden gates closed shut with a thunk. He had barely even registered walking across the threshold. His escorts had not entered with him, but a new pair of soldiers stepped out from the shadows to flank him. They wore the same deep red as the guards at the gate, not the black of the City Guard that Aiden was used to seeing.

He saw more movement out of the corner of his eye and realised that these forested gardens were far from empty. Sentries, almost invisible, patrolled silently amongst the hedges and trees, clearly armed with swords and bows and quivers of arrows. Aiden felt the distinct sensation of eyes watching his every move as he followed the soldiers further into the Palace grounds.

Aiden's attention was drawn to a single man striding down the gravel pathway towards them. His every step was measured and he was, thought Aiden, a man who walked with the relaxed air of a hawk waiting to strike. He was dressed in deep brown with a well-worn leather coat that came down to his knees, the hems swirling out behind him.

On either side of Aiden the guards shifted, muscles tightening. Aiden's mouth felt suddenly dry. The man stopped before them on the path, the sun glancing off his short sandy hair. He smiled, but it did not lessen the tension in Aiden's limbs. It was a thin smile, as though only a mask for some other emotion. Cunning intelligence gleamed in his grey eyes and though he could not have been much older than thirty, there was something in his gaze that spoke of an ancient power. Aiden lowered his eyes, feeling that this man could discern his deepest secrets with just one look.

The man nodded courteously to the guards and said in a clear voice, "I'll take him from here."

Wordlessly the guards left, leaving Aiden alone with the man. He twisted his fingers nervously while the man watched him, grey eyes unblinking. Aiden wished himself back on the other side of the gate.

The man held out his hand. "Welcome Aiden Brokksson. I am

Falkor."

Warily, Aiden shook his hand, feeling the ice-like strength behind the courtesy.

"You may be curious as to who I am," said Falkor, turning to lead the way towards the Palace. "I'm a wizard. *The* wizard you could say. The King's advisor on all things magical. And more."

Aiden nodded. The explanation had not put him any more at ease, especially not after the stories his parents had told the night before.

"I have heard you know a thing or two about magic," Falkor said, not waiting for Aiden to reply. "The guards may check you for weapons, but they never see the most dangerous one."

Aiden followed the wizard out of the trees, keeping a step behind and trying to ignore the veiled threat in Falkor's voice. He could now see the full extent of the Palace, a big rectangular building with a grand doorway in the centre, a wide stair splayed out before it. But it was not towards the Palace that Falkor led him. Instead they were walking across the grass to the strange archway Aiden had noticed earlier. They entered its shadow and Aiden suddenly realised that he could see none of the guards. He glanced back at the sunlit gardens, his heart beating loudly in his ears.

"You see Aiden," Falkor continued, still speaking as though it was a trivial conversation, "you have brought a dangerous weapon into the Palace and I need to check you're not here to kill the King." Falkor paused and stared at Aiden with those piercing grey eyes. "You do seem very nervous."

Before he could react, Aiden found himself pinned against the wall. Gort, the binder, twisted tightly around his wrists and ankles and up his arms and legs in a golden rope of light. He tried to squirm out of its reach, a cold sweat breaking out across his back, but he found that he could not move. The wizard stared into his eyes, unblinking. The blinding silver glow of another rune sparked in Aiden's eyes. Suil, the prophet. For a moment confusion broke into his panic. What was the wizard going to do with Suil? Then a searing pain shot through his head and Aiden could do nothing but screw up his eyes. He tried to lift his hands, but Gort glowed and tightened around him, burning against his skin. The pain in his head persisted, a ceaseless, blinding ache. What was happening to him?

"Why are you here?" said Falkor.

Through the pain Aiden's mind did not understand the question, but somehow the words were ripped from his mouth. "I was… sent for." The pain lessened instantly and his eyes sprang open to stare coldly at the wizard. Falkor had *made* him speak. He had used Suil to steal the truth from his lips.

"Tell me then," said Falkor, ignoring his expression. "Why is a cloakmaker's son so skilled in magic?"

He should not answer, thought Aiden. His body writhed against the stone arch as he fought to stay silent. He closed his eyes, but it made no difference. He could still feel Suil scouring his thoughts and putting words in his mouth. "I like… drawing the runes," said Aiden.

"Which runes?" said Falkor instantly.

"Any of them," Aiden choked. He felt helpless, powerless. He had no defence against such an attack.

Falkor's eyes narrowed. "How many do you know?"

Aiden hesitated but the pain seared behind his eyes more sharply than before. "All of them," he blurted out.

"And who taught you?" said Falkor, his voice thundering in Aiden's ears.

Aiden screwed up his eyes. "No one," he gasped. "No one taught me anything."

"Impossible," Falkor whispered. "How did you learn to use them?"

"I taught myself," said Aiden defiantly, before Suil could steal his words. He opened his eyes to face the wizard.

Falkor considered him, searching Aiden's face for the truth. Aiden met his stare and gulped, but he refused to drop his eyes. Then, as suddenly as the pain had come, it vanished. Falkor released him without warning and Aiden fell to the ground, his knees smacking painfully onto the paving stones below. The light of the runes dissipated and he flexed his arms freely once more. The wizard stood over him, silently watching.

6. In the Service of the Eagle Riders

"What was that?" said Aiden, trembling with shock and anger. He felt suddenly weak from the immense effort of fighting against Suil and Gort. For the first time in his life Aiden thought of the runes with a whisper of fear. He had never thought to use them for something like that before. He supposed, in the back of his mind, he had always known it was possible… but that was from stories and legends of long ago. He had always been proud of himself and his hidden skill, but now? Now he realised just how very little he knew. And how completely he was at this wizard's mercy.

"My job is to protect the King," Falkor said, his grey eyes still scrutinising him, unblinking. "I had to be sure you weren't a threat."

Aiden glared at him. If they had thought he was a threat then why bring him to the Palace in the first place? Why not just throw him straight into a prison cell as they were bound to do? He clenched his fists, hoping anger would hide his fear.

Falkor contemplated him. "You know Aiden, I think we're going to get along."

Aiden raised his eyebrows, an incredulous laugh escaping his lips. Had the wizard forgotten that he had just tortured him for information? But Falkor ignored it and reached down to pull Aiden to his feet. He dusted him off, nodding his head in the direction of the Palace. He led the way towards the main door.

Aiden followed a few steps behind, drawing in shaky breaths.

Why was he following this man? He should leave now before something worse happened. He looked around and realised he had no choice. Any attempt to escape and the sentries would only drag him back. His mind reeled at the thought of what Falkor might do then. He understood now why people feared wizards.

The creak of a door snapped Aiden out of his thoughts. Up ahead the main entranceway to the Palace opened and the Eagle Rider who had saved his life stepped out. Relief flooded him from head to foot. This man had rescued him, bandaged him, and was almost certainly not going to torture him.

"Arthur," said Falkor, nodding as they reached the base of the steps.

The Eagle Rider smiled, a slight crease between his eyes as if he had not expected the wizard to be there. He turned to Aiden and his smile brightened. "Hello Aiden," he said warmly. "It's good to see you again. I am Captain Arthur of the Eagle Riders."

Aiden nodded and sidestepped Falkor up the steps, trying to put Arthur between him and the wizard.

"How is the arm?" Arthur asked, nodding to Aiden's shoulder.

"It's healing," said Aiden, returning his smile. Now that he was no longer alone with the wizard he felt a lot safer and found that his curiosity was returning. Why had he been summoned? And why had he been greeted in two very different manners?

"Good," said the Eagle Rider. "Let's walk. The King awaits us."

The King! Aiden almost stumbled over the top step. That explained things, sort of. But why did *the King* want to see *him*?

Aiden followed the Eagle Rider and the wizard into the Palace. The doors opened into a grand hallway, the ceiling reaching for the sky. Stairs spiralled out of view on either side and the walls were wood panelled, carved with twisting vines and strange creatures. A number of doors were interspersed around the hall with one set of double doors gilded in gold at the centre. But it was to a smaller, plainer door that Arthur led them. Two men stood guard, wearing deep red cloaks emblazoned with the King's crest. They closed ranks as Arthur, Falkor, and Aiden approached, blocking the doorway. Aiden had wondered when someone was going to tell him he was in the wrong place, that he had no right to be in the Palace at all.

"This is Aiden Brokksson," the Eagle Rider Captain said to the guards, "and he has been summoned by the King."

The guards' cold gaze surveyed Aiden.

"He is a magic user," one of them said. It was both a statement and a question.

"He will pose no threat to the King while myself and Falkor are present," said Arthur.

The two guards dipped their heads and slowly opened the door, revealing a long corridor with windows on one side looking out to the courtyard, and doors on the other side hiding countless secrets. Aiden fell into step behind the two older men as they walked through. He glanced back as the soldiers closed the door behind them, marvelling at the fact that he had been allowed this far into the King's private world.

"They are the Palace Guard," said Falkor. "Only the most skilled are allowed to join. They are the King's personal guards and warriors. If we had not been with you, they would not have let you in. And do not think you could have outwitted them with the runes. They have been trained."

Aiden glanced over his shoulder one more time, a slight frown creasing his brow. Did Falkor really still think he was here to enact some plot against the King? He had not even known he was going to see the King until a few minutes ago. He wanted to challenge the wizard about it, but Arthur and Falkor had fallen into quiet conversation in front of him. As he watched them he got the distinct sense that they were talking about him. He strained his ears to make out their words, drawing Muin, the listener, behind his back and letting the tingle of the rune travel from his fingertips up his arm to his ears.

"You didn't need to meet him at the gate," said Arthur's quiet voice, slowly becoming clear. "I thought you knew it was I who was taking him to the King."

"Of course," said Falkor. Aiden could imagine the sly smile on his face. "But you know me Arthur. I heard there was magic involved so I had to come and see him for myself."

Arthur sighed. "And is your curiosity satisfied?"

"Let's just say that I will be watching him with great interest," said Falkor, peering over his shoulder with a cunning glint in his eye.

Aiden gulped and quickly looked out of the windows, letting Muin fade to nothing. When he turned back Falkor's attention was elsewhere, but he had a feeling that the wizard was not an easy man to fool.

They walked for a few minutes more before stopping at another door flanked by two more Palace Guards. This time the guards did not try to block their way, they just nodded politely at the Eagle Rider Captain and the wizard. Arthur stepped up to the door and knocked firmly on the wood three times before entering. Aiden felt Falkor's hand on his back pushing him forwards after the Eagle Rider.

The door swung open before him to reveal a bright room with tall windows looking out onto the gardens. The light gleamed on the polished wooden panels of a desk, reflecting the green and yellow colours of a crest with a winged crown encircling a tree. The royal crest. Aiden lifted his eyes to the man behind the desk. Although seated he seemed tall, his broad shoulders filling the chair he sat upon. Keen blue eyes appraised Aiden as he entered and he sensed both Arthur and Falkor straighten in this man's presence. Aiden had only ever seen the King from a great distance, but he had no doubt that it was Brandr son of Akki who he now stood before.

Captain Arthur approached the desk with confidence, giving a small bow to the King. Aiden followed, his steps small and unsure. It was only Falkor's presence behind him that kept him moving forwards.

"Your Majesty," said Captain Arthur. "Let me introduce Aiden Brokksson."

Falkor put his hand on Aiden's shoulder and pressed him forward. Aiden did not know what to do. His mouth felt uncommonly dry. He half smiled and bowed his head, attempted to say something, faltered and fell silent. He should not be this terrified, he thought. Brandr was a good King, fair and just, if a little distant from his people.

"You may sit," said the King, his voice measured but not unkind. When Aiden looked up he thought he saw the glint of a smile in his eyes.

Aiden perched on the seat in front of the King's desk and clenched his hands together. Arthur drew up another chair beside him and sat down, leaning back comfortably. Falkor remained standing behind them. The King's eyes flicked to the wizard.

"Are you staying Falkor?" the King asked.

The wizard nodded, almost imperceptibly.

The King gave an unconcerned nod and turned his attention back to Captain Arthur and Aiden. Brandr sat back in his chair and clasped his hands across his stomach. Aiden realised that his own hands had gone all clammy.

"Do you know why I have sent for you?" said the King.

Aiden shook his head. "No. But I'm guessing it has something to do with the burning building." If he was in trouble surely they would not have brought him before the King himself. Unless it was serious trouble.

The King gave a small smile, his true thoughts hidden behind an impassive mask. "It does indeed."

Aiden shuffled on his chair and tucked his hands beneath him.

King Brandr continued. "Word has reached me that you saved two lives in the fire, at considerable risk to yourself, and that you later helped to uncover evidence, despite the fact that the street was off limits."

Aiden looked down, waiting for the inevitable rebuke, but he did not sense any anger from the King.

"I am impressed Aiden," said the King. Aiden looked up to meet his eyes and found that the impassive mask was gone and replaced by… gratitude? Aiden was not quite sure but in a second the King's thoughts were once again closed off to him.

"I have heard much about you, but I wanted to meet you for myself," said Brandr. "And of course, the very fact that Falkor is here with you, suggests there is more to you than meets the eye." The King glanced again at the wizard, who had remained standing a few paces behind them. Falkor smiled enigmatically. King Brandr raised his eyebrow ever so slightly. Aiden's arms and legs tingled at the memory of his encounter with the wizard. Why was Falkor so interested in him?

King Brandr leaned forward so that his elbows were resting on his desk. Sunlight filtered in through the window, reflecting off the silver streaks in his dark hair. "Tell me Aiden, what made you run into certain death to rescue two people that you didn't even know?"

Aiden did not answer immediately. He tried to remember what he had been thinking as he lay on the street, the sound of the explosion ringing in his ears. His memories were a blur of emotions, but one thought that had never crossed his mind before he entered the building, was the thought that he might die. It was only at the very end that he had realised that. Aiden glanced up and his eyes met the King's expectant gaze.

"My death wasn't certain," Aiden said eventually. "It was

probable, but I didn't think about that at the time."

A slight frown creased the King's forehead. "So why did you go into the fire?"

"I went in because no one else would," said Aiden, with more certainty than he had felt all day.

"Ah," said Brandr, leaning back in his chair again. "And you were willing to do that twice." He seemed to fall into deep thought and Aiden was not sure whether or not he should answer. At last the King spoke. "You have done me a great service. The woman, whose life you saved, was a close companion of my late wife and I am indebted to you for rescuing her."

Aiden felt heat rise in his cheeks.

"I wish to offer you a reward," the King continued. From the corner of his eye Aiden saw Arthur sit up straighter. "You have demonstrated courage, resourcefulness, and selflessness in the face of great danger, worthy of one of my best soldiers."

Aiden frowned. Where was the King going with this?

"I wonder if there could be a place for you in the Feather Guard," said the King, turning to Arthur.

It was spoken as a suggestion, but Aiden could not mistake the authority behind those words. Arthur sat forward in his chair and gave Aiden a measured look. Aiden dropped his eyes.

"Someone with Aiden's particular skills would be greatly valued in the Feather Guard," said Arthur slowly and Aiden got the feeling that the Captain was choosing his words very carefully.

The King stroked his chin thoughtfully. "Falkor what do you think about this matter?"

As he answered, Falkor's cunning gaze did not leave Aiden. "I think I would rather have Aiden Brokksson as a friend than an enemy."

The King nodded. "It is settled then. Aiden shall become a member of the Feather Guard... as long as that is his wish also."

Aiden stared blankly at the King. Of all the things he had imagined might happen in this room, this was not what he had expected. But was it not what he had often dreamed of?

"Well?" said the King, his eyes bright with anticipation.

Aiden realised he had been silent for a long time. He looked up at the King. "It would be a great honour."

At his words both Arthur and the King stood. Arthur began to pull the chair from under Aiden before he had even begun to stand. Aiden's mind was whirling. Had he said the wrong thing? What was happening? The King emerged from behind his desk.

"Kneel," said Arthur, pushing gently on Aiden's shoulders.

Aiden dropped to the floor, his eyes flicking between the Eagle Rider and the King.

"Repeat after me," said Arthur.

Aiden frowned but spoke the words that Arthur said. "I, Aiden Brokksson, swear loyalty to the King of Teraan. I promise to be faithful at all times, to uphold his rule, to love what he loves, to shun what he shuns and never, by my actions or my words, bring harm to him. I now pledge my service to the Eagle Riders and to the Feather Guard."

King Brandr smiled. "Then you, Aiden Brokksson, are now in the service of the Eagle Riders."

Aiden stood and gave a small bow to the King. "Thank you, Your Majesty."

"Excellent," said the King. "I will leave the arrangements to you Arthur. I must return to my other tasks."

Arthur nodded and together he, Aiden, and Falkor bowed to the King. Brandr dismissed them with a nod of his head, his mind already returning to the paperwork on his desk. Aiden followed the Eagle Rider Captain back along the corridor, retracing their steps until they were outside. Once there Aiden let out a deep breath.

"You look like you're in shock," said Arthur with a laugh.

Aiden shook his head. "That was not what I was expecting."

Arthur smiled at him. "I'm going to put you to work next to my son Tristan. He'll oversee your training when you arrive."

"Thank you," said Aiden. "But can I ask, why did you decide to take me on? You must know the only thing I know is cloakmaking."

"You will learn new things," said Arthur. "Like the King said, it is your courage, resourcefulness, and selflessness that have impressed me."

"And you taught yourself the runes," said Falkor, tilting his head so that the light flashed in his grey eyes. "Not just anyone can do that."

Aiden shifted uneasily, still wary of the wizard's strange fascination with him.

"Now, arrangements for your new post," said Arthur, ignoring the wizard. "How about you return the third morning from now? Seventh hour. That will give you time to get your affairs in order and hopefully your shoulder will be fully healed by then. The rooms in the Eagle Rider Building are small, but you can bring a small bag of personal possessions. We'll have some uniforms for you by the time you arrive. I'll have Tristan meet you at the gate to the Restricted Zone."

Aiden nodded, his mind buzzing with all the information. "Seventh hour, three days from now."

Arthur smiled. "Now I must go."

The Captain began to walk away and Aiden felt the enormity of the situation engulf him. He was a member of the Feather Guard. He could almost imagine the Silver Eagle soaring around his head in joyous flight. His stomach churned and he could not distinguish between his excitement and his nerves.

Suddenly, his elation vanished as Falkor's hand pressed on his back, steering him towards the Palace gates. He tensed, half expecting an attack from behind. Was the wizard going to interrogate him again before he could start his new job? Aiden glanced nervously at the archway in the middle of the lawn. They passed it and Falkor came to a halt by the gates.

"You will see much magic used here," said Falkor, "more than you could ever imagine… but I'm warning you—do not use the runes lightly in the Palace. There are many here more powerful than you and they will not hesitate to use magic against you. They will not stop to ask questions."

Aiden felt a tremor pass through his body. Until now the runes had been his friends and the only consequences had been the anger of his father. Now there were bigger things at stake. The time for sketching innocent runes on the rooftop was gone. Aiden met Falkor's gaze. "I understand," he said.

"And Aiden," said Falkor, almost as an afterthought. "If you are going to eavesdrop on a wizard, you'll have to be more subtle."

Aiden shuddered. He had not fooled Falkor for one second.

Falkor grinned at the sudden fear that must have shown on his face. "You would do well to watch me. You might learn something useful."

Aiden drew himself together and met Falkor's gaze. "So we are to watch each other then."

Falkor laughed. "Yes, I suppose so. Although the difference is that I will always know when you are watching, but you will not always know when I am watching."

Aiden smiled hesitantly, unable to discern if Falkor was making a threat or a joke. The wizard turned and headed back towards the Palace. Silently, two of the Palace Guard emerged from the trees to escort Aiden through the gate and out of the Restricted Zone.

7. Father and Son

Aiden's steps shifted between a swift, eager trot and a slow, measured walk as he made the journey home. He had met a wizard and a King and an Eagle Rider, been into the Palace and now he was a member of the Feather Guard. One minute excitement bubbled through him so fiercely that he thought he would burst if he could not tell someone soon. Next minute came the niggling feeling in the back of his mind that something was not right. It was all he had dreamed of, so what was bothering him?

His chest suddenly felt very tight. Yes, he had gained all that he had dreamed of, but he was going to have to leave behind everything he had ever known. What would his family think about him leaving? Would they think he was abandoning them? In a way he was. He was only a few months away from finishing his apprenticeship and now he would never be a cloakmaker alongside his father.

By the time Aiden reached his street, his pace had slowed almost to a standstill. He hesitated outside his front door. What if they were disappointed? What if they did not want him to go? But the thought of *not* going was unthinkable.

He pushed open the door. There was a flurry of movement as both his parents stood to greet him. They must have been waiting. And worrying too, Aiden thought, seeing the anxious searching in their eyes as he approached.

His mother embraced him. "You're back," she whispered, releasing him, but keeping a hand resting lightly on his arm. "What did they want?"

Aiden gave a small smile and looked from his father to his mother. He pursed his lips. "Well…"

Andor burst into the room and ran over to grab Aiden's arm. "What happened?" he asked looking up with wide eyes.

Aiden hesitated. Would Andor still be excited when he found out or would he wish that soldiers had never come to his house to take his brother away? Or was it merely just his own doubts beginning to surface? It had seemed so perfect in the Palace, kneeling to make his oath, but had he really known what it would cost him?

"Hurry up and tell us," said Andor, tugging Aiden's arm.

"Well…" Aiden began. "I've been made a member of the Feather Guard." He lifted his eyes slowly, both dreading and longing for the expressions on his family's faces.

"You mean actually working for the Eagle Riders?" said Andor, his mouth dropping open.

Kari put a hand to her mouth and sat back down again. Aiden stepped over to her and took her hand, his smile faltering a little.

"What are you thinking Mum?" he asked.

She enclosed his hand in hers, her eyes glistening. She knew this meant he would be leaving, but she smiled nevertheless. "I'm thinking that you have been given a great honour and that I'm very proud of you."

Aiden smiled back at her, a glimmer of his excitement returning.

He glanced over at his father. Brokk came towards him and put a hand on his shoulder. What rebuke would it be this time?

Brokk smiled. "You have made us all proud. Well done son. Well done." He pulled Aiden into a hug and all the tension drained from his body.

"But what happened?" said Andor, his eyes bright. "What was the Palace like?"

Aiden sank into the chair next to his mother and began to recount the events of the morning, not least his conversation with the King. He could hardly believe that the words were coming out of his own mouth. If he had been ten years younger everyone would have said he had made it up. His parents listened, rapt, their worried frowns softening as Aiden told them about the King's gratitude and how he had been offered a place in the Feather Guard.

"And they want you to start three days from now?" said Kari when he was finished, folding her arms. "That's not very much time."

Aiden shook his head. "I know. I hope you're not too sad."

Kari smiled and reached over to hug him again. "I'm going to miss you, but I'm more proud of you than anything. I think we should celebrate. We'll have a special dinner for your last night and invite Aran and Sanna and Branwyn."

Aiden stood quickly. "I need to go and tell Branwyn." She would hate it if she did not hear the news from him first.

"On you go then," said Kari, patting his shoulder. "And invite them to dinner while you're there."

Aiden nodded and rushed to the door, his feet slowing as he crossed the street to the baker's. Of everyone, Branwyn would be the hardest to say goodbye to. She had been there, across the street, his whole life and suddenly that was all going to change. He almost could not even imagine it.

Aiden stepped through the doorway into the warm smell of the bakery. His Aunt Sanna stood behind the counter chatting away to a woman with a basket under her arm. Branwyn was busy beside them, wrapping loaves of bread in cloth pieces and passing them to the woman. She gave Aiden a smile, rolling her eyes at the two older women. Aiden shrugged sympathetically, before leaning against the wall and folding his arms. He would miss their unspoken conversations behind the spritely chatter of his aunt.

The woman with the large basket left, Sanna calling a cheery goodbye after her. His aunt waved to him before disappearing through the doorway to the kitchen where Aiden's Uncle Aran was working the ovens.

"What are you doing here?" said Branwyn, stepping round the counter and wiping her floury hands on her apron.

Aiden grinned. He could not help it. "Guess who met the King this morning."

"You don't mean you," said Branwyn, raising her eyebrows.

"I do."

Branwyn gave a short laugh of disbelief. "Don't wind me up."

"I'm not," said Aiden, trying to stop himself from grinning.

Branwyn's eyes searched his face. "Come on. Tell me what you're really after."

"It's true Bran," said Aiden, taking her by the shoulders. "Do I have to march you over to my Dad and get *him* to tell you?"

Her laughter died down into a bemused smile and his pushed his hands away. "Enlighten me then. Why did you meet the King?"

"You still don't believe me," said Aiden, taking a step back. He spread out his arms. "But you are now looking at a member of the Feather Guard." He bowed.

Branwyn said nothing.

"It's true," said Aiden again, earnestly this time.

"You really mean it," said Branwyn, slowly lifting a hand to cover her mouth. Then, all of a sudden, she snapped out of it and jumped on him, giving him a fierce hug. "Aiden that's amazing."

He smiled and hugged her back. They stepped apart and Aiden looked at her ruefully.

"What is it?" she said, her face turning into a frown.

"I'll be leaving in three days," said Aiden, "to live in the Palace."

Branwyn's frown softened, but she did not smile again. "Ah," she said. She looked up at him. "A big part of me wants you not to go, but I know it's what you've always wanted."

"It's not so far away," said Aiden. "It's not like we'll never see each other again." The words were as much for him as they were for her.

Branwyn shook her head. "No. But I'm still going to miss you."

"Well I'd hope so," said Aiden, grinning again.

Branwyn pushed him playfully. "You better miss me too then."

Sanna called over, returning with a large tray of fresh rolls. "Branwyn I'm going to need your help with this."

Branwyn waved back at her. "Just coming Mum."

Aiden followed Branwyn back to the counter, smiling at his aunt. "Mum's asking if you want to join us for dinner two nights from now. We're celebrating."

"What are you celebrating?" said Sanna, turning to begin stacking the rolls in baskets behind her.

"Aiden's become a member of the Feather Guard," said Branwyn.

Sanna stopped what she was doing and looked up at him. A smile spread across her face. "Really? Well that is worth celebrating." She called through to the kitchens. "Did you hear Aran? Aiden's become a Feather Guard."

The red-cheeked face of his uncle peered through the door. "Aiden? How on earth did that happen?"

"Dad!" said Branwyn, pretending to sound shocked. "Do you doubt Aiden's skills and bravery?"

Aran shook his head, rolling his eyes. "I think you know that's not what I meant."

"Thanks for your confidence Uncle," said Aiden, with a grin.

"Of course we'll join you for dinner," said Sanna, waving her husband back to the ovens before he could talk himself into another corner. "I'll get Branwyn to make something nice for pudding."

"You better make something good," said Aiden, poking Branwyn's arm.

She gave him a cool stare. Aiden hid his laughter behind his hand and waved to Branwyn and Sanna as he left the bakery. Outside he felt his smile falter. He really was going to miss all this. But, he reminded himself, there were new and exciting things yet to come. He was in the service of the Eagle Riders now. Anything could happen.

Over the next two days there was an oddly muted atmosphere in the house, a strange mixture of excitement and nostalgia. Aiden's mother fussed over him and took extra care to see to his injuries, even though he was almost completely better now. His father kept to his work and Aiden joined him, trying to savour every last minute. Andor was constantly distracted, but Brokk did not reprimand him. They laughed and joked as they worked and Aiden almost wished it would never end. Yet he often wondered how his father was really feeling. Was he sad that Aiden would never finish his apprenticeship? Undoubtedly, thought Aiden.

As his last afternoon at home passed by, he felt the sting of sadness in the back of his eyes and throat. He was packing his life into a bag and leaving everything else behind. A small bundle of clothes, the tiny sewing kit his mother insisted he take, a waterskin, and a knife in a leather sheath. And two keepsakes, to remind him of home. A little wooden Eagle he and Andor had carved together and the old flint arrowhead he and Branwyn had found once on one of their adventures. Aiden brushed his fingers over them, pressing his lips into a tiny smile, before adding them to the bag.

All too soon evening arrived. His aunt and uncle and Branwyn came round for dinner and there was much chatter and laughter as they shared the meat and vegetable stew with bread. Aiden sat between Branwyn and Andor with his back to the window. It was growing dusky outside and the shutters were closed, but the kitchen was lit by the flickering glow of the fire and the lanterns that hung around the walls. Aiden soaked in every minute and beamed a smile at Branwyn when she produced an apple pie for their pudding.

"Your favourite," she said, throwing an arm around his shoulders.

Although Branwyn and her parents stayed until late, Aiden was still not ready when it came time for them to leave. There was much hugging and well-wishing on the way to the door. Branwyn caught Aiden's arm just before she left.

"I'll walk you to the Palace in the morning, okay?" Her face was earnest.

Aiden nodded and smiled. "Thanks."

The house felt unnaturally quiet after they had gone. Kari sent Andor up to bed and began clearing up the plates and bowls that were still scattered across the table. Aiden slipped out the back door into the garden, feeling a sudden urge to be in the fresh air. He would have gone up to the roof, if he had not been worried about hurting his arm again before starting with the Feather Guard. He slumped down at the base of the tree, ignoring the cold dampness of the earth as it began to seep through his trousers. Above, through the gently swaying branches, he caught a glimpse of the first evening stars.

The click and creak of the door sounded from the back of the house. Although it was dark Aiden could make out the shape of his father silhouetted against the grey walls.

"Aiden?" Brokk called.

"I'm by the tree," he called back to his father.

Aiden watched as Brokk carefully made his way through the darkened vegetable plots until he stood by him at the tree.

"How are you?" said Brokk, his voice surprisingly soft.

Aiden shrugged. "I'm alright Dad," he said. Well almost, he thought. It was finally starting to sink in that he was leaving home.

Brokk sat down on the damp earth beside him. Aiden looked

over to his father, but it was hard to see the expression on his face through the shadows. In a way he was glad. He did not think he wanted to see sadness there.

"You know Aiden," Brokk began, "just because it was the King who asked you to go tomorrow, doesn't mean you have to go."

"But what if I want to go Dad?" Aiden replied. He wished his father would not try to talk him out of it. It was hard enough already.

"Then I would not want you to be sad on account of me and your mother," said Brokk, fixing him in a steady, heartfelt gaze.

"I just don't want to let you down," said Aiden. That was what scared him most. "I don't want you to be disappointed because… because I'm giving up on cloakmaking for Eagle Riders and well… magic."

Brokk shook his head and smiled. "Son, I am not disappointed in you, nor have you let me down. I think we both know you were never born to be a cloakmaker. In the last few days you have shown me what you are capable of and you have made me proud. Aiden, I may not like you using magic—and I can't promise that will change—but I cannot deny that you have a remarkable skill with it. If this is where your heart truly lies, then I say go to the Palace, work for the Eagle Riders, and do your family proud."

For a moment Aiden felt like he was floating, like a load had been taken from his shoulders. His father was telling him it was alright. He could leave tomorrow and not worry about those he left behind.

"Thank you," said Aiden, leaning over to hug his father. Brokk wrapped his arms around him and Aiden felt like a small boy again, protected from the world by his father's embrace.

"Now Aiden," said Brokk. "Help your father up. This cold ground is not good for my bones."

Aiden laughed and got to his feet, before taking his father's hands and pulling him up too.

"Come inside," said Brokk, putting an arm around his shoulders. "You're going to want a good night's sleep before tomorrow."

Aiden smiled to himself, shaking his head. There was the father he knew. The father who sometimes drove him mad with his common sense and discipline. He would miss him all the same.

8. Destiny

Early the next morning, Aiden stepped out into the street to find Branwyn waiting for him. She stepped forward, dawn light bathing her face golden, and linked an arm through his. "Excited?"

"Sort of," said Aiden, "but it doesn't feel real yet."

He turned back to his family, who had followed him out. His mother pulled him into one final hug.

"Do good," she whispered into his ear.

"I will Mum," he said, squeezing her tight and then stepping away.

He reached out to tousle Andor's hair. "Look after them all."

Andor batted his hand away.

"Come on Aiden," said Brokk, turning him towards the street again. "You don't want to be late."

Branwyn took his arm again and he followed her, keeping his eyes resolutely ahead. The sun had almost reached the horizon and the cool breeze blew the scent of spring through the streets. The wind whispered to him of adventure and far off places. He smiled to himself. Maybe this was the beginning of his very own adventure.

Soon Aiden and Branwyn found themselves on King's Avenue, the towers of the Palace growing ever closer. Aiden could feel the nerves tightening in his stomach and he was glad of Branwyn's company. The big gates to the Restricted Zone came into view and Aiden thought he could make out a solitary figure leaning on the wall waiting. As they drew closer the figure stood up taller and waved.

"Who's that?" said Branwyn.

"I think it's Tristan," said Aiden.

The figure at the gates had begun to walk towards them and Aiden recognised the confident step of Tristan Arthursson. He was dressed in a dark blue jacket with the golden feather of the Eagle Riders on his chest and a sword swinging at his side.

"Aiden," said Tristan, giving him a warm smile. "It's good to see you again in more friendly circumstances. And you too Branwyn," he added, inclining his head to her.

"Hello again," she said, smiling slightly and slipping her arm out from the crook of Aiden's elbow.

"I'm sorry we're taking Aiden away from you," Tristan said, his eyes not leaving her.

Branwyn shrugged and grinned at Aiden. "Don't worry, I can take care of myself." She turned to Tristan. "It's Aiden I'd be worried about."

"Hey," said Aiden, giving her a small shove. "You're going to miss me really."

"Of course," she said, with a smile that made her eyes sparkle. She grabbed him in a hug and Aiden hugged her back. "Now go and live your adventure," she said, pushing Aiden towards Tristan.

Aiden waved at Branwyn, blinking away the tear in his eyes. He turned to face the Palace gates, following Tristan the short distance to where sentries stood guard.

"You're going to need this," said Tristan, passing Aiden a strip of blue cloth. Aiden turned it over in his hands and saw the same golden feather embroidered there. "Until you get some uniform that's your ticket through the Palace gates. So don't lose it."

Aiden showed the crest to the guards at the gate and they let him through without question. Once inside the Restricted Zone he carefully tucked the square of cloth into the pocket of his trousers. The streets of the Restricted Zone were alive with people running to and from buildings, shouting to one another, collecting weapons and armour as they went. Aiden's head whipped from side to side, his eyes narrowing in confusion. He stepped closer to Tristan.

"What's happening?" he asked. He had never seen so many soldiers in one place outside of the training grounds.

Tristan gave him a bemused smile and shrugged his shoulders. "Changing of the watch. The dawn patrols heading out."

"Is it always this crazy?" Aiden asked.

"Yes," said Tristan, with a small laugh. "Don't worry though. You'll get used to all the routines of this place soon enough."

Aiden nodded. He had no idea about life as a soldier or about life at the Palace. What was he actually doing here?

Tristan led him through the Restricted Zone, weaving his way among the throngs of men. "So is Branwyn your girl?" he asked.

"No," said Aiden, grinning.

"Oh," said Tristan. "I just thought, because you always seem to be together…"

Aiden shook his head. "No. Branwyn's my cousin. We grew up together."

"Oh," said Tristan again, sounding faintly relieved.

"Who did you think she was?" said Aiden.

"Well," Tristan glanced away. "After I met you both in the ruins, the Eagle Riders sent someone to check if she was Brathadair, but I never heard the report."

"Branwyn—in the Brathadair!" said Aiden with a laugh. "She's a baker. And she was only in those ruins because I dragged her along."

"Well you should tell her to be careful. She doesn't want people to start thinking she's with the Brathadair," said Tristan.

Aiden's laughter died away. Was Tristan warning him about

something in particular or just being overly concerned?

The street took a turn and suddenly the intricate gates and pinkish wall of the Palace were before them. Aiden reached into his pocket for the crest. At the gate the guards checked his crest, turning the cloth over in their hands and scrutinising him from head to foot before reluctantly allowing him to pass.

"There was a time, not that long ago, when they wouldn't have looked twice at a crest like that," said Tristan, his voice wistful.

"Why do they care now?" asked Aiden, his footsteps crunching in time with Tristan's on the gravel path.

Tristan frowned. "It's all the Brathadair activity."

"But it was just one building," said Aiden.

"Yes, that's what we've been letting people believe. But there have been other things in the last couple of days, not so dramatic, but still the Brathadair sign has been seen."

Aiden bit his lip. The old faction was returning, bringing chaos and destruction and fear. And it was bad enough that the King was keeping it secret from his people. What else might have been hidden from the people? He followed Tristan around the edge of the main Palace, his mind paying little attention until he glimpsed another building through the trees. His eyes snapped up. The Eagle Rider Building—his new home.

The Eagle Rider Building was built from the same pinkish sandstone as the Palace, but here creeping vines trailed over the domed roofs, spreading green and red leaves like feathers across the stonework. Hooked spires emerged from the points of the roofs like giant talons or beaks. Aiden's steps slowed and his eyes grew wide, though it was still not enough to take everything in.

Tristan led the way towards the grand double doors of the porch, his steps sure and easy as if it was any old cottage he was about to enter. Aiden followed him through into a cool and airy entrance hall, stepping lightly as if he was worried about bringing mud in on his boots. How could he possibly belong here? Passages led off to either side, but the space was dominated by another set of grand double doors, even bigger than those they had entered by. Fearsome Eagles were carved into the woodwork above. Tristan stepped up to the doors and put his hand on the wood, giving Aiden a serious look.

"This is the Eagle Hall," said Tristan. "The heart of the Eagle Rider Building." Tristan leaned on the door and it creaked open a little way.

"Wait," said Aiden, taking an urgent step forward.

Tristan gave him a puzzled look.

"Will there be Eagles through there?"

Tristan laughed. "Maybe. It's not called the Eagle Hall for nothing."

Aiden nodded, feeling slightly foolish. Of course there would be Eagles in the Eagle Hall. Tristan opened the door and beckoned Aiden through. Aiden felt his mouth drop open as he stepped from the small entrance hall to the great, bright, open space of the Hall. It was long and high and seemed much bigger than it had from the outside. The walls were a sandy coloured stone and were dotted with alcoves and balconies that were strewn with what looked like heather and twigs. Eyries, Aiden guessed. Moss grew between cracks in the stonework and the floor was streaked with traces of mud and the occasional feather. Aiden gazed up and saw that part of the roof was open, a door to the sky. Sunlight and wind streamed in and the air smelt like the forest.

"Aiden, come meet some of the Riders," said Tristan, tugging his arm and dragging his mind back to the ground.

Aiden saw that a small group of people had just entered the Hall from the other side. They were walking towards him and Tristan, their boots making a dull thud on the stone floor. Arthur was foremost, but unlike the other times Aiden had met him he was dressed casually in a plain white shirt and brown trousers and he carried no weapon at all. Arthur put a hand on Tristan's shoulder as he reached them. He was still slightly taller than Tristan, but had his hair been less grey they would have looked almost identical. Aiden inclined his head to the Eagle Rider Captain.

"I hope Tristan has been showing you around," said Arthur.

"Yes. This place is amazing," he said, looking again to the sky door and the clouds scudding by outside.

"Let me introduce two of my lieutenants," said Arthur. "This is Lief, my second in command, and Maire." He pointed first to the small wiry man with a cloud of white hair and next to the woman whose short curly hair was falling into her eyes.

"A pleasure to meet you," said Aiden, bowing.

Captain Arthur nodded. "Well, I'll let Tristan continue. Don't forget to check in with Cuinn, Captain of the Feather Guard, and then I'm sure you've got much to do before your meeting with Odmund."

"Odmund?" said Aiden, speaking to the Captain even as he began to walk away. But Arthur and his lieutenants were already deep in some other conversation. He looked at Tristan. "Who is Odmund?"

Tristan grinned. "You'll find out soon enough."

Aiden raised an eyebrow but followed Tristan back towards the main doors. He glanced back up at the alcoves in the wall and up to the sky door. "Where are the Eagles?" he asked, feeling slightly disappointed.

"Out flying or sleeping," Tristan replied, not even bothering to look back. "It's not unusual for the Hall to be quiet."

Aiden sighed. He knew he would meet the Eagles soon enough, but part of him was sad that they had not been there to meet him. He shook his head. But why would they be there to meet him? He was not important.

Next Tristan led him out through the double doors and along a passage to the left. They took a set of stairs and entered a corridor lit by lanterns. They did not go far before Tristan stopped.

"You'll probably end up visiting most of these rooms at some point," Tristan explained. "This is where the Captain and his lieutenants have their studies and where the council chamber and records rooms are. For now though we're just going to stop here. This is Cuinn's office. He's Captain of the Feather Guard." Tristan pushed Aiden towards the door. "He'll want to meet you."

Aiden frowned. There was something about the way Tristan had pushed him towards the door and then backed away that made him uneasy. "Aren't you coming too?" he said.

Tristan shook his head. "It's probably better if I don't. I'll just wait out here."

Why? What was Tristan not saying? Before Aiden had a chance to ask, Tristan reached out and knocked on the door for him.

"Come," came a deep voice from within.

Aiden entered, holding himself as straight as he could.

The man sitting behind the desk was broad and muscled with a thick bearded face. His eyes looked up from a series of papers and scanned Aiden from head to toes with an unimpressed air.

"You must be the new recruit," he said, his voice sounding distinctly unimpressed.

Aiden nodded. "Yes sir." He tried to speak clearly, surely, despite the shakiness he felt inside. Would this man see through him? Did he have the power to send him home and make all of this an untouchable dream once more?

Cuinn rubbed a hand through his beard, the expression on his face barely changing. "Well, I suppose you look capable enough, though if it hadn't been the King's express wish I'd be having strong words with Arthur about recruiting you. You're too old to start new. And I don't like charity cases, so I'll be treating you like every other soldier here. If you can't keep up you're out. Don't expect any special treatment because you made an impression on the Captain."

Aiden nodded and licked his lips nervously. He did not want any special treatment, but at the same time could he really manage without? He knew nothing about being a soldier.

"Good," said Cuinn, his face lightening as he leaned back in his chair. "You'll be shadowing Tristan until I'm confident you know what you're doing. Any questions, go to him first."

Aiden nodded again.

"Dismissed," said Cuinn, looking back down at the papers on his desk before Aiden even had a chance to move.

Aiden turned and exited into the corridor. He clicked the door closed, blowing out the air he had been holding in his lungs. He raised his eyebrows at Tristan.

"Don't take it personally," said Tristan, grinning. "Cuinn didn't think you should be trusted, but since it was the King's request there's not much he can do. You'll soon learn that Cuinn doesn't like to be told what to do."

"I can see that," said Aiden, rubbing his arms. "But why didn't you want to go in? Surely he can't have anything against you, you're the Captain's son."

Tristan laughed as he set off back down the corridor. "Cuinn has everything against me *because* I'm the Captain's son. He's always complaining that I get special treatment. It doesn't help that in this case my father did specifically request that I oversee your training. So I was doing us both a favour by not joining you in there."

"Oh," said Aiden, following Tristan back down the stairs.

Tristan smiled over his shoulder. "Don't worry. As long as you do your job well enough Cuinn'll have no real reason to complain."

Aiden gave a small smile and hoped that he *was* able to do his job well enough.

Back downstairs they went straight across the small entrance hall to an almost identical stairway at the far side. This one led up to an almost identical corridor with lanterns hung on hooks between the doors. This time though Tristan took Aiden along the full length.

"This is me," said Tristan, tapping on the third to last door. "And this is you," he said, tapping on the second to last door.

"And who's that?" said Aiden, pointing at the last door.

"That's Euan," said Tristan. "His father is the Rider Halvard. He's only twelve, so he's just started as an apprentice a month or so ago. Just like I did eight years ago."

"And what about all those other doors?" said Aiden, glancing back.

"The rest of the Feather Guard," said Tristan, smiling. "You'll get to know them soon enough."

Tristan turned the handle to Aiden's room and went in. Aiden gazed around his new home. It was a small room but it had a full window letting in the bright rays of the sun. The walls were wood panelled and a pair of lanterns hung from the roof. A low bed sat in the corner laden with a pile of colourful blankets and a wooden chest sat under the window. Folded on top of the chest lay a pile of clothes and a midnight blue cloak.

"Welcome to your new home," said Tristan. "It doesn't seem like much just now, but I'm sure you'll make it yours. Your uniform is all here—shirts, trousers, boots, and a jacket and cloak in Eagle Rider blue."

Aiden nodded.

"Well, I have a few things to do so I'll let you get your uniform on and settle in. I'll meet you outside the Eagle Hall in about half an hour. Then we'll go and see Odmund." Tristan grinned again and left the room, closing the door behind him.

Aiden dumped his bag on the floor and sat down on his bed. He reached over and unfolded his uniform. Linen shirts and tunics, not unlike the kind his mother made for him. The boots looked good, brown leather that came half way to his knees, though he suspected they would take some wearing in. The jacket and cloak excited him most. Both were made from tough dark greyish blue material with flecks of light scattered across. Not light, thought Aiden, touching it. Runes: Dair, strength, Fearn, the shield, Iogh, the resilient.

Aiden quickly changed into his new uniform, slipping into his new jacket. It fitted snugly, buckling across the front with hooks for a sword belt at his waist. He strode across the room a few times, enjoying the feel of the jacket billowing as he turned. He stopped by the window and pressed his hands flat upon the cool glass panes. A swathe of grass spread out below him and beyond that a tangle of dark branches topped with bright green leaves swayed in the wind. The Palace was not visible, but his room was high enough that he could see out into the City. It felt strange being on a different side of the wall from his family. After a few minutes he turned back to his room and decided it was time to see if Tristan was at the Eagle Hall yet.

Back down at the grand double doors there was no sign of Tristan, nor anyone else. He casually leaned against the wall, hoping he would not have long to wait. The minutes dragged on and Aiden's gaze repeatedly wandered to the great double doors. Maybe he could just slip in for another look while he waited. The fearsome carved Eagles above the door beckoned him. He pushed the door open a tiny crack and squeezed through the gap, letting it close quietly behind him.

He barely moved, feeling like an intruder in this massive room. The Hall was quiet, but as Aiden stood he heard the rustling of feathers from above. He looked up quickly and saw a Great Eagle take flight from one of the eyries. Its wings were massive and powerful, muscles rippling under soft golden feathers. Aiden froze, hoping he had not been seen. The Eagle was descending, coming ever closer. The air pounded around him, blowing his hair back from his face. The Eagle landed on the ground a few feet from where he stood, towering over him. Aiden looked up and was fixed in a sharp yellow gaze. He shifted uncomfortably and the Eagle took a hopping step towards him.

"I have not met you before," said the Eagle in a deep but slightly musical voice. "Why are you here?"

Aiden wanted to step back, but forced himself to hold his ground. He gulped before speaking. "I... I've just started... in the Feather Guard."

"But why?" said the Eagle, tilting his head to one side.

Aiden frowned. "The King appointed me..."

"... for saving a life," the Eagle finished.

Aiden said nothing. It was not what he had been going to say, but he could not deny the truth of it. He looked at the Eagle again but found he could not hold his gaze.

"Do you know why you are really here?"

"No," said Aiden, shaking his head. "I keep thinking there's been a mistake."

"Time makes all things clear," the Eagle said enigmatically.

Aiden hoped so, but he wondered what the Eagle knew and how he knew it. His eyes met the Eagle's and for once he did not feel compelled to look away. The silence of the Hall wrapped them both.

"You have a great destiny Aiden," said the Eagle, spreading his wings and lifting himself high into the air with a few powerful beats.

The sound of the door came from behind, but Aiden did not turn. He watched as the Great Eagle flew to the opening in the roof. His shadow lingered for a second, a silhouette against the darkening sky. Then he was gone.

Tristan appeared at his side. "Why am I not surprised to find you in here?"

Aiden turned to him. "Which Eagle was that?"

"That's Jormandar, he flies with Leif. What did he want with you?"

Aiden shrugged. "I'm not really sure."

Tristan raised an eyebrow at him. "You know my father always jokes that Jormandar can see the future."

"Really?" said Aiden, wondering.

"It's not true," said Tristan, laughing. "Come on, let's get going. Odmund awaits."

9. Swordmaster

They left the Eagle Rider Building, Aiden following Tristan across the Palace gardens and out through a small, well-guarded gate into the Restricted Zone. There were no streets here, only a scattering of tracks and fields separated by fences with wooden huts interspersed. To their left, standing sentinel over the fields, was the great walled arena where Aiden had snuck onto the roof and learnt how to cast Uath, dread.

"This way," said Tristan, taking a track leading away from the arena. The ground was hard packed from the passing of hundreds of feet, the grass worn bare. Groups of people sparred in the fields, swords clacking, while others leaned on the fences watching. A man in the field beside them cried out in sudden pain. Aiden looked round quickly to see another man standing by, arms raised in victory.

Aiden ran a few steps to catch up with Tristan. They were nearing a secluded field half circled by a long wooden hut. A group of young boys and girls, who looked around his brother's age, stood on the thin grass in three lines. They remained motionless until a sharp command set them all moving, their wooden swords following a set pattern through the air.

Tristan slipped into the field through a gap in the fence and went to lean comfortably against the wall of the hut. Aiden followed, watching the children as they moved in unison, swords tracing a graceful arc before them. The majority were dressed in simple black and grey tunics, but a few wore red or green, and even a couple wore the same blue as Aiden's new uniform. Their faces were tightly drawn with concentration, but Aiden smiled at a boy whose sword flicked out a little too enthusiastically and almost knocked over the girl beside him.

"This is training for the newest recruits," said Tristan, leaning over. "Maybe half of them will complete it by the time they reach eighteen."

Aiden raised his eyebrows. "And you've brought me here because…"

"You're a new recruit," said Tristan, grinning.

Aiden gulped. Would he be good enough to complete the training? It almost did not matter. He would certainly not master anything before he turned eighteen.

Tristan stood suddenly, smoothing the grin from his face. "Here comes Odmund. The greatest swordmaster of our time."

A man crossed the field towards them, his pace seemed almost leisurely except for the precision emanating from each step. He was tall, broad and muscular, with closely cropped hair above a chiselled face that made it impossible to say how old he was. For all Aiden knew he could have lived a hundred years.

Tristan straightened and tucked his hands behind his back. Aiden smoothed down the front of his new jacket with clammy hands. The swordmaster, he saw, wore only loose fitting leggings and a leather jerkin, his thick arms bare and criss-crossed with scars. In one hand he lightly held a smooth wooden staff.

"Odmund," Tristan greeted, inclining his head. A note of respect crept into Tristan's voice, something Aiden had not even heard when he had spoken to the Eagle Riders.

"Tristan," said the swordmaster, returning the greeting with the hint of a smile. "How is your dual sword fighting coming along?"

"Well, I think," said Tristan. "Though I've not had the chance to test it out on anyone yet."

Odmund nodded. "Ask Muircadh. I'm sure he'd be up for the challenge."

"I will, thank you," said Tristan.

Very slowly Odmund turned to Aiden, the slightest of creases forming around his eyes. "Who are you?"

"Aiden Brokksson," he replied, standing straighter and trying not to glance sideways at Tristan. Was the swordmaster not expecting him?

"Our new recruit," said Tristan.

Odmund's eyebrow twitched slightly upwards. "Step forward then." The swordmaster placed the end of his staff gently on the ground and scrutinised Aiden over the top of it, as if measuring him against the unbroken grain of the wood. Aiden forced himself to be still and meet Odmund's eyes despite the fears roiling within his chest. How could he meet the standard? How could he learn in such a short time? Any minute he would be sent home to his old life to face everyone's disappointment, including his own.

Odmund rubbed his chin. "Have you used a sword before?"

Aiden gulped. This was it. This was the moment the world realised he was in the wrong place. This was the moment reality returned. "No sir," he said.

A slight frown creased the swordmaster's brow. "What were you apprenticed in?"

"Cloakmaking. Sir." Aiden clasped his hands behind his back and dropped his eyes.

"Very well," said Odmund. He picked a sturdy wooden sword from the stack by the hut and tossed it to Aiden. "Now face me," he said in a voice that set Aiden's hands and feet moving before his mind even understood. "Attack."

Aiden raised his sword, knees bent, and watched the

swordmaster. Odmund made no move other than to lean forward on his staff. Aiden pressed his lips together, swinging the sword and putting as much strength behind it as he could muster. Odmund sidestepped easily and gave him a stinging rap to his ribs with the staff as he stumbled past. Aiden caught himself and swivelled to face the swordmaster again.

"Brute force will not always win you the fight," Odmund said.

Aiden tried again, this time lightly darting forward, flicking out his sword while trying to change direction quickly. Odmund met the first swing and then, with an uncanny swiftness, he moved into the space Aiden had turned to and knocked the staff across his shins, making him stumble. Aiden caught himself before he fell and lashed back out with his own sword only to feel Odmund's staff crack across his knuckles. The wooden sword dropped from his hand and Aiden stifled a gasp of pain.

"Better," said Odmund, standing over him. "Now defend."

Aiden grabbed his sword and stood as Odmund came at him, staff whirling around his hands. Aiden blocked the blows as best as he could, but the swordmaster moved too quickly. His breath came in gulps and his arms grew heavy as he lifted the sword again and again. He could not keep this up for long, but he would not give up. This might be his only chance to impress the swordmaster.

He took a step back, giving just a moment's respite from the shower of blows, then he lunged forwards, swiping low at Odmund's feet. He jumped past the flailing staff and turned to catch the swordmaster in his back. But again Odmund anticipated him and was already facing him. The staff knocked solidly into Aiden's stomach and pushed him backwards to the ground.

Aiden scrambled back to his feet, but Odmund held out his arms. "Enough," he said. "Aiden you're a reckless fighter, but it's a brave recklessness, not born of stupidity. I think with some training you'll soon find yourself a proficient swordsman."

Aiden nodded, panting. He bit his lip before a foolish grin could spread over his face. He had passed.

"Come back tomorrow, ninth hour, and join the other recruits," said Odmund, turning back to the other recruits.

Aiden nodded again, smiling now that the swordmaster had turned away. This was really happening.

"Well done," said Tristan, clapping him on the shoulder.

"Thanks," said Aiden.

"Don't look so surprised," said Tristan with a grin. "You rescued those people from the fire, you'd think a little sparring would be easy."

Aiden gave a small laugh. "You'd think."

They returned to the Eagle Rider Building and Tristan showed Aiden around some of the other parts of the building, including the kitchens, the armoury and equipment store, and various other store rooms. Eventually they arrived back at the Eagle Hall where Tristan introduced him to some other Feather Guards, Suilan, a dark-eyed man in his late twenties whose uniform was ripped, frayed, and muddy, as if he spent more time in the forest than anywhere else, and Torryn, a lithe woman in her thirties.

Tristan left shortly after with Suilan to go on patrol, leaving Aiden with Torryn to learn the basics of Eagle harnesses. Aiden shot more than one longing glance at the door before Torryn cuffed him around the head and told him that no Feather Guard ever went out on patrol until they knew how to harness an Eagle. And so the rest of the day passed getting tangled in leather straps and buckles until Aiden's mind could take no more. Maybe when there was an actual Eagle to put it on, it would make more sense.

He did not have long to wait. The next morning Aiden was woken early by a knock from Tristan. He dressed quickly and followed him out, his stomach giving a disgruntled rumble as they bypassed the door to the kitchens. Tristan instead led him to the

Eagle Hall where Aiden frowned at the sight of the rows of hooks holding various pieces of equipment and harnesses.

"Members of the Guard take turns to prepare the Eagles for patrols," said Tristan, reaching to take down one of the leather harnesses. Aiden remembered Torryn explaining that each Eagle had their own personal harness, but he could not remember which that hook belonged to.

A rustling came from above and Aiden looked up to see an Eagle taking flight from one of the eyries. He stepped back involuntarily as it came to land beside them, wing beats blowing his hair back from his face.

"This is Catanta," said Tristan, inclining his head to the Eagle.

"The new recruit," said the Eagle, her voice warm and slightly musical, even though her beak seemed to clip the end of every word.

Aiden bowed his head too, but his eyes soon crept back up. He could not help it. Catanta was smaller than Jormandar, but her beak was still poised well above his head and her outstretched wings could easily cover him entirely. She blinked and turned her head to the side as Tristan approached with her harness. Aiden watched closely as he lifted it onto her back so that it sat in the space between her wings. He carefully smoothed the straps before tying them securely across her chest. Aiden's fingers itched to help, to feel the smooth sweep of her feathers, but he remained still, not sure if he was allowed yet.

A few moments later Lieutenant Maire came hurrying into the Eagle Hall, fastening a blue cloak tightly about her shoulders. "Thank you Tristan," she murmured, barely stopping before leaping onto Catanta's back. Catanta lifted them into the air with a rush of wind. Aiden craned his neck, watching them until they disappeared through the opening in the roof.

"She was in a rush," said Aiden.

Tristan laughed. "It's the morning patrol. Maire's always in a rush."

Aiden smiled.

"Speaking of which," Tristan continued, "you might want to hurry. Odmund doesn't like latecomers."

Aiden jumped round. He could not afford to make a bad impression—not when he had so much to learn. He dashed down to the training grounds, ignoring the puzzled glances of the guards at the gate. But as he rushed up to the fence of their field he sighed with relief. There were only a few other recruits and no sign of the swordmaster.

"You must be Aiden."

Aiden jumped and turned to face the young boy who addressed him. He was of slight build, even smaller than Andor, and his round face with rosy cheeks looked far too young to be carrying a weapon, let alone using one.

"I'm Euan Halvardson of the Feather Guard," he said. "Son of the Rider Halvard. Odmund said you might be early and I was to show you some of the steps if you were."

"Emm, can you do that?" said Aiden, with a twinge of disappointment. "I mean, doesn't Odmund need to show me things?"

Euan shrugged. "It's just the warm up. First thing any of us learnt and we've been doing it every day since, so I think I know it pretty well now." He began before Aiden had another chance to refute him, stretching high and then low, planting his feet firmly at a comfortable distance apart. He beckoned for Aiden to join him.

Aiden ducked through the fence and stood alongside him, copying his movements. And so they continued, alternately moving arms and legs through stretches and fluid movements, gradually building up speed until the whole body was moving at once. At first Aiden stumbled through a few of the moves, but as they continued his limbs began to recognise patterns and move more easily. Other recruits gathered around them, joining in, until Aiden found himself at the centre of a whole field of young recruits.

A shout brought them to a halt and they quickly formed into orderly lines. Aiden stood by Euan and hunched his shoulders a little, suddenly aware that he was by far the tallest and most noticeable person on the field. Odmund's eyes swept the lines.

"Stand straight Aiden," he shouted. "A cowering man does not win the fight."

Aiden lifted his head ignoring a couple of glances and smirks from the other recruits. He hoped they had not seen the flush of heat that had rushed to his cheeks. He kept his eyes forward. His father had told him to do his best at this new position and if that meant swallowing some pride then that is what he would do.

The lesson began. Odmund demonstrated a short series of moves and then they copied, not just once but repeating over and over again until all could perform it without hesitation. All the while the swordmaster walked between the lines adjusting stances, grips on swords, and the positions of arms and feet until he was satisfied.

Aiden's back tensed as the swordmaster watched him for what felt like an agonisingly long minute. He sensed glances from the other recruits but tried to ignore them. Odmund moved closer and pressed his staff between Aiden's shoulder blades. "Loosen up." Then he tapped the back of his knees, making him crouch lower. The swordmaster moved on, pacing the field silently.

They repeated the moves again and again, unconsciously falling into time with one another. Still Odmund said nothing. Aiden's arms began to ache. He wished the swordmaster would call a halt or a change, anything to relieve the growing tightness in his arms.

The swordmaster approached him again, brows forming a stern line. Aiden focused on his sword, but Odmund caught the wooden point as Aiden moved and pulled it in slightly closer to his body.

He nodded for him to repeat. Point out forwards and then up and to the side, as if catching an opponent's swing mid-air.

"You can't protect yourself if your sword is far away," Odmund said. Again he caught Aiden's sword and pulled it in closer, this time gripping his arm too and forcing it through the positions. Aiden relaxed and felt the way his arm moved through the air. It reminded him of how Halfdan the blacksmith had taught him Teine, fire, by guiding his hand through the shape. Sword fighting was no different. It was just shapes and memory and practice until his mind no longer needed to think.

At last Odmund seemed satisfied or at least he did not correct Aiden again, but they repeated the same series of moves until the end of training and Aiden sensed more than a few grumbles aimed in his direction after the swordmaster had left.

Tristan appeared by the hut as Aiden put away his wooden sword.

"How was your first sword training?" he asked.

"Not quite what I expected," said Aiden, rubbing his arms.

"Was that your first time ever?" said Euan, his eyes widening as he walked over to join them.

Aiden nodded, looking at the ground.

"I thought it was odd that you were taking so long to pick things up, but that explains it," said Euan.

Tristan grabbed Euan and wrestled him under his arm. "Even without any training, I'm sure Aiden was better than you were when you started."

"I know, I know!" Euan cried, twisting free. "That's what I mean. He was really good." He smiled at Aiden, a full carefree smile that lit up his eyes.

Aiden searched Euan's face for a hint of sarcasm, but could find none. He smiled back. It seemed he had made a friend on the training field.

"Come on," said Tristan. "Let's go to the kitchens and get some food. I'm sure you're both starving."

Aiden followed them back along the beaten path, through the maze of fences and huts. There were still people everywhere, honing their skills with weapons of all kinds. Aiden watched them as he passed, wondering if one day that would be him. His eyes were drawn to a pair of girls, fighting in one of the fields. Even from a distance it was clear they were breathing hard and sweating, their hair scraped back from their faces in braids. They swung swords at each other with a single-minded fierceness. Just as he was about to turn to Tristan and ask who they were, one of the girls met his eyes and for a second locked her gaze with his. Then she gave a cry of anger as the other girl knocked her off balance. Aiden quickly looked away and jogged a few steps to catch up with Tristan and Euan.

"Who were those girls back there?" he asked them, not daring to look back.

Tristan glanced back briefly and smiled. "Ah. That's the sisters Marsaili and Niamh. Personal guards to Princess Serineth. Fearsome aren't they?"

Aiden nodded, still not daring to look back. Something of his fear must have shown on his face because Tristan laughed. "No need to look so scared. They're alright really. Just don't ever give them a reason to fight you."

Aiden grinned. "That shouldn't be a problem. I don't plan on getting into any fights. Especially not with my sword skills."

Tristan and Euan laughed. "Euan better stick clear of them too," said Tristan, giving the younger boy a light push.

"Do you see much of the Princess around?" said Aiden, glancing back at Marsaili and Niamh now that they were further away. It had not occurred to him before that he now lived more or less in the same place as the royal family. "In the City, people say that she never even leaves the Palace."

"Well, they're not entirely wrong," said Tristan. "I used to play with her when I was really little, but I can't think when I last saw her. The King is very strict with her. He never says it out loud, but everyone knows he's scared that she will meet the same fate as her mother."

Aiden silently agreed and stepped after Tristan through the small gate back into the Palace grounds. The conversation ended as if it was almost traitorous to speak such things within the Palace walls. He put the thoughts out of his mind as they headed back to the Eagle Rider Building and its kitchens.

After lunch there was a short meeting of the Feather Guard, where Cuinn announced that the Rider Council had been summoned and that all ten Eagles and Riders would be returning to the City in the following days. Aiden and Tristan were sent to the Eagle Hall to begin readying the empty eyries for the return of their occupants. Tristan told him that some had not been used for months and Aiden was slightly hesitant about just how much dust that meant they would be cleaning.

They reached the Eagle Hall and Aiden frowned at the high ledges and alcoves. He could see no ladders or ropes to bring them up. Tristan just smiled at his confusion and led him to the back of the Hall to a seemingly ordinary section of stone wall.

"This is just one of the many secrets of the Eagle Rider Building," said Tristan, pointing to some scratches on the stonework.

Aiden's eyes widened. It was Fearn, the shield. Tristan tapped the rune briefly and it lit to his touch. Then he seemed to pass into the wall. Aiden touched the rune himself feeling the tingle of the old magic under his fingertips. Then the stones that had appeared to be stones faded, revealing a narrow opening with a shadowy flight of stairs behind.

"This leads up to the eyries," said Tristan. "Only the Riders and

Feather Guard are told of its existence. Eagles don't suffer strangers in their domain."

"But I'm a stranger," said Aiden, following Tristan up the darkened passage.

"You won't be for long," said Tristan, with a companionable grin.

Yet to Aiden's disappointment they did not meet any of the Eagles. Tristan took him only to the empty eyries where they swept out the dust and old branches, and scrubbed the floors, before bringing up supplies of fresh branches and moss for the Eagles to build their new nests.

The task lasted them till dinner when they joined the rest of the Feather Guard in the kitchens. Aiden was introduced to many of the others, but the only one he really remembered was Muircadh, a tall bearded man in his forties who had been Tristan's mentor when he first started. He told countless stories of his exploits, only half of which Aiden truly believed.

The next day and those that followed were much the same. The overwhelming newness of everything gradually lessened and Aiden began to fall into step with the rhythm and routine of the Eagle Rider Building. He learnt about harnesses and equipment and quarter-spears. He cleaned endless eyries and rooms, harnesses and swords, cloaks and boots. He brought food to people and to Eagles. He was sent on errands and delivered messages.

Some days Aiden helped Tristan with the message hawks. The Feather Guard took turns to feed and exercise the hawks, and to send and log any messages that came in or went out. It was more complex than Aiden first thought. Certain hawks were only trained for a few different locations, as indicated by marks on their legs, and they all responded to different whistles. Aiden managed to learn a few of the signals, but he was almost certain he would have forgotten them by the time he was next there.

Overall it was not so different really from being a cloakmaker's apprentice, except that under his father's supervision all he could do was dream about Eagle Riders. Now he lived amongst them. Aiden's one disappointment was that he was not yet allowed out on patrols. Tristan went every second day and although he described to Aiden the route through the City and forest fringes, and explained the signs of wild magic creatures they looked for, it was never enough to still Aiden's thirst for adventure.

For the moment Aiden would have to make do with sword training. It was both his favourite and most dreaded part of every day. He loved the satisfaction of learning another step, of stretching his body, of feeling his strength grow, yet he was always the slowest, always two steps behind everyone else. Odmund did not move on until all had mastered the move and every day it was Aiden who held them back. Sometimes he wondered how much longer the stony-faced swordmaster would put up with him. Yet a week had passed and Odmund had not thrown him out.

They moved through the familiar steps of the warm up routine and on to sword exercises, imaginary thrusts and parries, swipes and slices, quick steps and turns. Aiden's breath came in gasps, his arms aching to the point of dropping. Odmund called a halt, but instead of dismissing them he divided the recruits into pairs, facing each other, then set them to sparring.

At first Aiden was excited by the change. It felt like an achievement, a progression. But as he began to spar with Euan it felt like all the work of the week was undone. He used the moves he had been taught but Euan knew them too and anticipated almost every one. It was not long before he could feel bruises forming on his ribs and arms. A few minutes more and he felt his sword flailing wildly in frustration, breaking from the patterns he had been learning all week.

Finally Odmund dismissed the recruits. Aiden followed them

to leave, but he was stopped by the end of Odmund's staff pressing into his stomach.

"You're going to have to learn faster than the others," said the swordmaster, bringing the staff up, forcing Aiden to look him in the eye. "They have years ahead of them to learn. You have less than a year until you come of age. Then you're going to find yourself put in situations where you will be expected to know how to handle a sword. And if you don't, you're going to get hurt."

Aiden frowned. "You don't really expect me to master years worth of skills in just a few months, do you?"

Odmund folded his muscled arms. "I think you have it in you."

Aiden shrugged. "I barely scored a hit on Euan today."

Odmund smiled. "No. But you did score a hit and that's more than I would expect of someone with only a week's basic training. Come early tomorrow and I'll give you some extra training."

Aiden raised his eyebrows. Odmund had actually smiled at him. He could not be doing so badly. He did not know if he *could* master sword fighting in the months ahead of him, but he was certain that he would not give up trying. And maybe with the extra training... He nodded resolutely to Odmund and the swordmaster wordlessly dismissed him.

The other recruits had already vanished back to their barracks in the Restricted Zone and Euan was nowhere in sight, so Aiden headed back up to the Eagle Rider Building alone. He hoped there were no tasks to be done immediately. He longed to sit quietly in the kitchens and savour some warm bread and stew. He made his way back through the small gate into the Palace grounds. The guards recognised him and let him through without question. Aiden smiled. He was starting to belong.

Suddenly the air around him seemed to crack and shudder. He looked up sharply to see a plume of dark smoke scarring the horizon. Aiden clenched his fists. It was another explosion.

10. The Message

Tristan's head snapped up from the Eagle harness he was mending, the great crack ringing through his ears. Everyone in the Eagle Hall stopped, poised between tasks. Tristan stood, the leather harness dropping from his hand. Slowly he began to walk towards the door, his steps quickening until he was running. He burst out of the Eagle Rider Building finding the same hushed silence outside. A dark plume streaked the sky. He clenched his fists. Another explosion.

Cuinn's voice cut across the heavy silence. "To the Eagle Hall. Alert the Riders. Ready all the Eagles. We'll need harnesses and armour and something heatproof for the Riders to wear."

Feet scuffled on the gravel. Someone grabbed the clapper of the warning bell and rang it loudly, the deep sound reverberating through the walls. It set Tristan's heart racing. The Feather Guard had work to do.

Back in the Hall the air was filled with Eagles, wind gusting at all angles as they swooped to the ground. Tristan ducked as he ran across to avoid the beating wings of Korak. At the back wall he met Suilan already gathering Captain Arthur's armour and quarter-spear. Tristan took the quarter-spear and lifted the harness that belonged to Kael, his father's Eagle, from its hook. He re-entered the fray, a blue flash amidst a sea of feathers.

Kael ducked his head as Tristan approached so that he could lift the harness onto the Eagle's back. The thick padded area sat neatly in the space just between his wings and various straps dangled down, buckles jangling. Tristan buckled the straps snugly against the golden feathers of Kael's chest and fastened the quarter-spear into its sheath. When he stood up, his father was there pulling on gloves and wrapping a wet scarf around his neck, while Suilan tightened the straps of his breastplate.

Arthur nodded and squeezed Tristan's arm once, quickly. He jumped onto Kael's back, Kael spread his wings and lifted them both into the sky, blowing Tristan back a step. One by one the other Eagle Riders followed up and out through the door in the roof. Sound like a windstorm through treetops filled the Hall before falling suddenly silent.

Tristan ran a hand through his hair. The first and most important task was done. The frantic movement of the Hall calmed, members of the Feather Guard smiled and nodded to each other, picking up discarded items. A short distance away he saw Aiden hanging up some Rider's cast off cloak. When had he arrived? Tristan bit his lip. He had not told Aiden the drill for situations like this. This should have been a chance to train him, but he had barely noticed him in all the commotion. Tristan waved him over.

"What happens now?" said Aiden, his eyes wide and bright.

"Now we wait," said Tristan, holding out his hands. He gave a sympathetic smile as Aiden's face clouded over. "You better get used to it."

"But shouldn't we go and help?" said Aiden, frowning at him.

Tristan shook his head slowly. "The Captain will have left orders."

"Surely they need every bit of help they can get?" said Aiden.

Tristan looked up to the door in the roof. There was something infectious about Aiden's reckless energy that made him feel like a young recruit again. He saw smoke tingeing the sky black and, although he knew they would have their orders soon, all he wanted to do was run out and help his father. The corner of his mouth curled into a smile. The Eagle Rider's did not really *need* him. Or anyone. He was yet to hear of a problem that was beyond their skill. Aloud he said, "The Eagle Riders are capable of a lot more than anything you or I could do."

"I'm going anyway," said Aiden, turning and starting to walk hastily towards the door.

"Aiden, no," said Tristan. He ran after him and caught his arm, dragging him round to face him. Why did he have to be so stubborn? He shook his head. "Didn't you hear a word I just said? I know you rescued folk from the first fire and maybe now you think it's your responsibility to do it again, but it's not. We have to trust that the Eagle Riders have it under control. Do you trust that?"

Aiden looked at the floor and Tristan let go of his arm, recognising the look on his face. He had felt it many times before. It was that desperation to do something, anything to help. Over the years he had learnt to control that urge and follow orders, but sometimes he missed the boy who would have run into any fight without thinking twice.

"I do trust them," said Aiden. "It just doesn't feel right doing nothing. Don't you want to help?"

"Of course I want to help," said Tristan. He wished as much as Aiden that he could go and fight the fire alongside his father. "But we have to wait for our orders. We'll have our task and it will be what's needed, but if we don't wait for orders we'll all just be running around in chaos."

Just then Cuinn called to assemble the Feather Guard and they all gathered in the centre of the Hall.

"There is still much to be done," said Cuinn. "Suilan will lead a patrol into the City. Find where this explosion is and report back immediately. We'll need to know what extra equipment is needed, what casualties there are. Elthen, assemble your healers. Muircadh take some men and liaise with the Palace Guard and the City Guard. I'll go to the King and Falkor. Torryn take a group up to the hawks. We'll need quick communications. Take Euan with you too."

With a flick of his arm Cuinn sent the Feather Guard running.

"We're with Suilan," Tristan said to Aiden, steering him towards the group gathering by the door.

"Tristan, Aiden," came Cuinn's voice.

Tristan's shoulders tensed and he turned slowly.

Cuinn stared at him, the muscles in his jaw flexing. "The Captain asked specifically that you and Aiden remain here."

Tristan nodded and pinched his lips together. By the narrowing of Cuinn's eyes that was not the orders he had wanted to give.

"Any messages come, you're to act upon them. Anyone needs anything, you're to arrange it. I suggest you start by looking out the medicine chests, so Elthen can collect what she needs as soon as the healers are assembled."

Again Tristan nodded. By the door Suilan frowned once in his direction before giving the signal to head out. Tristan bit the inside of his mouth. Why did he have to remain in the Eagle Rider Building running errands while everyone else was out *really* helping? He quashed the thought almost as soon as it formed. This was where he was needed and he would do the task to the best of his ability.

Next to him Aiden looked over, his face grim. "I don't see how this is going to help."

Tristan smiled ruefully. He should not let Aiden see his disappointment. "Following orders isn't always easy. But I trust that my father knew what he was doing when he gave us those orders."

They headed out to the storerooms in search of the medicine chests and heaved them one by one up to the Hall. By the time they had finished Elthen was back with a contingent of healers from the Palace and City Guards. At the same moment Euan came rushing down from the aviary, a message from Suilan in hand.

"Explosion destroyed City library. Send more healers and medical supplies."

Tristan set his jaw as he turned to help Elthen and the other healers pack the essentials into small bags. They headed out quickly, leaving Tristan and Aiden to look out the rest of the blankets, ropes, and buckets, and stack them onto a small cart brought by the City Guard.

The Eagle Hall grew quiet after the last soldiers left for the library. Tristan tried to busy himself, readying the Hall for the inevitable rush of people that would arrive as soon as the worst was over. He and Aiden set up a long table, brought food and water and the spare medicine chest. He could think of nothing else to do. Occasionally Euan's footsteps clattered down the stairs from the aviary but the messages must not concern them since he never came into the Hall.

There was nothing to do now but wait. Tristan sat down in one of the chairs by the table and rubbed his eyes. This was the worst part. Across from him Aiden restlessly paced the length of the Hall.

"You're desperate to go to the library aren't you?" Tristan called over to him.

"How do you stand it?" said Aiden, still pacing. "I feel useless."

Tristan smiled and leaned back in his chair. "You sure it's got nothing to do with rescuing another pretty girl?"

Aiden stopped and folded his arms. "No."

Tristan laughed.

Aiden rolled his eyes at him and started pacing again. "I guess you must be used to this."

Tristan nodded. He barely knew any other life. "I've been working here since I was twelve. I've grown up learning to follow orders without questioning them and without knowing the whole story."

"I just wish I could be up there with them," said Aiden. "In the sky. Actually flying."

Tristan followed his gaze through the opening in the roof. The clouds scudding by were still tinged with black. Was it his imagination or did the air smell of smoke?

"I wish I could be up with them too," he said.

Aiden turned. "Do you think you ever will? I mean, be an Eagle Rider?"

Tristan hesitated. He had not told anyone other than his father of his wish to fly. He knew Cuinn would only hate him more for it. But there was something in the clearness of Aiden's eyes that he felt he could trust. "I hope so. But it's not an easy thing to become an Eagle Rider."

"But surely with your Dad as the Captain you'd have a pretty good chance? Couldn't Kael take you flying?" said Aiden.

"Flying," said Tristan, almost spitting out the word. Aiden really had no idea. He shook his head firmly. "No. Eagles only fly with one person and people only fly with one Eagle. It wouldn't be right for Kael to take me flying."

"Oh," said Aiden. "I didn't realise it was that strict."

"It's alright," said Tristan, relaxing back into his chair. "Just don't ever mention that idea to a Rider or an Eagle. Anyway, there's still ten Riders. They won't be looking for anyone new until old Leif decides to retire."

Aiden sat down in the chair next to Tristan. "How do you become an Eagle Rider then, if you can't practice?"

Tristan smiled. He had never thought of it like that before. "Well, firstly you have to be accepted into Rider training by at least half of the existing Eagle Riders. The training itself is the toughest regime any of Teraan's soldiers will ever have to face, tougher even than the Palace Guard. Only the Riders know what it fully entails. Then, if you survive the training, becoming an Eagle Rider is still dependent on there being an Eagle who has gone through the equivalent training. If person and Eagle decide together to continue, then there is further joint training before you are allowed to fly together. If you pass all of that then you are allowed to say the oaths and fly together. Only then are you an Eagle Rider."

Aiden sat back and raised his eyebrows. "That's a lot tougher than I'd thought."

Tristan gave a bemused smile. How could he ever have thought it would be easy?

"Have you been accepted for the Rider training?" said Aiden.

Tristan shook his head. "No. My father says I'm still too young. Anyway, I think I've got my hands full just now trying to train you."

"Me?" said Aiden aghast. "I can't be that terrible."

They both laughed.

It was evening before the Eagle Riders and the rest of the Feather Guard returned, smokey and exhausted. They drifted in in twos and threes and the Eagle Hall was transformed from an empty silent place of waiting to a chaotic bustle of hungry Eagles and irksome Riders. Four Eagle Riders had left that morning but now eight had returned, and though they had been expected soon for the Rider Council, their early arrival meant there was much more to do. At least Euan was happy with the return of his father, Halvard, and from the reports, the arrival of Astrith, the best healer among the Riders, had been timely. And Tristan had to admit he much preferred to be on his feet, doing, than sitting and waiting.

It was some time later before Tristan found himself with a moment to stand still. Most of the Feather Guard had been dismissed and the Eagles had now disappeared up to their eyries, though Catanta remained on the ground while Astrith dressed a deep cut on her foot. Jormandar too had stayed and hopped over to join the Riders around the long table where Cuinn, Falkor, and the Captains of the Palace and City Guards also sat.

Tristan and Aiden stood by the wall a short distance away silently watching and listening to the low murmur of voices drifting around the Hall. Tristan wished he could make out their words. What were they planning? The Captain of the Palace Guard was saying something heated, banging his fist on the tabletop as he spoke. Next to him Falkor sat comfortably in his charred coat with his feet propped up, watching with a cunning glint in his eye. Arthur ran a hand through his greying hair, frowning. He looked tired, but almost certainly a plan would be forming in his mind. He would want to find who set that explosion and catch them before they could do it again.

A few minutes later there seemed to be some sort of decision made. Maire beckoned over for Tristan and Aiden to join them. Captain Arthur raised his head, his face still lined with soot. He gave Tristan a brief smile. "I trust you were both here this afternoon and have not overtaxed yourselves."

Tristan nodded. So his father did have reasons for keeping them away from the action.

"Good," said Arthur. "You are to spend tonight at the library. There will be soldiers there too, posted at the barricade, but I want you to investigate the building itself. We still don't know why these explosions are happening, whether it's just to spread fear or if there is something deeper afoot. Look for anything unusual, anything that reminds you of the other explosion." Arthur paused, as if suddenly unsure. Out of the corner of his eye Tristan thought he saw Falkor nod. The Eagle Rider continued. "I know, Aiden, you have not been officially trained in magic, but you have permission to use runes if necessary. And both of you, if you come across anyone creeping around you are to fetch the soldiers. You are not to engage them, no matter who they are. Is that understood?"

Tristan and Aiden both nodded.

"On you go then," said Arthur, gesturing tiredly to the door.

Tristan and Aiden left the Hall and collected what they needed, making sure they had their swords and cloaks and gloves. After picking up a small bag of provisions from the kitchens they headed out from the Palace. It was nearly night, the air cool and the sky an inky blue above them.

The way to the library was not far and over the years Tristan had made the journey many times, getting books for the Riders and sometimes for himself. He slowed as they neared the barricade, trying to swallow away the bitter tang of ash in the air. The old rambling building stood ahead, or at least some of it still did. The north wing appeared intact, although the pink sandstone of its walls was blackened and cracked. The spire of the central dome which housed the main reading room still pierced the sky, but the south side had collapsed inwards like someone had cracked a giant egg. Beyond that the south wing was in a ruinous state, though at least the bare framework of the building still stood. Parts of the roof were gone and the stonework around the windows was ragged. Tristan flicked the corner of his cloak over his shoulder. The air was thick with the residual heat of the fire.

They dropped their packs outside the darkened doorway, Tristan beckoning Aiden to follow him inside. He blinked as his eyes adjusted to the gloom, coughing as the tang of smoke caught the back of his throat. Somehow the two tapestries in the entranceway had survived with just a little charring around the edges, although their bright colours were dulled by a fine layer of ash. He guessed that the heavy doors and thick walls must have stopped the fire from spreading uncontrollably through the entirety of the old building.

Tristan opened the door to the reading room ahead and quickly jumped back as stone cascaded towards him. It was blocked. He turned instead to the door on the right and entered the south wing.

The explosion had almost certainly happened in one of those rooms.

The first room was a sad sight and Tristan felt an ache starting in the back of his throat at the sight of all those books reduced to ash on the floor, scraps of half burnt paper flapping about in the breeze. He scuffed his foot through the debris. "I used to come here when I was little," said Tristan, his shoulders slumped. "Why would anyone want to destroy this place?"

"I don't know," Aiden murmured, light flashing at his fingertips as he drew Ailm, the seer.

Tristan raised his eyebrows. Everyone had said that Aiden was good with runes, but how could he create something so clear and bright when he drew it so quickly and so roughly? Tristan's magic tutor would have cuffed him round the head for something like that. Tristan turned back to his side of the room, carefully drawing Ailm and wishing it would not flicker quite so much. He shifted the rubble and half burnt books with his toes. At least with the rune he could pick out things he would not otherwise have seen in the dark, although every movement sent billows of ash into the air.

After a fruitless search they moved into the next room, finding much the same picture. If Tristan remembered correctly each wing of the library contained eight rooms, four to the front and four to the back. There were no corridors, only a series of doors leading from one room to the next. At the end of the south wing there was also a small reading room, a crescent shaped annexe added by King Cormac a hundred or so years ago.

The third room was in an even worse state of repair. A ragged hole gaped through the ceiling, only some of the floorboards remaining, splintered and charred, but holding on around the edges.

"Why?" Tristan mused to himself again. "Why would someone do this?"

"Maybe they're trying to get rid of anything that the King might use against them," said Aiden, his voice no more than a whisper. "There must be books of magic and the like here that could almost be counted as weapons."

Tristan stooped to pick up one of clumps of tattered pages. He wiped ash from the leather cover, feeling the indents of where the title was printed. "A History of Teraan's Forests," he read aloud. That could not be so dangerous to the Brathadair.

"Maybe they just want to make a point," said Aiden again. "A show of power, to scare everyone."

"Could be," said Tristan. "But why?" He laid down the book and picked up something else. It was a little statue of a tree. It must have been important because he could see the pedestal it had fallen from. Under the light of Ailm something flashed across its base. "Maybe it wasn't about the books," said Tristan. "We forget that there's artefacts kept here too. Some of them magical." He held up the tree.

Aiden took the statue and turned it over in his hands. "It's got Ur, the renewer, carved in its base. Magical, yes, but it didn't cause this fire."

Tristan shook his head. "No. But maybe it's one of the things the fire was meant to destroy."

Aiden nodded, placing the little tree back on its pedestal.

"Let's keep going," said Tristan.

They moved through to the last room on that side of the wing, passing a door that had been half burnt from its hinges. Everything here was dark and covered in a thick layer of ash. Barely a book survived. Only splinters of wood suggested that there had ever been shelves and bookcases on the now black and cracked walls. The doorway to the small reading room beyond had disintegrated, the stonework gouged out on all sides.

"Here," said Aiden, moving quickly forward. He picked up a piece of rubble.

Tristan looked at it through Ailm, seeing the bright glow of magic. "Can you make out which runes?"

Aiden nodded. "It's the same as before. Teine, Peith, Nuin, and Uath. There's more too."

"This must be the centre of the fire," said Tristan. Right at the entrance to Cormac's reading room. Did it mean something or was it coincidence? But why not set the explosion in the larger central reading room?

"See if you can find any more of these runic stones," Tristan said to Aiden. "I'm going to have a look through here."

Tristan entered Cormac's reading room and peered around. The fire must have raced round the wooden panelling and consumed all within. Even the big desks Tristan remembered were gone. He hoped there had been no one there when the explosion happened, but the library was a busy place and that room had been a favourite. He turned to leave, but stopped himself. Was that… a footprint?

Tristan's head snapped up, sword ringing from its sheath. The shadows in the corner of the room suddenly shifted and what seemed like a black-winged shape raced at him across the room. A great force thumped against him and Tristan found himself falling to the ground, his sword dropping from his grasp with a clang. His head cracked against the floor and even as black spots danced in front of his eyes Tristan saw the shape leap past. It was just a man, but he must have been using magic to aid him.

Tristan rolled over and jumped to his feet. Through the doorway he saw Aiden launch himself at the man, grabbing his legs and tumbling them both to the ground. Snatching up his sword Tristan rushed towards them. Aiden was not ready for this. "Be careful! He's…"

A mighty flash of runic light filled the room. When Tristan looked again, his vision was marred by bright spots and Aiden was lying on his back amidst the rubble, groaning. Tristan knelt by him and shook his shoulder gently.

"He's a magic user," said Tristan belatedly.

"Yeah? Thanks for the warning," said Aiden, frowning and rubbing his eyes.

"Stay here. I'm going after him," said Tristan, already sprinting towards the door.

"But Arthur said…"

"The soldiers won't get here in time," Tristan called back. And anyway, it did not matter now that his father had told him not to engage. He was engaged already and this man could be their only link to tracking down the Brathadair.

Tristan ran back through the rooms following the clouds of ash left in the man's wake. Ahead he almost ran into a bookcase as it fell across his path, paper and ash bursting around him. He raised a hand to shield his face. The flutter of the man's cloak disappeared into the next room. Tristan jumped over the bookcase and skidded against the door as it slammed shut. He grimaced. He was too close to fail now. He rattled the handle and felt the wood crumble.

Tristan rushed into the next room, ducking back suddenly as runelight caught the corner of his eye. A whoosh of air brushed across his cheek as the man's hand, armed with runes, sailed inches from his face. Tristan swiped out with his own sword, using the movement to right his balance. He heard the snick of the blade through cloth. The man backed up a few paces, a vicious sneer on his face and a dagger of light, formed from the runes Nuin, the spear, and Peith, the thunderbolt, in his hand.

They circled each other, ash floating in the air around them. Tristan swallowed, his mouth dry. He held out his sword, moving slowly, waiting for the man to make the first move. Did he have the skill to win this fight? The circle tightened and sword and dagger clinked warily against each other, flickers of runelight spurting where they touched. Tristan silently thanked Odmund for making him get the runes of Dair, strength, Peith, the swift, and Luis, the protector, etched into his blade.

The man lunged, but Tristan quickly brought up his sword to meet the dagger. Sparks flew as they clashed, crackling and leaping into the air like burning embers amongst the ash. The man struck again, three blows in quick succession, each one forcing Tristan to step back even with the advantage of his longer blade. Tristan swung his sword but the dagger countered, twisting round his blade with unnatural speed. Again Tristan drew back, blocking again. He was not prepared for this. He should have followed his father's orders.

The man jumped towards him, dagger raised two-handed above his head. Tristan raised his sword, bracing the tip of the blade against his palm. He met the attack, but it jarred him to his core. His knees buckled and he felt his feet slip out from underneath him. As he fell he swung his sword and felt it bite into something solid. The man grunted and pulled back a little.

A yell sounded from the doorway and Aiden burst in throwing Peith, the thunderbolt, ahead of him. The man ducked, losing control of his runic dagger and casting the room into darkness once more. Tristan heard a yell, then a thump, and then another grunt. He rolled onto his feet and grabbed his sword all the while blinking furiously until he could make out the shapes of Aiden and the man tussling on the ground. He stepped over and forced his boot down on the man's chest, pinning him to the ground. He pressed the tip of sword against his neck. "Hold still or I'll run you through." He hoped his voice sounded steady, despite the trembling he felt inside.

Instantly the man went limp. Slowly and carefully Aiden sat up and released his grip. Aiden glanced up at Tristan, a slight grin on his face, but Tristan kept his eyes trained on the man. He was taking no chances with a magic-user.

"Get the rope," Tristan told Aiden.

Aiden disappeared, returning a few moments later with a rope that he began to wrap around the man's hands. Tristan still did not move his sword, nor lower his gaze. There was something sinister about the man and the way in which he met his stare, unblinking and unafraid.

Suddenly the man lunged forwards, his hands pulling free of the rope and knocking the sword away from his neck. Tristan grabbed for the man, fingers catching the folds of his cloak, dragging him back. In the same instant Aiden drew Gort, the binder, and picking up the rope, threw both towards the man. The golden rune twisted around the rope, animating it so that it became like a snake, winding itself around the man's arms and tightening.

Tristan dropped the cloak warily as Gort spiked towards his hand. Did Aiden know what he was doing? Was he in control of the rune? But Aiden let Gort spread only until the man's hands were tied fast. He glanced back and Tristan nodded in approval, trying to smooth out the expression of shock that must surely be covering his face. How on earth had Aiden known how to do that?

Sheathing his sword in one swift motion, Tristan stepped back towards the man. He should take charge now. He grabbed the man by his shoulder and pushed him roughly ahead. Aiden led the way outside and they called to the soldiers who came rushing over, flustered that someone had managed to sneak past them. They kept the man under close watch while Tristan wrote a quick message to his father and sent it with a message hawk back to the Eagle Rider Building.

Tristan returned to his prisoner, crouching in front of the man who was now sitting between two soldiers with his back to the barricade.

"What are you doing here?" said Tristan.

The man's eyes flicked up to stare at him, but he said nothing. Tristan unsheathed the small dagger from his belt and laid it firmly against the man's cheek.

"Kill me and you'll never find out," the man said, the corner of his mouth twitching into a grin.

Tristan pressed his mouth into a grim line and stood slowly, sheathing his dagger. He took a few steps away and looked to the sky. It was enough just to have caught the man, he did not need to make him talk as well.

Within the hour the Captain of the Eagle Riders and his three lieutenants were at the library. Grimly, Mathias and Maire took the prisoner from the soldiers' care and marched him away. Arthur and Leif remained behind.

"I thought I told you not to engage," said Arthur, folding his arms, his eyes solely on Tristan.

Tristan stood straight and tucked his hands behind his back. "He engaged us first Captain. We were investigating Cormac's reading room and he came out of nowhere. If I'd known we had him trapped in there I would have got the soldiers first."

Arthur stared at him for a long slow moment and then his eyes softened. "Good work then son."

Tristan inclined his head, glancing over at Aiden. "I couldn't have done it alone." For a second he had almost doubted Aiden, but his skill with the runes truly was as remarkable as he had been told. And if Aiden had not chosen to follow him, even when he had told him to stay, there was no knowing how things might have turned out.

Arthur smiled. "Well done both of you. Now lets go and have a look at this reading room."

"This way," said Tristan, leading the way back into the darkened, desolate hallway.

Tristan, Aiden, Leif, and Arthur returned to the small crescent shaped annex that had once been Cormac's reading room. Arthur drew Teine, fire, and let its brilliant orangey silver glow illuminate the room. Tristan turned slowly, gazing around the room. It seemed no different than it had before. What had the man been doing here?

And then he saw it, an uncontrollable shiver running down his spine. "Look," he said, pointing to the wall.

A large piece of red cloth had been fixed to the wall above the doorway. Last time Tristan was there he must have been knocked down before he had seen it. Now it was clear as day in the light of Teine. Thick black charcoal lines covered the fabric: the Brathadair symbol, the upside down crown, and a message that made Tristan feel cold inside.

Tristan whispered the words aloud. "Out from his tomb, the great wizard is coming." He could not explain how or why, but the simple words filled him with dread.

11. Voices in the Dark

Aiden and Tristan returned to the Eagle Rider Building with Arthur and Leif in the early hours of the morning. Aiden's mind kept turning over the message in his head, wondering if it was somehow linked to the story his father had told him about Sorcier and the Brathadair. The Brathadair hoped that one day Sorcier would return, but did the message really refer to the dark wizard? Sorcier was dead. Aiden did not know what to think. His rational mind warred against the crazy possibility that somehow Sorcier *could* come back from his tomb.

Back at the Palace, Arthur dismissed Aiden to his bed with a pat on the shoulder. Aiden wandered slowly up to his room, eyes heavy and limbs shaky as he sank gratefully into his blankets. The visit to the library brought back vivid memories of the other burning building and he dreamt once more of the tawny haired girl and the shadowy hand of some unknown figure reaching out to grab her. He dozed uncomfortably for a few hours until the morning light streamed in his window, rousing him to wakefulness. Groaning and rolling over, he wished he could fall back asleep. Then he sat up straight, his eyes wide open. He had promised Odmund he would come early for extra training.

Aiden jumped out of bed and fumbled into his shirt, trousers, and boots. He managed to get out the door, but his feet dragged and he felt far too slow as he navigated the stairs. Outside he rubbed his eyes, forcing himself into a sprint across the Palace gardens. The guards at the north gate glanced at each other with eyebrows raised as Aiden sped past.

"Late for Odmund?" one called after him with a laugh.

Aiden ignored them. He really hoped he had not ruined his chances with the swordmaster.

Down at the training grounds Odmund stood statue-like by the hut, his great muscled arms folded across his chest. Aiden stopped just short of the fence, trying to still his breathing.

"You were supposed to be here early," said Odmund, his head turning even as the rest of his body remained still.

"I'm sorry sir," said Aiden, entering the field. "I was out on Eagle Rider business last night and I overslept."

Behind him came the low chatter of the other recruits arriving. A few glanced in Aiden's direction. He kept his eyes forward, wishing they would disappear.

"You're lucky Arthur told me of your Eagle Rider business," said Odmund, seeming to unfold before taking up his staff from where it leaned against the hut. "Now join ranks."

Aiden nodded quickly and snatched up a wooden practice blade, joining the others as they began their warm up. They blurred into a sinuous mass moving quickly and smoothly from one step to another. Aiden stumbled along after them. What was the next step? By the time he remembered they were already ahead again. He shook his head, trying to lift the heaviness from behind his eyes.

As they had done the last few days, they split into pairs towards the end of the lesson to practice against a real opponent. The focus helped, as did the threat of a rap across the knuckles, but even still Euan seemed to dance around him, taunting him almost. Aiden swung and missed, falling two steps forward before catching himself. He kicked the ground, letting out an angry cry. Why could he not move fast enough? Across the field he saw a tiny narrowing of the swordmaster's eyes. He turned back to Euan, but the glower did not leave his face.

They went through the set moves again, clack, clack, clack, and then both tried to disarm the other. Aiden lasted two blows before the wooden sword went flying from his hand. He watched blankly as it dropped to the ground.

Suddenly Odmund's staff butted into his stomach and he doubled over, gasping.

"Your enemy won't care if you're tired. You drop your sword and he'll run you through." The swordmaster's voice was eerily calm. "Now pick it up."

Aiden flinched, the words jabbing like the point of a sword, but he did not look up. He crouched slowly to retrieve his sword. Odmund's feet stayed firmly where they stood even as he called to dismiss the other boys and girls. Aiden straightened up to face him.

"We will have your extra practice now," said Odmund, his steady eyes fixing upon Aiden, daring him to refuse.

Aiden wanted to throw the sword away, to collapse in a heap, to tell Odmund he was through with training for the day, but he stopped himself. The swordmaster's face was impassive, but his hands twisted tightly round his staff. *He's waiting to see if I will give up*, thought Aiden. Yet as Odmund's knuckles turned white Aiden saw that he was also willing him not to.

Aiden took a deep breath, trying to pull himself together. How had the lack of a few hours sleep robbed him of all sense? But that was not all. He missed home and the ruins of the library had only made him remember his close encounter with death in the other burning building. He tried to imagine what his father would say to him now. *Just keep going Aiden. You'll get through.* Aiden nodded.

Odmund's grip on his staff relaxed and he beckoned Aiden further onto the field.

"We'll start with defence," said Odmund. "Let's see your

positions."

Aiden stood with his sword raised in front of him while Odmund attacked slowly from different angles, calling instructions to him on how to adjust his stance and when to bend his wrist and when to turn his shoulder. The attacks gradually increased in speed and Aiden felt like he blundered from one move to the next, just barely keeping up. His mind could not hold all the instructions. He missed a strike and grimaced as the staff cracked against his ribs. He whacked his sword against the ground. The more he tried the less he seemed to be getting anywhere.

"You're thinking too much," said Odmund. "Your mind is tired so don't use it. Let your instincts take over."

Aiden tried to let his mind go slack, focusing only on the movement of his body, switching off the thoughts that told him to move more to his right or to lift his arm higher. Some of the tension drained from his shoulders. There was a rhythm to their sparring that he did not need to think about. He let his body take over, his muscles remembering and reacting before he had a chance to think.

Finally Odmund held up his hand to stop. "Better." The corner of his mouth curved into a smile. "You did well once you decided in your mind that you could."

Aiden nodded and bit back a smile. "I thought I wasn't supposed to think at all."

Odmund gave a tiny shake of his head and waved him away with a flick of his hand. "Go. Get some rest. I'll see you tomorrow."

Aiden smiled and put his sword back in the stack. He could see now why Tristan held Odmund in such high regard. He left the field, wandering back along the path to the Palace. In the next field the sisters Marsaili and Niamh fought each other, their swords mere flashes of silver. Aiden slowed to watch. They swung at each other with such ferocity that he almost winced each time they clashed.

They made his tiny victories today seem pitiful in comparison, yet he could not draw his eyes away. He recognised hints of the moves he was learning in the intricate steps they danced around each other.

"Hey Marsaili, you've got an admirer," called one to the other.

Heat rose in Aiden's cheeks and he hurried his steps. On the field the taller of the two replied with two heavy swings of her sword, knocking her sister's sword to the ground and punching her roughly in the stomach with the butt of her own. Only once her sister was flat on the ground did she stop and drive her sword point-first into the earth. She wiped sweaty strands of golden brown hair from her forehead with the back of her hand.

"Wait up," she called, feet pounding after him.

Aiden slowed and pressed his lips together. He turned to face her.

"You new here?" she said, leaning over the fence, grey eyes flashing.

Aiden nodded. He guessed she was Marsaili, the older of the two. She had a scar along her right cheekbone that reminded him of a line of war paint. He wondered who had been good enough to score a hit against her.

"Like what you see?" said the other girl, joining her sister at the fence. Her face was rounder than her sister's and her hair and eyes darker. Niamh. She laughed, flicking her braid over her shoulder. Aiden's face felt hot. He could not quite tell whether he was being laughed at or not.

"Emm…" he began.

"You're the new Feather Guard," said Marsaili, leaning closer, a coy grin on her face.

Aiden smiled and managed to stop himself backing up a step. "What gave it away?" he said, pinching the embroidered golden feather on the front of his shirt.

"You're not what I imagined," said Niamh frankly, tilting her head to the side.

"Not twelve you mean," said Aiden, raising an eyebrow. He had already had that line from a few of the Palace Guard.

She wrinkled her nose. "No. Not heroic enough."

Aiden frowned.

"That's a bit unfair Niamh," said the first sister, definitely Marsaili. "It doesn't take anyone special to run into a burning building."

Aiden's mouth dropped open a little.

"But he did it twice!" said Niamh. Although she spoke to her sister she glanced at him, the beginnings of a grin at the corner of her mouth. Again Aiden could not tell if she was truly impressed or just laughing at him. Aiden clenched his jaw, hoping they could not see the heat rising in his cheeks.

"I'm sure you'd have done the same," said Aiden.

"Of course we would," said Marsaili, slowly straightening up. She reached a hand over the fence. "I'm Marsaili by the way."

Aiden shook the outstretched hand, feeling the solid strength behind her grip. She could probably knock him unconscious with just her bare hands.

"And I'm Niamh," said the other.

"Aiden," he replied, eyes flicking between the two. At least he had got their names right.

"Welcome to the Palace, fire-boy," said Marsaili with a smirk.

Niamh jumped back from the fence, tapping Marsaili on the arm with her sword. Marsaili followed more slowly. "You know Tristan, right?"

Aiden nodded.

"Well, tell him he should come and spar with us again."

Niamh called back across the field, "We promise not to show him up in front of Odmund again."

"Okay," said Aiden, with a half smile. He had no difficulty

imagining Marsaili completely annihilating Tristan with a few clean sweeps of her sword.

Aiden headed back to the Eagle Rider Building, hoping to find Tristan in the kitchens and question him further about this sparring match with Marsaili. The kitchens were busy, members of the Feather Guard chatting animatedly amongst themselves and calling across to a couple from the Palace Guard who were stationed there that day. Aiden grabbed his food and found Tristan at his usual table in the corner, sitting with Suilan.

"Euan tells me you were late for training this morning," said Tristan. "I'm surprised you're back in one piece."

Aiden laughed. "Yeah, not as surprised as I am." He put down his bread and looked up at Tristan. "But I also heard that you got beaten by a girl."

Tristan's eyes narrowed. "Now who might have told you such a thing?"

Aiden shrugged. "I heard it straight from the mouth of the girl who beat you."

Tristan laughed and sat back. "Oh you mean Marsaili. Well, there's no shame in being beaten by her. She's frightening to fight against."

Suilan nodded. "I've not met a man who said they could beat her, except those that are old enough to have faced her when she was younger."

"What about Odmund?" said Aiden, leaning in.

"Well no one knows," said Suilan. "But we'd all pay money to see it."

"She didn't challenge you to a fight, did she?" Tristan asked.

Aiden shook his head. "No. But she did challenge you to a rematch."

"Oh really," said Tristan, folding his hands behind his head. "Clearly wiping me out once is not enough."

A shadow fell across their table from behind and Aiden turned around to find Cuinn standing over them. Tristan dropped his hands and wiped the smile from his face. Aiden quickly swallowed his mouthful of bread.

"Tristan, Aiden," he said. "I know you were due to go out on patrol this afternoon, but since you were out all night I've got Muircadh and Torryn to take Euan out instead. I'd like the two of you to go to the archives. Lieutenant Maire has made a start on researching this mysterious wizard, but she has other things to attend to this afternoon. She'll brief you when you get there."

Tristan stood with a curt nod and Aiden copied him, trying not to let the frown show on his face. Cuinn must have sensed it, for he gave Aiden a long hard stare before moving away. As soon as the Captain was gone Aiden's shoulders slumped. Finally a chance to go on patrol and he was being sent to the archives instead.

"You'd better finish up quick," said Tristan.

Aiden rushed the last few mouthfuls of his bread and cheese. He followed Tristan up the stairs into the side corridor that hosted the Riders' quarters and a few larger rooms. One of the doors sat ajar and Tristan pushed it open revealing the council chamber. It was a long windowless room with a sliding wooden partition along the far wall that opened onto a ledge in the Eagle Hall, allowing Eagles to join the meetings. For now the partition was closed and the room filled by a large table, the surface of which was hidden underneath a giant map showing the whole country of Teraan. The Rider Maire was standing over it, rubbing her chin thoughtfully. She glanced up and smiled as they entered.

"Come to take over?" she asked.

Tristan nodded.

"I should say well done to you, Aiden, on your first successful mission last night," she said, tucking her curly hair behind her ears.

"Thank you," said Aiden. "Has the man we caught said anything yet?"

Maire smiled, but her eyes remained serious. "Not to worry. Arthur and Falkor will find out what he knows."

Aiden shuddered. He remembered Falkor's methods for finding out information and wondered how long it would take for the man to divulge his secrets.

"Now let me explain," Maire continued. "We're trying to work out who the 'great wizard' referred to in the Brathadair's message is. I've spent the morning compiling all the reports that have been labelled as mentioning a wizard of old. There's a lot of history to read through, but we need to figure out if any of these wizards were linked to the Brathadair and, of course, we need to see if there's any mention of a tomb." Maire placed a hand on top of a large pile of crinkled and dusty papers sitting on the table beside the map. "This is what I've got so far, but if you get through this there may be more in the archives."

Tristan nodded sharply, but Aiden found himself staring at the pile of papers, a frown spreading across his brow.

"You can read, can't you?" said Maire, bobbing her head into his line of vision.

Aiden blinked. "Oh yes. My father taught me when I was younger..."

Maire smiled. "Well you'll be glad of it now."

Aiden smiled, suddenly taken over by the sense that somehow his Dad was still looking out for him.

Aiden and Tristan took a pile of papers each and set to work. Aiden found that they were reports written by Eagle Riders about incidents that had happened over the years. Despite his fears they were not nearly as difficult nor as dull as he had imagined. He found it quite fascinating to read the words of Riders long dead, to hear how they spoke and learn about the Teraan City of their time. He read about incidents from the later years of King Cormac's reign, grandfather to the current King Brandr. They too had been plagued by the Brathadair causing explosions involving magic, destruction, and fire. From the incidents it seemed that leaving messages in the wake of destruction was not new to the Brathadair. Almost all the Riders then had noted messages foretelling the wizard Sorcier's return.

After a few hours of reading, Aiden shared his findings with Tristan. Tristan had been reading about more recent events, but the reports were oddly similar. Although the names of other wizards appeared, they came and went with the years. Yet Sorcier's name endured.

"Do you think the Brathadair's threats ever came true? Did Sorcier ever come back?" said Aiden, rubbing his temples.

Tristan shook his head, leaning back in his chair. "Not from what I've read. But it seems the Eagle Riders took it very seriously back then."

"Which makes sense," said Aiden. "After all Sorcier was probably still alive back then. But now…?"

Tristan shrugged.

It was the same dilemma Aiden had been tossing over in his mind since the night before. More in hope than certainty he said, "Maybe it's just some discontented folk using the old Brathadair symbols to make people afraid."

"Maybe," Tristan mused, half to himself. "What I want to know is where is Sorcier going to come back from? Clearly he's not here anymore, so what happened to him?"

"The stories go that the Eagle Riders defeated him," said Aiden, remembering what his father had told him.

"Yes," said Tristan. "But why haven't we read about that in any of these reports?"

Aiden shrugged again. "We're looking in the wrong reports?" he suggested.

Tristan nodded and collected more reports from the archive next door, adding them to the never-ending pile of paper stacked on the table. Aiden half regretted his suggestion, but he found his curiosity was enough to keep him reading. Everyone knew the Eagle Riders had defeated Sorcier, but how and where and what had happened to him afterwards? Had the truth of the story been lost over the years so that even the Eagle Riders did not remember it?

Aiden and Tristan spent the rest of the afternoon reading and were no closer to an answer. Riders and Feather Guards came in and out of the room, bringing reports of the more recent Brathadair attacks and creating a pile of runic stones in the corner, which Aiden recognised as those he had found in the burning building and the library. Later, they heard that Sigurd and Svana, husband and wife, and last of the Riders to answer Arthur's summons, had arrived. Aiden wished he could go down to the Eagle Hall to meet them, but Tristan showed no signs of abandoning their task and so he stayed. Not long after, Arthur himself, accompanied by the wizard Falkor, came to check on their progress before the Rider council convened.

Tristan stood to give their report, his voice measured as he spoke. "There have been a few dark wizards and a few great wizards mentioned over the years in the Eagle Riders' reports, but only one name that has come up again and again, and always in association with the Brathadair."

"Sorcier," said Falkor, interrupting.

"Yes," said Tristan, his mouth pressed into a grim line. "What the reports don't tell us is what became of Sorcier."

"They wouldn't," said Arthur. "The reports of that are kept in the Eagle Riders' private archive. You have both done well though." The Eagle Rider Captain glanced away, a pained expression flitting across his face.

"Was there ever really any doubt?" said Falkor, clasping his hands behind his back and raising an eyebrow at Arthur.

"I had to be sure first," said Arthur, returning his gaze with a grim stare. Aiden's eyes widened. They could not really think that Sorcier would come back. The dark wizard was long dead. It had to be someone else just using his name to instil fear.

"Thank you," said Arthur. "That's enough for today. You two should get a good rest tonight. You've been working hard these last two days."

Aiden nodded gratefully, following Tristan from the council chamber. They went for food together in the kitchens, but it was a quiet meal, neither speaking much, both sharing in the silent worry of what was to come. Aiden returned to his room shortly after, standing for a moment, gazing out of the window. What were Branwyn and Andor and his parents up to at this very moment? They would know about the library by now, but had they heard about the message left inside? What would they think it meant? What did he even think it meant? He went to bed mulling over these thoughts, but coming to no real answers.

The next day, after his morning tasks, Aiden went down early to see Odmund. They worked on his technique and he tried to let his body settle into the rhythm of sparring again. Later when Euan and the other recruits arrived he put Odmund's advice into practice and tried not to overthink too much. At first he saw no change, but when they turned to sparring in the last half hour he found he was getting hit less often and by the end of the lesson he was surprised to find only a small ache in his arms. He must finally be getting used to holding a sword.

He caught Euan at the end of training and elbowed him in the side. "You're not beating me quite so often," he said with a laugh.

Euan mumbled something and starting walking back to the Eagle Rider Building.

Aiden frowned. That was not like him.

"Hey what's wrong?" said Aiden, running after him.

"It's nothing really," said Euan, his voice quiet. "Just my Dad's gone away again, on a mission."

On a mission, thought Aiden, wondering. But the Eagle Riders had only just returned for the Rider council. "What's it about?" he said aloud.

Euan shrugged. "He didn't tell me."

Aiden wondered where he had gone. And why? What could possibly be important enough to take an Eagle Rider away from Teraan City, when the Brathadair threat was growing every day?

Later Aiden asked Tristan about it. Tristan reported that both Halvard and Kanook along with Johann and Arvid had left that morning, but he knew no more about it than Euan had.

"Has your father not said anything about it?" asked Aiden, sure that there must be more to it.

"He doesn't talk to me about everything," said Tristan, folding his arms. His expression softened. "But no, he's not spoken to me about this. Which means it's either nothing to worry about or it's really bad."

Despite the unrest, the next few days blurred into one as Aiden's life became part of the wider routine of the Eagle Rider Building. Every morning he was up at dawn either being sent to feed the hawks or help one of the Riders prepare for a patrol. He soon mastered how to put a harness on an Eagle and was becoming even more familiar with the cleaning and maintaining of all the equipment. He took his turn with Tristan to exercise the message hawks and had mastered a couple of the whistles well enough that the birds would fly to his hand. His sessions with Odmund continued, sometimes joining with the other recruits and other times getting private lessons from the swordmaster. He was improving, but every time he seemed to master something Odmund would add another challenge.

Surveillance of the Brathadair continued. Maps of the City and of the wider country dominated the walls of the council chamber. They were quickly filling up with markers showing past and present Brathadair attacks and hideouts. The Brathadair themselves were not silent. Nothing on the scale of the first burning building or the library was attempted, but their presence in the City was felt nonetheless. One night the gatehouse on King's Avenue was attacked and the City awoke to find three words scrawled over and over again around the City Walls: HE IS COMING HE IS COMING HE IS COMING. Another day, the grain store in the outer City was burnt down and the King had to arrange the royal reserve to be made available to the people. Rumours of the return of Sorcier began to spread throughout the City.

On the morning of the fourth day since the attack on the library, Aiden entered the Eagle Hall and stopped short. He had been expecting Tristan and maybe Mathias and Korak, but not a gathering of Riders, Eagles, and Feather Guards. They spoke in low tones and there was a tension amongst them, making them stand too stiffly or gesture too sharply. Aiden wondered whether he should approach. Before he could decide Tristan broke away from the gathering and came over to him.

"What's going on?" Aiden asked.

Tristan's eyes were grim. "Halvard and Johann should have sent a message hawk by now."

"Has something happened to them?" said Aiden.

Tristan held up his hands.

Just then Arthur entered, flanked by Cuinn. Aiden and Tristan fell silent, watching as the two Captains crossed the Hall and joined the other Riders and Eagles. Aiden twisted his hands together. Tristan frowned. Arthur spoke to the group, but his voice was too low to hear. The Riders' faces were impassive and Aiden was not familiar enough with Eagle expressions to know what they were thinking. A few minutes passed and then the group dispersed, walking and flying away with what Aiden could only describe as renewed purpose.

Cuinn walked towards them.

"There's been a change of plans," said Cuinn, handing Tristan a crumpled piece of paper. Tristan's eyes scanned the paper and Aiden glanced at it over his shoulder. It was a list of things, dried fruit and meat, water-skins, ropes, blankets, and more, all accompanied by scores of tally marks. Tristan's eyes went wide and he jerked his head up suddenly, looking Cuinn in the eye. Aiden snatched the list from his hand, wondering what it was he had seen.

"This is an expedition list," said Tristan, the hint of a question in his voice. "Enough for all the Eagle Riders."

Cuinn nodded. "That man you caught. He finally talked."

"And?" said Tristan.

"And the Eagle Riders have decided that they all need to take action. With Johann and Halvard's possible disappearance we can take no chances," said Cuinn.

"Where are they going?" Tristan asked.

"Only the Eagle Riders need to know that," said Cuinn. "This is all that matters to you two now." He tapped the expedition list that was still in Aiden's hand. "The Riders plan to leave tonight, so don't take your time. I want you two to organise the food supplies."

"Yes sir," said Tristan.

Cuinn half turned but stopped. "This takes precedence over any other tasks or training you might normally do."

"Of course," said Tristan. He waited until Cuinn had gone before turning to Aiden. "Don't worry. I'll speak to Odmund."

Aiden smiled gratefully.

The rest of the day passed in a whirlwind of activity. Aiden and Tristan moved between kitchens and stores, before heading out into the City to purchase the rest of the supplies. Back in the Eagle Hall Suilan and others organised the weapons, while Torryn oversaw the harnesses and equipment. Elthen and Astrith stripped the medical chests almost bare trying to decide what to take, before returning at least half to the boxes. Up in the aviary Muircadh picked out suitable message hawks for the trip. By the afternoon the Hall was filled with more things than Aiden thought possible. He wondered how they would ever carry it all on their journey, but then began the process of checking and testing and discarding.

By early evening the busyness of the Eagle Hall died down to be replaced by nervous anticipation. Packs of provisions and equipment lined the walls in readiness, waiting to be secured onto the Eagles' harnesses. The Eagle Riders were milling around, glancing at each other, checking and rechecking bundles, tightening the harnesses. The Eagles moved quietly about the floor of the Hall, flexing their wings and ki-ing softly to each other. Finally, Arthur gave the signal for the harnesses to be loaded. The Feather Guard ran to their tasks. Aiden went to follow, but the Eagle Rider Captain grabbed his arm.

"I need you to go and fetch Falkor," said Arthur. "I need to speak with him before we leave."

Aiden nodded eagerly. He had never been to the wizard's quarters before, but Tristan had shown him the door around the back of the Palace should he ever be sent there. He ran from the Eagle Rider Building into the darkness outside and cut across the grass towards the back corner of the Palace. A tiny breeze rustled the trees to his right, but otherwise the night was still and cool.

He had almost rounded the corner when a strange noise, like a muffled cough, sounded from somewhere nearby. Aiden slowed and looked to the trees, shadowy trunks reaching like black fingers into the mass of rippling leaves. He saw no one. Frowning, he drew Muin, the listener, in the palm of his hand, hiding the light of the rune from anyone who might be watching. Some distant part of his mind protested that it was not a good idea to use magic just before finding Falkor, but it was too late now. He half closed his eyes, focusing on the sound while still walking.

Voices trickled through to him. "Our man played his part well," said one voice, a man. The sound of it tugged at Aiden's memory.

"Good," said another, this time unfamiliar, but sharp and calculating. "All is ready at Cairn Ban?"

Aiden's feet slowed even further. Cairn Ban? Where was that?

"The trap is set," said the first voice. "The Riders won't stand a chance."

Aiden stumbled. Cairn Ban must be where the Riders were going. But no one had been told—not even the Feather Guard.

"Excellent," said the second voice.

Aiden's ears were wide open and fizzing, his mind racing. Who were these two men? Why did they want to set a trap for the Eagle Riders? And why did they want to send them to Cairn Ban? Questions buzzed through his mind, but he could think of no clear answers to any of them. He knew he should warn someone, but should he continue on to Falkor or go back to the Eagle Rider Building?

The voices continued, quieter this time. He must have passed their location.

"What happens when Brandr finds out?" said the first voice.

The second voice laughed coldly. "Brandr, the fool, won't have a chance to do anything. I'll do away with his trusted wizard and then... well Brandr won't be King for much longer..."

Aiden's heart hammered in his ears. These men wanted to do much more than trap the Eagle Riders. They were plotting to overthrow the King. And right now Aiden was the only person who knew. He remembered the conversation he had had with Jormandar on his first day in the Eagle Hall. The Eagle had spoken of destiny. Was this his destiny?

Aiden extinguished Muin in his fist and turned abruptly back the way he had come. There was no time to find Falkor. He had to stop the Eagle Riders from leaving. His feet jittered across the grass, itching to burst into a sprint, but he forced himself into a measured walk. He was nearing the spot where he thought the voices had come from. Maybe he could catch a glimpse of the men. If they were inside the Palace gardens it meant they were trusted and that meant they could be anyone.

Movement flickered ahead, the shape of a man emerging from the trees. Aiden kept his head down, as if he had not seen, but the man's path lay between him and the Eagle Rider Building. If he timed it right he would see the man's face. His heartbeat quickened. It also meant that the man would see him. What if he realised he had been overheard? Aiden did not doubt that he would be killed.

There was nothing to do but keep going, anything else would only raise suspicions. Aiden forced a steady pace into his feet. The man continued towards him. Aiden's shoulders tensed and squirmed. He wished he had a sword, even a wooden practice blade. But as the man came closer he lifted his head to wish Aiden goodnight, passing him by with no concern. Aiden nodded in reply, trying to keep his expression vague, even while he memorised every detail of the man's thin face, from his dark hair to his pale blue eyes. Spindly arms and legs had peeked out from beneath flowing robes and it was clear to Aiden he was not a soldier.

Once the man had disappeared from sight around the corner of the Palace. Aiden broke into a sprint. The Eagle Riders, the very people who had taken him in and made him welcome, were in danger. He needed to find Arthur, someone, anyone, and warn them before it was too late.

12. The Conspirators

Outside the Eagle Rider Building a group of people had gathered: ten or so figures milling around in the darkness, blocking the main door. Aiden almost froze in panic, thinking the enemy had already come to take down the Eagle Riders. But someone in the crowd raised a hand and waved to him. Relief washed over him at the familiar blue of the Feather Guard. But why were they all outside?

Tristan stepped out of the crowd, grinning. "I almost thought you weren't coming back."

Aiden ignored him. "What's going on? Have the Riders gone yet?"

Tristan shook his head. "The King and Falkor are in speaking with them. We'll see them when they fly out."

"We have to stop them from leaving," said Aiden, turning from Tristan before he had even finished speaking. He pushed past the other Feather Guards, ignoring the frowns and scowls directed his way. He made straight for the door, bursting into a run once he was free of the crowd. The crossed spears of two of the Palace Guard jumped into his path and he skidded to a stop on the gravel. His eyes widened. "Let me through."

"No one may enter while the King is inside."

"I'm a Feather Guard," said Aiden. "I have an important message for the Eagle Riders."

"Then you'll have to give them the message after the King's

gone."

"After will be too late," said Aiden, hearing his desperation crack his voice. The Riders could leave any minute and he was the only thing between them and the trap. The two Palace Guards did not move. Aiden breathed in slowly and took a small step back. There was only one way to get past these guards and he was probably going to regret it later.

Suddenly a hand caught his arm. He looked to see Tristan there, anxiety lining his face.

"Aiden, whatever you are going to do, don't."

He said the last word so slowly and firmly, Aiden almost wanted to obey him. But if Tristan really knew what was going on he would not be trying to stop him. There was no time to make him understand.

"I'm sorry," Aiden whispered. Then he brought up runes he had secretly been drawing in his hands and threw them at the guards. Peith, the thunderbolt, carried by Eadha, the wind, with Dair for extra strength. The runes whipped around Aiden in a great whirlwind, knocking down any who stood too close. Tristan slumped heavily at his feet and Aiden wished there had been another way. But the guards were down and the rest of the Feather Guard were staring at him in shock. He had to reach the Eagle Riders while he still could. There was no time for anything else.

Aiden pushed through the door into the Eagle Rider Building, sprinting the few feet across the small entrance hall to the grand double doors that led into the Eagle Hall. But before he had made it, Aiden found himself on the floor, a shooting pain in his ankles as if someone had whipped a flaming rope around them. He scrabbled onto his hands and knees but a second lash brought him to the ground again. He struggled, confused, then saw the golden gleam of Gort, the binder, wrapping around his body. There was another guard. He opened his mouth to speak, but before he could utter a single word the spear butt of the remaining guard crashed down between his shoulder blades. His forehead smacked off the ground, leaving his head ringing.

Aiden lay still on the ground, taking a moment to gather his strength. All he had to do was get through the next door. Before Gort could reach his hands Aiden drew Uath, dread, and threw it at the guard. The room grew dark for a moment and the guard took an involuntary step back giving Aiden enough space to crawl forward. He drew Ruis, the dancer, and the light of the rune flitted ahead of him like some small creature and pushed open the grand doors to the Eagle Hall. A rustling storm of wind battered his face and with sickening dismay he realised it was the Eagle Riders taking to the sky. Gort still wound its way around his body, stiffening his limbs and choking his voice. If he could just get up and shout and catch their attention. With all the strength he could muster Aiden envisioned Peith in his mind, sending the thunderbolt crashing through the magic that bound him. Gort exploded around him in a thousand tiny sparks, lifting a weight from his body but leaving him tingling all over. The force of the magic knocked back the guard who had been a few paces behind, already raising his spear to knock Aiden down again. Aiden jumped to his feet. Across the Hall he saw Falkor, the wizard's eyes cold as steel, staring straight at him. Aiden saw him raise his hand, the glow of a rune already on his fingertips.

"Falkor," Aiden yelled across the room. "It's a trap! Don't let them go! Falkor listen—"

The force of Falkor's blow knocked him to the ground again, but he saw the cold light fade from the wizard's eyes as the words reached him. The wizard turned his head sharply skywards, but it was already too late. The darkness of night streamed in through the sky door. Aiden slumped to the floor, suddenly exhausted. Soldiers of the Palace Guard surrounded him, expressions of fury and anger on their faces, the sharp ends of their spears pointed in Aiden's direction. Aiden ignored them. The only thought running through his head was that he had failed.

Aiden was not sure how much time had passed before the guards standing over him stepped aside and a steely eyed Falkor grabbed him by his shirt and pulled him to his feet. "I'll deal with him," said Falkor to the guards. They glowered, but nevertheless stepped back, allowing Falkor to march Aiden out of the Eagle Hall.

Just outside the door they ran into a man wearing a long black robe. Aiden ignored him. He did not care who he was or what he wanted. All that mattered was that Aiden had failed the Eagle Riders. He wanted so badly to reverse time, to go back and try again. Maybe he should have told the guards about the trap instead of using magic. Maybe then they would have let him in in time.

"What's going on here?" said a voice that sent a jolt of recognition through Aiden.

Aiden's head jerked up. It was him. It was the same thin face, dark hair, and pale blue eyes that he had seen coming out of the trees in the Palace gardens only moments before.

"Not to worry Hakon," said Falkor, his voice hard. "I have it under control."

"Nevertheless I still should know. I am the King's advisor." Hakon glanced at Aiden, meeting his eyes not with a frown or a scowl, nor any of the confusion his words were meant to display. His eyes were as clear and pale as ice, and the tiny twitch of a smile told Aiden that the man knew exactly who he was and what was going on. It was just an act, yet for it to be carried out so successfully by someone so close to the King was almost unbelievable. Aiden looked away, his mouth dry, his fingers cold. He had just made a very powerful enemy. The man, Hakon, knew that he knew, which meant unless Aiden could convince Falkor of the truth, he was surely dead.

Falkor held Aiden still, not speaking, until Hakon sidled past them and into the Eagle Hall. Aiden felt Falkor's hand between his shoulder blades pushing him forwards and left down the passageway and into an empty room. The door closed with a resounding thud and the key scraping in the lock. Falkor turned, folded his arms across his chest and regarded Aiden with an uneasy stare. "You had better be sure of exactly what you're saying," he said.

Aiden gulped and gave an almost imperceptible nod. He could remember all too clearly the last time Falkor had questioned him and this was far more serious. He glanced at the locked door. No one else would come to his aid. And even if Tristan or Euan saw what was happening, would they even want to help him after what he had done?

"Why do you think the Eagle Riders are going into a trap?" said Falkor. He did not move, did not draw any runes, just stood there, arms folded, eyes cold. Aiden had no idea what the wizard was going to do, or what he was capable of.

"Arthur sent me to find you," said Aiden. "But there were two men talking in the gardens. They were talking about a trap for the Eagle Riders and one of them said they were planning to overthrow the King."

"And this trap. Did they say where it was?"

"Someplace called Cairn Ban," said Aiden.

"Cairn Ban?" said Falkor, taking a sudden step forward, unfolding his arms. "You're sure that was it exactly?"

Aiden nodded. A cold sweat broke out on his back. He clasped his hands to stop them shaking. Did Falkor believe him or not? What was going to happen?

"How did they say they were going to overthrow the King?" said Falkor.

"They didn't say how," said Aiden. "They only said that he wasn't going to be King for much longer. I didn't wait around to ask."

The wizard's eyes glinted in the lamplight of the room. "If what you say is true, then the King and all of us here are in very great danger," said Falkor. "But what if *you* are the spy, trying to stop the Riders from going where they are needed? You have been caught up in an awful lot of Brathadair attacks. Maybe that's not a coincidence."

Aiden shook his head, cowering backwards until he felt the wall at his fingertips. "I promise you, I'm telling you the truth."

"You know what's got to happen," said Falkor, advancing on him.

The wizard's hand was raised, Suil, the prophet, burning brightly there. Aiden gulped. He did not want it, but if it meant Falkor would believe him then he would allow it. He dreaded to think what would happen to him if he did not manage to convince the wizard.

Aiden stared at Falkor, trying not to screw up his eyes as the shooting pain of Suil slipped into his head.

"Are you Brathadair?" said Falkor.

"No," said Aiden, the word scorching over his tongue.

"And all this about the trap?"

"I promise you. It's the truth."

Falkor released him and Aiden slid down the wall to the floor. Falkor gave him a moment before crouching down next to him. For a second Aiden thought he might have patted him on the shoulder, but the wizard did not move any closer.

"Aiden it's important that you concentrate now," said Falkor. "Did you see the men who were planning this trap?"

Aiden froze for a second, remembering the look Hakon had given him in the corridor. Would Falkor still believe him when he told him that one of the King's advisors was at the centre of this plot?

"You know who they are," said Falkor, reading into his silence. "Aiden you must tell me." Falkor grabbed his shoulders and shook him.

Aiden looked up at the wizard. "I only saw one of them, though I thought I recognised the other man's voice."

"Who did you see? Could you recognise him again?"

Aiden nodded. "We walked into him a minute ago. That man in the hall. Hakon."

"Hakon," said Falkor, almost spitting the word, hatred hardening his grey eyes. "We have to take this to the King. But you can't be seen. The whole Palace Guard and Feather Guard thinks you're a traitor right now. If what you say is true then Hakon has to believe that I think that too."

Falkor stood and pulled Aiden to his feet. The wizard drew runes with both of his hands, Fearn, the shield, and Luis, the protector, then Onn, the joiner, and Ailm the changeling, and placed them above Aiden's head. Then he repeated the process at Aiden's feet.

"What are you doing?" said Aiden.

"Making it so that you can't be seen." Falkor finished the runes and let them drop onto Aiden.

Aiden felt the light tingle of the magic as it washed over him. He looked down at his hands but could see no difference. "Falkor, I can still see myself."

Falkor lifted one eyebrow. "Yes but no one else can. Make sure you walk as close to me as you can."

They left the small room, Aiden walking far closer to Falkor than was comfortable. He tensed when they reached the entrance to the Eagle Rider Building. There were lots of people still there, talking in small groups, trying to make sense of what had happened. Though some glanced up at Falkor, their gazes passed through Aiden and he walked past unseen. Outside Tristan sat on the ground, staring despondently at his feet, his head in his hands.

The first twisting of regret clutched at Aiden's stomach. He had not wanted Tristan to get caught in the magic. But there had been no time to stop and explain to him, and Aiden feared that he never would have time.

Falkor and Aiden crossed the gardens and entered the courtyard of the main Palace. They passed through a small doorway, the guards allowing them through without question. They hurried along the empty hallways, lamplight flickering as they went by. Aiden had not been back in the main Palace since his first meeting with the King and although the corridors seemed familiar, he did not think he had been in this place before.

Suddenly Falkor stopped and Aiden walked right into the back of him, glad that there was no one else around.

"Good, you're still here," said Falkor.

Aiden frowned. "I thought you could see me."

"And risk having every other magic user in the Palace see you too?" Falkor laughed.

"But what if I get separated from you?" said Aiden.

Falkor shrugged. "Doesn't matter anymore. Now get in here."

Aiden wished he had been watching the wizard more closely because somehow he had opened a door in the wall. There was a dark passageway beyond. Aiden stepped into the opening and stopped.

"There's no light?"

"It will come as you walk," said Falkor. "Now go straight. Don't take any turns and I'll meet you at the far end."

The door began to close again.

"Wait, Falkor," Aiden called. "Am I still invisible?"

"Yes," said Falkor, with a sigh. "Now go. I doubt you'll meet anyone anyway."

Aiden followed the length of the passageway, the way lit by faint marks of Teine, fire, which came to life as he walked by. It was a good thing no one else was around or else the light would have given him away, despite the invisibility. Although there were other doors and passages along the way, Aiden kept to the central way. It was impossible to know how far he had travelled in the dark but eventually he came to the end of the passage, where only a closed door lay ahead. He waited for what felt like an age, wondering if Falkor was really coming back. Maybe he had somehow strayed from the path and was waiting at the wrong door. Or maybe he had unwittingly walked into a prison of the wizard's design.

Suddenly the door opened and light flooded in. Aiden screwed up his eyes at the sudden brightness and to his relief saw that it was Falkor on the other side of the door. The wizard's eyes were searching.

"Aiden are you there?"

"Yes," said Aiden, stepping out into the room beyond. "I almost thought you weren't coming."

Falkor drew Ur, the renewer, and cast it in Aiden's direction. The rune landed on Aiden's left shoulder, not quite his head, where it should have, but it was uncanny how Falkor knew where he was without even being able to see him. The light tingled across his skin as the magic dissipated. It was then that he really took in his surroundings and saw who else was in the room with them. It was a small room with a small window and a couple of large soft armchairs. Sitting in one of the chairs was the King. Aiden instantly fell silent and bowed his head respectfully.

King Brandr made no greeting. He looked pointedly at Falkor. "The only reason we are having this meeting Falkor, is because after Arthur and my daughter you are the person I trust most. So there had better be a good reason for this."

"Brandr, Aiden has overheard a plot to overthrow your Kingship," said Falkor, his voice calm, unwavering.

The King sat back in his chair, completely silent.

"It seems they don't expect you to be King for much longer and they were heard discussing a trap for the Eagle Riders, set at Cairn Ban."

King Brandr's expression gradually darkened. For a second Aiden saw a glimmer of fear, but it was replaced quickly by steely resolve.

"And you believe him?" said Brandr. "He tried to force his way into the Eagle Hall using magic."

"Only because there was no time," said Aiden, a desperate pitch reentering his voice. "I had to warn the Eagle Riders before they flew into a trap."

"I believe him," said Falkor.

"Very well," said Brandr, folding his arms. "Who was it you heard?"

"It was Hakon," said Falkor.

"Who?" said Brandr, his eyes thunderous. He turned to Aiden. "Are you certain of this?"

The weight of the King's gaze lay heavy upon him and Aiden's mouth was suddenly dry. "I am certain," he said, his voice sounding small and insignificant in his ears.

"Hakon has been one of my closest advisors for many years," said the King. "Are you sure you are not mistaken?"

Aiden swallowed. The question held a carefully masked threat. But Aiden knew what he had heard and knew who he had seen. He could not lie.

"I saw him," said Aiden. "And he knows it." The last words slipped out almost without him realising.

Both the King and Falkor regarded him silently. Then Brandr turned to look at Falkor.

"I believe him," Falkor said quietly to the King. "Arthur believed in him."

"I am inclined to agree with you," said the King, "but I am loath to believe that Hakon is capable of such treachery. This could yet be a misunderstanding."

"It is possible," Falkor conceded, "but look at what else has been happening. An inside man would explain why the Brathadair have been so successful. And how else would Hakon know where the Eagle Riders were going. Only you, me, and the Riders themselves knew that."

"Hakon has given me no reason to be suspicious," Brandr countered.

"That will be his plan," said Falkor. "Now is our chance to stop him."

"I cannot arrest him without evidence," the King shouted at Falkor. "I know you have not always seen eye to eye with Hakon, but you cannot let personal grievances get in the way."

"You should not ignore this threat Brandr," said Falkor. He spoke quietly and yet it was somehow more menacing than Brandr's angry shout.

"And I am not going to," said the King, more quietly. He paused for a moment, as if gathering his thoughts. "I will give Hakon the chance to show his true colours. You and I, Falkor, must act as if we know nothing of this threat. Secretly though, you will watch every move that Hakon makes and report back to me." The King turned to Aiden. "Sadly this pretence must have unfortunate consequences for you Aiden. If your warning proves true, you will have done the Kingdom and myself a great service, but for now no one can know that. Which means I must act as if tonight's commotion is entirely your fault… you will be dismissed from all service at the Palace and sent back to your family."

Aiden's mouth dropped open and his eyes fell, shocked and confused. Something like numbness began to spread through his body. He had thought that once the truth was out things would get better. His actions would be excused. He would rejoin the Feather

Guard and help them in their efforts to save the Eagle Riders. He thought he would have a chance to explain his actions to Tristan and they would both laugh about it later.

The King's voice grew kinder. "If Hakon sees that you are still here, he will know what you have told me and you will not be safe. Nor will I, for that matter."

Aiden met the King's gaze and nodded. He tried to tell himself it was for the best, even if he did not like it.

"If we make it through this, you will be reinstated in the Eagle Rider Building in a place of honour," said the King. He held Aiden's gaze, trying to reassure him, but Aiden felt nothing but empty sadness.

"No one else can know of this plan," Falkor said to the King.

Brandr nodded. "Falkor, you and I shall discuss strategy in more detail later, but for now, you must escort Aiden back to his home. Do not let him speak to anyone in the Palace. And Aiden," said the King, turning to him once again, "not even your family can know about this. Do you understand?"

It was like a knife being slid into his heart. First, he could not say goodbye to Tristan and Euan and Odmund, and now he could not even tell his family why he was being dismissed from the Palace. He could not bring himself to look at the King. He could feel the numbness breaking apart into fiery anger.

"Do I have your promise Aiden?" said the King, firmly.

Aiden slowly raised his eyes. "I will tell no one," he said, biting back the emotions that made him want to scream at the King.

"Good," said the King, leaning back in his chair. "Falkor, you know what to do."

The wizard clamped his hand on Aiden's shoulder and steered him back towards the dark opening and the passageway. Aiden felt like it was swallowing him up. It could for all he cared. Anything would be better than having to return home and let everyone think he was a failure and, worse, a traitor.

At the end of the passageway Aiden barely noticed Falkor renewing the veil of invisibility around him. He followed the wizard out of the Palace and back to that empty room in the Eagle Rider Building, where Falkor released the magic.

"I'll get someone to send on your things," said Falkor. "I can't let you back up to your room."

"Then why bring me back here?" said Aiden, scowling.

"No one can know you met with the King," said Falkor, his voice betraying no emotion.

Aiden shrugged and shook his head. "You could have at least let me walk to the gate still invisible."

"Sorry," said Falkor. Aiden could not tell if he meant it or not.

The wizard dragged Aiden's hands behind his back and bound them with Gort. Then he pushed him towards the door and into the corridor. Aiden kept his head to the ground, not looking at anyone they passed for fear of seeing the resentment in their eyes. Outside the night had deepened and the stars felt cold and distant. All was silent but for the crunching of gravel below their feet. They left the Palace without incident, but the cold looks Aiden received from the sentries told him word had already reached them about his 'betrayal'. He hung his head. He knew it was not true, but he felt the shame of it nevertheless. The final blow came at the gate when, without a word, Falkor took a knife and ripped the crest of the Eagle Riders from his jacket.

It was better once they were out, walking among the familiar shadows of King's Avenue. Without a word Falkor loosed the runes that bound Aiden's hands and walked beside him, a few paces away.

Aiden gave a wry smile and rubbed his wrists. "Don't let all this be for nothing. Catch him before he gets away with it."

"Hakon the traitor," Falkor spat, unleashing an anger that had been kept carefully hidden while in the presence of the King. "He won't be getting away with anything so long as I'm watching."

Aiden glanced at the wizard and saw fury in his eyes. "Hakon said he was going to get rid of you too," he said quietly.

"Oh really," said Falkor, sounding faintly amused. "I think he'll find it's not easy to get rid of a wizard."

The rest of the journey they walked in silence. A few houses away from Aiden's own home Falkor stopped and looked at him earnestly. "You must stay away from the Palace and stay out of any Brathadair activity. And stay alert. There is still a chance that Hakon will come after you."

Aiden frowned and could not keep the worry from his face.

"Keep your eyes open and your magic sharp," said Falkor.

"Is it not magic that got me into this situation in the first place?" said Aiden with a wry laugh.

"Maybe so," said Falkor, "but it may be your only protection." Then the wizard turned abruptly and headed back to the Palace.

Aiden walked the last few paces to his house, his footsteps heavy. He could see light shining dimly from between the shutters. The door was closed but not locked and he did not give himself the chance to think before stepping into the flickering candlelight. The workshop was empty, but at the sound of his entry Brokk appeared silhouetted in the light from the kitchen.

"Aiden," he said, a smile brightening his face.

But Aiden could not find it in him to smile back. His throat felt too thick. Brokk stepped forward quickly and led him into the kitchen. His mother rose from the table and caught him in a warm embrace. He hugged her back, not wanting to let go. Eventually he stepped back and Kari's eyes were drawn to the ripped patch on his shirt.

"Aiden, what's happened?

Aiden sat down at the table and wiped his eye. What he should tell his parents? He hid his head in his hands. He wished he knew what to say.

"Aiden?" said Brokk.

He lifted his eyes to his parents. There was a sudden clatter on the stairs and Andor burst into the room. His face was bright, eyes wide with anticipation. "You've come to visit!" he said, rushing over to sit opposite Aiden at the table. "You have to tell me everything."

Andor's smile cut him deep. It reminded him of all that he had lost. And the unfairness of it all. He was just getting to know the place—just starting to feel like he belonged—but then he had to let his curiosity get the better of him. He just had to hear what those men were saying. He wished he had heard nothing.

The room was silent, all eyes upon him. He had to say something. Start with the truth, he thought. The simple, unavoidable truth.

"I've been dismissed from service," said Aiden, his throat closing around his words. He looked away. He did not want to see their sadness too.

"What?" said Andor, thumping his fists on the tabletop. "They can't do that."

"They can," said Aiden, rubbing his face.

"But why?" said Brokk. Aiden glanced up at his father. He wore a deep frown, his eyes dark, but Aiden sensed that his anger was not directed at him.

Aiden sighed and dropped his head back into his hands. What to say? He had promised the King and Falkor he would tell no one, not even his parents. How could they ask that of him? He had risked his life to tell the King what he knew and what thanks had he got? He had lost his job, had to let his friends think him a traitor, and he could tell his family none of it. The King did not even know his family—did not know that they could be trusted. I am the one in danger, thought Aiden. His family were certainly not going to betray him. He almost made up his mind to tell them everything, but suddenly another thought entered his mind. What if telling his family put *them* in danger?

"I don't want to talk about it," said Aiden, balling his hand into a fist, willing them to accept his answer without further questioning. "Just know that it wasn't my fault... I was just in the wrong place at the wrong time."

Brokk frowned at him for a second, as if trying to understand. He held up his hands, then let them drop to his sides. "You've had a hard day Aiden. We'll talk about it in the morning."

Aiden nodded briefly and stood up from the table. He wanted to be by himself, away from their puzzled sympathy. He took the stairs two at a time and in seconds was on the windowsill, climbing up to the roof. The familiar smoothness of the slates greeted him and he sank down into their cool embrace. This is home, he thought. The world cannot catch me here.

And so he lay there, watching the sky, letting his fears, his anger, his sadness pour out until he had no tears left to cry. And even then he did not move.

A distant shout brought Aiden to sudden wakefulness. At first he was not sure where he was. Open sky was above him, the wind blowing across his face. For a second he thought he was flying... then he remembered. He was on the roof, at home. He must have fallen asleep, for it was dawn now and Branwyn was waving to him from the street. He waved her away, groaning. Another person to avoid explaining things to.

Aiden shuffled into a sitting position, and wiped sleep from his eyes. He felt stiff and numb, but the thought of going inside was not something he was ready to consider. Going back inside would make everything real. Some part of him was still waiting for Falkor or Arthur or Tristan to turn up at his door and say it was all a mistake, that it had just been a test. The thought of Tristan sent a sharp ache shooting through him. He remembered the look of despair that had been on his face as he sat outside the Eagle Rider

Building. Would they ever be friends again?

"Aiden?" Branwyn's voice came from below, but closer this time. Aiden rolled over onto his stomach and peered over the edge. Branwyn's round face looked up at him from his bedroom window. From her rueful smile Aiden knew someone had told her already.

"Are you coming down?" said Branwyn.

Aiden wished she would not look at him with such sympathy. He shrugged. "Maybe later."

"It won't change what happened," said Branwyn, tilting her head to one side.

Aiden shook his head.

"What did happen?" said Branwyn. "Your mum said you wouldn't tell them anything last night."

Aiden pursed his lips. "I can't say," he said and rolled back onto the roof where she could not see him. "Go away."

"Aiden," said Branwyn, sharply. "Don't ignore me."

Aiden did not reply. He lay on his back and closed his eyes. There was silence for a moment and Aiden wondered if she had gone away. He felt a pang of regret. Branwyn had a way of always making him feel better.

He heard the sound of footsteps at the window. Branwyn's voice called out to him. "Give me a hand Aiden. It's been ages since I climbed up on this roof."

Aiden rolled his eyes, but he could not stop the smile from spreading across his face. He shuffled back to the edge of the roof catching Branwyn's arms and pulling her up. Once up she caught him in a sudden hug. The stiffness slowly began to fade from his limbs.

"So tell me what happened," said Branwyn firmly, planting herself next to him on the roof.

Aiden shook his head. "You can't know. It's dangerous." This was why he had not wanted to speak to her. She was just going to pry until he told her something. He should not really tell her anything.

Branwyn frowned at him. "Well don't tell me the details then."

Aiden sighed. She was not going to give up. But maybe she was right. Maybe he could tell her something without endangering her with the details. "I heard something I shouldn't have, okay. And it was dangerous for me to stay."

"Oh," said Branwyn, sounding almost disappointed.

"It would be dangerous for you to know," said Aiden, softening his tone.

"You should tell your parents that," said Branwyn. "They're worried about you."

"And if I tell them they'll be even more worried."

Branwyn frowned at him and he felt the stirrings of guilt, although he did not know why.

"Not talking about it won't make this whole thing go away," she said. "You have to decide what the greater danger is—telling someone or keeping it a secret."

Aiden chewed his lip and stared out across the City. "Right now, I don't know."

Branwyn leaned into him and wrapped her arms around him. "It will be alright in the end."

"Yeah?" said Aiden, with a short laugh. "Right now it's rubbish."

Branwyn pressed her lips together in sympathy and gave him a sad look.

Aiden looked away. He did not want her sympathy. He wanted things put right. "It's just so… unfair," he said, struggling to find words to sum up how he was feeling. "All I did was the right thing. I went above the call of duty and put my own neck on the line. And what thanks do I get?"

Branwyn frowned at him. "Aiden I know it feels like the world is against you right now, but you can't change what happened." She peered into his face, forcing him to look at her. "You have to know that whatever's happening is not finished yet. Not unless you give up and let it be finished. You did the right thing before and I'm sure that the right thing now doesn't involve sitting around on this roof and moping."

Branwyn's eyes were fierce as she finished speaking. Aiden looked away across the City, feeling unable to meet her gaze. Eventually he felt her stand and heard the shuffle of her feet as she edged across the roof and clambered back down to the window. Aiden stayed sitting where he was. It was all very well for her to say those things, but really what could he do? The situation was out of his hands.

But later that morning, long after Branwyn had gone, Aiden found that something she had said was still stuck in his mind. *You have to decide what the greatest danger is.* It did not matter whether he told his family or not, the real danger would be in being unprepared for what might happen if the King's plan failed. Preparing was something he could do.

13. Secrets

Tristan swung his sword at the target post sending wood chips flying. Every strike made a satisfying thud and sent a judder along his arm. He put all his weight behind the swings, his breath becoming heavier and heavier. After a few more strokes he took up a second sword in his free hand and began to swing both his arms in unison. His left arm still felt clumsy, but he was determined to master dual sword fighting. He went through the different swings methodically, drowning out any thoughts with the constant movement.

"Tristan," a voice shouted behind him.

Tristan whirled around, bringing both swords with him. They collided with a dull thud against Odmund's staff. The swordmaster twisted his staff and thrust downwards, pinning Tristan's two swords to the ground.

"We're not on the battlefield," said Odmund.

"Sorry," said Tristan, letting the swords drop to the ground.

"You've been out here for hours," said Odmund.

Tristan stood up straight and rubbed his arms. "I'm not going to get better unless I practice."

Odmund reached down to pick up the swords and handed them back to him. "I've been watching you all week. You're not doing that badly."

Tristan swung one of the swords lightly at the target post. "Maybe not with the swords." But with everything else, things were not going well. Aiden had betrayed them all and it was Tristan who had been responsible for him. He should have seen it coming, but all he had seen was a friend. Could he really expect everyone to be as loyal to the Eagle Riders as he was? No wonder his father had not thought him ready to start the Rider training.

"Show me what you've been practicing," said Odmund, turning Tristan from his thoughts. The swordmaster lifted his staff and sunk down into a slightly crouched position.

Tristan raised his two swords and readied himself. He would be better. He swung at Odmund letting his frustration strengthen his arms. He sliced across with the two swords, the metal of the blades rasping against each other. Odmund's staff became trapped between them and Tristan allowed himself a tiny grin as he leant on the swords, forcing Odmund to step back. Then suddenly he stumbled forwards as Odmund twisted his staff and the weapons that had been so tightly locked came loose. Tristan felt heat rise in his cheeks, but he ignored it, turning quickly to meet the swordmaster's next strike.

"Keep your left arm higher," said Odmund.

Tristan lifted his arm and swung again, harder and faster than before. He staggered his blows, giving Odmund no time to rest between swings, but it seemed to make no difference. He changed the pace, he dropped low, he swung high, he sidestepped around him, but Tristan could not find the way past Odmund's defences. He could not beat him. His arms grew heavy and a great tiredness washed over him. He stepped back and let the tips of his swords drop to the ground.

Odmund folded his muscled arms, his staff resting lightly on his shoulder. "You've got some impressive skills there Tristan. You'll be a match for most of the Palace Guard soon. You'd probably even get a hit on Marsaili."

Tristan tried to smile lightly, but his grin felt more like a grimace. He was a match for the Palace Guard, but he was not yet good enough to be an Eagle Rider. Tristan sheathed his swords and nodded to Odmund. "Thanks. I better get back to my duties now."

Odmund just raised an eyebrow at him as Tristan made his way from the training field and back along the beaten earth track that led to the Palace. His steps slowed as he approached the north gate and made his way through the Palace gardens. The Eagle Rider Building lay in the distance, peeking out from behind the branches of the trees. Even from this distance he could sense the emptiness of the Eagle Riders' absence.

The crunch of feet on the gravel path startled him and he stepped aside to let two men pass. It was Hakon, the King's advisor, and the Captain of the Palace Guard. They were deep in conversation, but Tristan did not fail to notice the tiny narrowing of their eyes as they walked by. He looked away. No doubt they remembered him as the one who had almost let the traitor get to the Eagle Riders. The one who had been too blinded by friendship to see the dangerous magic user beneath. Tristan put a hand to his head feeling a flash of sharp pain behind his eyes. Then it was gone. It happened every time he remembered that night. Every time he remembered the bright rune that Aiden had thrown at him.

Tristan rubbed his forehead, trying to shake the feeling. Movement in the trees caught the corner of his eye and he turned, seeing a flash of sandy hair and a long brown coat. He frowned for a minute, wondering what on earth Falkor was doing and then shook his head. He was a fool to think he could ever understand the wizard's business.

He returned to the Eagle Rider Building and made his way up the stairs to the council chamber. No one else was there and he was glad of it. The work that he and Suilan had begun the day before still lay on the table unfinished. He sat down heavily in a chair and picked up where he had left off, comparing the old library catalogue of magical artefacts to the inventory that had been compiled after the attack. Torryn had had the idea that maybe the Brathadair had been after some object of power and Tristan was inclined to agree. Aiden had thought that too, Tristan remembered, when they had first investigated the library, but he pushed that thought away.

There were many items from the old catalogue that were missing. Most, however, had been delicate things of little power that had probably been destroyed in the fire. Their disappearance did not trouble him. He was just about to give up when a word further down the list caught his eye.

The Feather Key.

There was no notation beside the entry, nothing to give Tristan any indication of what the object was or what it had been used for. It must have been an Eagle Rider artefact once, he suspected. There were records of those sort of things in the archives, so Tristan went next door and began to rummage through the scrolls and bundles of paper stacked on the wooden shelves. He checked the index of magical objects, then the index of magical weapons, but there was no mention of a 'feather key'. He even tried the records from old King Ectan's collections. Still nothing.

Tristan leaned his head against one of the wooden shelves in the archive room. Maybe it was not important. It was a feather. It probably had not survived the fire. He lifted his head and was about to leave when something silver caught his eye. It reminded him of runelight but it was softer and somehow more pure. The light fluttered like a bird flexing its wings and then was still again.

Tristan approached the light, which seemed to hover just above one of the old bundles of paper. He frowned. They had been through this part of the archive already, although he himself had not read this particular bundle. He stretched out a hand to lift the papers from the shelf and the light went out. Curious, Tristan took the papers to the table and flicked through them. They were old reports from during the war with Sorcier, mostly battle reports and lists of casualties. He shook his head. He was not going to read through all that. He stood to take them back to the shelf. But what about the light? He would read one—the one from the bottom of the pile. He pulled it out and smiled to see it was only a few lines long, clearly something that had been copied from a message hawk: *Sorcier defeated. We take him now to his prison. Let us hope the feather key works.*

"Feather key," said Tristan aloud. He laughed. What were the chances?

Then he stopped to think. The feather key was for Sorcier's prison. And it was missing from the library. After a Brathadair attack. That was not good at all. Undoubtedly that was where the Eagle Riders had gone. But had they known about the Feather Key before they left? What had they flown into?

His mind darted in all directions at once. Could that explain what had happened to Halvard and Johann? Had the Brathadair somehow managed to release Sorcier? Could Sorcier even be released if he was dead? Was his father prepared for what he might find when he and the other Riders arrived at their destination?

Tristan stood clutching the report in his hand. He would take this information to Cuinn and hope that the Captain of the Feather Guard was in a receptive mood. For the Eagle Riders it could be the difference between life and death. Tristan collected the artefact list from the council chamber, then walked the short distance along to Cuinn's study. Tristan kept his pace measured and his hand was unwavering as he knocked on the door.

"Enter," came the muffled voice.

Tristan opened the door and stood straight, shuffling the papers into a neat bundle.

"What is it?" said Cuinn, barely lifting his eyes to look at Tristan.

"I think I know what the Brathadair were after in the library," said Tristan slowly.

Cuinn put down the pen he was writing with and clasped his hands. "Well?"

"An item called the Feather Key is missing. The only mention of it in any of the records is as the key to Sorcier's prison."

Cuinn raised his eyebrows and held out his hand for the papers. Tristan passed them over, stepping back and chewing his lip while Cuinn scanned the lists himself. After a few minutes Cuinn put down the papers and laid a hand flat over the top.

"You have some very scant evidence here," said Cuinn. "But I'll admit it's possible." He flicked through the papers. "Keep working at it. I'll look into this further later."

Tristan frowned. "But sir, shouldn't we warn the Eagle Riders?" If there was any chance it was true then surely the Eagle Riders needed to act before the Brathadair could.

A brief frown flitted across Cuinn's face. He looked away. "It would change nothing. The Eagle Riders are already on their way to Sorcier's prison."

Tristan's chest tightened. He had easily guessed that his father had gone somewhere dangerous, but somehow knowing the truth made it worse. Now it felt real. He tugged the hem of his jacket. "Did the Riders know about the Feather Key before they left? Did they know what they were flying into?"

Cuinn shook his head. "I honestly don't know. Arthur did not divulge all his plans."

"Then shouldn't we send word to them?" said Tristan his voice rising. He flexed his fingers, wishing this was a problem he could solve as simply as picking up a sword.

Cuinn rubbed a hand through his beard and avoided meeting Tristan's gaze. "We can try."

"Try?" Tristan wrinkled his brow. "Why do you say that as if it's difficult?"

Cuinn folded his arms and sighed. "Your father was supposed to send word every day. It's now been more than a day. There must be something stopping the hawks from getting through."

A sudden nausea overtook Tristan and he took a step back. "They're message hawks—nothing *stops* them."

Cuinn lifted his head sharply. "Then we must assume that something has stopped the Riders from sending the hawk in the first place. But it has only been a day. I don't think it's cause for worry yet."

Tristan opened his mouth to speak but no words came out. Never in his entire life had he known his father to miss a report or a hawk to be delayed. How could Cuinn think it was not cause for worry? Tristan clenched his jaw. "The Eagle Riders' lives may be at stake. Don't you think we should do something?"

"There's already enough to be done here. Until we know more, I cannot spare resources on something that may prove to be nothing."

Tristan's frown deepened and he stepped towards Cuinn's desk. Very quietly he said, "How can you just sit here and do nothing?"

Cuinn stood, his chair scraping over the floor. "You should watch your tongue boy. Just because your father is the Captain, it does not give you leave to challenge me."

Tristan pressed his lips together, muscles quivering. "It doesn't matter who I am or who you are. We are Feather Guards and we should be doing all we can to help the Riders."

Cuinn lifted his chin and folded his arms across his chest. "You mistake the fact that I am not acting on this with the notion that I am doing nothing. Do you think I spend my days sitting here with my feet up? No. I am helping the Riders. I'm keeping this place going. I'm doing every little task that they left behind. The Riders are miles away. Even if we knew for sure that they were in danger—which we don't—what more can we do from here? Nothing. They are beyond our help." Cuinn sat back down and snatched up his pen. "Dismissed."

The last word was spoken with such finality that Tristan straightened himself and left the room. What more could he say? Cuinn did not believe that the Eagle Riders were in any real danger and Tristan knew that he of all people could not convince him otherwise. He pressed his hands to his head and then lashed out, punching the nearest wall. How could he not believe? If his father had not sent a message then something truly bad must have happened. But what? Why had none of them sent word? Were they captured or injured or trapped? What about his father? Was he still alive? Tristan frowned. He should send word to his mother. But what should he tell her? That his father was missing? Or worse, that his father could be dead?

And what about the Feather Key? There was no doubt it had been taken from the library. They thought they had caught the man responsible, but there could easily have been others that they did not know about. They would have had no difficulty in getting the Feather Key to the place of Sorcier's prison while the prisoner was interrogated.

Cuinn was wrong. Something had to be done about it. But what? Falkor, thought Tristan. If anyone in the Palace knew what to do it would be the wizard.

With determination lengthening his stride, Tristan left the Eagle Rider Building and crossed the short distance to the Palace. He passed through the courtyard and entered through a sturdy wooden door at the far corner, emerging into a small entrance hall. A colourful tapestry with golden tassels hung on the wall, hiding bare stone beneath, while torches stood in their brackets on either side. Two soldiers of the Palace Guard were stationed there and they nodded at Tristan as he entered.

"Eagle Rider business?" one asked as Tristan approached.

Tristan nodded. It was not a lie exactly. He *was* there about the Eagle Riders. It was just that the Palace Guard were very particular about who they let in. He had never before been allowed past without some evidence of a direct order or without his father. Confidence was the way past the guards, he decided. "I'm here to see Falkor," he said, casually folding his arms. "I have a message for him."

A flicker of a smile passed between the two. "Didn't you get the news? Falkor's not here."

Now Tristan frowned. He was sure he had seen the wizard only an hour or so earlier. "Where is he?"

"Gone," said the other guard. "No one's seen him for days."

"Maybe the Brathadair have scared him off," said the first guard with a laugh.

"Are you messing with me?" said Tristan. "Because I really do have important news for Falkor."

The guards bit back their laughter, shaking their heads. "Falkor really is gone. Couldn't tell you where to find him."

"Well can I at least go up and check?" said Tristan.

"No."

The guard's hand tightened ever so slightly over the hilt of his sword. Tristan inclined his head and forced a smile to his lips. He turned away. There would be another way in. Besides, some instinct told him that Falkor was not really gone.

Tristan waited until he was out of the Palace courtyard before he ran back to the Eagle Rider Building. He took the stairs to his room two at a time. Inside he began to rummage through his chest, pulling out blankets and clothes and dumping them on his bed. At the bottom his hand closed around a cool piece of metal—the key to his father's study. With the key in hand Tristan headed to the far side of the Eagle Rider Building and up the stairs to the Riders' quarters. He waited until the corridor was clear before running lightly down to his father's door. The key turned seamlessly in the lock and clicked open.

Tristan slipped inside. He crossed the room to the big wooden desk and stopped, a sudden ache in the back of his throat. It was far too empty and tidy with his father away. What if he never did come back? Tristan pushed the thought to the back of his mind. He would do all he could to stop that from coming true. He pulled open the drawer and grabbed another ring of keys, pocketing them and heading back out the way he had come.

Moments later Tristan was back in the Palace courtyard. He crossed over to a small door and paused for a moment, steeling himself for what he was about to do. One glance over his shoulder and then, before he could back down, he slotted a key into the keyhole and heard the crack as the old bolts turned aside. He crept through into the old disused servant's hall.

The room was dark, illuminated only by shafts of light breaking through cracks in the shutters. A dead and blackened fireplace sat at the far end of the room, separated from him by a long wooden table, scuffed and scratched from years of use. He ignored all this and carried on to the passageway beyond. It was darker there and eerily silent. Tristan hurried along, stifling a cough as dust rose into the air.

At the end of the passage was a locked door. Tristan crouched down to peer through the keyhole. On the other side was the clean and brightly lit corridor of the new servants wing, which led to the private quarters of the King's closest advisors. It was empty, so Tristan fished out the key he had taken from his father's desk and fitted it into the lock.

The lock was stiff and Tristan screwed up his face as he tried to turn it. Maybe he had taken the wrong key. Then suddenly it found purchase and twisted sharply with a loud clunk that set his heart racing. Tristan froze and waited for what felt like an eternity until he was sure he heard no footsteps on the far side. Then carefully he pulled the door open, wincing as the old wood creaked. He peeked out. No one there. And, as he thought, the old passageway had taken him past the guards.

As quickly and calmly as he could Tristan stepped into the corridor and closed and locked the old door behind him. He hurried on, turning a couple of corners before at last he saw the first steps of the spiral stair that would lead up to Falkor's room. But he stopped instantly and jerked back, pinning himself to the wall. A pair of Palace Guards were coming along the corridor towards him. He clenched his hands into fists to hide the trembling in his fingers. There was nowhere to hide. How could he explain why he was there?

But his time was up and the guards rounded the corner, lifting their short swords in surprise as they saw Tristan.

"What are you doing here?" said one.

Tristan smiled lightly. "It's alright. Feather Guard."

"You didn't answer the question," said the second, advancing upon him.

Tristan tried to hold his ground but could feel his feet itching backwards. "Eagle Rider business," he said.

The guard's mouth twisted into a mocking grin. "Is that what your friend told you before he knocked you out with a rune?"

Tristan's smile faltered. So it was true. Everyone thought him a failure. His shoulders tensed but he held himself still. He needed to focus on the task at hand. "That has nothing to do with this," he said, trying to keep his voice even.

"But how do we know that you're not an accomplice in this?" said the first guard.

"Maybe you staged it all," said the second. "And now that everyone trusts you, you come into the Palace and do the real damage."

"That's not true," said Tristan sharply. He paused and then said more quietly, "I am *not* a traitor. My father is Captain of the Eagle Riders."

The first guard shrugged. "You wouldn't be the first son to fall out with his father."

"How'd you get in here anyway," said the second guard. "I don't remember anyone letting you in."

"I let him in," came a voice from along the corridor.

Falkor strode towards them, his coat flaring out behind him. The wizard's cunning grey eyes were as sharp and cold as ice. "Let him through," said Falkor with the tiniest of sighs.

The guards scowled but reluctantly parted. Falkor pushed Tristan past them and began drawing a complex net of runes. Tristan watched as the glow of their lights intensified into one blazing ball, which Falkor then threw back at the guards. The wizard did not wait to see the effects of his magic but pushed Tristan further down the corridor.

"To make them forget," said Falkor, glancing at Tristan's puzzled face. "I'm not supposed to be here. But then neither are you."

Tristan opened his mouth to speak, but Falkor put up a hand to stop him. The expression on the wizard's face did not invite argument. Tristan held his tongue. Falkor led the way up the narrow spiral stair, stopping further on in front of a plain wooden door. The wizard touched his fingers lightly to the wood and a rune lit up briefly. The door swung open soundlessly. Falkor stepped in and pulled Tristan after him.

A lamp sputtered into life, flickering light across a bed strewn with crumpled blankets and a desk scattered with books lying open at various pages. A plate of half eaten food lay on the sill by the shuttered window. Falkor flipped two of the books closed, turning very slowly to face Tristan.

"What are you doing here Tristan?" Falkor twisted his fingers together. "I hope you realise the risk I had to take to get you out of trouble."

"I *was* actually looking for you," said Tristan, glancing nervously at the wizard's hands. "Why don't you want people to know you're here?"

Falkor smiled enigmatically. "Just be glad that I trust you enough to let you know I'm here. I could have let those guards drag you away to the dungeons or wherever they were going to take you."

Tristan shifted uncomfortably.

"So what do you want?" said Falkor leaning back against his desk, his voice suddenly overly amicable. It unnerved Tristan more than the wizard's anger ever could.

"I want to know what's happened to my father," said Tristan.

Falkor frowned. "He went on a mission. You don't need me to tell you that."

"No," Tristan agreed. "But I discovered today that an object called a Feather Key is missing from the library. It was thought to be the key to Sorcier's prison. That's where the Riders went, isn't it? Now Cuinn tells me that word from the Riders is overdue. Don't tell me that's just a coincidence."

Falkor paused, his eyes narrowed and focused. He shook his head and very carefully he said, "No, I don't think it is."

Tristan's stomach clenched. "Then what's happening? Is there really a chance that Sorcier could come back?"

Falkor's eyes flashed and he turned around, absently flicking the pages of a book. "Those questions are bigger than you know Tristan. And you're not going to like the answers." Falkor stilled, hand poised above the page. "I don't think I'm going to like them either."

Tristan's eyes narrowed. "Why?"

For a moment Falkor was utterly silent, as if making up his mind about something. Then he spoke. "Why do you think Aiden left?"

"What's that got to do with it?" said Tristan, glowering.

"Because on the night Aiden left, he overheard people planning to overthrow the King. Part of that plan involved a trap set for the Eagle Riders at a place called Cairn Ban. Sorcier's prison and his tomb. To try and fool our enemies into thinking we knew nothing of this plan, Aiden had to leave. But, if the Eagle Riders have fallen silent, I can only assume that they have been caught by this trap. Whether or not Sorcier is coming back, I don't know. But there are Brathadair within the Palace walls, closer to the King than you would imagine. And if you say the Feather Key is missing then it is not good news."

Tristan felt his mouth dropping open as he tried to take in all that Falkor was saying. Brathadair in the Palace, close to the King. The Eagle Riders caught, trapped. And Aiden, not a traitor after all. "What does all that mean? What must we do?"

"It means I must speak to the King immediately," said Falkor, striding suddenly to the door. "And you shouldn't be here anymore."

Tristan pinched his lips together. Falkor could be so infuriating sometimes. He followed the wizard out into the corridor, taking the opposite direction from where the two guards had been posted. Torches had been lit in their brackets and outside the courtyard lay in shadows as the last of the daylight faded to night. It felt like an age since Tristan had stood outside mustering the courage to sneak into the Palace. Falkor walked silently ahead, pausing occasionally at small sounds in the passageway, but they met no one. Eventually the wizard drew them to a halt.

"Are you taking me to see the King?" Tristan whispered, frowning at the door to the Royal wing of the Palace.

"No," said Falkor. "You won't be seeing anything." He held out a strip of cloth with the rune Fearn, the shield, sewn into the fabric. "I need you to wear this blindfold."

Tristan raised his eyebrows. "I've seen the Royal wing before."

"Not where I'm going to take you."

Tristan sighed, but allowed Falkor to tie the blindfold around his eyes. It was tighter than he would have liked, but he did not dare adjust it. The wizard's hand on his back pushed him forwards and he stumbled a little as he put his feet forward onto unknown ground. They walked for a few minutes until Tristan heard a soft click and felt a slight gust of air. Falkor pulled him in a new direction and even despite the blindfold he sensed a deeper darkness around them. The click came again and then the blindfold was taken from his eyes. He blinked a few times until he could pick out the sides of a windowless passageway, lit only by dim runes of Teine, fire, carved into the walls.

"Don't ask what this place is," said Falkor. "Just follow the passage till the end. It will take you out into the Palace grounds. Once out you will not be able to reenter the way you came, so don't even try. The fire runes will light up as you pass them so you won't be in complete darkness."

Tristan nodded. "Thank you."

Falkor gave a slight nod. "Now go."

Tristan turned and began to walk along the passageway, the runes on the walls growing brighter as he passed before fading quickly behind him. Tristan did not need to ask what this place was. It was obviously a secret passageway for the Kings of Teraan. He glanced over his shoulder, but already Falkor and the entrance had vanished. He kept on, not so much because he had purpose, but because he did not know what else to do. How could he know who to trust anymore?

A silver flash caught his eye, far brighter than any of the runes along the walls. Tristan stopped and backed up a few steps. An unmarked doorway nestled into the wall, but there was nothing there that could have made such a flash. He pushed gently against the door, expecting it to be locked, but it swung open smoothly at his touch. Beyond was a small dark room, barely four feet across. There was nothing there except two tiny slit windows placed roughly at eye level. Then he heard a voice.

"What news of the Eagle Riders?"

Tristan stepped into the room. He recognised that voice. The tiny window beckoned and he stepped up to peer through the slit. It was the King's study and there at the desk below sat King Brandr himself and across from him, Falkor. Tristan's eyes widened. Had Falkor meant him to find this place or was it just coincidence? No matter, he thought. Either way he was going to stay and listen.

14. Treachery and Rebellion

"What news of the Eagle Riders?" said King Brandr, his voice muted slightly by the walls of the small room.

Tristan peered down at the top of his head and guessed that the tiny window was near the ceiling of the King's study. Falkor sat across from the King at the desk, his brows creased. "There should have been a message yesterday," said the wizard, "but none came." He glanced out the window, as if distracted. "I think we have to assume it was a trap. They're probably captured… or worse."

Tristan shuddered at Falkor's quiet words. He could not imagine his father and Kael as prisoners to anyone. In his mind they had always been invincible. Dread clouded his thoughts. What if they were dead?

"But what could possibly take down all ten of the Riders and their Eagles?" said the King, echoing the question in Tristan's own mind. "They are the best, my finest warriors. In my lifetime they have never been defeated."

"Only a very powerful wizard could do so," said Falkor. "And one with a great deal of cunning and trickery. Such a thing would be beyond my skill."

"Then who could?" said the King, his voice almost a whisper, as if he dreaded the answer.

Falkor hesitated, glancing out the window again. Tristan wondered what had caught the wizard's eye. "There has been no one that powerful since Sorcier," said Falkor, shaking his head. Tristan frowned. For a moment it had seemed like Falkor was going to say something else.

The King sat back in his chair with a long sigh. "It always comes back to Sorcier. I know there are stories that say he will come back, but I don't believe it. It's just fear-mongering. A way for the Brathadair to distract us while they snatch power out from under our fingers."

"Maybe," said Falkor. But there was something in the way he said it that made Tristan think the wizard was less than sure. "Tristan told me today that the Feather Key has been discovered missing from the library. We can only assume that the Brathadair have it. It's been long enough. It's probably at Cairn Ban already."

"What do you believe then?"

"I know nothing for sure," said Falkor. "But it may not be as impossible as you think for Sorcier to come back."

The King was silent, musing over this thought. Tristan felt a frown creeping across his brow. He too had thought Sorcier's return impossible. But was it? The discovery of the Feather Key changed everything.

The King leaned forward over the desk, his voice dropping lower so that Tristan had to strain to hear him. "And what about Hakon? Have you discovered his plans yet?"

Hakon? What about Hakon? Tristan's mind tried to fit this information with the disappearance of the Riders and suddenly the pieces fell into place. Falkor had said there were Brathadair within the walls, close to King. Hakon must be one of them. He leaned forward and wished their voices were not so muffled.

Falkor shook his head. "It worries me that if there are traitors within our walls they have been able to hide so well."

"But you do think he's involved in this plot against the Riders?" said Brandr, a steely edge to his voice.

Falkor nodded slowly. "I think he's the mastermind behind the whole thing."

"If what you say is true, it worries me that I have been so blind to it. Hakon has been a close advisor for over ten years. A friend even." The anger in the King's voice turned to sorrow. "After they killed my wife, Hakon was instrumental in helping to bring down the Brathadair. And now you say he is one of them?"

"We've all been blind to it," Falkor replied.

The King shook his head. "The only reason we think Hakon is involved is because Aiden says he overheard him. What if he was wrong? We have no evidence."

Tristan squinted through the slit window, as if seeing more clearly would help him to understand. So it was Hakon that Aiden had overheard. Tristan clenched his fists. He did not know what to think about his once-friend anymore. Although his betrayal hurt, it seemed easier just to be angry with him.

Falkor shook his head. "He was right about the Eagle Riders. They've been gone five days and now they have fallen silent. Something has gone wrong."

The thought of it hit Tristan again and he felt a shakiness, a weakness, spreading through his limbs. What if after this mission his father was not coming back? He clenched his fists again and stood straight. No, he would not believe it.

From below the King spoke again. "Whether or not we believe Hakon is who we think he is, we still need to decide our next move.

"I think—" Falkor began.

A cry rent the air. Tristan's hand jumped to his sword hilt even though he was safely hidden in the tiny room. He peered through the window trying to see what was happening. Both Falkor and the King were on their feet, a dangerously bright rune already illuminating the wizard's hand. The clang of metal upon metal reverberated through the walls. Dread settled in the pit of Tristan's stomach.

"I think the enemy has decided our next move," said Falkor, moving cautiously over to the window. "The Palace Guard are fighting amongst themselves," he reported. He turned back to the King. "It's begun."

Brandr seemed to falter for a moment and then mustered his resolve. "My daughter is safe, isn't she?"

"Yes, she left a few days ago."

Brandr nodded curtly and crossed over to the far side of his study. He unsheathed a blade from its stand in the corner. Tristan gasped. It was the Sword of Teraan. It had not seen battle for many years.

Suddenly something solid and sharp crashed through the window sending fragments of glass everywhere. Tristan flinched, despite the wall that separated him from the danger. A crossbow bolt or a rock, he could not quite see. A flaming arrow followed it through the ragged opening. Falkor drew Suil, water, and threw it at the smoking spot where the arrow had landed. Between the hiss of flames and the cries of battle outside Tristan heard the click of the door in the room below. A pair of Palace Guards ran in.

"What's going on?" said the King.

But instead of answering, the guards drew their swords and advanced. "Don't try anything wizard," said one. "Your time is over."

In one fluid motion Falkor drew his sword and dispatched the men with neat swift strokes. He turned to the King. "We need to leave now."

The King nodded tersely and followed Falkor to the door. Tristan twisted his head, trying to see where they went. He could just make out the door. The limp bodies of two other guards lay in a pool of their own blood, arrows sticking out of their chests.

Tristan stepped back from the tiny window, his mind reeling. He covered his mouth and gulped back the bile that had risen in his throat. He had been in fights before, but this time was different. This time there was no clear enemy. In a split second friends had become foes and he did not know who to trust. How far had the Brathadair's treachery spread?

There was no time to figure out the answer, not when the King was in danger. If his father had been here he would have rushed to the King's aid. But his father was gone and that meant it was down to him. He drew his sword, the movement stilling all the tremors in his body. He ran back down the passageway.

Ahead Tristan saw a flash of light and the shadows of two people. Of course, he thought. This was the King's escape tunnel. "Falkor," he cried out, alerting the wizard to his presence.

"Tristan?" said the King, drawing close, a frown plastered across his face. "What are you doing here?"

"No time. We need to get the King to safety," Falkor said, turning back to push the door closed.

Suddenly a spear head thrust through the opening. Falkor grunted and slammed his shoulder against the door, but the spear wedged against the wall, holding it open.

"Break it," the wizard shouted.

Tristan raised his sword, but the King was there before him, hacking at the spear head with the Sword of Teraan. It snapped and the door slammed shut.

"Go," said Falkor.

They turned and headed along the passage, the fire runes in the walls lighting up as they went past. At the end of the passageway, just beyond the tiny room, a flight of stairs zig-zagged down into the dark. It led them down until Tristan felt they had gone further than the two floors from the King's study to the ground. Eventually Falkor turned into a stone walled tunnel and, although Tristan could not be sure, he sensed they were leaving the Palace behind.

The passage ended abruptly in what appeared to be a dead end, but Falkor put a finger to his lips and sketched Muin, the listener, in the air above them. They stood in silence for several minutes, the only sound in Tristan's ears his own blood pumping. Falkor was intent on the rune above him and the King just stood, statue-like, against the wall, lost in his own thoughts. Tristan shuffled uncomfortably. Falkor turned to them, Muin fading away into the darkness.

"Well?" said the King.

"As far as I can tell there's no one lying in wait for us just outside. But then the Brathadair have clearly had help from a powerful wizard so that could mean nothing."

"Let's assume the worst," said Brandr. "But if we make it out, this hatch is just near the north gate. That's our way out of the Palace."

"But that goes through the training grounds," said Tristan. "Won't we be seen?"

"It's night. We'll just have to hope they're not looking," said Falkor. "Now let's go before we're completely trapped."

"I'll go first," said Tristan, suddenly aware that he was probably the most expendable of the three men there. A shiver passed through his body when neither Falkor nor Brandr argued otherwise.

Falkor unbolted a catch in the ceiling, runes sparking as the bolt slid back. Tristan stepped forward, steeling his resolve. There was a small step in the corner and he used it to climb up until he was crouched under the ceiling. Slowly he pushed against the hatch with his shoulders and felt it lift seamlessly upwards. A small cloud of earth, moss, and fallen leaves rushed in the gap, almost making him choke, but there was no other movement. He peered out and up. Nothing but darkened sky and pale moonlight through the branches of trees.

In one quick movement he pushed the hatch the whole way open so that it flipped and lay flat on the ground behind him. Then he pulled himself up and rolled away, lying for a moment flat on the ground, waiting for the inevitable pain of an arrow. Nothing happened. Small noises of battle filtered to him through the air, but for now, it seemed he was alone.

"It's clear," Tristan whispered.

In a few moments both Falkor and the King were out of the tunnel. Falkor closed the hatch with a small thud and a flash of runes as he resealed the magical locks. Tristan looked at the spot where the tunnel had been and knew that, even if he tried, he would probably never find that entrance again.

The passageway had brought them out into the trees that formed the outer rim of the Palace gardens. Falkor crept ahead, beckoning, ducking under low branches. Tristan and the King followed slowly, wincing with each rustle of dried leaves and twigs underfoot. A few moments later the trees thinned and there lay the path leading to the arched portal of the north gate. The wooden door was barred and guarded by a full patrol of soldiers wearing the red cloaks of the Palace Guard. Tristan's heart leapt, but in the same instant he felt sick in his throat. Other people wearing the same red cloaks lay dead at their feet. These were no longer Palace Guards: they were Brathadair.

"They're trying to trap us in the Palace grounds," Falkor whispered.

"What about the east gate," said Tristan. "It's behind the Eagle Rider Building. The other Feather Guards may be able to help us. I know they are loyal to the King."

"You know that, do you?" said Falkor, scathingly. "Just because you are loyal Tristan, it does not mean that the other Feather Guards are. You've seen what's happened to the Palace Guard."

Tristan fell silent. He knew those men and women. He could not imagine them betraying the King, betraying his father, betraying him. But, after all that had happened, he was sure of nothing anymore.

"It's still a good idea," said the King. "You have Arthur's optimism and, though I fear the Brathadair have spread much more deeply through our ranks than I care to admit, we should still try it. I don't like our chances in open battle."

"We are not helpless Brandr," said Falkor.

"No," said the King, "but even your command of the runes may not be enough if we are surrounded. Many in the Palace Guard can use the runes well too."

Falkor made no reply as he moved off through the trees, roughly following the line of the path away from the north gate. He stopped. "We'll make a run for it across here."

The gap between the trees where they hid and the trees on the far side of the path was narrowest here, but to Tristan it still seemed a long way. "Can't you shield us with runes?" he whispered.

Falkor shook his head. "The King is right. Many in the Palace Guard can use magic and they are looking for us. The minute I start using the runes they will know where we are."

Brandr nodded solemnly. All three turned their eyes to the path looking both ways for the flickering of torches or the red flash of a cloak.

"Now," said Falkor.

They darted across, straight into the trees and stopped, ducking down into the shadows of the roots. Tristan glanced back at the heavily guarded gate, but the soldiers remained where they stood. Slowly he wiped a hand across his forehead.

Falkor led the way further through the trees. Their quiet steps felt too loud and yet too slow at the same time. Even keeping to the shadows, they could still see out across the lawns to their right. Every so often torchlight glanced through the branches and they froze. Each time Tristan wished he could blend into the bark of the trees. Yet somehow the Brathadair passed them by wihtout noticing them.

Tristan, Falkor, and the King circled slowly round until they caught sight of the Eagle Rider Building ahead. Tristan stopped. A fierce battle raged on its doorstep. He flinched at the clangs of metal and human cries. He was a Feather Guard in the service of the Eagle Riders. He should be there with his comrades, helping to defend the Eagle Rider Building. He pushed the guilt away. If his father was here he would see the King safely away. And that was what he must do, even though the thought of leaving the Eagle Rider Building to its fate filled him with great sadness. At least not all of the Feather Guard had turned traitor. At least some had stood to fight.

Suddenly there was a noise to their left, the crack of a branch as a figure moved through the trees. Tristan froze, ducking down. But this time there was a ring of steel and the cry, "Over here. I've found them."

Falkor wasted no time in pushing the King forwards. They broke out onto the open lawns, secrecy thrown aside. The man who had sounded the alarm jumped at them, but Tristan swung the hilt of his sword straight at the man's head. He dropped to the ground, eyes flickering. Tristan glanced at him and then raced after Falkor and the King, his insides turned cold. He had once sparred with that man in the training grounds. What had made him turn traitor?

Tristan quickly caught up with Falkor and Brandr, but already there were cries coming from all directions. The night was black, clouds now covering the moon and stars. He could make out little beyond the circle of torchlight at the door to the Eagle Rider Building.

An arrow whistled overhead, slicing through the air. Tristan leapt aside as it thudded into the ground in front of him. If it had not been dark... Tristan gulped. He dodged again as other shafts dropped down from the sky. Ahead Falkor brought the runes to life in a beam of light tinged orange and sparking. It burst through the night and Tristan saw a person fly backwards and land with a thud. Arrows rained down glancing off a bright sphere surrounding Falkor and the King. It glowed with each hit and then suddenly went dark.

Shouts came from behind and Tristan chanced a look back. The torch outside the Eagle Rider Building had been thrown onto the ground, scorching into the path. He could not tell who the bodies lying on the ground at the door belonged to. Were they dead? Brathadair from that fight were now racing after the King too. With a sickening thought Tristan realised he could be the only Feather Guard left in the City.

More light flashed ahead in brilliant streaks. Brathadair fell with pained cries. Falkor darted across the grass shooting a rune upwards at a man firing down upon them from one of the smashed windows of the Palace. A shadow jumped out at the wizard and he met the soldier with a clash of steel. With two hands on the flat of his blade Falkor pushed the man back. Tristan ran towards him, but where was the King?

Falkor nodded ahead and Tristan saw a figure running forwards alone. He changed his course, sprinting to catch him, but his speed was not enough. He saw the King stumble and fall even before he heard the agonising cry escape his lips. Tristan rushed over, flinching into himself as another arrow passed just over his head. Falkor reached them a moment later.

"What happened to your shield?" said Tristan, the words flowing out of his mouth before he realised their unhelpfulness.

"Too much happening…" Falkor murmured.

A groan drew Tristan's attention back to the King. His face was very pale and sweat plastered his hair to his forehead. Tristan gulped at the sight of the wound. A thick bolt, probably from a crossbow, had neatly sunk through the King's leg, its barbed head slicing through muscles, tendons, and bone. A sticky pool of blood already darkened the ground beneath him.

Silently Falkor snapped the end off the bolt and hauled the King to his feet. Tristan grabbed his other arm. They dragged him a few paces towards the lee of a lone tree that stood in the middle of the lawn. A pair of soldiers charged at them. Falkor thrust out his arms, runelight crackling along his fingers and shooting outwards, knocking them both down. A third appeared from the other direction and Tristan whirled to meet him. He twisted his sword, slicing the man's arm so that he dropped his weapon and stumbled backwards. Fear flashed across the man's face and he scrambled away as quickly as he could. Tristan did not follow. He could just make out a ring of soldiers drawing slowly closer, tightening the noose around them.

Falkor crouched by the King and drew Beith, the healer. Brandr clutched the wizard's arm. "You must go… without me."

"No Brandr," said Falkor. "My duty is to you." He lifted his head and shot a bolt of runic light towards the advancing soldiers. They faltered and stopped as fire flared on the ground around their feet.

"No Falkor, both our duties are to Teraan," said the King, his voice strong despite the grimace on his face. "You know as well as I that I cannot walk on this leg and you cannot hold them back forever. One of us must live to escape. Serineth can't be left to face this alone. She is the future. She will be a much better ruler than I ever was. Falkor, my judgement has been clouded of late. I have… trusted the wrong people."

Falkor shook his head, shooting again towards the advancing enemy. This time a man fell and was pulled back by his comrades. Falkor shot again and again in different directions. The ring slowed to a stop.

"No Brandr. I can get you out," said Falkor. He ripped a strip of cloth from the bottom of his coat and wound it around the King's leg.

The King winced and put his hand on Falkor's to stop him. "Leave me," he said with more urgency. "I won't make it, but if they catch me I don't think they'll kill me. I know things about this Palace, about Teraan, that no one else does. You they'll kill and you can't keep this up forever, no matter how strong you are." The King took up the Sword of Teraan and pushed it into Falkor's hands. "You must take this sword to my daughter. Help her."

Falkor's hands closed uncertainly around the sword. Tristan glanced back and forth between the wizard and the soldiers. The crunch of gravel drifted through the night signalling another band of reinforcements.

"Falkor," Tristan said, his voice low with warning. The wizard had to leave before his chance was gone. Tristan looked down at the King and Falkor kneeling beside him. He had never seen Falkor so indecisive, his face creased with worry, with fear.

"I'll stay with the King," said Tristan with more bravery than he felt.

"No," said Brandr, with a force that surprised Tristan. "No," he said more gently. "Your father would not forgive me if you stayed here and died."

"My father may already be dead," said Tristan, not sure where he found the strength to say those words.

"Or he may not," said the King. "You must bring back the Eagle Riders, for I fear we will need them before the end."

Tristan opened his mouth to argue, but the King held up a hand to stop him.

"Tristan, the Palace has fallen and the Eagle Rider Building has fallen with it. You are now Captain of the Feather Guard. It is up to you."

For a moment Tristan felt strong enough to face anything. Then he remembered the fallen torch on the doorstep of the Eagle Rider Building and felt the sting of tears in his eyes. At what cost had this title come to him?

"Falkor," said the King. "You know what you have to do."

Falkor took the King's hand one last time. "I *will* come back for you Brandr." Something unspoken passed between them. Suddenly Falkor jumped to his feet, pulling Tristan away from the King. "Stay close," he said.

They ran straight at the line of advancing Brathadair, swords raised, Falkor blasting soldiers aside with the blinding light of runes, knocking a hole through the ring. Tristan felt his sword cut through armour and flesh, but he did not stop to look at the damage. He kept running through the gap they created, sprinting past the Eagle Rider Building and towards the east gate.

The clamour behind them grew as men scrambled after them across the gravel, armour clinking. By the gate a mass of Brathadair awaited them. Tristan's feet slowed, but Falkor kept running, runes sparking to life in his hands. The line of soldiers faltered ever so slightly at the sight of the wizard. Tristan took courage from their hesitation and pushed his feet faster. He drew a quick rune in the air, Fearn, the shield, and hoped that he would get by unscathed. He raised his sword, but just as he thought they would run into the enemy Falkor unleashed a great blast of runic magic that sent men flying in all directions. Tristan stumbled as the shockwaves swept past, but he made it to the gate unscathed.

"Get the bar," Falkor yelled.

Tristan barely slowed as he ran headlong into the wooden planks of the gate. With all his strength he pushed up at the wooden beam that held it closed. It groaned as they moved it slowly upwards. Tristan felt tears streak from his eyes as he leaned into it. Beside him Falkor cried out in frustration, the rune Dair, strength, glowing through his hands. Suddenly the beam lifted and dropped to the ground. They pushed open the gate and raced through.

Tristan lifted his sword quickly to parry a blade which appeared from the shadows on the other side. He sliced and dodged, not bothering to win the fight, only giving himself enough time to get away before more of the enemy arrived. Falkor was close at his heels, throwing Peith, the thunderbolt, forwards before whirling to throw another at those now chasing them from behind.

They sped through the Restricted Zone's deserted barracks and empty echoing streets. Yet there were signs of battle here too: splintered doors hanging on broken hinges, fires crackling in windows, red stains across the cobbles. There were bodies too, but Tristan's eyes shied away from them. He did not want to know who they were.

The shouts of men sounded not far behind them, along with the thud of more feet than he could count. He caught a flash in the corner of his eye and ducked as a poorly cast rune crashed onto the cobbles behind them. They were not out of danger yet.

"This way," said Falkor, dragging him quickly into a narrow passage between two buildings. They slipped through the gap, Tristan barely noticing as he scraped his knuckles on the rough stone that hemmed them in. Then they were out, into the next street and then into another passage overshadowed by a wooden walkway. On the far side, the wall of the Restricted Zone stood tall, just a few feet above head height. Once past it their chances of survival would increase dramatically. The tops of trees out in the City beckoned to him, speaking of hiding places and safety. At the wall Falkor crouched down and held out his hands, nodding up at the wall.

"What about you?" said Tristan, realising that the wizard meant to give him a boost up and over the wall.

"I'll jump with runes," said Falkor. "Now come on."

There was a shout from behind and without looking round

Tristan sheathed his sword, put his foot in Falkor's hands and launched himself into the air. His hands caught the top of the wall and he pulled himself up and rolled over the top. He dropped down the other side, landing on the ground with a thud. He drew his sword again, but there was no one there to challenge him. A second later Falkor was at his side, urging him onwards. They made a dash for the nearest street and veered down between the houses, leaving the Palace out of sight behind them. They ran solidly for several more minutes, ducking into the tree covered lanes between the streets as often as they could. Eventually, Falkor drew to a stop in the deep shadows provided by a great oak tree. He bent over and put his hands on his knees, taking a deep shuddering breath. His face was pale in the darkness.

"Are you ok?" said Tristan, gulping in air and putting out a hand to steady himself against the tree.

Falkor nodded. "It's just the runes. They take their toll, especially in battle. It's at times like this working with an Eagle would be nice. Help to sustain the level of magic required."

Tristan nodded, though it disconcerted him more than he would say to see Falkor admit weakness.

"Come on," said Falkor, straightening up, as if sensing his thoughts.

"Where are we going?" Tristan asked as they began to run again, although at a slower pace than before.

"First," said Falkor, "we are going to get Aiden. And then we are getting out of the City."

Tristan kept running. Aiden. The Eagle Rider Building may have fallen but Aiden lived. That meant he was not the only Feather Guard left in the City. Despite the confusion he still felt when he considered his once-friend, the thought filled him with a strange comfort. Compared to the treachery he had just witnessed, Aiden's betrayal seemed nothing.

15. Across the Wall

Aiden ducked under the thick bushes and through the rubble of the ruined entranceway. He squinted in the sudden darkness, but the spiralling steps of the abandoned tower were familiar to him. He ran his hand along the wall as he climbed, the grit of the stone rough under his fingers. Branwyn clambered in after him, scowling as she tugged on a twig that had become entwined in her hair.

"So are you going to tell me what we're doing here?" said Branwyn, stepping up behind him.

Aiden smiled. "I said I'd show you. We're almost there."

Branwyn raised her eyebrows. "You do remember we used to play in here all the time when we were younger. I have seen it all before."

"It's not the tower I want to show you."

They continued up, spiralling past the dusty light beams that shone in through the windows. Aiden turned at the third doorway subconsciously drawing Teine, fire, as he entered the room beyond. Branwyn ducked in behind him.

"This is what I wanted to show you," said Aiden, spreading his arms wide, the rune growing brighter and sending flickering shadows across the room, enhancing the pale sunlight that crept in through the slit windows in the far wall.

"Hmm?" said Branwyn.

Aiden smiled, walking to the far corner by the windows and

carefully setting the rune to float in the air above his head. He reached down and pulled back a heavy black blanket. Underneath it was a plain wooden box that had been roughly nailed together.

"Not my finest work," Aiden admitted. "But I added some runes to the wood that will keep the contents dry and free from mould and bugs and stuff."

Aiden lifted the lid and Branwyn leaned over, peering inside. It was full of blankets, some spare clothes, dried meat and fish and fruit, some travel bread, a pair of waterskins, and two knives.

Branwyn glanced sharply up at him. "What's all this for?"

"Precautions," said Aiden. And though he had spent the last few days gathering the things together, it still did not feel like enough.

"But what for?" said Branwyn, her frown deepening.

In case the Eagle Riders fail and the Brathadair really do take over the kingdom, thought Aiden.

"Aiden what's going on?" said Branwyn. "Tell me." She stared at him, hands on hips.

Aiden closed the lid of the box and sat down on top of it. He had known he would have to tell her. And he was prepared.

"It's got to do with the reason I left the Palace," Aiden began.

"I thought so," Branwyn murmured to herself.

"I overheard some of the King's advisors talking. It turned out they were actually Brathadair and they were plotting to overthrow the King." Aiden's voice sounded strangely calm as he spoke, even though his words made it all sound more real.

"What! But how? When? Won't the Eagle Riders stop them?"

Aiden shook his head slowly. "The Eagle Riders are gone. I don't know for sure, but I think the Brathadair set a trap for them. I couldn't stop them in time."

"Gone," said Branwyn, sinking into the space beside him.

Aiden did not reply. Somehow it did not seem possible that the Eagle Riders could be gone. In all the stories and songs nothing could defeat the Eagle Riders. They were masters of the land and the air. They could wield the runes better than any man.

"Are you going to tell the others about all this?" said Branwyn, breaking the silence.

"No," said Aiden firmly. "At least not yet. I don't want to worry them. It might not happen. But I wanted to make sure someone in your family knew it was here, in case—"

"Don't say it," said Branwyn, interrupting him. "It's bad enough thinking it."

Together they stood and draped the heavy blanket back over the box. Aiden let Teine fade to darkness above his head and they made their way back down the stairs. It was a quiet walk home.

That night sleep was elusive, as it had been every night since Aiden left the Palace. He tossed and turned in his blankets, countless worries swarming around his head and eating into his dreams. He missed the training sessions with Odmund that had once tired him out to the point of exhaustion.

Eventually he must have fallen asleep for he woke suddenly to blackness and pounding. He squinted his eyes at the window, but there was no light coming in through the cracks in the shutters. It was still night. He sat up, his clothes sticking to his skin, and saw Andor stirring in the bed across from him.

"What's going on?" Andor whispered.

Aiden rubbed his eyes. The sound had not been in his head.

He swung out of bed and carefully drew out a knife from under his bed. Andor raised his eyebrows, but Aiden put a finger to lips, urging him to stay quiet. He tiptoed across the room, creaking open the door to catch a glimpse of light on the stairs ahead. His father was already up. He hurried after him.

The pounding was louder downstairs, although the knocks came in sporadic bursts, as if the person outside was torn between making too much noise and not enough. Aiden slipped into the shadows by the door, knife in hand, and nodded to his father.

"Who is it?" said Brokk quietly, the candle flickering in his hand.

"We're here to see Aiden," came the muffled reply.

Brokk glanced at Aiden, his brows furrowing. Aiden shrugged. The voice was too muffled to make out. He could not think who it could be unless...

"Who are you?" Brokk hissed.

"It's Falkor and Tristan," said the muffled voice.

Aiden started forward. "Open it a crack," he whispered.

Brokk undid the latch and pulled the door inwards ever so slightly. Aiden peered out into the darkness of the street. There were the two dishevelled faces of Falkor and Tristan, smeared with grime and spattered with... blood.

"Who else is here?" said Falkor.

"Just my Mum and brother," said Aiden, pulling the door open further so they could slip inside.

Tristan's shoulders sagged as the door clicked closed behind them. Aiden tried to catch his eye, but Tristan avoided him, keeping instead near the door, his hand still resting on the hilt of his sword.

"What happened?" said Aiden, turning to Falkor.

Falkor's gaze flitted about the room. He paced to the kitchen door and glanced through, though Aiden was not sure what he saw in the dark. "I'm afraid Hakon's plan has succeeded."

Aiden's mouth dropped open. "But you were going to catch him." The words slipped out before he could stop himself.

"And he evaded me," Falkor snapped, his voice hard like stone cracking against stone. Untold fury glinted in his grey eyes.

Aiden shrunk into himself, not sure if Falkor's anger was directed at him or at his more distant enemy.

There was a small noise as Kari descended the stairs and appeared in the doorway to the kitchen, candle in hand. Andor snuck down behind her still wrapped in his blanket.

"What's going on here?" said Kari, her eyes shifting between the people in the room.

Falkor hesitated. He spoke, his voice now flat and devoid of emotion. "The Brathadair have overrun the Palace. Half, maybe more, of the Palace Guard have turned traitor. The King is captured and the Eagle Riders have disappeared. Does that explain it?"

Brokk's mouth opened and closed as if he was trying to speak, but no words came out.

"But what's all this got to do with Aiden?" said Kari.

Falkor blinked slowly, turning to Aiden, his voice lifting a little with surprise. "So you didn't tell them?"

"You made me promise to tell no one," said Aiden, a flash of fire in his chest. "Not even my family and friends." At that Aiden looked over at his friend, but when their eyes met Tristan turned quickly away to peer out through a crack in the window shutters. Aiden stared after him, trying to sense what he was thinking. He remembered too well the disbelief and shock on Tristan's face when he had thrown the rune, blasting his way into the Eagle Rider Building. Did Tristan still feel betrayed even though he now knew the truth? Tristan's face was haggard in the shifting shadows of the candlelight, giving nothing away. Aiden hoped things could be put right again.

"Well," said Kari. "I think it's about time you did tell us what's really going on. Or at least someone should," she added, glancing pointedly at Falkor.

Silence stretched around them. Falkor's jaw twitched as if it was an effort for him to speak. Aiden frowned. If the wizard would not tell them then he would.

Falkor rubbed his chin and began. "Aiden was sent home from the Palace because he overheard Hakon, the King's advisor, plotting to capture the Eagle Riders and overthrow the King. He used magic to try and prevent the Eagle Riders from leaving, but since he was not authorised to use runes in the Palace grounds he was stopped. He was then sent home for his own safety, until we could determine whether Hakon really was the one behind all these Brathadair attacks. Sadly everything Aiden overheard has now come true."

Brokk and Kari exchanged worried looks.

"You mean the King has been overthrown?" said Brokk.

Falkor nodded, his shoulders slumping ever so slightly. "This very night. We almost escaped, but the King was shot through the leg. Tristan and I had to leave him behind."

"And the Eagle Riders?" said Aiden. "What happened to them?"

"They're gone," said Tristan, finally looking at Aiden. "Disappeared. Captured. Dead. I don't know." His voice was tight, pained, so that Aiden almost did not recognise it.

"I'm sorry," Aiden whispered. How could he imagine the immense loss it would be to Tristan. It would be like losing his family ten times over.

"Don't be," said Tristan flatly. "Just prove to me that you weren't the cause of it."

Aiden nodded. He would have to work to regain Tristan's friendship. But he would regain it, he promised himself.

"So what happens now?" said Brokk.

"We need to leave the City," said Falkor, glancing over at Tristan. "I must go to the Princess and ensure her safety."

"And I go in search of the Eagle Riders," said Tristan, straightening. "I am Captain of the Feather Guard now."

Aiden's breath caught in his throat. If Tristan was in charge then what did that mean for the rest of the Feather Guard? Was he the only one left? Tristan looked at him, long and hard.

The room was quiet for a moment.

"You better get your things then Aiden," said Brokk.

"No," said Kari, darting forward and taking hold of Aiden's arm.

Brokk reached after her and pulled her slowly away. "Kari. He has to go," said Brokk. "Doesn't he?" he added, looking to Falkor and Tristan.

Falkor nodded. "He is a known magic user, loyal to the King. Hakon will be on the look out for him too. But we must go now."

"Now?" said Kari, reaching for Aiden again.

Aiden nodded, biting his lip as he looked at his mother. He stepped backwards, away from her and turned, taking the stairs two at a time. Under his bed he found the bag he had made ready for an occasion such as this. He quickly changed into some travel clothes, slipped his feet into his boots and pulled on his favourite cloak. He scooped up the bag slinging it over his shoulder. He gazed around his familiar room one last time, but he knew the longer he stayed the harder it would be to leave. He jumped back down the stairs and saw that Kari had packed another sack of food to give to Tristan and Falkor.

And then the moment he had been dreading. Goodbye.

He stood in front of his family and suddenly his throat grew tight. How could he leave them behind? He felt frozen to the spot, gripped by the terror that he might never see them again. How could there be life without them?

Aiden hugged each of them in turn, trying to memorise each of their faces. His mother's round rosy cheeks and short golden hair, glistening in the candlelight. She kissed him on the forehead and the wetness of her tears dripped onto his face. Brokk pulled him into a rough hug. The creases around his eyes that had once been so stern, now seemed to carry the weight of the world.

Last he turned to Andor, his green eyes wide, scared but trying to be brave. Aiden ruffled his hair. "Here, let me show you something." He drew a rune in the air, slowly so that Andor could see how it was drawn. The pale silvery shape hung shimmering in the air. "This is Fearn, the shield." Andor copied the movements and drew his own rune in the air. It shimmered alongside Aiden's though it was not as bright. "Fearn can protect you from all sorts of things, so remember its shape well." Andor smiled and nodded. Then Aiden brought the rune down and placed it lightly on Andor's forehead. It sparked as it touched his skin and split into hundreds of tiny fragments that went shooting across his face and down his neck and body.

Aiden took a step back. Tears flowed silently down his mother's face. Brokk stood beside her, looking pale and serious as ever. Aiden gulped. He was leaving and he might not ever come back. "Mum, Dad, Andor," he said. "You remember the abandoned tower that Branwyn and I used to play in?" They nodded, so he continued. "In a room on the third floor is a box with supplies of food and blankets and such. It's a safe house for you all and Branwyn and Uncle Aran and Aunt Sanna. If things get dangerous—"

Suddenly Falkor touched his arm and motioned him to be quiet. He doused the candles between his fingers. "There's a patrol coming," he whispered. "We go now."

Aiden took one last look at his family. "Tell Branwyn... tell her I'm sorry I couldn't say goodbye. And I promise you all, I will come back."

It was a promise as much to himself as it was to them.

Brokk and Kari smiled and nodded and Brokk put one arm round his wife as she wiped her eyes and the other round his younger son. "Go," he said.

Falkor ushered Aiden and Tristan out of the back of the house. They sped across the garden and out onto the pathway beyond. Back on the street feet pattered more closely and Aiden dreaded to think how close they had come to being caught. He hoped against hope that his family would not relight the candles and that the Brathadair would quickly pass them by.

Aiden hastened along the overgrown path behind the houses. He risked one final glance over his shoulder, but it was too black to see anything. The darkness smothered him, wrapping all around him, tripping him on tree roots, straining his eyes. Flickering light cast their shadows suddenly ahead of them and they ducked further under the trees. Had the soldier followed them or was he just checking the lane? They waited, poised in the shadows, until he turned away back to his patrol.

They moved on quickly, their pathway ending at one of the larger streets. Falkor went on ahead to check that the way was clear. All was quiet so they stepped out onto the street. The cold air nipped his face and the back of his throat. Beside him Tristan was breathing heavily, his face pale. He looked exhausted.

They had seen no one since the house, but every now and then, through the gaps between buildings, they caught sight of torches and heard the muffled cries of men. The trio made it to the end of the street and then to the end of the next. Suddenly there was a light at the next corner, catching them in its glow. The soldier shouted, a loud and clear call into the night.

Falkor urged them into a run. "Stick together and make for the Wall, but avoid the gateways. I'll lead them off and meet you there." The wizard angled off into a side street casting some sort of runic light behind him.

Aiden and Tristan ducked into a shadowy alley and broke into a run. Neither stopped to look back. They hurtled through the City, always moving, always forwards. In the streets around them they sensed as much as they heard the thud of booted feet over the cobbles, the clink of armour, and the scrape of swords. Angry shouts sounded from all directions, some far off, but some close enough to echo off the walls. There was the creak and splinter of someone's door or gate being broken through and the nearness of it sent a jolt of fear through Aiden's limbs.

"This way," said Tristan, grabbing his arm and dragging him into another darkened alleyway as soldiers brandishing torches and swords rushed into the street they had just been traversing. Above Aiden heard shutters clunk open and a gravelly voice shouted something unintelligible down at them. They ran on regardless, jumping through the garden and climbing the short fence onto the path beyond. A few steps down and a raised lantern appeared at the end of the path. Aiden stopped and Tristan ran into the back of him.

"Go back," said Aiden, flapping his arms. "Quick."

They ran back, slipping through another garden and out onto a deserted street.

"They're everywhere," said Aiden. Tristan did not respond.

Further along they saw the door to a house hanging awkwardly from it's hinges. Sobs sounded from inside. Soldiers appeared in the doorway, one wiping red smears from his sword on the leg of his trousers. Time slowed for a minute and Aiden saw a vicious sneer spread across the man's face.

A ring of steel sounded in Aiden's ear and suddenly Tristan was advancing on the soldiers. Aiden reached after him and dragged him by the cloak back into the shadows. Tristan struggled in his grasp, pushing him away.

"Don't try to stop me again," he said in a low voice, his eyes fierce.

"We need to get out of here," said Aiden.

"He was my friend," Tristan whispered, his face grim.

Aiden gave a slight shake of his head. "We can't take them all."

"You could use your magic," said Tristan, his voice turning sharp. "You used it on me, why not on them?"

Aiden frowned, guilt stabbing through his chest. "We'd only announce to everyone where we are."

Just then a bang sounded and a great flash lit up the sky.

"The wizard," shouted one of the soldiers. In a great rush they drew their weapons and ran out onto the street, away from where Aiden and Tristan hid in the shadows.

Tristan glowered after them, but eventually he sheathed his sword and murmured, "Come on."

They ran again, taking a different road. Tristan was very quiet, his face a pale shape in the darkness. Something nagged at Aiden's mind. Maybe they should have attacked the soldiers? He shook his head. That did not feel right either.

After awhile there were no signs of pursuit and a few minutes later Aiden and Tristan sprinted the last few yards to the Wall. They embraced the rough stone, sheltering in the deep shadows it provided. They were some distance from any of the main gates and Aiden hoped that whoever was patrolling the battlements was occupied elsewhere. Gradually their breathing slowed and a silence and stillness descended. A tiny noise made them both jump, but it was nothing. Aiden wiped sweaty palms on his trousers and pressed himself further into the shadows. Then Tristan, a few feet away, went taut.

"Someone's coming," he whispered, almost too softly for Aiden to hear.

Aiden tried to mould himself to the Wall, all the while tensing his muscles to run at any moment. He found himself holding his breath. The soft pad of a single set of footsteps came closer.

"Aiden? Tristan?" whispered a voice.

A great sigh escaped his body. It was Falkor. Aiden extracted himself from the Wall and allowed himself to breathe again. The wizard beckoned them further along. "All the gates and stairs are guarded. We'll have to climb," he whispered.

There was an old tree up ahead, thick and gnarled, and Falkor led them under its branches. He pointed up and Aiden began to climb, followed closely by Tristan. The bark was rough under his skin, but there was something comforting in its coarseness. Aiden edged along the branch that brought him closest to the Wall and waited for Tristan and Falkor to join him. Falkor produced a rope and tied it securely around the main trunk. He tossed the other end to Aiden and gestured for him to tie it round his waist.

"You need to jump to the top of the Wall then I'll lower you down," Falkor whispered.

Aiden gulped as he looked over to the Wall. The parapet stood at least thirty feet high with crenellated battlements facing out into the City. There was space for a person to walk along the edge, but if he missed, it was a long fall back to the ground. Aiden edged further along the branch, tensing as it began to bend under his weight. He shuffled up from his crouch, until he was almost able to stand. Then, before he could let himself think, he jumped the gap to the top of the Wall. His feet touched the stone and his arms grabbed the parapet. He swayed precariously for a second before gaining his balance. Then he clambered over the battlements and lowered himself over the edge until his arms were straining. A pain shot through his shoulder, a residual pain from his injuries in the burning building. Then the rope went taut around his waist and he let go, allowing Falkor to lower him to the ground.

As his feet touched the ground he quickly slipped the rope from his waist and watched it snake back into the tree. Aiden clung to the shadows at the foot of the stones. He had crossed the Wall, but he was not yet out of the City.

A sudden shout rent the air. They had been seen, but from where? The skiff of an arrow through the air made him duck instinctively, but it came from inside the Wall and could not hit him. Yet the others had no such protection.

Aiden looked back up. Tristan made the leap from the tree and Aiden heard the skid of one of his feet slipping off the edge. But he recovered and righted himself. Tristan ducked as an arrow shot by, followed swiftly by another. He turned to lower himself down from the battlements but then cried out, his voice piercing the night. Aiden watched as he stumbled and fell. He no longer had any grip on the stonework of the Wall, but dangled from the end of the rope about five feet from the ground. Aiden reached up to steady him. The shaft of an arrow protruded from the back of his leg. Blood dripped onto the ground below.

Falkor appeared on the wall-top, leaning down towards them.

"Tristan's been shot," Aiden called up urgently.

"Catch him," said Falkor, cutting the rope with one clean slice.

Tristan collapsed onto Aiden, stifling another cry. Falkor jumped nimbly from the top of the Wall and dropped to the ground casting a rune ahead of him to slow his fall. He turned back, shooting Teine, fire, at the remains of the rope, burning it up so no one could follow them. In a second, he was at their side. He snapped off the shaft of the arrow and drew a quick rune of Iogh, the resilient, pulling Tristan to his feet.

"Can you walk?" said the wizard.

Tristan nodded and through a grimace hobbled onwards. Wordlessly Aiden followed, clenching his fists to try and stop them trembling. They had not yet left the City and already the faint light of dawn was colouring the eastern sky.

16. The Alder Gate

Aiden had barely fled a few feet from the Wall before he heard cries behind them and the ·rustle of branches as the soldiers climbed the tree and jumped to the Wall. The whizz and click of arrows hitting the ground by their feet intensified. Aiden scrambled after Falkor and Tristan behind the nearest building. They paused. Falkor glanced behind then ducked quickly back and pointed down a path to the left.

They ran along the path, then back onto a street, turning one way then another through the maze of buildings and lanes. Torches flashed between the houses. They ran on, twisting through the streets until the cries dimmed behind them. And in the silence Aiden's skin prickled.

As they drew nearer to the edge of the City they stopped more frequently, clinging to shadows that were rapidly fleeing the rising sun. The houses were thinning, the City fraying at its edges. A few houses started to show signs of wakefulness, shutters opening and smoke puffing from chimneys. Beyond them Aiden could sense the open fields and their escape into the wild.

Falkor's eyes narrowed. "We're too far east," he murmured. "We need to cut south, towards the forest."

Aiden frowned, glancing back at Tristan. In the faint glow of sunrise he could see his companions' faces more clearly. Falkor's was flecked with blood, his eyes a steely glint, his resolve unwavering.

But Tristan limped heavily behind and now he leaned against a wall, his face plastered in a sheen of sweat, twitching every so often in a spasm of pain. He gingerly touched his leg and his fingers came away bright with blood. It was still some way to the forest. Would he make it?

Tristan caught his eye and with a frown pushed off from the wall. "Let's get going then," he whispered, leading the way along the street. Wordlessly Aiden followed as they moved off in the new direction.

The sounds of pursuit faded as they skirted round the edge of the City. The forest drew closer, its shadowy mass silhouetted ahead of them. The sky was no longer black but a pale blue tinged with red. Glancing back Aiden saw the City in the red light of dawn. Smoke plumed from the Palace. The dark banners of the Brathadair now flew from its battlements and their great black mark scoured across the pink stone. He gulped back a swell of emotion. There would be time later to mourn, once they were safely away in the forest.

The next moment there was a shout. Aiden knew without looking that they had been seen again. Falkor waved him ahead, a rune glowing in the palm of his hand, ready to strike. Aiden heard it whistle through the air and the cry of the man it hit. But there were more and Aiden forced his strides to lengthen.

Aiden heard a thud and a groan, too close to be one of the soldiers. Glancing back he saw Tristan face down on the ground. Falkor stopped beside him and shot Nuin, the spear, at an advancing Brathadair soldier. Already Tristan had dragged himself up onto his elbows and knees, but his face was twisted in a grimace. Aiden sprinted back, hauling him the rest of the way to his feet and wrapping his arm across his shoulders.

Aiden set off again, Tristan leaning heavily on his side, his uneven strides cutting across Aiden's rhythm with jerky movements. Sweat soaked through Tristan's shirt and Aiden frowned at the shudder he felt every time his friend's injured leg caught the ground. He tried to push them onwards, but he could not seem to move his legs fast enough or lift his feet high enough. His lungs burned as though crushed beneath some great weight.

Falkor remained a few paces behind them urging them onwards and turning every so often to throw Peith or Nuin or some other runic combination at their pursuers. All the while he kept a glowing shield of Fearn in the air around them. It sparked as arrows hit, but they bounced off harmlessly.

Aiden poured all his strength into their strange lopsided run. He barely noticed as the houses became shaded under a thick canopy of leaves or when, further on, the green became deeper, the ground overgrown, and the houses disappeared altogether. Aiden pulled Tristan onwards, muscles straining, heart beating wildly. He followed a barely discernible earthen path through the undergrowth of heather and bracken. Twigs scratched and grabbed at his ankles, trying to pull him down. The air was close, sticking to his skin, and no matter how much he gulped in, it never seemed enough.

Behind came the crashing of the soldiers as they chased. But there was something else too: a heaviness and a blackness to the air. A dread crept over him and he was too terrified to look back. Tristan's grip tightened on his shoulder and Aiden knew he could sense it too. The fear gave new strength to their failing bodies. They ran blindly, even Tristan forcing his injured leg to work.

The tiny path petered into nothing and even then they kept going, battling through thick heather. Tristan's weight dragged on Aiden and from the corner of his eye Aiden saw the grimace across his face. Then Tristan's good foot caught in the branches and his injured leg, unable to take his weight, buckled beneath him. Tristan collapsed onto Aiden bringing them both to the ground. For a moment they just lay there.

It was then that Aiden realised that the wood had grown quiet. He rolled onto his knees and sat up slowly, glancing around. The dread he had felt before was just a faint buzzing in the back of his mind. His thoughts returned. Where were their pursuers and more importantly where was Falkor?

A groan escaped Tristan's lips as he rolled onto his back. Aiden looked down at him. His eyes were closed, squeezed shut, pulling a frown across his brow, and his chest rose laboriously with every breath. He held his right leg awkwardly above the ground.

A tiny snap of a twig echoed through the trees and Aiden crouched down amongst the heather. He peered around until he saw a figure in the distance. A sigh escaped his mouth. It was Falkor. He was casting a rune and placing it on the trunk of a tree. Aiden's spine tingled, but he pushed the feeling away and sat up again, waving to Falkor.

The wizard walked over, picking his way carefully through the heather. When he was close enough Aiden whispered over. "Are they still following us?"

Falkor slowly moved his head from side to side. "I think for now they are gone."

"What were you doing?" said Aiden, nodding at the tree Falkor had come from.

"I have been casting Uath among the trees," said Falkor, coming to stand above them.

Dread, thought Aiden. That was what he had felt. That was the fear that had driven him on. And possibly the same fear that had driven their enemy back.

"How is he?" asked Falkor, bending down on one knee next to Tristan.

Tristan's eyes flickered open. "I'm fine. I just need a rest."

Falkor's eyes glanced to his leg and then back to his face. "We should look at your leg before we go on. Stay here. There's a stream nearby. I'll get some fresh water. Aiden, try and make him comfortable."

Tristan propped himself up on his elbows as the wizard trudged off into the trees. He began to shuffle himself into a sitting position. Aiden reached out a hand to help him, but Tristan shook his head. "I'm fine," he said sharply. He shuffled back a few more times until his back rested against a tree. Silence stretched around them broken only by Tristan's strained breaths. Once that silence would have been companionable, but now there was an uneasiness between them. Tristan's trust was gone.

Falkor returned shortly with fresh water dripping from their waterskins. He passed one to Aiden and he gulped it down ravenously. Tristan sipped at his more slowly. Falkor knelt by Tristan's leg and lifted it by the knee, pulling off his boot so that he could see the splintered end of the arrow protruding from his calf. Tristan kept his face expressionless, but his fists were clenched so that his knuckles had turned white.

"Aiden, a knife," said the wizard, holding out his hand but not turning his eyes from Tristan's injury.

Aiden quickly fished one out of his pack and placed it in the outstretched hand. Falkor began to gently cut away Tristan's trousers, peeling the fabric away from the sticky mess of blood. Falkor stopped and just stared for a moment at the wound. Then he pressed a hand suddenly to Tristan's forehead, forcing him to look up. Tristan batted him away.

Falkor caught his wrist. "Tristan look at me and tell me honestly how you feel. And don't say you're fine."

Tristan hesitated. "Tell me what's wrong," he said slowly, his voice heavy.

"The arrow has been poisoned," said Falkor. "And now the poison is in your blood."

Tristan fell silent.

"Are you sure?" said Aiden, interjecting. He did not want to believe him. "Maybe it's from the running? We've come a long way."

"See for yourself," said Falkor, leaning aside. "That is not a natural wound."

Aiden peered over the wizard's shoulder and looked down at the messy sight of Tristan's leg. He gulped back bile. He had not seen many wounds in his time, but even he knew that this was bad. The skin was red and inflamed, with crooked blue veins twisting out from it. The wound itself was dribbling blood as well as a yellowish fluid from around the broken stump of the arrow.

"Can't you take out the arrow?" said Aiden.

Falkor shook his head. "If I had done so he would have bled to death by now. No I think his best chance is for the arrow to stay and for him to fight the poison."

"And can I fight it?" said Tristan.

"It's not impossible," said Falkor.

Tristan closed his eyes, leaning his head back against the tree. Very quietly he said, "If you have to go on without me... I understand."

"No," said Aiden sharply, shocked that Tristan would even think it. "Falkor tell him," he said, appealing to the wizard.

Falkor hesitated and in a moment of dread Aiden realised that the wizard really was considering it, as if leaving him behind was a real possibility.

"Aiden's right," said Falkor eventually. "We're not leaving you behind."

"We left the King behind," said Tristan, his eyes raised in challenge. "What makes me so special? Is it not the same injury, just worse for the poison?"

"Yes," said Falkor. "But the circumstances are different. Here we are not surrounded by enemies. We are not contending with a rain of arrows. We are no longer sprinting through shadows or climbing walls. If we stop for a moment we will not be caught or killed. In the Palace all those things were true and we would not have made it."

Silence fell at Falkor's words, broken only by the wind rustling leaves in the canopy above their heads. Aiden wondered if Falkor was trying to convince himself as much as Tristan.

"Do you want us to leave you?" said Falkor eventually, a hint of a smile in his voice.

"No," said Tristan, with a shake of his head.

"Then that's the end of it," said Falkor.

The tension drained from Aiden's shoulders.

"Now I'm going to clean and dress the wound," said Falkor.

Tristan sat tensed and still as Falkor cleaned out the wound with the cold water he had collected from the stream. Then he drew Beith, the healer, above it so that its silvery light soaked into his leg. He wrapped it with fresh bandages until only the tip of the arrow was visible, then he left to wash his hands in the stream. Aiden stayed with Tristan, sitting across from him, watching. Tristan's eyes closed and, though he lay still, his breathing was laboured. Every so often his leg spasmed, a grimace passing across his face.

Falkor returned a few minutes later and crouched in the heather next to Aiden. "We need to keep going," he said quietly. "I don't know how long it will take them to pick up our trail again."

"But where are we going?" said Aiden. "Will Tristan even make it?"

"We're going to Torelia," said the wizard. "There is a healer there. If we can get Tristan to her then all may yet come good."

"How far is it?" Aiden had not heard of the place before, but then he had rarely ventured far from the City.

"Two days, maybe three."

Aiden frowned and glanced back at Tristan. He sincerely hoped it was not too far.

"Tristan's strong," said Falkor, catching his gaze. "He'll make it."

Falkor pulled Tristan to his feet and pressed a stout stick into his hand. "Aiden take his other arm," he said. Aiden hoisted his pack onto his back, taking Tristan's free arm over his shoulders. Falkor led the way to the stream, ushering them ahead through the waters. "I'm going back to cover our tracks," said the wizard.

After some time of splashing through the shallow waters, feet growing cold and numb, Falkor caught up with them and pointed away through the trees. Aiden pulled Tristan onto the dry bank and they walked on, the wizard remaining at the back, carefully sweeping away their trail with a mixture of runes and old tracker's secrets. Aiden's feet dragged beneath him and his head was thick with exhaustion, but every tiny noise jolted him back to alertness. Tristan trudged beside him leaning more heavily on Aiden's shoulders as the time passed. Once or twice Aiden had to catch him before he fell.

An hour or two later they came across a small hollow amidst the trees and Falkor called a halt. "We'll rest here for a while. Our tracks are well covered. You two should get some sleep if you can." Falkor took a seat in the heather a few paces away and allowed himself to lean against a tree.

Tristan slumped down into the heather, bunching up his cloak for a pillow. Within seconds his eyes were closed. Aiden found a comfy spot in the heather and settled down. He tried to sleep, but there seemed to be no escape from his thoughts. He turned his mind away from his injured friend and the burden of secrets and betrayal that had come between them, but then all he could think about was Andor and Branwyn and his parents. The uncertainty of their fate did nothing to put him at ease. He drifted in and out of vivid dreams, where he somehow failed to save Tristan and failed to stop the Brathadair from tearing down his home. In the last one Hakon caught him and gripped him hard, shaking him. Aiden awoke with a start to find Falkor standing over him.

"We need to keep going," said Falkor.

Aiden nodded and got to his feet, ignoring the heaviness in his eyes and the dull ache that had invaded his muscles. It was still light, though the shadows felt longer now. Late afternoon, he guessed. They had rested for a few hours at most. Falkor roused Tristan, who groaned as he opened his eyes, a great shudder passing through his body. Aiden frowned at his pale face.

"I'll carry you for a while," Falkor said to Tristan. "I fear that too much walking will only spread the poison further through your body."

Tristan nodded, his eyes dull. Once, Aiden thought, there would have been a spark of pride and protest at the thought of being carried. Now he let Falkor hoist him over his shoulder.

They set off again, deeper into the forest. Tall red-barked pines surrounded them and smaller white-trunked birch with shimmering leaves. Low sunlight slanted through the canopy and it would have been beautiful had there been time to stop and look. Aiden wished he could stop and speak to the trees. Surely birch, who had once taught men the rune of Beith, the healer, would know how to help Tristan. In the old stories people had been able to speak to the Tree Spirits, but Aiden did not know how. He doubted anyone knew anymore.

Aiden's mind turned to other old stories of the wild. Legend and history told of the Cat-Sidhe and the Cu-Sidhe, Wulvers and Kelpies, River Folk, Tree Spirits, and Fae. Once there had been wars between them and men and it was said that they had all been pushed to the most remote parts of the country. But in this never-ending expanse of trees Aiden could almost believe that he had strayed into their territory.

Falkor pushed on, keeping their pace at a march. Aiden hastened after the wizard. How could he still keep going after all the fighting and healing and rune casting he had done, before they even began this headlong race through the forest? But even Falkor had limits and he seemed to stumble and put his hand out to steady himself against a tree. He set Tristan on the ground, passing him to Aiden.

"Are you ok?" said Tristan, as Falkor crouched down and rubbed his eyes slowly with one hand.

"I'm fine," said Falkor. "I've just drawn so many runes my energy is almost spent."

"I'll walk for a bit," said Tristan, pinching his lips together to hide the grimace as his bad leg touched the ground.

"No," said Falkor glancing up sharply, but his grey eyes seemed paler than usual in the evening light.

"I'll lean on Aiden," said Tristan. "You can't keep this up."

Falkor hesitated, but did not deny it.

"We could rest here awhile?" said Aiden, hopeful.

"No," said Falkor again, standing. "We keep going. But you'll have to help Tristan again."

So they continued again with Tristan leaning awkwardly on Aiden's shoulder. Falkor led the way a few paces ahead, scouting the best path in the quickly growing darkness. Progress was much slower than before. Tristan's bulk weighed heavily upon Aiden, disrupting the rhythm of his steps. Tristan tensed with every step, wincing at every jolt. It became harder and harder to see where they were putting their feet. Aiden's own strength was waning, his eyes struggling to focus.

Eventually, when it was too black to see, Falkor called a halt. Aiden set Tristan carefully to the ground. He was shivering, his teeth clacking as great tremors passed through his body. Aiden took a blanket from his pack and wrapped it around him. Falkor recast the runes over Tristan's leg, but did not attempt to change the bandages. To Aiden's eye they seemed to be making no difference, but he said nothing. Tristan was keeping himself alive by will alone and Aiden was afraid that if he showed any doubts then Tristan would lose hope. They quickly ate a cold meal in silence before settling into the heather to sleep. Aiden's eyes dropped closed almost before his head had even reached the ground, exhaustion dragging him into a deep sleep devoid of all dreams.

Falkor woke them again in the grey light of pre-dawn. There were dark circles under the wizard's eyes and Aiden wondered, with a sudden pang of guilt, whether Falkor had slept at all the night before. Tristan was harder to rouse. He shuffled restlessly amidst the heather and though he opened his eyes, they were unfocused and he squinted away from the light. His face was pale, but his cheeks were red and fiery hot. Aiden was not sure if he even noticed when Falkor picked him up and set off again into the trees.

Around them the forest grew wilder, the undergrowth thicker, the paths deer tracks only. They had not seen another person for almost two days now. Aiden had never been in so remote a place.

Falkor pushed them on through the day with only small stops, enough for a drink and a quick snack, but no more. They swapped Tristan between them as often as they could, though Tristan himself barely noticed. He mumbled to himself as they walked, sometimes calling out to things that were not there. His eyes flickered and blue veins stuck out not only on his leg, but also on his wrists and face. Tristan was slipping further and further into a dream world from which he might never return.

They walked under a thick forest canopy and Aiden felt like they were going in circles. The trees never seemed to change and the undergrowth merely alternated between scratchy heather and bracken with leafy fronds reaching as high as Aiden's waist. Sometimes when Aiden looked up he could see the sky above. It was blue enough, but the sunlight never quite managed to reach them. It felt like a great shadow had been cast over all of Teraan.

Night drew in again, but Falkor did not call a halt. He glanced often and anxiously at Tristan, draped over his shoulder. Aiden stumbled along behind, his feet deadweights. Only his will and determination kept him going. Falkor too was unsteady on his feet, a pale shadow wavering between the trees.

"Falkor we can't keep this up much longer," said Aiden, his voice a coarse whisper.

"It's not far now," came Falkor's voice through the darkness, though how Falkor could tell Aiden did not know. "For Tristan's sake we can't stop now."

Aiden made no reply. There was nothing to say. All he had to do was keep putting one foot in front of the other. They trudged on and time fell away around them until all there was were shadows and rasping breath and the never-ending dull ache throughout his body.

"Halt," an unseen voice shouted from the trees. "State your business or an arrow will find your heart."

Falkor stopped and slowly lifted Tristan to the ground, passing him into Aiden's care. Tristan leaned heavily into him and Aiden's tired muscles cried out with the strain.

With a tiny, barely perceptible flash Falkor drew Fearn, the shield, and threw it back over them before stepping forwards. Another more visible rune shone brightly in his hand: Peith, the thunderbolt. Aiden hoped he would have the strength to hold it.

"I am Falkor, the King's wizard and you would do well not to hinder us," said Falkor, his voice full of threat.

"Prove it," the unseen voice called back.

Without dropping Peith, Falkor drew another rune, Suil, the prophet. He held it aloft. "I am Falkor. May the river's waterfall refresh you if you are friends or strike me down if I lie."

Suil burst into bright sparks that flew around the forest, lighting up the trees in stark white light. Aiden caught glimpses of men in the shadows, ducking away, but no one cried out. The light died away as suddenly as it had come.

There was a small rustle of leaves and a man, or at least the shadow of a man, stepped out. The deep darkness after the sudden light left Aiden's eyes almost blinded, but even once the afterglow of Suil died away it still felt like his eyes bounced off this man. As he stepped closer Aiden could make out more of his features. He was tall and lean but well muscled. A dark beard covered his chin and long hair was tied loosely behind his head. He had his sword drawn, but it was not held threateningly.

"I'm sorry about the welcome Falkor," said the man. "But with all the rumours reaching here recently I had to be sure."

"Allan," Falkor greeted, clapping arms with the man. "You are right to be wary. Brathadair have taken Teraan City and the King with it."

"How?" said Allan, anger sharpening his voice.

"I'll explain later," said Falkor. "But Tristan Arthursson was injured in our escape. He holds on to his life by a thread. We need to get him to Torelia as quickly as we can."

Allan instantly turned and signalled into the trees with a quick flick of his hand. Silently and swiftly four men materialised from the forest, long cloaks whispering about them. One unclipped his cloak in a fluid motion and set it on the ground. They lifted Tristan from Aiden's arms, his head lolling back as they laid him onto the cloak. He moaned as his infected leg touched the ground. Then, taking a corner each, the four men lifted Tristan into the air and sped off into the night. Allan signalled again into the trees and Aiden heard tiny rustles as other men moved off.

As the forest grew still again Aiden felt Allan's dark eyes appraising him.

"Tristan I have heard of," said Allan. "But who's this?"

"Aiden Brokksson," said Falkor. "Feather Guard. If it were not for him the Brathadair attack on the City would have been much worse."

Worse, thought Aiden. Surely it was bad enough already?

"I thank you then, Aiden Brokksson," said Allan, stepping up to him. "I am Allan, Captain of the Torelian Border Guard."

Torelian. It was that word again. The place he had never heard of before.

"Come," said Allan, turning into the trees. "You must tell me all that has happened in the City as we walk."

They started off into the trees and though Aiden's legs ached he felt lighter than he had for days. He fell into step behind Falkor and Allan, listening as they spoke in low tones about all that had happened. Falkor recounted the story of the man they had caught in the library and the message left scraped on the walls. He told of how Halvard and Johann had gone to Cairn Ban and not returned, then of how their prisoner had talked of a great Brathadair army amassing at Cairn Ban to await Sorcier's return and how that had sent the rest of the Eagle Riders flying out to stop them.

Allan said little but looked back occasionally when Falkor explained Aiden's part in overhearing the conspirators and the plot against the King and the Eagle Riders. Yet although it was him they spoke of Aiden felt like he was miles away from everything that had happened. Only when Falkor came to describe the attack on Teraan City did things start to feel more real. An overwhelming sense of the unstoppable came over Aiden. The Eagle Riders had gone to face an army, but in doing so had left the City and its King to be captured. They were all dancing to the Brathadair's tune and Aiden wondered if their next move would already have been anticipated by their enemy.

"Did the Princess arrive safely?" said Falkor as he came to the end of his tale.

Allan nodded. "She arrived a few days ago, before we knew the true extent of the treachery."

"Good," said Falkor. "She is the future now. She must be kept safe."

The men fell silent. They walked for a few minutes more and Aiden wondered when they would reach Torelia amidst the seemingly endless expanse of trees. Then, suddenly, looming before them was a gate. It was so close Aiden wondered why he had not seen it before. But as they came closer he saw that it was made of alder branches—alder, the giver of Fearn, the shield and the secretive. The gate was slender and made of intricately twisted branches. It blended seamlessly into the forest forming a beautiful, yet mysterious archway. Aiden followed its curve with his eyes and saw that branches twisted away into the forest on either side, an almost imperceptible barrier pushing people's very thoughts away from this place. Aiden had no doubt that those inside the barrier would be able to see the forest much clearer than those without.

"What is this place?" Aiden whispered, without realising he said the words aloud.

"It is Torelia," said Allan. "One of the King's secret refuges. Very few people know of its existence."

"Does Hakon know?" said Aiden.

"He knows it exists," said Falkor. "But he's never been and the magic of this place means that no one but a select few can remember its location after leaving its borders."

Aiden gazed with fresh wonder at branches of alder twisted unassumingly through the forest.

"He can see the barrier," said Allan, matter-of-factly.

Falkor nodded. "He has an eye for magic."

As they approached the gate, two guards wearing cloaks of twisting greens materialised to challenge them. They were quickly allowed through and Allan led them onwards to the secret outpost of Torelia. As they walked Aiden became aware of platforms hidden in the trees. He gazed up, occasionally seeing a green-cloaked figure shift in the trees. Away from the alder gate Aiden began to hear the low roaring of rushing water. The sound became clearer and louder the further they walked, yet Aiden could not catch a glimpse of a river anywhere. It was unnerving, but no matter how much he strained his eyes he could see no more than a few feet ahead.

All of a sudden, the trees broke apart, the ground dropped away and there, at last, was the river. Aiden's head spun as he realised he stood at the top of a treacherous gorge. Not far to their left a great misty cascade of water tumbled down into the canyon, moonlight glistening softly off the smooth wet rocks. Allan took them to a precarious path leading down the cliff and Aiden's balance was shaky as his eyes jumped from the ground at his feet to the tremendous drop on his right. They headed down towards the great waterfall and the roaring of the river seemed to swallow up every other sound.

Before they were even half way to the bottom Allan turned into the cliff itself. A narrow cave led them into a warren of tunnels, twisting in all directions. Allan lit a torch and held it aloft, its light piercing the blackness of the tunnels. At the back of the cave they took the right branch of the tunnel and continued downwards for a few minutes, still heading towards the waterfall. The sounds of the river were muffled here and the light of the torch danced off rough hewn stone. Occasionally they passed more caves, some covered by wooden doors, some by heavy pieces of cloth, but there were others left open to the moonlight and Aiden caught the roar of the river as they went by.

Eventually, Allan stopped and lifted back a heavy dark blue cloth to reveal the entrance to a small cave. "Aiden, this cave is yours for the duration of your stay. You should find everything you need inside. I'll send someone with food in the morning," said Allan.

Aiden stopped. "What about Tristan?"

"I'll make sure he gets to the healer," said Falkor. "In the meantime you should rest. We'll talk more in the morning."

Aiden opened his mouth to protest, but the glare in Falkor's grey eyes was enough keep him silent. He slipped into the cave, letting the cloth drop down behind him. Falkor and Allan's footsteps faded away down the tunnel, then all he could hear was the rush of the river.

Aiden suddenly felt very tired. He gazed blankly around the cave. It was a small space, with a bed nestled into the rough stone wall and a small table and chair on the far side. Moonlight filtered in through an uncovered opening opposite him and he approached it to find it led out to a ledge overlooking the river. He returned inside, dumped his pack on the chair, tipped off his boots, and sank into the pile of blankets on the bed. Within minutes he was asleep.

17. Left Behind

Branwyn awoke piece by piece. She shifted in bed, her blankets wrapping around her. Her eyes flickered and frowned. The first grey light of dawn was only just seeping in through the cracks in the shutters. She could smell the tang of yeast from downstairs where her father must be making the bread doughs. Why had she awoken? A pained cry sounded from the street, followed by the scuffing of feet. Branwyn rolled over and closed her eyes. Probably drunkards. Then there was the rasping of metal and the dull clang as it hit something. Branwyn opened her eyes again and after a moment sat up. Silence. And then the sounds came again.

She stood quietly, drawing her blankets around her shoulders, and padded over to the window, pulling the shutter open a crack to peer out. Cool air rushed in, making her shiver. Then her eyes caught movement a short way along the street. One man was wildly flailing his blade against two soldiers of the City Guard. Branwyn wrinkled her nose. Why did the man even bother trying to fight the guard? She moved to close the shutter again, not wanting to witness his eventual defeat, but something caught her eye and she stopped. She looked again at the men.

But her eyes had not deceived her. All three of the men wore the garb of the City Guard.

What had seemed a common brawl suddenly made no sense. Branwyn found herself rapt, her bed forgotten. The fight separated for a moment and the men circled each other. Aiden's warnings of the day before came rushing back. But did that mean that at least one of those men was Brathadair? Then who?

The lone man rushed at his assailants again, trying to take them by surprise, but they were not easily tricked. The two guards drove him back, beating him down with their swords. Branwyn flinched as each blow landed on the man. She wanted to look away but found herself trapped with him in his plight. A cut opened on his forearm and then another down his side, rushing blood. He seemed unable to lift his sword above head height. One guard went for his knees, but he dodged back. Then, his face hardening, he lifted himself tall and Branwyn sensed he was preparing for something.

In a move that sent a grimace of pain across his face, the lone man lifted his sword. "Brathadair scum," he spat. He ran at the two guards, knocking through them and pounding down the road. Suddenly he dropped, face to the ground and did not move. In one glance Branwyn saw the knife sticking out of his back and the other guard, arm outstretched.

Branwyn ducked back from the window, sinking to the floor. Time seemed to float around her. The man had died. Right there in her street. And killed by two Brathadair, dressed as City Guards. She knew what she had seen and yet somehow she could not comprehend it.

Suddenly, she heard the door open downstairs and her father's voice out on the street.

"What's going on?" he called, his voice sharp and irksome. She could imagine his face reddened from lighting the ovens, his hands floury from the dough.

An unnameable panic arose in her chest and in an instant Branwyn was on her feet again and peering out the window. No Dad, no, she thought. Did he not realise it was the Brathadair who had won the fight? What would the men do?

Branwyn watched as the taller of the two bent down and retrieved his knife from the dead man's back, wiping it casually on his sleeve before turning to face her father. The cold indifference on his face was terrifying.

"He was loyal to a false King," said the guard. "And it got him killed."

"What false King?" said Aran.

There was the hint of a smile around the guard's mouth, as if he had been hoping for this. "Brandr, who used to sit on the throne." The guard flipped his knife in his hand.

Branwyn could not see her father, but she willed him to say no more. Let him come inside. Then there was the flash as the knife was thrown and the resounding thud as the door slammed shut. Branwyn clapped a hand over her mouth to stifle her cry. She stood perfectly still. The guard who had thrown the knife walked towards their door. Wood splintered as he pulled his knife from their door.

"Remember who the false King is and we won't have to come back," the guard said through the door.

Through the crack in the shutters Branwyn saw the two Brathadair wander away, lifting the dead man by his arms and dragging him away as they left. Once they were out of sight, she dropped her blanket in a heap and ran down the stairs, straight into the open arms of her father. She felt tears wetting her cheeks.

"I thought he was going to kill you," she cried into his shoulder.

Aran said nothing, but Branwyn could feel him shaking, even as she cried. There was a creak on the stairs behind and Aran reached out a hand to Sanna, pulling her into the hug. "I'm ok," he whispered.

"They were Brathadair," said Sanna, her voice thick. "What did they mean 'Brandr, who *used* to sit on the throne?'"

"I don't know," said Aran.

Branwyn stepped back so that she could see her parents faces.

"Aiden will know," she said. "He told me some of it yesterday, before he knew if it was true."

"And you didn't think to tell us?" said Aran.

"I had hoped it wasn't true," she said, feeling tears prickling her eyes again.

Aran wiped his hands down his apron, taking it off and passing it to Sanna. "I'm going to see Brokk."

Branwyn's eyes lit up. "Let me come too." She had a sudden, desperate, urge to see Aiden. To know that he was safe. If the Brathadair were killing City Guards then what would they do to him if they found him?

Aran shook his head. "Not now Bran. I don't know if it's safe."

Branwyn turned beseechingly to her mother. "Mum?"

Sanna shook her head. "Your Dad's right. We don't know what's going on out there."

"But it's just across the street."

"And I was almost just killed for stepping outside my door," said Aran. "So you and your Mum are staying here. Bar the door behind me and only open it again when I return."

"Dad wait," said Branwyn.

Aran turned back to her.

"Aiden also told me that he had made a safe house in case… in case we needed to escape. He showed me yesterday. In the abandoned tower."

Aran nodded, turning abruptly to the door. He glanced both ways along the street before walking out. Sanna dropped the wooden bar across the door behind him. Branwyn rushed through to the front window and bit her lip. She watched her father dart across the street and, as he slipped safely through the door to Brokk and Kari's house on the far side, she let her body relax. Then there was silence.

Branwyn could not say how long she stood there watching,

shifting from foot to foot. She was distantly aware of the sun rising, casting a stark brightness across the empty street. Barely a noise stirred the air. A long sigh came from the door and Branwyn turned to see her mother bringing the first tray of bread from the kitchen.

"It must be true," Sanna whispered. "Or else we'd have had customers by now."

Branwyn looked back outside. It was true that she had seen no one pass since the fight. But what did that mean? What was going on in the rest of the City? Suddenly she jumped at the touch of a hand on her shoulder. It was only her mother, who had joined her without her hearing.

"It's going to be alright Branwyn," said Sanna.

Branwyn frowned. "How do you know?"

Sanna gave her a smile. "We have to believe it. And you forget we have the Eagle Riders. I don't doubt they will rescue our King, if indeed he has been taken."

The Eagle Riders. The thought sent a rush of fear through Branwyn. "The Eagle Riders are gone," she said, hearing her voice almost crack.

Sanna's smile faltered. "What do you mean?"

"I mean the Eagle Riders are gone. Aiden said they left the day he was… the day he left."

"But surely not all?" said Sanna. "There is always at least one here."

Branwyn shook her head. "Not this time."

"They'll come back," said Sanna, but as silence fell around them Branwyn saw the smile finally slip from her mother's face. That, more than anything else, brought the reality of the situation crashing around her. Up until this point her parents had been bigger than any of her troubles. Now they were in the same uncertain and scared place as she was.

"There's your father," said Sanna, moving away from her towards the door. Branwyn followed more slowly.

Aran stepped in, his face drawn, eyes sombre, and put an arm instinctively around his wife's and Branwyn's shoulders.

"What is it?" said Sanna.

"Did you speak to Aiden?" Branwyn said, her spirits lifting at the thought of him.

Aran hesitated before replying. Then he said, "Aiden wasn't there."

Branwyn's brow wrinkled in confusion. Why would he not be there? Her mind jumped to the first, most terrible thought—that he was dead. She reasoned to herself that it could not be so. But after what she had just seen anything was suddenly possible. In the space of a second her emotions went full circle.

Aran continued. "Aiden left last night, with the King's wizard and one of his Feather Guard friends."

"Tristan…" Branwyn murmured.

"Yes that was the name," said Aran.

"But why?" said Sanna.

Aran took her hand. "The Brathadair have taken over. They have the King."

Sanna took the news silently, but her fingers gripped more tightly to Aran's. Branwyn herself felt numb inside. Aiden was gone and all that he had feared was coming true. He was not dead, but then he was not safe either. She did not know whether to be scared or angry.

"What do we do now?" said Sanna.

"Brokk and I think we should all go to the safe house Aiden prepared. At least until things quieten down."

Sanna nodded as if this was no surprise. "I'll pack some things quickly."

Branwyn stayed rooted to the spot.

"Are you ok?" said her father, taking her by the shoulders.

"Is Aiden going to be ok?" she asked, looking up at him and feeling like she was a little girl again.

Her father pulled her into a hug. "He's with the King's wizard and Brokk thinks they managed to escape."

It was not a real answer, but it was something to hold onto.

"Now go and pack your things," said Aran, pushing her gently towards the stairs. "I'm going to fire-down the ovens."

Branwyn headed to her room, dressing quickly and folding some clothes into a small bag. She gazed around her room, wondering what else she should take. What was even important? Her silver pendant. Her favourite blue scarf. She threw in a couple of other small things and then stood, unsure.

Her mother appeared in the doorway.

"Are you ready?"

"I feel like I'm forgetting something," said Branwyn.

"Don't worry about it Bran. I'm sure we'll be back before you know it."

Branwyn gave a small nod and tugged herself away. Despite her mother's optimism it somehow felt very final. And she could not help but remember how the smile had slipped from her face earlier. Did her mother really believe they would be back soon? Or was she just saying that to reassure her? Branwyn did not know, but she followed her anyway to the foot of the stairs where her father was waiting for them.

Aran opened the door a crack and peered out before leading the way across. It was just a short journey over the road, one Branwyn had made more times than she could remember, but never before had it filled her with such fear and foreboding. The street was empty so they darted across the road, feeling like thieves in the night. Brokk opened the door quickly. His face was pale and haggard, as if he had not slept at all. Branwyn glanced back as she entered the house and saw a tall dark plume of smoke rising from the direction of the Palace. At the sight of it she felt her skin prickle. That was why the streets were empty.

"Wait," came a muted shout from behind them.

Branwyn stumbled after her father into the house, suddenly picturing the dead soldier with the knife in his back. But instead of closing the door behind them, Brokk held it open. She turned, peering between the shoulders of her parents. It was the blacksmith, Halfdan, who lived further along their street. He had a satchel over his shoulder and a barely concealed sword in the folds of his cloak. Across the street his family huddled in the shadow of a building.

"You've heard?" said the blacksmith, eyeing their own bags.

Brokk nodded.

"We're leaving town," said the blacksmith. "My son, who's been working in the armouries in the Restricted Zone, came home this morning, saying the Brathadair have taken over the Palace. He says riots have broken out and they were starting to get out of control. The Brathadair seem to be rounding up anyone who isn't loyal to them. My son says they are forcing soldiers to make the choice between joining them or death. If you've had any connection to the Palace you'd be wise to get out of here while you can."

Brokk nodded again. "Thank you and good luck."

The blacksmith nodded, glancing furtively over his shoulder. "And you."

He left quickly and quietly to rejoin his family. Branwyn watched them begin to make their way along the street before Brokk closed the door with a loud clunk. They set their bags down in a small pile by the door, next to Brokk and Kari's things. Kari appeared from the kitchen with one final pack to add to the pile.

"We're doing the right thing," said Brokk, looking round at the weary and worried faces of his family.

Aran nodded solemnly. "But what route should we take out past the Wall? How far do you think the riots have spread?"

Branwyn left them to their discussions, taking the stairs to her cousins' room, where Andor sat gazing out of the window. She squeezed his shoulder and sat down next to him but neither she nor he said a word. What was there to say anyway?

In the silence Branwyn's mind wandered, racing the empty streets outside, searching for some sign of Aiden. But all she could see was that small patch of blood where the other man had fallen. What if that happened to Aiden too? If he was caught or died she might never know. He might never come back. Branwyn stopped herself. Aiden had left hours ago. He would be well out of the City by now. She shook her head, trying to shake off the fears that threatened to paralyse her.

"Look," said Andor, suddenly pointing.

Branwyn looked out and saw a patrol of ten or so soldiers marching along their street. They wore the deep red of the Palace Guard, but were they really Palace Guards? One man at the front had the glow of runelight about his fingers. The rest followed him, looking to him for instructions. Then he looked up and pointed towards them.

Branwyn and Andor ducked out of sight. Branwyn's breath caught in her throat. She did not think they had been seen, but they were coming this way. Andor gazed at her, eyes wide. He scrabbled across the floor, jumping to his feet once he was out of sight of the window and leaping down the stairs in two great bounds. Branwyn scrambled after him, her feet clattering over the wooden steps. Downstairs in the workshop she heard Andor saying, "There's soldiers in the street. Coming this way. I think they pointed to our house."

Branwyn rushed in to silence and to expressions of unmasked terror on her parent's faces. It lasted for an instant only and then there was a sudden burst of movement. Branwyn's bag was thrust into her hand and she felt someone guiding her elbow back towards the stairs.

"Quickly, upstairs and hide," said Brokk.

It was her mother's hand leading her to the stairs. Sanna squeezed her arm gently and with one tear-brimmed smile told her to stay safe and be brave and that she was loved all at once.

"Don't come out unless you are sure it's safe," said her father.

"Take care of Andor," said Kari, placing one of his hands in hers.

"And if something happens…" Brokk struggled for words. "Go to the safe house."

"Nothing will happen," said Branwyn, feeling tears choke her voice. She did not believe her own words.

Conversations were cut short by an angry banging on the door.

"Go now," said Kari urgently.

Branwyn pelted up the stairs with Andor close behind her. They darted into Aiden and Andor's room and tried to still their breathing. Branwyn jumped as a great splintering crash resounded through the house. She clutched Andor's hand tighter. They had broken down the door. Raised voices began to filter up through the floorboards.

"Brokk, the cloakmaker," said one.

"Yes," came Brokk's reply. To Branwyn's ears he sounded pitifully small and scared.

"Where is your son, Aiden? And the wizard Falkor? They have aided the King in his treason. And don't bother denying it. We know Falkor came here. We've tracked him with magic and the runes never lie."

"The King's treason!" Brokk spluttered. "What about your own treason?"

Branwyn clamped a hand over her mouth. She knew instantly that her uncle had said the wrong thing. He had given himself away, revealed that he knew more than he should. She could almost imagine the Brathadair man sneering over him in victory.

"Sir, bags," said another voice. "Looks like they're preparing to run."

"Where is your son?"

"He's gone," said Brokk, defiantly.

"Search the house," said the Brathadair.

Branwyn's eyes went wide and she felt suddenly cold all over. They were just standing in the middle of the room. They should have been hiding, not listening. Sounds of the search spread through the house. There was a crash and the splintering of wood, followed by a ripping noise. More bumps and clunks reached them and things were thrown around carelessly downstairs.

"Check upstairs," someone called.

Branwyn and Andor glanced at each other, frozen momentarily by the same mind-numbing fear. Then at the same time they both whispered, "The roof."

They rushed over to the window and pulled open the shutters. Branwyn winced as the wood clunked against the stone wall. Andor scrambled out first and Branwyn pushed his feet up from below. She tossed up their bags. Then, carefully, she balanced herself on the windowsill and, using the tips of her fingers, pulled the shutters back towards her. Her hands trembled with the effort.

The footsteps of the Brathadair clunked on the stairs. At last the shutters were back in place. She reached up, Andor's hands grabbing hers, and began to haul herself up. She rolled, rather ungainly, onto the roof and froze. The footsteps had reached Andor's room. She shuffled herself very slowly further onto the roof.

They heard rummaging from the room below and the thuds of things being knocked onto the floor. Then the shutters were flung wide again and both Branwyn and Andor flattened themselves to the roof. There was an agonisingly long moment where Branwyn did not dare to move. Her skin prickled as if she was being watched, but she was sure they could not be seen.

After what felt like an age a voice shouted, "There's no one up here."

The noises grew fainter as the men returned downstairs, but Branwyn still did not dare to move. Muffled voices filtered up through the house, but Branwyn could no longer make out what was being said.

"I wish we could hear what was happening," Branwyn whispered to Andor.

Andor nodded, his expression growing thoughtful. He shuffled on the roof and sketched a rune. At first Branwyn saw nothing except the creases on Andor's forehead deepen. Then the rune started to glow, weakly at first, but it grew stronger. And with it came the sounds from below.

"…if you don't tell us … you will all be … as traitors and punished…"

"We are not the traitors here," said Branwyn's father defiantly.

"Tie their hands."

Sounds of a scuffle broke through. She heard indeterminate shouts that could have been either her father or Brokk trying to prevent their imprisonment. She glanced fearfully at Andor and saw her expression mirrored in his face. He lost control of the rune and suddenly the rooftop was silent. Wild scenarios ran through Branwyn's head all of which ended with the death of her parents and aunt and uncle. She scrambled to the edge of the roof and was almost climbing back down when Andor grabbed her. She glanced at him in surprise.

"Wait."

She struggled against him for a second, pulling free, and then froze as people began to spill from the house. Soldiers dressed in the red cloaks of the Palace Guard came out dragging her parents and Brokk and Kari with their hands tethered behind their backs.

She could see her father twisting against his bonds and her mother trying to hold her head high despite the soldier pushing her down. The soldiers dragged them along the street, pulling them further and further away. Branwyn scrambled towards the edge of the roof again. She could not lose them.

"Branwyn no," said Andor, clutching at her. "You'll get caught too."

Branwyn heard the desperation in his voice. She remembered how Kari had placed Andor's hands in hers and told her to look after him. She could not leave him now, no matter how much she might want to go after her parents. She stopped and felt the wrench of her heart as she let the figures of her parents dwindle. She felt tears stinging down her cheeks as she tried to etch every contour of their faces into her memory. Neither her father nor mother looked back and though it pained her she knew, deep down, that it was their last act of defiance and love. They would not give away her hiding place.

Eventually Branwyn drew her gaze back to Andor. His face was ashen, his eyes glistening. They should get down from the roof, she thought, and this time Andor did not resist her attempts to climb down. He followed her and they moved quickly through the house, pausing downstairs to gaze at the destruction the soldiers had left in their wake. Andor ran through the kitchen, touching the broken things scattered across the floor. His hands trembled and he fell down on his knees in the middle of the carnage. His shoulders began to shake. Branwyn put a hand on his shoulder, drawing him into hug. She let him cry silently into her shoulder for a minute, then pulled back.

"We need to go," said Branwyn. "It's not safe here anymore."

Wordlessly they slipped out onto the street. The daylight was stark and eerily silent and Branwyn clung to the shadows as they walked. Shops were still boarded up and the shutters that had been open were quickly pulled shut as they approached. Wind whistled through the houses and rustled through the trees, sometimes bringing with it shouts and cries that barely sounded human anymore. Minutes later they arrived at King's Avenue.

"Look," said Andor, grabbing her arm and pointing. From the rosy walls of the Palace a thick cloud of black smoke streamed into the air but, terrible as that sight was, it was the black marks painted across the red stone of the towers that filled her with dread. She recognised the symbol from when she and Aiden had gone to the burning building and Tristan had shown them the mark of the Brathadair. It had been small then, but now, scrawled across the Palace itself, no one in the City could doubt that they had taken over.

A trail of carnage led down King's Avenue heralded by harsh cries and the bitter taste of smoke. People, some soldiers, some not, lay scattered among the debris of stone and broken furniture all lit by the crackling light of small fires. Further away, at the Wall, a mass of people swarmed around the gate. A sense of deep foreboding grew in Branwyn's mind. It looked to her like a battle and she had no desire to be any closer than they already were. Yet it was the way out and they had no choice but to go on. She took Andor firmly by the hand, as much for her sake as for his, and continued forwards.

As they neared the carnage they kept close to the edge of the street, ducking through debris, rather than skirting around it. There was movement all around, flashes of colour and steel and noise. Nearer the gate Branwyn almost lost her focus, trapped instead in a seemingly endless cycle of ducking and spinning and dodging and hiding. But every time it seemed they would be attacked they somehow escaped. None of the fighters cared about two children navigating the battlefield. At last Branwyn saw a clear path through the melee and under the archway of the gate.

Branwyn made a break for it, keeping a firm grip on Andor's

hand, sprinting through the fighting until finally they were in an open street with the battle behind. Even then she kept running until the noise of the battle had grown dim. It was only when Andor tugged on her arm that she slowed.

"Come on," she said, gently drawing Andor behind her. "We're almost there."

They zig-zagged through the last of the houses until they reached the abandoned tower and there they pushed through the bushes at the entrance and slowly climbed the spiral steps. Aiden's box was there just as he had left it. Only yesterday, thought Branwyn. So much had changed since then. Something clutched at her throat, threatening to choke her. Her eyes brimmed with tears, but she squeezed them shut and pushed back the feeling. For Andor's sake she could not cry yet.

Branwyn took some blankets out of the box and tried to make the little stone room more comfortable. They sat, neither speaking. Branwyn shifted from one position to another, unable to get comfortable. A deep restlessness pervaded everything. She walked to the slit window, gazing for a moment over the empty streets before returning to her seat. It was no good looking. They were not going to come.

The day passed slowly and Branwyn's mind ran through the sequence of events. What could she have done to save them? She should have told her parents yesterday about what Aiden had said. But she had not believed it would be true. They would not have believed her either. Or maybe first thing they should have all gone across to Brokk's and then they could have left before the Brathadair came. Only to be caught in the street, said a small voice in the back of her mind. No, the thing she regretted most was not going after her parents when they were caught. She would have been caught too, and that was not what they would have wanted, but how could she know now where they had been taken? She wished she could have called out to them, told them she loved them.

Eventually, day turned to night and Branwyn lit a candle, sitting it in the corner of the room away from the window. Andor curled up on the blankets and laid his head on a pile of clothes. After a while his breath slowed and deepened. Branwyn drew his cloak over him gently. She wondered how he could sleep.

Branwyn stood and took the last few steps up to the open top of the tower. Darkness enveloped her. Even the fires at the Palace and along King's Avenue had now been snuffed out. She shivered in the chill air but did nothing more than wrap her arms around herself, sinking to the floor and letting numbness seep into her bones. She longed for tears to release the pent up emotions of the day, but she felt nothing: not tiredness, not cold, not feeling. She contemplated sitting until she had faded away completely.

"I have nothing left," she whispered into the night. The City had been taken over by enemies, her family were prisoners, she could not go home, she was alone and afraid.

A warm tear streaked across her cheek and then another and another. This time she did nothing to stop it. A shuddering breath wracked her body. She wanted to scream out her anger, but she was too afraid to make a sound. She held herself and rocked back and forth, her eyes and nose streaming, despite futile attempts to wipe her face with her sleeve.

Sometime later, she found herself lying on her side on the bare stone floor, her tears dried on her face. She could not say how long she had lain there, but she felt very cold and very tired. With some effort she lifted herself and shakily walked back down the steps to the little stone room. The candle had blown out, but the soft sound of breathing told her Andor still slept. She wrapped a blanket around her shoulders and huddled down next to him, at last feeling the pull of sleep.

18. Torelia

In the light of the new morning Aiden gazed down on Torelia. The waterfall filled his ears with endless roaring and sent a fine spray into the air, catching rainbows in the sunlight and coating the nearby rocks so that they glistened. The swirling water entranced as it tumbled down from its great height, taller even than the old watch towers of Teraan City. The river flowed a clear greyish-blue, rushing to the northwest, its waters flecked with the remnants of froth from the great cascade. On either side the stony cliffs of the canyon rose up, a few hardy plants clinging to the cracks in the rock. At the top the ground opened out briefly, making way for a path, before the giant sentinel shapes of trees crowded the horizon.

Cautiously Aiden stepped closer to the edge of the ledge and looked out and up. The cave he stood in must have been about half way up the cliff and he began to pick out other caves scattered along the gorge. Some were high up, like his, but others opened down near the water. There were people down there, walking along the narrow banks of the river. They approached the waterfall, hugging the foot of the cliffs, and disappeared behind the curtain of water. Of course, thought Aiden, his eyes brightening, there is a cave behind the waterfall.

Aiden left his little cave, following the tunnel beyond that led straight from the cliff face at the top to the space behind the waterfall at the base. The cavern was massive. Aiden took two steps and stopped, craning his neck up at the high ceiling, which flickered constantly with reflections of light through the waterfall. His gaze turned to the torrent of water, eyes widening. It was so close and yet its roar was not deafening him and the cave was dry. He studied the waterfall intently and began to pick out silver sparkles in the water. They would be easily mistaken for sunlight to the untrained eye, but Aiden recognised them immediately as thinly veiled runes. And once he realised that, he saw them everywhere, forming a silver net across the entire opening to the cavern.

Aiden wandered over to the waterfall until the river was barely a few inches from his face. Still he could feel none of its wetness nor hear anything more than a dim roar. He caught the silver sparkle of a rune out of the corner of his eye. Behind it the water fell, a mesmerising, never-ending flow. He reached out a hand to touch it and the sudden icy cold gushed through his fingers. He snatched his hand back, bringing a trail of drips into the cavern. He glanced around quickly, but no one seemed to be watching him.

Aiden dried his hand on his trousers and walked towards the edge of the waterfall. There, where water met stone, he found a tiny gap formed by an arch of runes with a couple of steps hewn from the stone leading down into the gap. He stepped lightly under the arch, tensing slightly as the water crashed down above and beside him. But he remained dry and continued forward until another step took him up onto the riverbank. As soon as his feet brought him out of the tunnel cold spray buffeted him and he could hear nothing but the rumble of the water as it churned and frothed. He looked back at where he had come from and saw that the archway of runes was almost completely hidden by the rocks and the spray. He darted back inside, marvelling again at the dry ground and the quiet, allowing himself to pace slowly along the water's edge, a smile twitching at the corner of his mouth.

"Not many people see them," said a voice, jumping Aiden from his reverie. It was Allan. "The runes keep out the noise and the spray, otherwise this cavern would be almost useless."

Aiden nodded. "It's impressive."

"Come," said Allan. "Falkor wants to speak to you."

Aiden dragged his eyes away from the runes. "What of Tristan?" he said, a sudden stab of guilt bringing a frown to his face. He should have thought of his friend sooner.

"I'm afraid that will have to wait. Tristan's with the healer now and she's not to be disturbed," Allan said with a grim smile. "Come. Falkor is waiting."

Aiden hesitated a second then followed Allan back up the tunnel that led to the cliff top and the forest. A little way into the forest they came to a cluster of long, low buildings. Aiden almost did not see them at first, their walls built from timbers that still had a shell of bark and their roofs so thickly overgrown with leaves like trees. A small group of men were gathered in the midst of the buildings and someone led a pair of small hardy ponies out from the largest building. Falkor nodded a greeting to Aiden and Allan as they approached. The other three men, dressed in plain travelling clothes, Aiden did not recognise.

"What's going on?" Aiden whispered to Allan.

"They're going back to Teraan City to gather information on the Brathadair attack. They hope to bring back any survivors."

As they arrived the men mounted their horses. One man, who looked far too big for the small pony, rode over and leaned down to speak.

"You're Aiden?"

Aiden nodded.

"I'm Rook, one of the Feather Guard stationed here. Falkor says your family may have gone into hiding in the City."

Aiden nodded again, more vigorously. "If they had to flee they would have gone to an abandoned watchtower in the outskirts of the City." He described the place in more detail and Rook listened closely, rubbing a hand over his beard.

When Aiden was finished Rook reached down and squeezed his shoulder. "I'll keep an eye out for them. Don't worry. If they're there, I'll find them and I'll bring them here."

"Thank you," said Aiden. A rush of relief swept through his body, relaxing muscles he had not even realised were tense. Their mad dash through the forest had left the events of the City so very far behind and suddenly the thought of his family's safety filled him with hope. Yet there was also the niggling sense of guilt. He was safe already and he should have thought of them before exploring the magic of the waterfall. He should go and see Tristan now too. He had put that off too long already, despite what Allan said.

Aiden looked up to see the three men on their ponies cantering off into the forest. Only Falkor and Allan remained.

"Ah Aiden," said Falkor. "I have a task for you."

Aiden approached the wizard who was still dressed in the same blood spattered coat he had worn their whole journey. How much rest had Falkor managed to get last night? There were dark circles under his eyes, yet even that could not dull their cunning glint and his hands were steady as he produced a piece of paper that had been folded over many times to form a tiny square. "This is a message for Skaldar of the Great Eagles telling him about the capture of the King and inviting him here to hold council with the Princess and myself. It should rightly be sent by the Feather Guard. You'll find their base across the river in the south forest. It's hard to miss."

Aiden took the paper in his hand. "How's Tristan? He was pretty bad when we got here last night."

Falkor nodded. "My magic only just kept him alive. There's only so much Beith can do unless the wielder truly understands the injuries and the healing process. But he's with Anniina now. Some say she's the most skilled healer in Teraan," said Falkor.

"And what do you say?"

Falkor hesitated. "She's skilled enough to save him... that's all that matters. Now go. We both have important matters to attend to."

Aiden started off on the path that led back down to the great cavern, but Allan called after him. "There's a bridge across further up the river. It's quicker than going through the caves."

Aiden nodded his thanks and headed off up the river. He passed the point where the water plummeted over the edge and saw just beyond it a stone bridge, or rather two stone archways that spanned the river, resting on a little island in the middle of the current. He walked across, the cobbled floor of the bridge worn smooth by the passing of countless feet, while the parapets were covered with green lichen. He paused momentarily on the island, realising that it was bigger than it had seemed from the shore. But there was nothing there so he continued on to the far bank.

In the forest he found a tiny deer track cutting through the heather and began to follow it, once more passing the great waterfall. It was only a little way further when he saw the place he was looking for. An ornate cabin, built from slats of wood nestled into the branches of a huge old beech tree, with a spiral stair leading up to it. A wooden platform ringed the cabin and formed a bridge to a second cabin in the neighbouring tree. Slender branches made a railing around the walkways and spiralled down the stair. At the base of the tree were the ashy remains of a campfire and a couple of stools made from fallen logs. In the trees surrounding the cabins Aiden saw more platforms made from intertwined branches that reminded him of bird's nests. Eyries.

As he approached the camp a woman's face appeared in the doorway of the cabin, her narrowed eyes widening into a smile upon sight of him. Instead of walking round to the stairs she nimbly swung down on a rope, landing on the ground with a bounce.

"Hello," she said. "You must be Aiden. We heard you had arrived, but we hadn't expected to see you for a few days. Not until you had recovered from the trip and all that."

Aiden shrugged. "It's Tristan who might not be up and about for a few days yet."

"Oh yes. We heard about that too," she said, brushing some strands of sandy hair out of her face. The rest of her hair was loosely tied in a braid, although most of it was falling out of place. She wore a rather well-worn jacket in the faded midnight blue of the Eagle Riders. Aiden thought she looked to be around thirty, but he could not be sure.

"I'm Signy, Feather Guard," she said, offering him her hand.

"Is it just you?" said Aiden, looking around as he shook her hand. Back at the Palace there had been lots of people working in the Eagle Rider Building.

"Well, Rook's usually here too. He's my superior officer, but he was sent back to the City," she said, smiling brightly. "So it's just me for now. Not that there's ever that many people here at all. Torelia can be an awful quiet place most of the time. The arrival of the Princess the other week was the most exciting thing that's happened for years. And now you're here too."

"But other people live here too, don't they?" said Aiden.

Signy nodded. "There's always a core of guards here looking after the place, but what's the use of a secret refuge if everyone knows about it and comes to visit? It only gets busy when one of the royals comes and that doesn't happen very often. Of course we do have the occasional Eagle Rider passing through too."

"What do you do all the time when there's not a royal here then?" said Aiden.

"Don't ask me about the guards," said Signy with a laugh. "Who knows what they do half of the time. Me and Rook though, we look after the Eagle Riders when they pass through. And there's always the odd Cu-Sidhe or out of control Wulver in the forest that needs dealt with. We also look after the hawks and deal with their messages."

"Speaking of messages" said Aiden, holding up the paper. "I have one for Skaldar of the Great Eagles."

"Oh," said Signy, her eyes widening. "It's not often we get messages for the Great Eagles themselves. We'd better get a hawk ready."

Signy led the way under the cabins in the trees to a small aviary formed from netting draped around a tree. There were a few hawks roosting on the branches, but when Signy whistled softly they came flying down to her. She chose one and took it out from the netting, stroking it gently once on its head. Aiden took the message and secured it into the little pouch on the hawk's leg.

"Will the Eagles be able to manage a message like this?" said Aiden, in his head picturing an Eagle trying to open the tiny buckle on the case with beak and claw, while the message hawk flapped in terror.

Signy smiled and shook her head. "The hawk will go to the Feather Guards stationed out near the eyries and they'll pass on the message. I think this little guy would get a bit of a fright if we sent him directly to the Eagles." Signy stroked its head again and it flapped its wings impatiently. She drew Peith, the swift, over its head, whispering the place it was to go before throwing it into the air. The hawk shot into the sky and dwindled from sight above the trees.

"Now for the great waiting game," said Signy quietly, watching the hawk disappear. She turned to Aiden. "I suppose I should give you the tour now."

She took him up the spiral stair and into the main cabin. The first room was bright and airy with two windows letting light in to shine on the desk and chairs. Inkwells and pens and a stack of paper under a stone sat there waiting for messages to be written and sent. A log book lay open on the middle of the table and Signy quickly noted down the message they had just sent. The floorboards creaked softly underfoot as she showed him into the other room. In there were shelves of books and, dangling from hooks around the walls, were assorted weapons, tools, cloaks, jackets, and Eagle harnesses.

"It won't be as much equipment as you're used to in the City, but its enough to meet most of the Riders' needs when they come," Signy explained.

Next she took him out across the walkway to the other cabin. The planks seemed to sway and bounce precariously under Aiden's feet and he was glad of the railing, slender as it was. The other cabin was slightly bigger and built with the trunk of the tree at its centre. It was divided into six almost identical rooms, each one with a bed and a trunk. It reminded Aiden, with a stab of nostalgia, of his room back in the Eagle Rider Building.

"Rook and I live up here," said Signy. "It's not much, but I'd prefer it to those dark caves any day. Well except maybe in a storm." She laughed. "You're welcome to a room up here too."

"Really?" said Aiden, with a start of excitement.

"You are a Feather Guard aren't you?" said Signy with a smile.

"Well, yes I suppose," said Aiden. He trailed off. Was he really though? He had been forced to leave until the truth was discovered and though Tristan and Falkor had brought him here, did that really mean he was now reinstated?

Signy gave him a look.

"I had to pretend to leave the Guard so that Falkor could draw out the Brathadair," Aiden explained, somewhat clumsily. "No one's officially reinstated me."

Signy laughed and waved a hand at him. "Well that's easily sorted. Wait here a moment." She disappeared into the other cabin and returned a minute later with a midnight blue jacket in hand. "It's a bit tatty and it might be too big, but welcome back to the Feather Guard." She smiled and whirled it round his shoulders.

Aiden slipped his arms into the sleeves. It was a bit big, but he did not care. It was Eagle Rider blue and the golden feather gleamed on the front. "Thanks." Aiden beamed. "I'll bring the rest of my things up later, but I better go and see Falkor now and tell him his message has been sent. And I've been trying to get to see Tristan all day."

Signy nodded. "Probably a good idea. But come back later if you can. I'm sure there's some work we can do if Falkor doesn't have other tasks for you. And you'll have to bring Tristan once he's better too. Rook tells me he's our Captain now, so really he should be the one giving out orders."

"I will do," said Aiden smiling, though at the same time a tremor of apprehension passed through his body. What would Tristan think of his reinstatement in the Feather Guard? Had he forgiven him yet for what happened in the Palace? And would Tristan's sudden promotion in rank change him from the competent and easy going friend Aiden remembered?

Aiden headed back through the forest and down the passageway that led to the great cavern. Once behind the waterfall again he paused, realising he had no idea where to find Falkor or even where to start looking. He gazed around, but there were too many openings leading to tunnels and caves to choose from. Instead he walked over to where a young guard with a long spear was standing sentry.

"You can't go up there," said the guard as Aiden approached. "The Princess' chambers are strictly off limits."

Aiden held up his hands. "I wasn't planning to go up there. I'm just looking for Falkor. Have you seen him?"

The young guard relaxed his grip on the spear. "Falkor's in

council with the Princess right now. He's been in there all day. You can leave him a message if you like."

Aiden nodded. "You can just tell him his message has been sent."

The guard nodded and stood up straight.

Aiden wandered off to another part of the cavern and wondered what to do now. He had no idea how long Falkor would be, so he would have to find Tristan on his own. He gazed around, taking his bearings. There were two main entrances to the cavern that stood on either side of the river, one to the north and the other to the south. These opened into the sloping tunnels, which led to the cliff top and forest, and to the flat tunnels, which ran along the base of the cliffs. From what he had seen so far, these tunnels were all mostly the same: a torchlit passageway dotted with little wooden doors and curtains that led into caves, like his own, where the soldiers lived. Apart from these large entrances, the great cavern had other doorways that presumably led further into the rock behind the waterfall. He had already tried the central door and been denied entry, but the others were not guarded so he decided to try one.

He found himself in a high ceilinged cave that bubbled with noise and the warm smell of food. Big long tables, some already occupied by soldiers, were set out in rows, all pointing towards a fire at the far end where the cook darted about between pots. Smoke drifted upwards escaping through a number of small holes in the rock that must open somewhere in the forest. He slowly walked the length of the hall and decided to have some food before resuming his search for Tristan. The cook was a cheery woman who gave him a large helping of stew and he took some time to sit and eat it while listening to the soldiers gossip around him. It did not take long for someone to come and speak to him.

"New here?" said a soldier sitting down opposite him with a thud, his stew almost sloshing out of his bowl.

Aiden nodded. "I'm in the Feather Guard. I escaped from the City."

"So you're the lad who came in with Falkor. Some battle I hear."

"I think so," said Aiden. "I wasn't at the Palace when it happened."

"Count yourself lucky," said the soldier. "Terrible business, men turning on each other like that."

"And our King being captured," another man chipped in. "Who knows if they'll let him live or not."

"They'd be fools to kill him straight off," said the first soldier. "The King knows things that no one else does. Just think about this place. As soon as we're past the boundary we start to forget how to get back unless we've got the right magic. But not the King. He always knows how to get here."

So that was how Torelia was kept such a secret, Aiden mused. He noted to himself not to wander alone past the boundary. But the idea of such magical protection intrigued him and he wondered if he would only forget how to find Torelia or if he would forget Torelia altogether. It saddened him to think that one day he might not remember the beautiful waterfall and its forests and caves.

"… But he wouldn't give it up. Not with the Princess here," the second man finished.

"Will the Princess send an army back to the City?" said Aiden. "To free her father?"

The two soldiers glanced at each other and then back to Aiden. "There's not nearly enough of us here to mount that sort of attack. And without any Eagle Riders…" He left the rest unsaid.

"I don't know what Serineth will do," said the second. "Her father's kept her so hid away all these years, no one really knows what she's capable of."

"As long as she does something," said the first. "We'll all be doomed if someone doesn't take control."

Aiden had not thought of that before. He had always felt sure that the Brathadair could be beaten, but with no Eagle Riders and an untested Princess the task seemed a lot less possible. He sensed the two soldiers had followed his line of thought for they both became quiet and eventually left to return to their duties. Aiden finished his stew, speaking to the cook on his way out.

"Do you know Tristan Arthursson who was brought in last night?"

The cook nodded while spooning stew into the bowl of another soldier.

"Know where I can find him?" said Aiden.

"Oh yes," said the cook. "Anniina has him in a cave on the north side of the river. Take the bottom tunnel and it's the third cave with a wooden door. Mind you, I'd wait till Anniina's finished working. She doesn't like to be disturbed."

Aiden found the place easily and pushed open the thin wooden door to find a cave similar to his own, except instead of looking down on the river, it looked out across it. Tristan was lying on the bed, his wounded leg poking out from the blankets. His face was pale and sallow, his hair sticking to his forehead. A woman with an ample figure and long, greying hair tied back out of her face knelt by the bed. Aiden guessed she was Anniina, the healer. She was casting runes which seemed to draw the poison from Tristan's leg in trickles of yellow fluid, which she wiped away with a sodden cloth. Tristan flinched every time she did this and yet his eyes were closed, his face peaceful as if he was in a deep sleep.

"Why doesn't the pain wake him?" said Aiden.

"I'm keeping him asleep," said Anniina, her eyes never once leaving her patient. "Once he's rid of the poison I'll let him wake, but that may be some time yet."

"Is he going to be alright?" said Aiden.

"Of course," said Anniina, "though it will probably take longer than any of you want."

Aiden shifted nervously on his feet, wondering exactly what Anniina meant by that.

"Well not much point in you hanging around longer," said Anniina. "Tristan's not going to have anything interesting to say for quite a while yet and I'm in no mood for idle conversation."

"Sorry," said Aiden, heading back to the door. "I'll leave you in peace. But please let me know when he wakes. I'm Aiden by the way."

"I know who you are," said the healer.

Aiden paused by the door, expecting her to say more, but she did not. "Thank you," he said quietly. He slipped out the door and stopped in the tunnel outside feeling... disappointed? What had he expected? That Tristan would be conscious. That they could have spoken and relieved Aiden of his anxieties. But he had been warned, more than once that day, that Tristan was with the healer and not to be disturbed.

Aiden cleared away the thoughts with a shake of his head. He would go and get his things and move up to the Feather Guard cabin. He found his bag lying on the floor of the cave where he must have dropped it the night before in his exhaustion. It was strange that this was all he owned in the world. A cloak his father had made him, a knife, his waterskin, a carved wooden Eagle that he and Andor had made together, and two sets of clothes. One set being the muddy and slightly ripped clothes that he was currently wearing. He should probably wash them, he thought, and mend them.

He stuffed everything in his bag and left the little cave behind, stopping briefly at the river to wash both himself and his clothes, before taking the tunnel back up to the southern forest. He walked the short distance along the cliff top path and through the forest to the Feather Guard base. He could no longer see the river, but he was beginning to find that there was nowhere out in the forest that he could not hear it.

At the cabin Signy greeted him happily and let him choose a room before throwing a leather harness that needed waxing at him. They sat together around the burnt out fireplace, cleaning the equipment while Signy chatted away, not caring whether Aiden joined in or not. A while later, a soldier appeared with a bundle of messages to be sent out to some of the other towns and villages in Teraan, requesting aid. Signy sighed at the pile. "We're going to have no hawks left by the end of the day." But nevertheless they got the birds ready and set them loose into the sky.

As evening drew in Signy lit a fire and set a pot of soup to heat over the flames. Aiden gazed at the sky, watching as the stars began to appear. Were Andor and Branwyn and his parents gazing at the same stars this very moment? Would Rook find them in the tower? Had the Brathadair managed to take over the City completely? And what had become of the King? So many questions that only the stars knew the answers to.

The next day Aiden helped Signy with her tasks again and by the afternoon there was little to do, so he left to explore Torelia further. He kept to the woods this time and began to walk upstream. He passed the bridge he had crossed yesterday and saw another path winding away into the trees and decided to follow it. After a few minutes he had left the river behind and found himself enclosed by pines. The steady roar of the water grew faint and another familiar noise came to his ears. Clack, clack. It was a sound that made him instantly think of Odmund and the training grounds. Aiden picked up his pace and jogged through the trees until he came to a clearing where two guards were sparring. Behind them was a little equipment shed, lined with practice swords, wooden staves, bows, and arrows. A couple of targets, sacks of old straw, had been set up on poles. The guards paid him no attention, so he picked himself a practice sword and wandered a little way off to where he was mostly hidden from sight. He wanted to practice some of the moves Odmund had taught him, but he had no desire for an audience.

Aiden tested the air with a few swings of the sword, loosening up his muscles. Then he began to work through the warm up, smiling as the steps came back to him with ease. His muscles remembered their old routines and soon he was engrossed in swinging, lunging, blocking, and ducking, the other guards forgotten.

"You should keep your arm higher when you draw back."

Aiden jumped and whirled around to see a woman standing there, arms folded and leaning against a tree. A long golden brown braid hung down over her shoulder and there was a scar across her cheek that reminded him of a streak of war paint. Marsaili, the Princess' bodyguard. Or was it the other one, Niamh?

"You might want to stay alert to your surroundings too," she said, smiling and unfolding her arms, flicking the tip of a dagger between her fingers. "That is if you want to avoid a dagger in your back."

"How do you know I didn't know you were there?" said Aiden, lifting his chin defiantly.

She let out a snort of a laugh. "You don't even know which sister I am."

"I do," said Aiden, frowning at her laugh. Was his ignorance so obvious?

"Well?" she said, tilting her head and raising her eyebrows expectantly.

"Marsaili," he said not taking his eyes from her and hoping his earlier identification had been correct.

"Good guess," she said, smiling and stepping towards him, flicking her braid back over her shoulder. "You've got guts fire-boy, I'll give you that. And a knack for getting yourself out of tight places."

Aiden folded his arms as she walked over. "If you're talking about escaping the City, I had help."

"You're not the one who got shot," said Marsaili, beginning to circle him. "How is Tristan anyway?"

Aiden turned to keep her in sight. "The healer's keeping him asleep while she takes out the poison. He's going to be ok I think."

"Lucky."

"If you call getting shot in the leg with a poisoned arrow lucky," Aiden replied.

Marsaili shrugged. "He got shot when he was with the wizard, one of the few who could keep him alive. I call that lucky. I don't keep such magical company, so if I got shot like that I'd probably just have died."

Aiden shivered at her words. She spoke so freely about death, about her own and Tristan's. If Falkor had not been there Tristan would have died. He wondered if, beneath her fierce personality, that thought bothered her or not. Aiden tried to smooth the frown that must have been creasing his face.

"Still," Marsaili laughed, and Aiden got the feeling she was laughing at him, "at least if I knew I'd been shot by a poisoned arrow, I'd take down as many of the enemy with me as I could."

"I'm sure you would," said Aiden, feeling increasingly nervous with her walking around him like he was prey of some sort.

Even though he was expecting it, Aiden still did not see the flash of Marsaili's sword until the steel of her blade rested gently against his neck. His practice sword hung uselessly in his hand and his heartbeat was so loud he was sure she could hear it.

"You're dead," Marsaili whispered into his ear.

Aiden tried not to flinch.

Marsaili laughed and let her sword drop away from his neck. "No need to look so scared. I like you fire-boy and, in the interests of you not dying, I'm going to show you how this sparring thing is really done." She plunged her steel sword into the earth at the edge of the clearing and picked up a practice sword that she must have left by the tree.

Aiden lifted his own sword, trying to still the roiling of his stomach as he looked at the fearsome girl across from him. What was he getting himself into?

Marsaili came towards him and he saw her shift ever so slightly, as if she was going to strike him on his left. Could it really be that simple? He braced himself, lifting his sword, but at the last moment he gambled and moved to his right. He felt a brief moment of satisfaction as he caught her sword in an arm jarring blow. Then suddenly there was only pain as she hit again at his unprotected left side.

From that moment on Aiden found himself constantly outmanoeuvred. Unlike his sessions with Odmund, challenging as they were, this was not a fight Aiden enjoyed. Marsaili paid no attention to what moves he had learnt already, forcing him to constantly improvise as she danced around him, laughing. Every time she landed a hit or flicked his sword from his hand he found himself missing Odmund more and more. At least the swordmaster had tried to teach him and had found no such joy in his failings.

Eventually she stopped, laughing at the grim look on Aiden's face. "Don't hate me," she said. "You don't have time anymore to learn every thrust and parry. There's a war coming and if you don't learn to fight on instinct then you're going to be a casualty pretty quickly."

Aiden tried to calm his breathing. "So the Princess has decided to go to war against the Brathadair?"

"They started a war," said Marsaili, turning suddenly serious. "What choice does she have?"

"And what about the Eagle Riders?" said Aiden.

Marsaili shrugged. "That's the big unknown in all of this. It has been hundreds of years since Teraan has been at war without the Eagle Riders there to bring victory. The real decision for Serineth is when to go to war and whether or not to risk going after the Eagle Riders first."

Marsaili left after that and was quickly engaged in a sparring match with the two other guards that made Aiden's previous efforts look pitiful. He hung up his practice sword with a sigh of immense relief. Gingerly, he rolled up one of his sleeves and prodded the blue spots of bruises that were already forming. He wiped sweat from his brow and headed back to the Feather Guard base to join Signy for some food.

Over the next few days Aiden's life settled into a strange rhythm. It was not that his work was anything other than normal, it was the odd sense of nervous anticipation that shrouded everything. He waited for Tristan to wake, he waited for Falkor to give him a task, he waited for the Princess and her council to decide what to do, he waited for the Great Eagles to answer their message, and most of all he waited to hear the fate of his family. In the meantime he worked with Signy around the Feather Guard base or went to the little training ground to practice by himself or with Marsaili if she was there. He still did not enjoy his sessions with Marsaili, or her taunts and laughter, but he could not deny that he was getting a little better.

He spent his evenings roaming Torelia, but always, if he strayed too far into the forest, a Border Guard would send him back. Whenever this happened he would inevitably find himself in the great cavern behind the waterfall, gazing at the closed door to the council chamber where Falkor, Allan, the other captains, and the Princess sat figuring out strategy. He longed to know what was being said and he longed for action, but he quickly realised that even though it was he who had overheard Hakon's plot, he was still only a Feather Guard of the lowest rank.

Around midday on his fifth day in Torelia, he was again sitting in the cavern behind the waterfall watching the endless torrent streaming past. He was resigned to his waiting, hardly daring to hope that Falkor would appear or that the men from the City would return. At least there was the mystery of the waterfall to occupy him. It was the most complex runic magic he had ever come across. So far he had counted at least eleven individual runes, but he was yet to fully understand how they all fitted together.

Suddenly a man burst from one of the passages and walked with great purpose across the cavern. That was Tristan's passage. Aiden was on his feet in an instant chasing after the guard. He caught him just before he disappeared into another tunnel.

"Is it about Tristan? The Feather Guard," said Aiden.

The guard looked him up and down, his face softening. "I'm just fetching the healer because the young Feather Guard is awake."

The guard continued on. Aiden paused momentarily, absorbing the news before running across the cavern to the tunnel that led to Tristan's cave. Tristan was awake at last.

19. Fugitives

The days that followed Branwyn and Andor's escape to the tower seemed endless. They went often up to the roof, gazing over the parapet to the City below. People had gradually returned to the streets, though there was a wariness in their steps that had not been there before. Brathadair flags appeared along the Wall and the snippets of conversation that reached them in the tower, told that all the gates to the inner City were barred and guarded.

Branwyn and Andor spent many hours up there, watching, but neither dared to admit that really it was their parents they watched for. Branwyn would not give voice to that tiny hope, but neither could she crush it. And yet every day she wondered if they were still alive. She tried to smile for Andor's sake, but the expression felt sour on her face and she did not think Andor believed her anyway.

Andor did not speak of their parents either, but Branwyn knew he had not given up. He kept constant watch on the streets, continually darting over to the window to look outside or remaining on the roof long after she had retreated inside. A few times he begged to be allowed out of the tower, but she refused. She did not know how dangerous it would be. Instead, she saw him practicing the runes, though she did not always recognise the shapes and what they were for. She wondered if regrets and guilt plagued his young mind the same as they did to hers. She hoped not but then they both knew they had escaped and their parents had not.

On their fourth morning in the tower Branwyn passed out some breakfast, rummaging around the bottom of the box to find another waterskin. Her stomach twinged. There was no more. She closed the supply box quickly, hoping that Andor had not noticed.

"What's wrong?" he said, staring at her.

Branwyn tried to smile and gently shook her head.

"We're running out of food, aren't we," said Andor.

Branwyn let the smile drop from her face. "Water," she sighed.

"We're going to have to go outside sometime," said Andor, looking at her earnestly.

"I know," she said, sighing again. "We need to decide what we are going to do." She paused. "We can't wait here forever."

"We need to rescue our parents," said Andor, defiantly.

"And how do we do that?" said Branwyn. "I'm a baker. You're a kid. We're not Eagle Riders or wizards. We're not even soldiers."

Andor frowned, but to his credit he did not argue her point. Instead he said, "We need to find people who are. We can't be the only ones who've escaped."

"Alright," said Branwyn, after a moment. "But first we need to figure out how to look after ourselves. Most importantly, where are we going to get more water and food? The Brathadair have closed off the City and they control all the markets and stores."

"Isn't there a grain store on the outskirts somewhere?" said Andor.

Branwyn shook her head. "They burned it, remember."

"Oh." Andor's shoulders slumped. He lifted his head. "We'll at least get water from the stream."

"Yes," said Branwyn with a small smile. "We can start with that at least."

They took their cloaks, and a knife each tucked into their belts—though Branwyn had no idea what she would do if she had to use it. At the entrance to the tower she hesitated, fingers entwined in the twigs of the bushes. Maybe she should make Andor stay behind? He glanced back at her, his eyes a flash of green. It was the brightest she had seen him since before they left home. She ducked her head and pushed through the bushes after him. They would do this together.

They walked carefully through the houses to the small stream that ran nearby, avoiding the few people that they passed. No one paid them much heed anyway. It was soldiers they had to fear, thought Branwyn. At the stream Branwyn and Andor filled the waterskins, taking a long drink while they were there. Branwyn splashed some water over her face and felt a little better now that some of the grime was washed away. She stood.

"Where now?" said Andor, crouching to refill his waterskin once more.

"Maybe we should look for a market," Branwyn mused. Even if they could not get food there, they might pick up some information.

"What about the Brathadair?" said Andor, standing and brushing the dust from his knees.

"We'll have to be careful," said Branwyn.

They set off again heading closer to the Wall. The sky above was cloudy, giving a grey cast to the air. Branwyn pulled up her hood, tucking loose strands of hair under the folds of her cloak. As they drew closer to one of the arched gateways into the City, the murmur of voices softened the empty silence of the streets. For a second the noise was comforting, reminding Branwyn of the ordinary bustle of the City that had surrounded her every day of her life, but a second later her insides twisted and she almost felt sick. The voices could be anyone. They could be enemies. What if someone was looking for them? She shook her head. It was a silly idea. They were not important. There was no reason for it. But nevertheless she could not shake the jumpiness from her limbs.

A short way ahead the source of the voices became clear. A few meagre stalls were set up outside the gates, some with vegetables and fruits, others with bread and flour, and one with some grisly offcuts of meat. It seemed to Branwyn a rather pitiful affair compared to the markets of the City which had sprawled from street to street, lively with noise and smells and colour, but there were still more people here than she imagined. Behind them the Wall loomed, great wooden gates locked tight under the archway. On the battlements above, silhouetted figures of soldiers patrolled.

Branwyn led the way towards the stalls, her hand tightly gripping her satchel with their waterskins and the few coins she had brought with them inside.

"How much for the bread?" she said, stopping under the fluttering canvas of the first stall.

"Five silver pieces," said the woman, eyeing them with a suspicious gaze.

"Five!" Branwyn exclaimed. They had never charged that much for such a simple loaf of bread in their bakery.

"You won't find a cheaper price this side of the Wall," said the woman, folding her arms. "If you can't pay you can get lost."

"What about the flour?" said Branwyn, biting her lip. It would make things more difficult, but it would last them longer if they could make their own bread.

"Three for a small bag," said the woman. "And I won't go any lower than that."

Branwyn glanced at Andor. He gave a small nod. They had little choice it seemed.

Branwyn passed over the money and took the small canvas bag of flour in exchange. They moved off through the stalls, glancing at the fresh apples, but frowning when they overheard the price. Branwyn shook her head. They were too expensive. It was all too expensive.

"We could try and set a trap in the forest," Andor whispered to her as they gazed at the meat stall.

Branwyn nodded. It was the only way they might get enough food. "We might find some berries or a fruit tree while we're there too," she whispered back.

"Let's go then," said Andor, head tilting towards the forest. "There's no point in staying here."

Branwyn nodded, but she scanned the crowd one last time. They had found food, but not information. Part of her had hoped to hear something, anything, that might allay her fears. She lowered her head, tucking the flour into her pack. Her parents were gone and they were not simply going to reappear. When would she get that into her head?

She stepped after Andor. His light feet dodged through the crowd ahead. Andor turned to wave her after him. She smiled. Give Andor a task and a purpose and it seemed nothing could dampen his spirits. Yet as Andor turned again he thumped straight into a tall muscled man, with a dark green hood shadowing his face. Andor jumped back, but a thick scarred arm reached out and grabbed him. There was a sword hidden beneath the folds of his cloak.

Branwyn gasped and ran towards them. "Please, he didn't mean it," she stuttered out.

The man paused and lifted his head, his mouth open as if she had interrupted him speaking. There was a chiselled face below the hood with eyes grim and lined. Very slowly he released Andor's arm.

"I mean you no harm," he said quietly. "Only you remind me of someone I had hoped to find." At this he looked again at Andor.

Andor rubbed his wrist and glanced shyly up at him.

"Let's go," said Branwyn, resting a hand on Andor's shoulder to steer him away. Andor planted his feet more firmly and resisted her touch.

"Who are you?" Andor said, lifting his chin.

The hooded man looked around and waited until no one was close before leaning forwards. His voice was so quiet Branwyn almost could not hear. "My name is Odmund."

Branwyn frowned. Was that supposed mean something to them?

"Odmund," said Andor, repeating the word slowly. His eyes seemed to light up.

"And you must be Aiden's brother," said Odmund.

Branwyn's mouth dropped open. How did this man know Aiden?

Just then a commotion sounded a short distance away in the market. Odmund's head snapped up and his hand tightened on the hilt of his sword. One of the stall holders shouted after a man running headlong through the crowd, crashing through people in his mad haste. Branwyn pulled Andor out of the way before they were both knocked down.

A thud and a creak came from the Wall, the gates swinging open, and a group of soldiers marched through, calm, menacing, unstoppable. The crowd began to swarm. Stallholders threw protective arms across their produce. People scrambled to get away.

"Come on," said Odmund, his voice a sharp command. "It's not safe here." He took Andor's elbow and steered him onwards.

Branwyn stayed fixed. How was going with this man any safer?

"Branwyn, come on," Andor called back, his voice desperate.

Branwyn glanced back once and then moved, her feet stumbling as she urged herself into a run. They dashed down a street, not caring which direction they took so long as it was away. Shouts and cries came from behind but they were distant and eventually they slowed.

"That was close," said Andor, leaning forward on his knees.

Branwyn nodded, her heart hammering. Odmund paced the short length of street, his head turning slowing, eyes flicking from corner to corner. At last he turned to them.

"Do you really know Aiden?" said Branwyn, stepping in front of Andor.

"I taught him… at the Palace," Odmund said quietly. "But this is not the place to talk of such things. Come back with me. I have a safe place and you'll get more to eat there than a bag of flour."

Branwyn's mouth dropped open. He must have been watching them.

Andor tugged on her sleeve. "It's ok. Aiden told me about him."

Branwyn pursed her lips. "I'm not sure," she whispered to Andor, turning her back on Odmund. "How do we know he's not turned traitor."

Andor frowned. "We said this morning that we needed to find people who could help us get our parents back. This is our chance."

His wide eyes pleaded with her. Branwyn ran a hand through her hair. Andor was right. If they ever wanted to find their parents they were going to have to trust someone. She gave a small nod. "Alright."

Odmund bobbed his head in the direction of the forest and set off, not waiting to see if they followed. Branwyn and Andor scurried after him. After a few minutes they neared the edge of the City where houses were sparse and the forest crowded amongst them. There was a little cottage there with bowed walls and only half a roof.

"This is one of our hideouts," said Odmund, ducking as he passed through the doorway.

"Our?" Branwyn fingered the knife at her belt. Who else would they find in this cottage?

Odmund turned and raised an eyebrow at her, his gaze lingering on her knife. "That's brave girl, but there's no need. We're all like you—fugitives from the Brathadair."

Branwyn moved her hand away from her knife and pulled her

cloak closer about her shoulders. It was shady in the cottage and there was no fire to warm the bare stone walls.

"There's no one else here," said Andor, walking about the room and peering into the different corners.

"No. We stay on the move during the day. Makes us harder to find." Odmund took off his cloak and hooked it over the top of a long wooden staff that leant against the wall.

Branwyn perched on a rickety stool. "Who's 'we'?"

"Myself and a few from the Palace and City Guards who stayed loyal to King Brandr. We're still trying to gather and find out who escaped and who didn't."

"What about the Feather Guard?" said Andor.

Odmund planted his feet apart and folded his arms across his chest. He scrutinised them. "I've not found your brother if that's what you're asking."

Andor shook his head. "Aiden left with Falkor and Tristan four days ago."

Odmund's eyes widened and he sucked in a breath. "Falkor's alive? And Tristan?"

Andor shrugged. "They were four days ago."

Odmund's face seemed to lighten and though his lips pressed together, Branwyn thought it was from gladness rather than grimness. She snuggled into her cloak and gave a tiny smile. If there was hope for people Odmund had thought lost, then maybe there was yet hope for her parents.

"Now tell me," said Odmund. "What are your names?"

For the next little while Branwyn found herself telling Odmund their story. In fact it was Andor who did much of the talking, for she had not been there when Falkor and Tristan came for Aiden, but in a way she was glad. It still felt like her throat closed up whenever she tried to speak of her parents. Odmund nodded and said very little, but his eyes were attentive and he rubbed his chin often as if musing over their words.

"I'm afraid I don't know where they would have been taken," Odmund said once Andor had finished. "But it's possible some of my comrades have been taken there too. The Brathadair have killed many, but it was not so long ago that they were our friends. I believe some may have been taken prisoner in the hopes of converting them to the cause."

As midday approached others began to appear at the little cottage. Branwyn and Andor kept to themselves in the corner and though Odmund seemed to explain to the others who they were, he made no move to introduce anyone. A few distrustful glances were thrown their way and at one point Branwyn heard someone murmur, "We can't take in every abandoned child we find." But on the whole no one bothered them.

They ate lunch together and later Odmund suggested that they go with one of the women to help forage for food in the forest. Branwyn agreed and nudged Andor to wipe the scowl from his face. They might not stay with these people forever, but if they could learn at least something of how to find food in the forest then they would be better for it.

Later Branwyn expected them to head back to the little cottage with their gleaning baskets but instead the woman took them further into the forest where a small clearing was lit by a flickering smokeless campfire. Others were there already, some—but not all—she recognised from lunch time. More joined as the afternoon passed, bringing with them large packs and bundles.

One of the new arrivals was Halfdan, the blacksmith from their street. He greeted Branwyn and Andor with a warm embrace, his brow furrowing at the news of their parents. It seemed that Halfdan had taken his family away to one of the nearby villages and later returned with his oldest son to help any others who had escaped. That was when he had met Odmund and the others.

"We move camp every couple of nights," said Halfdan, "and even then we find new people every day. There's hope yet for your parents." He smiled sympathetically, but Branwyn was not sure that he really understood. Their parents had been taken by the Brathadair. They were not just wandering the City, lost somewhere.

"I'll get you some food," Halfdan continued, oblivious to the doubts in her mind.

Branwyn nodded, her stomach rumbling at the smell of hot stew after days of only dry bread and meat. She and Andor joined the ring of fifteen or so people sat on the ground around the campfire and ate ravenously the food offered to them. Once her stomach was full she tried to relax, but her feet twitched and she shuffled, unable to get comfortable on the ground. Andor sat next to her drumming his fingers, his green eyes flicking round the people in the camp. There seemed to be an unspoken agreement that they would stay here tonight, but Branwyn frowned. She wanted to be back at the tower. Maybe she just did not feel comfortable with all these strangers, but what if... what if their parents came to the tower and they were not there?

Branwyn leaned over to Andor and whispered in his ear. "I think we should go back to the tower."

Andor wrinkled his nose. "Now?"

"I know it seems silly," said Branwyn, biting her lip. "But what if they're trying to find us?"

Andor chewed the end of his finger, lifting his eyes to hers. He nodded.

It took some persuading to get someone to show them the way back to the City, but eventually Odmund conceded. Dusk was falling as they reached the outskirts. Odmund stopped under the trees.

"We'll keep an eye out for your parents," he said. "And if you need anything you can leave a message at the cottage. You're welcome to join us anytime."

Branwyn smiled. "Maybe we will."

It was a short walk back to the tower, though the emptiness that greeted them left Branwyn feeling hollow. Her shoulders slumped. Maybe they should have stayed by the warmth and company of the campfire.

Her uncertainty must have shown on her face because Andor wrapped his arms around her waist, hugging tightly. "Don't feel bad. We had to be sure." Branwyn smiled at his sudden affection. "Plus," he said, looking up at her. "I think our beds here will be comfier."

Branwyn laughed aloud.

They settled down, lighting some candles and joking quietly, pretending they lived in a luxurious castle. Branwyn's restlessness began to ease as they snuggled into their blankets. It had been a good day. They had found allies and just knowing that they were not completely alone helped a great deal.

"Do you think we'll ever find Aiden?" said Andor, his quiet voice breaking the silence.

"If he really has left the City, he's gone where we can't follow," said Branwyn. Her heart twinged a little as she said those words aloud.

"I wish we could follow him," Andor whispered.

Silence fell. An unknown voice spoke from the darkness of the doorway.

"Maybe I can help with that?"

Throwing her blanket aside Branwyn jumped up and faced the door. Every muscle in her body tightened, ready to run at any moment. A tall figure stood in the doorway and her panic renewed at his unfamiliar face, her mind assessing how easily they could push past him and down the stairs. Unconsciously she shifted onto the balls of her feet.

The man in the doorway stepped forward into the light. A long green cloak hung down from his wide shoulders and amidst the folds of material Branwyn's eyes caught sight of a sword belted on his hip. A reddish grey beard the same colour as his hair covered his face.

"My name is Rook," said the man, his beard twitching as he smiled. "I'm a member of the Feather Guard. I've come from the forest and I'm looking for the family of Aiden Brokksson."

"Aiden!" said Andor, sitting up.

"Shh," said Branwyn.

"I mean you no harm," said the man, spreading his empty hands out towards them. "Aiden is in a safe place and I have been asked to take you to him."

"Did Odmund send you?" said Branwyn.

"Odmund?" Rook answered. There was a glimmer of recognition in his voice but enough confusion that Branwyn knew Odmund had not sent him.

"How do we know we can trust you?" said Branwyn fiercely. It seemed too good to be true.

Rook shrugged. "I knew to find you here."

Branwyn hesitated, but it was true. Who else outside their family knew they would be here? Unless... but no, her parents would not have given them up. She would not believe that. She glanced at Andor and he nodded vigorously.

She spoke slowly. "I'm not saying I trust you, but if you are who you say then you won't mind telling us where to find Aiden."

Rook smiled through his beard again. "No I won't mind, but it's not something I can tell. It has to be shown."

"Why? Where is this place?" said Branwyn.

"It's in the forest," said Rook. "But where is the rest of your family? Aiden told me there would be six of you."

"Our parents were taken by the Brathadair," said Branwyn,

tasting the bitterness of her sorrow again.

"I'm sorry," said Rook, his eyes dropping momentarily. "I'm afraid there's nothing I can do for them, but I can take you both somewhere safe."

"To where Aiden is?" said Andor.

"Yes," said Rook.

Branwyn opened her mouth, searching for words that would stop this conversation. It was all happening too fast. What if their parents did get free and came here to find them gone? In the end all that came out of her mouth were the words, "Is it far?"

"It's far enough that you won't have to worry about the Brathadair waiting around every corner," said Rook, mistaking her concern.

"It's not that..." Branwyn trailed off. Maybe they should stay, she thought, doubts creeping in. How could they help their parents if they were miles and miles away? But even this close what could they really do? They would be stuck in this tower, constantly having to search for more food and water, or roaming the woods from camp to camp with Odmund. That was not what her parents would want for her.

"Well?" said Rook.

"We will come," said Branwyn, even though it felt like she was leaving her parents behind, abandoning them. "But first we have to see Odmund."

"Good," said Rook with a nod. "Are you ready?"

"Now!" said Branwyn, flustered all over again. She gathered herself together. "Erm yes. We'll just need a minute."

Rook nodded. "I'll wait outside." And with that he disappeared down the darkened stairway.

Branwyn and Andor began to gather together their things.

"Do you really think he's seen Aiden?" said Andor excitedly. "Where do you think he is?"

Branwyn shrugged quietly, but Andor was too excited to notice she had not really answered any of his questions. She turned her mind back to the things they needed to take with them. Spare clothes, yes, cloaks, definitely, the dregs of the food and water, though they would need to find more soon, and the two small bowls and cooking pot, some candles, the small pouch of healing herbs, and the knife. That should be enough. Lastly she rolled up the big heavy blanket and strapped it to the top of her pack.

Andor led the way to the door, but Branwyn paused. She took the knife back out of her pack and hastily began to scratch words into the lid of Aiden's box. *Gone to meet A. All safe. B + A.* Branwyn turned her back on the little room. At least now she felt sure that if their parents did escape and come here, they would know she was safe.

They met Rook just outside the entrance to the tower and Branwyn led the way to the point at the edge of the forest where they had last seen Odmund. She hoped she could remember the way through the forest to their camp.

"I'll just get a candle," said Branwyn.

"No." Rook closed a fist over her hand. "We don't want to be followed."

She nodded. He was right. If the Brathadair followed them it would put a lot of people in danger. She broke off into the trees, stumbling along a tiny track, heather scratching her ankles. Trees loomed out of the dark, black shadows in the night.

Suddenly there was movement in the trees and the ring of steel as weapons pointed in their direction. Branwyn threw up her hands and felt Andor clutching at her cloak. Rook stepped in front of them, pulling his hood down. He lifted a fold of his cloak to reveal a golden feather gleaming on his jacket. The weapons lowered and a big man with scarred arms pushed through the circle.

"You're back sooner than I expected," said Odmund. He lifted his head, eyes narrowing at Rook through the dark. "Who's this?"

Rook chuckled. "Don't recognise me with a beard?"

Odmund was silent for a moment and then his lips parted into a smile. "Rook." He clapped his arm.

Branwyn sighed, the last of her doubts about Rook fading into the night. He was a friend and that meant that he really had seen Aiden. And he was going to take them to him.

A signal was given and everyone began to weave their way through the trees back to the camp. They stopped there for some time, deep discussions being held at various places around the fire, none of which Branwyn and Andor were invited to join. Branwyn's eyelids were drooping by the time Rook returned to their side.

"What's happening?" she whispered.

"Some of us are going," said Rook. "Others are going to remain here and continue to spy on the Brathadair's doings."

"Are we going tonight?" said Andor, rubbing his eye slowly.

Rook crouched down next to him and nodded. He gently gripped his shoulders. "It will be some days hard walking before we reach your brother. Do you think you can manage that?"

Andor nodded. Rook smiled and glanced up at Branwyn.

She gave a wry smile. "I'm stronger than I look. I'll manage."

"Lets go then," said Rook, jumping to his feet.

"But where exactly are we going?" said Branwyn.

"To Torelia of course," said Rook, with a glint in his eye.

20. Arrivals

Tristan's eyelids felt thick and so heavy they did not want to open. He blinked slowly, allowing soft light to filter into his vision. Above his head was rough hewn stone. He was lying on a soft, lumpy mattress, underneath a thick green blanket. The tumultuous sound of rushing water filled the air. Where was he? Dim recollections of the last few days floated just out of reach at the back of his mind.

He propped himself up on his elbows and winced in pain as he moved his leg. That memory came flooding back. The Brathadair attack, the King's capture, their desperate flight from the Palace, and that unlucky scramble over the wall where he had been shot. This must be Torelia. He had made it after all. But how long had he been here, lying in this bed? His only indication of the time was the light filtering in from outside and that told him nothing except that it was day.

He lay back on the bed and found himself drifting in and out of sleep. He might have slept more deeply had his skin not felt as hot and clammy, or his throat as dry. Air caught the back of his throat and he sat up, coughing. He noticed that he was wearing a new shirt and as he pulled back the blankets he saw new trousers too, although they were cut away just above his right knee. The lower part of his leg was swathed in bandages. He inspected it but decided against removing the bandages.

Tristan shuffled over to the side of the bed, his muscles feeling stiff and weak. The journey had certainly taken its toll. How long had it been since he had last moved around? He swung his left leg to the ground. More slowly, he lifted his right leg down beside it. With one hand firmly on the cave wall he stood, fighting a wave of dizziness. He limped across the cave to a small table and found a waterskin, which he gulped down until his thirst was slaked.

The door to the cave was not locked when he pulled it open. He paused in the torchlit tunnel beyond. He had no idea where he was, so he decided to turn left. The passage ran ahead, neither ascending nor descending. He limped along, gingerly putting weight on his injured leg, wincing as he felt the skin pull tight around the wound. He had barely gone a few paces when someone appeared ahead of him. The man's face dropped with astonishment.

"I don't think you should be up yet," he said. "She won't be happy. Quickly. Back to your room. Before Aniinna comes."

Tristan frowned, not wanting to return to the little cave, but he had no strength to resist as the man took his arm across his shoulders and began to lead him back. He could not deny that it felt good to take the weight off his injured leg.

"Wait here," said the man, depositing him back on the bed. "I won't be long."

"Wait," Tristan called after him. "Can't you at least tell me where I am? What day it is?"

But the door was already swinging closed behind him and Tristan was left alone. He sighed and inspected his now throbbing leg. A red stain was beginning to show through the bandages. He frowned, but at least his short walk meant people would be coming soon. And people brought information. He wanted to know what had become of the City since he had left. Had the Eagle Riders returned? Had his father returned?

Suddenly the door swung open and Aiden burst into the room, a rosy glow on his cheeks. He wore a slightly oversized jacket in the blue of the Eagle Riders. Tristan felt a stab in his chest of both longing and relief. "It's good to see a familiar face."

Aiden smiled. "How are you feeling?" he said, drawing across a chair and sitting perched on the edge, leaning forward eagerly.

"Tired and sore," said Tristan, shuffling himself up to lean his back against the wall. "How long have I been here?"

"We arrived five nights ago," said Aiden. His brows creased slightly. "You were in a pretty bad way."

"Five nights!" he gasped. He saw the unspoken words in Aiden's expression. He had made it, but he had almost not. Silence dragged out between them and Aiden shuffled on his seat. It was not the contented silence they once would have shared after a day's hard work in the Eagle Rider Building. A part of Tristan's mind felt like he should still be angry with Aiden, but that was stupid now. Aiden had not betrayed the Riders or him, and now he had probably saved his life. He had to put things right, even if only for his own peace of mind.

"Thank you," said Tristan, the words feeling awkward and inadequate in his mouth.

Aiden grinned and shrugged. "Falkor carried you most of the way."

Tristan smiled at the thought. "I think I'm glad I don't really remember." He paused, searching for the words. "But it's for more than just that. I want to thank you for everything you did back at the Palace. I thought you'd betrayed us, but I know now that you didn't. You gave up a lot to try and stop the Riders from flying into a trap. That means a lot to me and I know it will mean a lot to my father too."

Aiden smiled sheepishly and shuffled in his chair. "I wanted to tell you why I left, but Falkor wouldn't let me. He said it was for everyone's safety."

Tristan smiled and shook his head gently. "That wizard and his mind games. It's like he enjoys handing out secrets to people and then watching them squirm."

"I know," said Aiden, grinning.

Tristan grinned back. Despite the throbbing pain in his leg he felt lighter than he had in days.

Just then the little door over the cave entrance creaked and swung open. A plump woman with a round face and long grey hair braided down her back came in, her eyes brightening when she saw Tristan. This must be the healer, thought Tristan, cringing inside a little. He had met her type before and no doubt she would want him to spend the rest of his days chained to this bed.

"You're awake," she said, walking quickly across the room and shooing Aiden out of his chair so that she could sit at his side. She placed a cool hand across his forehead and Tristan tried to duck out of her reach, but she paid him no attention. He frowned at being treated like a helpless little boy, especially with an audience. "The fever's gone," she remarked to herself. "Let me see your leg." Before he had a chance to say or do anything a tiny knife was cutting away bandages with sharp tugs that made his eyes prickle. Underneath, the wound seemed strangely small, just a ragged scab on his leg, now oozing with fresh blood after his foray into the tunnels.

"You've been up and about already," muttered the healer, "but it's good. Much better." She sat back in her chair and smiled at him. "I'm pleased to say that the poison is now gone, but you will still have to take is easy for the next few days."

Tristan hesitated. "How easy is easy?" He could already sense the dreaded bed-rest looming over him. Nice as this cave was, he had more important things to do than sit in it all day.

Aniinna frowned. "You soldiers are all the same. You don't know how to sit still." She leaned forward in her chair and fixed him with a bright blue gaze. "You may walk around a little but in your condition you should not go far. Nor should you go on your own."

At this she glanced pointedly at Aiden. "If you open the wound through any fighting or sparring you risk infection and infection means being confined to this room. You may even lose your leg."

Tristan smirked.

"You think I'm joking," said Aniinna, pointing a finger in his face, but through her sternness Tristan saw the corners of her mouth twitch up. She shook her head and leaned back in her chair again. "I'll put a fresh bandage on just now, but I want you to watch closely. If it goes bad when you're out then you need to know what to do. I trust you know the runes well enough?"

Tristan nodded.

Aniinna began by cleaning the wound with a damp cloth, a process that threatened to bring tears to his eyes with every stinging touch. He was grateful when she paused long enough to let him blink water from his eyes, before she showed him which runes to use. Out of the corner of his eye he saw Aiden take a step closer to see better as Aninna began to draw the runes.

"First is Beith," she said, drawing the rune with clear confident strokes so that it shimmered brilliantly before sparking into his wound and across his leg. Already he could feel an easing of the pain. "Next Ur, the renewer. Now it's important with Ur that you tell it to renew the right thing. Last thing you want is for it to start renewing the poison. So just make sure you are clear in your mind that it's your leg you want renewed." She finished drawing the rune. It had a pale golden glow about it that reminded him of a sunrise. "And last, something to protect you from further harm. Fearn will do the job here, but if this was a magical poison then I'd be recommending Luis." She finished off the last rune with a flourish. She turned suddenly, causing Aiden to jump. "Make yourself useful Aiden and fetch me new bandages.

Tristan bit back a smile as bewilderment spread across Aiden's face and his eyes searched frantically for the bandages.

"Just there on the table," said Aniinna with a shake of her head. She muttered to herself, "You'd think I'd asked for the moon."

Aiden brought the bandages and Aniinna wrapped up his leg again. The stinging was less this time and Tristan guessed that the runes were already doing their work. Finished, the healer stood and looked over him with hands on her hips.

"Don't walk far," she said, pointing a finger at him. "And if you do go out there's a crutch in the corner. Use it. I'll be back tonight to check on you and I'll know if you've gone too far, so don't push your luck."

And with that she bustled out of the room leaving the door to swing shut behind her.

Tristan turned to Aiden, a bemused smile on his face. "Well she's quite something."

"Yeah, that's Aniinna," said Aiden. "Just be glad you slept through the last few days."

They both laughed.

"Now," said Tristan. "I've got to get out of this cave. Let's go for a wander."

Aiden grinned and retrieved the wooden crutch from the corner, offering it to him with a glint in his eye.

Tristan looked once at it and set his jaw. His leg hurt, but if he could not stand a little bit of pain what sort of Feather Guard was he. "I can walk just fine."

Aiden's eyebrows twitched, as if he was thinking about saying something, but instead he shrugged and put the crutch back in the corner.

They exited the cave and made their way slowly along the stony tunnel, going in the opposite direction from the way Tristan had almost gone earlier. He limped along, a pace behind Aiden, inwardly cursing the shakiness in his limbs. It scared him a little to think how quickly his strength had fled him. A niggling thought in the back of his mind said he should have brought the crutch, but he pushed it away. He could do this. He would prove to himself that he could.

"So has there been any word of the Eagle Riders?" said Tristan. Any word of my father, he thought but did not say it aloud.

Aiden stopped. "I'm sorry... there's been nothing."

Tristan carefully held his face still. Had he really thought there would be? If his father was here he would have been at his side.

Aiden continued. "The worst part is that no one is doing anything about it. It's so frustrating. There's no plan to find them. By the sounds of it no one's even sure whether we *should* try to find them."

Tristan clenched his teeth and balled his hands into fists. How could people not care about what had happened to the Eagle Riders? They were the strength and wisdom of Teraan. They were its protectors. They were his family.

"We need the Eagle Riders," said Tristan. He needed them. "How can they have just disappeared?" Tristan shook his head, biting back the sudden emotion that threatened to overtake him. "I just wish I knew what had happened to them. Are they captured or trapped or..." He stopped, refusing to give words to his last thought.

"It's all this waiting and not knowing," said Aiden quietly. "Sometimes I think it would be better to know, even if it was bad news."

Tristan got the sense that Aiden was no longer talking about just the Eagle Riders. He had left his family behind in the midst of the turmoil. Brokk and Kari and Andor, who he had met briefly in the dead of night. And Branwyn. The thought of her made his chest grow tight and he was sad to think that she might be in danger.

"Any word of your family?" said Tristan.

Aiden shook his head. "Some men went back to the City a few days ago to gather information. They were going to bring news of my family or bring them here if things have got bad in the City."

Tristan nodded his understanding. It was yet another unknown to gnaw at the back of their minds. Tristan thought about his own mother and younger sister and brother. At least they would be safe in the little village of Colle where he had grown up. It was far enough away from the City that they would have had time to escape if they had to. But how could he know for sure? As he felt his heart begin to tug, the soldier's part of his brain took over. There was nothing he could do to help them without abandoning his duty to the Eagle Riders and to his King and his Princess. The best way to help them was to find his father.

Tristan looked up to see that while he had been lost in his thoughts, Aiden had pulled ahead of him and was waiting at the end of the tunnel.

Aiden folded his arms and raised an eyebrow. "You sure I don't need to go back for that crutch?" he said with a smirk.

A splutter of laughter escaped Tristan's lips. "No," he said firmly, feeling some of the tension drain from his body.

At the end of the passageway the tunnel opened out into a vast cavern, one side covered by a great sheet of cascading water. Tristan could not keep from gazing up at it.

Aiden pointed up at the waterfall. "A net of runes covers the whole opening. Keeps out the noise and the water. If you look closely you'll see them."

Tristan squinted up. There were flashes of light in the water, but surely that was just the sun. He focused on one point and eventually saw the shape of Fearn, the shield. How could Aiden see the runes so easily? He glanced at his friend, perplexed for a moment, then he gave up trying to make sense of it.

"Want to go outside?" Aiden asked, dragging his eyes away from the runes.

Tristan nodded and followed him slowly to the edge of the

waterfall, where Aiden showed him the narrow gap between the rushing water and the cliff wall. He followed him down the steps, keeping one hand on the cliff to steady himself. The rapid movement of the water so close made his head swim. He clambered stiffly out the other side feeling the skin pull painfully around his wound. They stood at the bottom of the gorge, stony cliffs rearing up on both sides, the river rushing endlessly past, coating them in a fine spray. He followed Aiden further along the riverbank, along a great slab of rock which ended in a pebble beach. Tristan savoured the clear river air and, despite all his misfortunes, was glad.

"Let's sit here for a while," Tristan called over to Aiden.

Aiden nodded and they found a couple of larger rocks to sit down upon. They sat in silence for a while with the sun on their faces and their thoughts filling with the sound of the river. A couple of off-duty soldiers nodded to them as they passed on their way down the river with fishing gear in tow.

"So tell me, what else has been going on while I've been asleep?" said Tristan.

Aiden gave a short laugh and Tristan sensed more frustration. "There's been a lot of messages and a lot of council meetings, but has anything really happened? No."

Tristan smiled sympathetically. It did not really surprise him. Aiden clearly was not used to politics. "Have there been no replies to the messages?" said Tristan.

"Well, I think some people have arrived from the nearby villages, but the first day we were here I sent a message to Skaldar of the Great Eagles and we've yet to hear from them."

Tristan nodded. Of course. Falkor was gathering forces around the Princess, not just to protect her but to build an army to take back the City. Still, unless they found hundreds of men, taking back the City would be a challenge without the Eagle Riders. Falkor surely must know that. He turned to Aiden. "It's not unusual for messages to the Great Eagles to take time. The eyries are some distance and then Skaldar will have to gather the Eagles. I wouldn't worry... yet."

Aiden frowned and Tristan could tell he was not convinced. But then without the steadfast presence of his father, he too was no longer sure of anything.

"But what about you?" said Tristan, trying to lighten the conversation. "Don't tell me all you've been doing is waiting for me to wake up."

Aiden laughed. "You wish! I've been up at the Feather Guard base helping Signy with her work. And I've been getting some sword fighting lessons from Marsaili."

Now Tristan laughed. "You've been fighting with Marsaili! How's that been going?"

Aiden opened his mouth to defend himself, but then sighed. "She's been beating me to a pulp." He lifted up his shirt to show him his blackened ribs.

Tristan screwed up his face. "That looks sore. But you know you could tell her to go a bit easier on you."

Aiden raised his eyebrows and Tristan smiled, knowing that that was exactly how he would feel too. You did not ask Marsaili to go easy—unless you wanted to be laughed at for the rest of your life.

"I need to learn somehow," said Aiden. "After all there's a fight coming whether we want it or not."

Tristan nodded. They were back to that again. The threat of war. "If we want to win we're going to need the Eagle Riders," he said.

"I know," said Aiden. "But right now it feels like we're wasting time. All these council meetings and it doesn't seem like anything is happening."

Tristan held up his hands. "It's the Princess who's got to make the decisions. And she's never had to deal with anything like this before." For the first time he felt a tiny wrench of fear inside. All he could picture was the scared little girl who had lost her mother, the Queen, to the Brathadair all those years ago and who had been hidden away from the country she would one day have to rule. Maybe this was what the Brathadair wanted all along. A country without a strong leader would be easily defeated.

"Look," said Aiden suddenly, pointing up to the top of the cliff.

Tristan squinted up to make out a line of silhouettes descending from the forest into the tunnels. Most of them held themselves like soldiers with straight backs and strong steps, but two were smaller and hunched over, their feet dragging along the ground.

Aiden was on his feet. "It's them," he said, barely able to contain his excitement. "They're back from the City."

Tristan stood more slowly. Aiden had already moved a few paces ahead, but then stopped to wait for him, his eyes flicking between Tristan and the waterfall.

"You can go ahead," said Tristan.

In a flash Aiden sprinted ahead along the riverbank. Before Tristan had even reached the end of the pebble beach, he vanished through the gap in the waterfall. Tristan followed more slowly, cursing again the arrow that had brought him to this weak and stumbling state. A few minutes later he emerged into the cavern to find a great commotion. People streamed in down the tunnel from the forest, but guards were also coming from all directions to hear any news for themselves. Falkor and Allan appeared from the council chambers on the far side of the great cavern and even the Princess showed her face, although Tristan noted that she kept herself mostly hidden by the door.

A joyous shout echoed through the cavern. Tristan turned and saw Aiden pushing his way through the crowd. He ran headlong into two people, scooping them up in a tight hug. Branwyn and Andor. Tristan felt a tightness in his throat. He knew he should be happy for Aiden, but he wished it was his father coming down that tunnel.

Aiden, Branwyn, and Andor broke apart, though Andor stayed hanging onto Aiden's arm. Branwyn began to speak and Tristan frowned as her face creased and tears welled in her eyes. Aiden drew her into a hug, but Tristan could still sense her sadness floating across the cavern. He wished there was something he could do to put it right. He looked away and rubbed his jaw. Put what right? He did not even know what was wrong. And she probably did not even remember him.

Tristan jumped as someone tapped his arm. "Tristan, you're here. I had feared the worst."

It was Odmund, his old teacher. He clasped Odmund's arm in greeting and the strong grip that was returned reassured him.

"I made it," said Tristan. "But not without a souvenir." He pointed at his leg.

"Don't worry about that. I'll have you back in fighting shape in no time," said Odmund.

Tristan smiled and Odmund clapped him on the shoulder before weaving his way through the crowd to where Falkor stood. A crowd was gathering around the wizard, but Falkor looked over and caught Tristan's eye. He held his gaze for a long moment. They had not spoken since Tristan had recovered. There was so much to say and yet so little. Tristan bowed his head to the wizard. He would be dead if not for him. Falkor nodded back and Tristan knew that he would ask for no more thanks than that.

Tristan scanned the crowd, searching for Aiden, Branwyn, and Andor once more, but they were nowhere in sight. He sighed. They had probably gone to be alone. He dropped his head and closed his eyes. It was not until they were gone that he realised he had been hoping to speak to them, to her. He turned and drew up short. Branwyn was there, face to face with him and before he was ready she caught him in a tight hug.

"Tristan you made it," she said, holding him close. She smelled like the pine forest. "And thank you for bringing Aiden to safety."

She did remember him. She released him from the hug and he hoped his surprise did not show on his face.

"It was really Aiden who got *me* here safely," he said, with a glance to his friend.

She smiled and tilted her head to one side. "I'm just glad you're both safe," she said, her voice firm even though her eyes were still red from crying. He wanted to hug her again, but something froze his arms at his side.

"Was it a hard trip?" said Tristan.

Branwyn shrugged. "It wasn't the journey so much…" She tailed off and wiped her eyes.

"The Brathadair have captured my parents and my aunt and uncle," said Aiden, his face grim. Tristan pressed his lips together. He knew how it was to have a father taken and would not wish that on anyone.

"I'm sorry," said Tristan. He knew those two words were not enough, but to say more would only belittle the grief Aiden and his family were feeling.

Aiden nodded.

"I'm going to take Branwyn and Andor to find somewhere to stay," said Aiden. "Will you be alright by yourself?"

Tristan nodded. "Don't worry about me. But you should take them to the Feather Guard base. I'm sure Signy can find some room for them."

They smiled their thanks and headed over to the tunnel at the far side of the great cavern. Tristan suddenly felt very lonely. He shivered, remembering the warmth of Branwyn's hug and the smell of the forest in her hair. Movement caught the corner of his eye and he looked quickly over his shoulder. Maybe she had come back. He jumped. Niamh's face was right behind him, close enough to almost bump heads. He shook his head at her, but a smile crept across his face nevertheless.

She squeezed his shoulders. "I almost had you there."

"Even when I've been asleep for the last five days, you still can't sneak up on me," said Tristan.

"Oh but I wasn't really trying," said Niamh with a wide grin. "We've got to be gentle with you crippled types."

"I am not *crippled*," said Tristan slowly.

Marsaili jogged over to join them.

"Ah, Tristan the invalid has awoken," she greeted him.

"I am not an invalid either," said Tristan, trying to hold onto his dignity, all the while knowing that the sisters would not let him quickly forget this.

"Well, I suppose you can still walk," said Marsaili. "Cripple was a bit harsh Niamh."

Tristan folded his arms. "At least I didn't miss the fight."

The sisters looked at each other, pressing their lips together as if suppressing their rage. In the end it was laughter that burst forth.

Marsaili looked at him, amusement on her face. "I can't argue with that, so I suppose you can have that small victory."

"And of course," Niamh added. "Retribution will come to those Brathadair scum, as soon as we get a chance."

"I don't doubt it," said Tristan. His eyes flicked back to the doorway where he had seen the Princess earlier, but she was gone now. "How is the Princess faring with all this? I see she didn't come down to meet those who came back from the City."

"She will," said Marsaili, following his gaze. "Just give her some time. It's not easy. Her father's been taken and suddenly she's expected to take his place. There's nothing that can prepare you for that."

"I know how that feels," said Tristan, thinking of his own father and how the King had made him the new Captain of the Feather Guard. By no means did Serineth have the monopoly on captured fathers. "But she's going to have to face the people sometime. We need a strong leader."

"And we have one," said Marsaili, taking a step towards him, her hand unconsciously brushing the pommel of her sword.

Tristan put his hands in the air. "I'm sorry. I'm just frustrated. I woke up to find that I've missed five days, my father is still missing, and in that time what real action has been taken?"

"You think we're not frustrated too?" said Marsaili, her voice sharp. "You think we don't want to go back to Teraan City and knock Hakon's head from his shoulders? We don't have the strength for that sort of attack."

"The Princess is doing what she can. She is gathering an army," said Niamh. "Messages have been sent across the Kingdom."

"Messages," said Tristan, raising his eyebrows. "What we need are Eagle Riders."

"Of course you would say that," said Niamh.

"Doesn't make it any less true," said Tristan. "Eagle Riders can do more than any army. And if we really do have a dark wizard returned, then we are going to need the magic of the Riders more than anything."

"And how do you propose we get the Eagle Riders back?" said Niamh. "There's barely a hundred men here. We can't spare any to go off on a wild journey to find the Riders, only to have them killed because the Riders were captured by a dark wizard that only they can defeat."

"I don't know," said Tristan. "But I'll think of a way. You tell the Princess that even if she can do nothing else, she should send someone to find the Eagle Riders."

The sisters shrugged, but Tristan knew that if they really did not agree with him then they would have been much more vocal. They would tell the Princess what he had said. Whether she would do anything about it was another matter altogether. But that did not stop him from forming a plan. Marsaili and Niamh left to return to their duties, leaving Tristan alone with his thoughts. He wandered around a little until he found the kitchens. Helping himself to food, he headed slowly back to his cave to eat and to think.

The first problem was that they had too few men. Easily solved. Send a very small rescue party—two, maybe three. The second problem was harder to solve. Magic. Only someone very skilled with magic could have taken down that many Eagle Riders. Which meant someone very skilled in magic was going to be needed on this mission. In other words, Falkor. But he would take some convincing. He had other duties too, not least guiding the Princess. Tristan would just have to convince him that rescuing the Riders was more important than everything else. He drifted off to sleep trying to think just how he could do that.

21. Envoy of Eagles

Andor scraped his bowl clean and smiled sheepishly at his brother. Aiden could not help but smile back. He gave the briefest of nods towards the far end of the hall, but it was enough to send Andor scurrying off through the Torelia kitchens to ask the cook for more. Aiden laughed quietly at him. He had not realised what relief it would bring to have his family with him. But even still, it was a happiness tempered with a heaviness of heart. His parents had not made it. Neither had Aran or Sanna. They had all been captured for refusing to give him up. Now he did not know what to do. He had family that he had to look after, but he also had family he needed to rescue. How to do both? The only thing he was sure of was that he was not going to abandon his parents or his aunt and uncle.

Across the table Branwyn sighed and dropped her spoon in her bowl. She was unnervingly quiet. But then something like this had never happened before. She had cried when she first arrived and though she had not broken down again since, she had lost her spark. She could feel it too, thought Aiden. This tearing between joy and sorrow.

"How did you sleep?" said Aiden, trying to break the silence.

Branwyn shrugged.

"We'll get them back. I promise you we will," said Aiden earnestly, reading into her silence.

Branwyn smiled sadly at him. "You can't really know that

though."

Aiden frowned and folded his arms. "I know that I'm going to go back and try."

Now Branwyn folded her arms. "And how are you going to do that?"

"Do what?" said Andor, returning to their table.

"I'm going to go back and rescue Mum and Dad and Aran and Sanna," said Aiden.

Andor's eyes lit up. "Can I come too?"

"No," said Branwyn, her eyes wide. "It's bad enough Aiden's thinking of going back. Aiden, you didn't see the City when we left. It's changed. It's dangerous now. And we couldn't even tell you where they were taken."

"I'll find out," said Aiden, trying to reassure her with a smile. "And you forget I know the Palace. I've had training. And I can probably use the runes better than half of Hakon's men."

"Our parents were captured so that we could all escape to safety. If we go back and get caught then their sacrifice will have been for nothing." Branwyn bit her lip.

Aiden looked at the floor. He had not thought of it like that before. But the idea of abandoning his parents to their fate was not an option, no matter what they had sacrificed.

"Branwyn," he said. "Andor." He reached across to take each of their hands. "I know our parents gave up everything to keep us safe, but I can't happily live in freedom knowing that they are in danger. Especially not when I know I can do something about it. Yes they made a sacrifice so that we could get away safely, but that sacrifice let us find each other and it will also allow us to make a plan to rescue them on our own terms, not the Brathadair's."

Their eyes gazed back at him with a fiery brightness and his own mouth burned with the resolution in his words. They would do it, he was sure. As long as this determination to rescue their parents stayed with them he was sure they could overcome any barrier.

"Ok," said Branwyn. "What do we do?"

Aiden paused. He had not really thought that through yet.

"I thought as much," said Branwyn. "I know you meant every word you said, but we can't just go charging back there without making a plan."

"You're right," said Aiden. "But we're all agreed that doing nothing is not an option?"

"Agreed," said Andor, throwing his hands into the air.

"Bran?"

She sighed. "Agreed. But only if we have a good plan."

"Making a plan is doing something," said Andor.

"Yes," said Aiden, reaching over to tousle Andor's hair whilst grinning at Branwyn.

Branwyn folded her arms. "Don't make me feel bad about this. You forget I know you well. Your dad used to think it was the runes that always got you in trouble, but I know it was just your recklessness. There's no space for recklessness here."

Aiden smiled at her. "I know. That's what we've got you for."

Branwyn's frown softened and she shook her head at him.

"We need to start by finding out where our parents are being held," said Aiden.

"That means going back to the City," said Branwyn. "And we only just got here."

"We don't all have to go back," said Aiden.

"But I want to come with you," said Andor. "I can use the runes too."

"But not as well," said Branwyn. "I don't think you should go."

"I agree," said Aiden, fixing Andor in a stare.

Andor pulled away. "It's not fair. I want to rescue them too." He shuffled along the bench until he was at the far end of the table and turned his back to eat his porridge.

Aiden raised his eyebrows at Branwyn.

"It's the right thing to do," she said quietly. "He's still a child."

"I can hear you," said Andor.

"Good," said Aiden. "Cause we still need you to help plan." Aiden turned to Branwyn and lowered his voice. "You'll need to stay behind with him."

"I know," she said, nodding.

A commotion from the tunnel caused Aiden to look round. The man at the entrance to the kitchens pointed up at the sky, his eyes bright. Men and women got up out of their seats, gathering around him, before breaking away to relate his news to others.

"What's going on?" said Andor, who had slid back along the bench while Aiden was not looking.

A soldier Aiden vaguely recognised walked over to their table. "Did you hear?" he said. "Skaldar and the Great Eagles arrived this morning. They are meeting with the Princess now." The soldier wandered off to the next table.

A smile crept across Aiden's face. "They got the message," he said. "They've come."

"What are you talking about?" Branwyn said.

"We sent a message to the Eagles five or six days ago, asking for their help. And they've come." Aiden was already on his feet, excitement bubbling at the thought.

"Where are you going?" said Andor.

"I'm going up there," said Aiden. "I want to hear what the Eagles have to say. And Tristan and Signy might need my help."

"What about this rescue we're planning?" said Branwyn, eyebrows raised.

"We're still going to plan it," said Aiden, squeezing her shoulders, "but after. Anyway the Eagles might have news of the City and what's happening in the rest of the country."

Before either one of them could question him further, Aiden

dashed across the kitchens and into the tunnel that led towards the waterfall. In the great cavern groups of soldiers milled around, talking animatedly, grinning and joking and pointing to the sky. Aiden grinned too. Half way across he ran into Signy.

"I've been looking for you," she said. "But I guess you've heard the news by now."

Aiden nodded. "Does Tristan know?"

"Yes, of course. He's at the meeting with them now."

"Where?" said Aiden. "Where are they?"

"The island above the waterfall," Signy replied.

Aiden slipped past Signy and continued running across the cavern.

"Wait," Signy called after him. "You can't go up there. You weren't invited."

Aiden turned back and shrugged. "No one's going to know I'm there. I won't set foot on the island."

Signy shook her head, gazing after him as he ran off into the tunnels.

Aiden sprinted up the passageway and out into the forest above. The clouds were low over the trees and the far shore of the canyon was shrouded in a misty blanket. He blinked as rain splattered into his face. Part of him wished he had brought his cloak, but he was not going back for it now. He ran into the forest, where the rain was not so heavy under the trees. He kept well away from the main path as he neared the island, drawing the runes of Fearn, the shield, and Luis, the protector, as he ran. He willed them to hide him from unwanted eyes as he placed one on each shoulder and let them spark across his arms and chest. He slowed to a walk and turned towards the canyon. The roar of the waterfall grew louder and soon he could see the froth as the water plummeted below. And there, shrouded in the mist of rain and spray, was the island.

Aiden found a spot at the base of a tree with a good line of sight to the island. He began to weave together a complex mix of Ailm, the seer, Muin, the listener, and Coll, wisdom. He drew them, one on top of the other, so that they fused together into one rune that would allow him to see, hear, and understand what was happening on the island. Then he held the runes between his palms and stretched them out to create what looked like a shimmering gold-flecked window. As he looked through this window the island became suddenly clearer and the noises of the forest and the river dulled around him.

Aiden's eyes grew wide, his lips parting. The Eagles were majestic. Even having met Eagles before could not take away his awe. The largest of the group stood at the centre, yellow eyes sharp, bright, and unblinking. Raindrops glistened on his golden feathers and he shook out his wings, sending spray flying. That must be Skaldar, thought Aiden.

The other Eagles were spread around the island, perched still as sentinels. Occasionally one would tilt its head at some unseen movement in the forest. At the midst of the gathering, standing just in front of Skaldar, with their backs to him, was a small group of people. Aiden recognised Tristan, his right leg poised gingerly on the ground while he tried not to lean too much. The hood of his blue cloak covered his head, but next to him Falkor, in his usual brown leather coat, seemed unbothered by the rain. Allan was there too and Odmund and another small hooded figure standing between two guards. Marsaili and Niamh. Which meant that was the Princess. He strained to get a better look at the elusive monarch, but she had her back turned to him and her face was hidden in the hood of a rich purple cloak.

Aiden focused on the runes in his hands, bringing Muin, the listener, to the forefront of his mind. Gradually voices began to whisper to him across the water.

"I am sorry this meeting could not be under more fortunate

circumstances," came the voice of a young woman. Aiden guessed it was the Princess, but even with the magic the voices were muffled, drifting from soft to loud as if he had water in his ears.

The Great Eagle inclined his head slightly. "It grieves me greatly to hear the news of your father, the King's capture." The Eagle had a deep, almost musical voice, and the soft clacks of his beak punctuated his words with a strange rhythm.

The Princess stiffened. "As it does me," she replied, her voice strained. "And that is why I have invited you here. I know you are a wise leader, Lord Skaldar, and I ask for your assistance in the fight against the Brathadair, who have caused my family and the people of Teraan so much anguish over the years."

"Neither have they been kind to the Eagles," said Skaldar. "In the last few days I have flown across the country to all the eyries of my people and have brought with me a bird from each place. I cannot command the Eagles to fight as your King would command his men, but there are many who are willing to help."

"I am honoured," said the Princess. She curtsied, her purple cloak billowing out around her feet and all the others followed suit.

"What news has there been from the City in the last few days?" said Skaldar.

Falkor stepped forward and bowed. "The Brathadair position is strong. Since the initial battle we believe they have taken full control of the Palace, the Restricted Zone, and the walled part of the City. The men we initially sent back found a few survivors and more recently a patrol has been dispatched to set up watch on the outskirts of the City. It is not clear whether the King lives or not, but I suspect we would have heard something if he was dead. It seems that those still loyal to the King have been imprisoned with him in the Palace."

Aiden's mind began to race. If people were being imprisoned in the Palace then that could be where his parents were.

"In my travels I have seen little evidence of the Brathadair in other parts of the country," said Skaldar.

Falkor nodded briefly. "I fear it is only a matter of time before they begin to spread. We need to move quickly."

Skaldar paused and surveyed the people before them. "It is all very well moving quickly, but if you do not have the strength to win, it will do you no good."

"But with your help surely..." said the Princess.

Skaldar's head tilted rapidly and his unblinking yellow eyes fixed the Princess in their gaze. "Our numbers are not great Princess, nor can we fight within the walls of your Palace. You are in need of more help than even I can give. Unless the Eagle Riders can be found. If we are to stand a chance against our enemies then they must fight at our side."

Skaldar's stare was unwavering and although he did not move or speak he seemed to grow in size. Even through the hazy film of the runes Aiden was transfixed. Then he froze. Skaldar's gaze had shifted beyond the Princess and was looking directly at him. He had been seen. He shifted onto the balls of his feet, ready to run. He glanced quickly over his shoulder and then back to the gathering on the island. But the Great Eagle's gaze was fixed once more on the Princess. Aiden frowned. He was sure he had been seen. Maybe he had imagined it. Then he realised that the Princess was speaking and he had missed most of what she had said.

"...do not have the man power to mount a full search—"

"Excuse me," said Tristan, stepping forward and pulling down his hood. Everyone fell silent and stared at him. Aiden clapped a hand over his mouth.

"Who are you?" said Skaldar.

Tristan bowed low. "Tristan Arthursson. Son of Captain Arthur of the Eagle Riders and now Captain of the Feather Guard."

Skaldar blinked once, slowly. "I have heard of you. Your father always spoke well of you. What is it that you wish to say?"

Tristan paused. "I believe the Eagle Riders can be found without needing to send lots of men. A smaller party would travel much faster and could infiltrate an enemy more easily. It would only take two men really."

"Who?" said Falkor.

"I would offer my services as a Feather Guard to undertake this mission, but I cannot go alone. If the Riders are prisoners of a dark wizard then it will take the assistance of one skilled with the runes to free them…"

"Me then," said Falkor.

Aiden bit his lip. Tristan's plan was a good one, but Falkor would have to agree, as would the Princess.

"You can't go Falkor," said Allan. "You are needed here. And the Princess needs your protection."

"I agree," said Odmund. "It may be a fool's errand. We do not know if the Riders are even still alive."

As they spoke their objections a cunning glint appeared in the wizard's eye. Falkor glanced at Tristan. "Tristan's plan is sound and although you may not like it, it may be the only way. If the Eagle Riders are still alive then they will need my help. And I'm sure the Torelian Guard will be more than capable of protecting the Princess."

Aiden grinned. Only Falkor could turn their rational objections into feeble excuses.

"It's up to you, Your Majesty," said Falkor, turning to face the Princess.

The Princess' head shifted from side to side, as if seeking an answer, but none was forthcoming. Eventually she spoke. "It seems to me that the rescue of the Eagle Riders is paramount to our achieving any victory against the Brathadair and so I am inclined to let you go."

"I think it is a wise decision," said Skaldar, who had been silent until this point. "There is one thing I would add. I ask that you would take one of my Eagles with you on this mission." Skaldar looked behind him and spoke to the other Eagles in their own language, a series of soft *kiis*, clacks and movements of his body. He turned back. "It is decided. Iolair, daughter of Jormandar, who roosts with the Feather Guard just now, will join you."

Jormandar, thought Aiden. That was Leif's Eagle, the one who had predicted a great destiny for him. He thought it strange for the Eagle to have a daughter.

"We would be honoured to have her company," said Falkor.

"It's settled then," said the Princess. "It was a well thought plan Tristan."

Tristan bowed low, but as he took a step back his foot caught on the uneven ground and he winced involuntarily. Frowns took shape on the faces of Allan, Odmund, and Falkor, and the Great Eagle's eyes narrowed.

"I'm fine," said Tristan, looking around wide-eyed.

"Maybe," said Falkor. "But it seems you are not as well healed as I had thought. How will you cope with a long hard journey?"

"I'll manage," said Tristan.

"You are injured?" said Skaldar.

Tristan nodded reluctantly. "I was shot during our escape from Teraan City, but I am almost fully healed now."

"This is a mission of great importance and speed is a necessity," said Skaldar. "Though I do not doubt your ability, it cannot be jeopardised. No matter how much you may wish to rescue your father, it may be wiser to send another man."

Tristan stood up straight, his face impassive. Aiden frowned in sympathy. This was Tristan's plan and Tristan's father. If it was Aiden and his father, he would not take no for an answer. He could see the others shuffling and glancing, but no one contradicted the

Great Eagle.

"You are right," said Tristan, his voice betraying nothing of what he must be feeling. Aiden's muscles grew tight. How could Tristan just accept it?

"Is there someone else you would trust to take on this mission in your stead?" Skaldar asked, looking first at Tristan and then at the Princess and Falkor. The small group glanced at each other.

Falkor spoke up. "I propose Aiden Brokksson should join Iolair and myself on this mission."

Aiden nearly dropped all the runes in his hands in astonished excitement and then again almost instantly as a wave of dread shot through him. He gaped. He could not go—he had to return to the City to find his parents. How could Falkor volunteer him without asking him first? He gathered his mind back together and focused again on the runes, his growing anger making them burn bright.

"... his skill with the runes will be invaluable," Falkor continued.

A frown knitted deeper and deeper across Aiden's forehead as he watched all those at the meeting nodding their heads in agreement. "No," Aiden whispered. He had just got Branwyn and Andor back.

Aiden's eyes snapped back to movement at the gathering. One of the Eagles crossed the island leaning close to Skaldar's ear and speaking too quietly for Aiden to hear. Both suddenly looked towards the place he was hiding. Aiden ducked fully behind the tree. He realised that in his shock he had let Fearn and Luis, his protectors, fade into nothing. They had almost certainly seen him this time. His mind raced, but finally it fixed on one certainty and he got to his feet and ran into the forest.

If they could not find him, they could not make him go.

Aiden ran into the forest until the breath was rasping in his throat. Only when he was surrounded by silent trees, the river only a distant roar, did he stop. At the foot of a tall tree he laid his forehead on the rough bark and closed his eyes. Anger simmered under his skin. What right did Falkor, or any of them, have to ask this of him when his own parents needed rescuing? And why him? Of all the people they could have chosen.

A niggling voice in the back of his mind said maybe this was the great destiny that the Eagle Jormandar had predicted for him. But how could it be? It was too... big. He had been a cloakmaker's apprentice until a few weeks ago. He was not fully trained. He could barely even win a fight. Surely someone would speak up and point out the foolishness of the plan. Maybe Marsaili would tell them about the regular bruisings she gave him in the training field?

Aiden slapped his palm against the tree trunk, opening his eyes and looking up. There was a wooden platform, now covered in thick moss, built into the tree. A sudden urge to climb overtook him and he jumped and caught one of the lower branches, swinging himself up. He reached the wooden planks easily but the urge was not satisfied. Aiden went higher, clambering upwards, the branches growing thicker around him. He ignored the pain as a sharp twig scraped along his arm. He wanted to see the sky.

Aiden's head burst through the canopy and he felt the whip of the wind and a splatter of rain on his face. He closed his eyes again and listened to the sway and creak of the branches and the soft patter of raindrops on the leaves. He breathed in the cool damp air and wished that his life could go back to how it was. He wished all his adventures to be dreams again. He shook his head and ran a hand through his wet hair. No, he did not really want his adventures to be over. He tried to pinpoint what he was feeling. Scared, he realised. And when he thought about it he realised he had every right to be. But what he could not decide was what scared him most—the thought of going with Falkor on a quest upon which the fate of Teraan rested or the idea of losing his parents, maybe forever.

As he sat in the tree the rain that had fallen for most of the day began to lessen. He stayed with his eyes closed allowing the quiet of the forest to sink in, trying to forget the things he had heard, as if forgetting his troubles would make them all go away.

"Aiden Brokksson?" came a voice from beside him.

The sudden noise and the gust of wind in his face startled him and he almost lost his balance. He looked wildly around and saw Skaldar and two of the other Eagles come to perch in the trees alongside him, their great size bowing the branches.

"You are Aiden Brokksson?" said Skaldar again.

Aiden nodded, too surprised to say anything.

"You were watching the meeting, so you must know why I have come."

"I…" Aiden began. He thought about denying the Eagle's claim but Skaldar's gaze was the same gaze that had fixed upon him before. He knew Skaldar had seen him. "I wanted to hear news of the City so I can return to rescue my parents," said Aiden. "And I wanted to see the Eagles."

Skaldar tilted his head to one side. "But you now know that you are needed for a rescue mission of a different sort. Is that why you are hiding out here in the forest?" Skaldar's bright yellow stare seemed to look into his soul. "None of us can run and hide from our destiny."

"I want to rescue my parents," said Aiden, hating the childish whine in his voice. "How can I go and rescue the Eagle Riders and yet do nothing for my own family?"

"I would see the two as one and the same," said Skaldar. "The return of the Eagle Riders means an attack on Teraan City is possible and with it the rescue of all those imprisoned there. Tell me you are not so selfish as to put the rescue of two people above this country's hope of victory."

Aiden frowned. "That is not how I see it. My parents are

prisoners because of me. I can't abandon them."

"That is a noble sentiment," said Skaldar. "Tell me though. What would your parents want you to do?"

Aiden hesitated. He knew with a deep certainty that if Brokk or Kari were there with him now they would not ask to be rescued. They would tell him to do his duty and make them proud. They would say that maybe he had escaped to fulfil this very task. He thought of what they would say if they ever found out that he had come to find them, instead of doing something that would benefit everyone. He suddenly felt ashamed.

"They would want me to go with Falkor to find the Eagle Riders," said Aiden, unable to meet Skaldar's gaze.

"Then that is what you should do," said Skaldar. "Now I must fly to gather the Eagles for war."

Aiden looked up sharply. "You're not going to escort me back and make sure I go on this mission?"

Skaldar tilted his head to one side. "I am not going to order you to do anything. It is for you to decide and for you to live with the consequences of your own decision."

Skaldar spread his huge wings and air rushed around him. The branches swayed and Aiden clung precariously to his perch. The Eagles took off and quickly climbed skywards. Aiden almost wished he could go with them and fly away from the troubles of the earth. But he knew Skaldar had left him with a choice and, no matter how hard the decision, it was one that he would have to make.

22. Erin

Aiden walked slowly through the dripping forest. His mind was made up and now all that remained was to tell Branwyn and Andor. His steps dragged but his anger was gone. Skaldar had given him his choice and he had made it of his own accord.

Before long he had arrived back within sight of the gorge. He was further downstream than he thought, the cabins of the Feather Guard nestled high in the trees a short distance away. A couple of Eagles roosted in the eyries, flicking water from their wings as they sheltered under the canopy. They cast their keen gaze down on him as he approached but quickly returned to preening their feathers.

As he drew closer, voices drifted down from the main cabin, not quite angry, but certainly anxious. It sounded like Branwyn and Tristan, and maybe Signy too, but they were too muffled for Aiden to hear what was being said. Candlelight flickered through the window and Aiden shivered, rubbing his arms. His sodden clothes stuck to his skin and he was finally starting to notice the chill of the rain. The voices from the cabin continued.

Aiden paused at the bottom of the spiral stair. He had a strange feeling that the anxious words being spoken were about him. "Hello," he called up.

The voices stopped and a face he vaguely recognised looked down on him from the window.

"It's Aiden," said the man over his shoulder to the others. He beckoned Aiden up to join them.

Aiden took the spiral stair, grabbing the railing, the wood slick beneath his feet. He had barely taken a few steps before Branwyn appeared in the doorway. She ran carefully down to meet him, feet clattering over the wood.

"Where have you been?" she said, her voice an anxious whisper as she caught him in a hug. She pulled away quickly. "You're soaking."

Aiden smiled at her creased brows. "It's been raining."

"Did you get caught eavesdropping?" Branwyn whispered as they started back up the stairs. "Falkor's been here looking for you. Tristan's supposed to report to him as soon as you're found. He's been pacing the cabin since he got back. He won't do anything until he's spoken to you."

They reached the top of the stairs and Aiden could finally see who awaited him in the cabin. Tristan was there, and Signy, and the other Feather Guard, Rook, who he had met only briefly. Andor sat cross-legged on the floor and he gave Aiden a small smile across the room. Signy stood from her chair and silently tossed a blanket to him, not meeting his eye. Aiden wrapped it around his shoulders, shivering despite its warmth. The air was thick with unspoken words.

Tristan stood and walked haltingly over to him. He still wore his formal Feather Guard uniform. "I was beginning to think you weren't coming back," he said. "But Branwyn tells me you're not the type to run away." There was a sternness to his face that Aiden had not seen before. This was Tristan, Captain of the Feather Guard, thought Aiden, not Tristan his friend.

"No," said Aiden, suppressing the urge to call Tristan 'sir'. "I am a Feather Guard. I wouldn't abandon my duty."

"Good," said Tristan. "Because there is a task for you."

Aiden drew his blanket tighter around his shoulders. The

question would come from Tristan then. But as an order not a question, from a superior officer to a soldier under his command.

Tristan straightened himself. "Falkor is leading a mission to Cairn Ban to learn the fate of the Eagle Riders and rescue them if possible. If not for my injury I would have been going, but since I cannot, another member of the Feather Guard must go in my place. It was the express command of the Princess that that person be you."

The eyes of the room fixed upon Aiden and the silence was so complete he could hear the blood pumping through his veins. For a moment Tristan's stern exterior dropped and there was a flash of pain in his eyes, a glimpse of the worried and frustrated man beneath. This was just as hard for Tristan as it was for him. Aiden nodded once. "I would be honoured to represent the Feather Guard in service to the Princess."

"No Aiden you can't," said Andor, jumping up. "What about Mum and Dad?"

Aiden turned to his brother and put his hands on his shoulders. "We'll still rescue them. As soon as the Riders are safe. But Mum and Dad wouldn't want me to run away from my duty just to rescue them, no matter how much I want to. With the Eagle Riders back we'll have a better chance of winning this war and rescuing Mum and Dad anyway."

"But can't someone else go?" said Andor, tears rising in his eyes.

"Maybe," said Aiden, pulling Andor into a hug. "But it's me they've asked and it wouldn't be right to say no."

Andor wiped his eyes and slumped back to the floor. Branwyn crouched down next to him.

A brief frown flitted across Tristan's face, but he blinked and it was gone. He stood tall once more to address the room. "Rook, Signy, I want the supplies and equipment ready by this evening. Aiden, make sure your own things are ready too and report back here. Falkor's coming later to check everything and he'll want to speak to you. I'll go now and tell him and Allan and the Princess that everything is settled."

Rook and Signy pulled up their hoods and ventured outside to begin preparing things for the journey. Aiden and Tristan followed them out. At the bottom of the stairs Tristan reached out to grip his arm.

"I know you were planning to go back for your parents," said Tristan. "Branwyn told me. I wish I didn't have to ask this of you."

"I know," said Aiden. "I don't hold it against you."

"Thank you," Tristan whispered. "I trust no one better than you to take this mission in my place… and I am sorry you can't go for your family. I know how that feels…" Tristan looked down.

Aiden squeezed his shoulder. "I'll do my best for the Riders, for your father, and I trust that you'll do the same for my family while I'm gone." Aiden glanced to the cabin where Branwyn and Andor remained.

Tristan smiled. "That I can do."

The rest of the afternoon passed in a flurry of activity as Aiden got himself ready for another journey. As evening drew in he met the others in the clearing under the Feather Guard cabins. Tristan and Falkor were there already with Rook and Signy inspecting a number of packs. Aiden joined them silently. They nodded a greeting, but Rook did not pause as he described the contents of the bags.

"…food in here, one pot and two bowls."

"I doubt we'll be doing much cooking," said Falkor.

"You can leave it if you want," said Rook.

Falkor shook his head. "It's fine for the moment."

Rook continued. "Two bedrolls. And I've put some medical supplies in here. Bandages and salve and some useful herbs, though hopefully you won't be needing them." Lastly Rook turned to

Aiden. "This is from Odmund. He said you didn't have a sword."

Rook passed him a long object wrapped in cloth. Aiden unwrapped it to find a sword with a slightly curved crossbar and a half moon pommel. He drew it from its sheath. It fitted snugly in his hand, a comfortable weight. Etched into the blade was Eadha, the wind or the river, patience.

"I hope you know how to use it," said Falkor, walking over to his side.

"Well enough," said Aiden, sheathing the sword and eyeing the wizard coolly.

Falkor raised his eyebrows, unconvinced. "You were a hard person to find this afternoon," he said.

Aiden glanced away. How much did Falkor know? "I was exploring the forest."

Falkor stared at him and the glint in his eye reminded Aiden of the day they had first met. "Well, let me remind you that the time for exploring is done. Unless you are fully committed to this mission then we will fail."

Aiden nodded, trying to keep his face passive, but it was as if the wizard could see into his mind. He could not decide to what extent to believe Falkor. Was he just saying those things to scare him into action or was it really true, that unless he was fully committed, the mission would fail? Until now, the thought that they might fail had not truly crossed his mind.

Falkor continued. "Come. I'll introduce you to the other member of our party."

The wizard led him a short distance into the trees. Aiden's breath caught in his throat at the sight of the sleek golden frame and sharp eyes of an Eagle. The great bird turned slowly as they approached, flexing wings that spoke of both power and grace. She was smaller than the other Eagles Aiden had met but then if he stood straight he would still probably find himself eye to eye with her. He was both fascinated and a little afraid at the same time.

"Meet Iolair, daughter of Jormandar," said Falkor. "She will be travelling with us."

Aiden felt himself bowing. "It is an honour to meet you."

The golden head tilted to one side and the sharp yellow eyes blinked softly. "You don't need to bow to me," Iolair said, in a musical voice. "I am not one of the great lords of the sky."

"You seem it to me," said Aiden, his face growing red.

Iolair looked up to the sky. "Then I hope it is my future you see."

Aiden frowned, not quite understanding what she meant.

"I have other things to prepare," said Falkor, breaking the silence. "Make sure you are both ready." Falkor gave Aiden one last hard stare before walking away.

Aiden was left alone with Iolair, who rustled her wings quietly and watched him, saying nothing. Aiden shifted from foot to foot not knowing what to say or do. Eventually he said, "I suppose I better get ready then."

"Yes," she said, neither agreeing nor contradicting.

Aiden nodded farewell, feeling slightly foolish and quickly walked back towards the Feather Guard cabins to finish getting ready. He kicked himself inwardly. That was his chance to really talk to an Eagle and what had he managed to say? A couple of trivial remarks before making his excuses to leave. He would have to do better next time. After all, he would be seeing a lot of Iolair over the next fews days and weeks.

That night Aiden struggled to find sleep. He curled up on his bed, listening to the creak of branches outside the cabin. Thoughts tumbled around his mind. He heard the soft breathing of Andor from his makeshift bed on the floor and he was relieved that neither Andor nor Branwyn had tried to talk him out of going. It was the adventure he had always dreamed of, but these were not the desperate circumstances he had imagined. In his dreams there had always been the warm comforts of home to return to but now there was not even that. There was no guarantee that he even would return.

After a while Aiden sat up and swung himself out of bed. He slipped outside onto the wooden walkway and leaned his arms on the railing, the cool damp of the night making his skin prickle. He stood, listening to the sway of the trees and the ever present rushing of the river. Behind him a door clicked gently open and a moment later he felt Branwyn's hand on his shoulder. He put an arm round her.

"You're doing the right thing Aiden," Branwyn whispered, as if she heard his thoughts. "None of us like it, but go knowing it's what they would want."

Aiden nodded and gazed out into the darkened forest. There was nothing but blurred shadows. Like his future, he thought. But then a flash of silver caught his eye. Just for a moment he saw the Silver Eagle of his dreams. Then it was gone.

By the time morning arrived Aiden's resolve had quickened and the flutter in his stomach was as much anticipation, as it was worry. Aiden met Falkor and Iolair at the stables in the forest where two horses laden with equipment were waiting for them. There was quite a gathering of people to see them off. Aiden glanced nervously over at Iolair, who perched quietly beside the horses. What would it be like to travel with the Eagle?

Someone tapped his shoulder from behind.

"Good luck," said Tristan, stepping forward. His eyes flicked once to Iolair with a glimmer of longing, but he quickly masked it with a smile.

Tristan should be going, not me, thought Aiden. He pulled Tristan into a hug. "I wish you were coming too," he said.

"You know I can't," said Tristan smiling reproachfully. "I'd be no use if my leg gave out."

Aiden smiled sympathetically. "Look after yourself… and the others," he added, glancing at Branwyn and Andor behind him.

Tristan nodded and clapped Aiden on the shoulder.

Aiden turned to Branwyn next. Her eyes were watery, but she did not cry. He was glad.

"Be careful," Branwyn said, hugging him.

"I'll try not be too reckless," said Aiden, smiling.

Then Aiden took Andor into a huge hug, lifting him off the ground. "Goodbye little brother. I'll miss you."

"Can't I come too?" said Andor, his voice muffled in the folds of Aiden's jacket.

Aiden shook his head. "Not this time." He placed him back on the ground, studying his face. They were almost eye to eye. When had Andor grown so tall? And when had his eyes become so serious?

Andor stepped away and looked down at the ground, the smile slipping from his face.

"I'll be back before you've missed me," said Aiden, his voice light.

Aiden waved to them all as he began to walk backwards. Finally he turned and jogged the last few steps to where Falkor and Iolair waited. Falkor barely paused before hoisting himself into the saddle of the horse and starting off into the forest. Iolair rose into the sky with a great gust of wind to follow them above the trees. Aiden put a foot in the stirrup and pulled himself onto the horse in a less than dignified manner. He got himself settled, nudging the horse forwards. He turned back and waved and was met by a chorus of "good luck" from Branwyn and Andor, Tristan, Rook, Signy, and others, many of whom he did not even know. Then the forest was around him and the voices faded away.

The day was cloudy and under the trees it was damp and shadowy, but at least the previous day's rain had stopped. Despite struggling to find his rhythm on the horse Aiden felt light-hearted, maybe even excited. It was good to finally be doing something. They picked their way through the trees at a gentle trot and quickly came to the magical boundary of Torelia and its intricate arched gateway. The Torelian Guard saluted as they passed through. Once through the gate Aiden glanced over his shoulder, but the alder archway was quickly fading back into the forest, hidden by the magical qualities of Fearn. Already the route to the waterfall seemed hazy in his memory, though at least he could still remember the magnificent sight of the rushing waters.

"It's best not to look back," said Falkor.

Aiden glowered at him. Falkor could at least show some hint of remorse at dragging him away from his family. But he was not going for Falkor's sake, Aiden reminded himself. He was going for the Eagle Riders and for Tristan and in the hope that the Riders could help him rescue his parents.

They rode in silence, following a track through the forest. After a few hours Falkor steered his horse off the path and into the heathery undergrowth.

"Why are we going this way?" said Aiden, frowning as he ducked to avoid a low tree branch.

"The track will take us a winding route through every village between here and Cairn Ban," said Falkor, not looking back. "If we want to get there quickly and unnoticed then we need to avoid the path."

Aiden silently agreed but could not help thinking that there was a reason the people of Teraan did not stray far from the path. There were worse things than even Cu-Sidhe and Wulvers in the deep wilderness.

As afternoon approached, the clouds began to clear and the trees started to thin. Aiden caught occasional glimpses of Iolair soaring above and, through breaks in the trees, the far horizon showed the towering shadows of the mountains, a place he knew only from stories. He craned his neck to see them better, but they were still obscured by the forest and all he could discern was the vague outline of rocky slopes.

"There are Eagles who live in those peaks," said Falkor, catching his gaze.

"Are we going there?" said Aiden.

"No. We'll make camp on the edge of the forest tonight. Tomorrow we'll pass through the foothills, but we won't climb them."

Aiden nodded. He wondered what it would be like—a vast expanse unbroken by trees or buildings. And the mountains, did they truly reach higher than the clouds as the stories told?

The last bright light of day coloured the sky as Aiden and Falkor came to the edge of the forest. They stopped the horses in a clearing, but Aiden carried on the short distance to where the trees broke and the moors began. His eyes widened at the view before him. Rocky mountains rose out of a swathe of heather and wild grasses, touching the very heavens. Two birds wheeled around a distant summit. There was not a cloud in sight, only the rosy light of the setting sun. Aiden felt captured by open expanse, unable to draw himself away.

"It's beautiful, isn't it," came the soft, musical voice of Iolair.

Aiden jumped and marvelled at how she had managed to land so quietly behind him.

She made no sign of noticing his surprise. She said, "My home is that way, in a small pine forest on the far side of the mountains."

"It is beautiful," said Aiden, gazing back out to the hills. An occasional tree cast a long shadow in the sinking sun. "I've never seen anything like it before."

Eventually, Aiden turned and walked the short way back into the forest to where they had left the horses. He dropped his small pack to the ground and began unbuckling their supplies from the horses' backs. He looked around. "Where's Falkor gone?"

"He went for firewood," said Iolair. "He told you, but I don't think you were listening."

Aiden patted his horse absently and avoided Iolair's gaze. After their first meeting, and now this, he hoped she did not think him an idiot. He unpacked what they would need for the evening, spreading out their bedrolls on either side of the place they would build the fire. Falkor returned shortly with an armful of firewood, dropping it in the centre of their camp. He left Aiden to start the fire, returning to the forest to collect more wood. The sun sank behind the hills and very soon it became dark. Aiden drew the mark of fire, Teine, and let it float above his head as he arranged the wood. Then he allowed Teine to sink into the pile of branches and burst into flame. He caught Iolair watching him, but the Eagle made no comment on his unconventional method of starting a fire. He sat by the flames, warming his hands and occasionally feeding another branch to the fire.

"Someone's coming," said Iolair suddenly, flapping her wings.

Aiden poked the fire absently with a stick.

"It's not Falkor," warned the Eagle.

Suddenly alert, Aiden jumped to his feet, looking deeper into the forest. He reached over to his pack and pulled his sword from its sheath. It was clumsily done. He became horribly aware of his inexperience and hoped that the little sword training he had received from Odmund and Marsaili would serve him now. Quiet laughter filtered through the trees, along with the slight jingling of a horse's harness. Aiden hefted his sword, trying to seem unafraid. A moment later a small figure leading a horse stepped into the ring of firelight, hooded and cloaked. Aiden took a step towards them, holding his sword out before him.

"Is that supposed to be frightening?" came a sarcastic voice.

The figure looped the horse's reins over a tree branch and then walked right over to the fire and casually sat down opposite him. Hands lifted to push back her hood.

"You!" said Aiden, gasping in surprise but keeping his sword held out. It was the girl he had saved from the burning building. Her reddish-brown hair was tied back from her face, but her eyes were as bright and blue as ever. And the cloak. He recognised it now, with its flashes of runes.

"Do you know her?" said Iolair, a sharp edge creeping into her soft voice.

"I saved her once, from a fire," said Aiden. "But I don't know her."

He cast his eyes over her face, trying to fathom its depths. All that crossed his mind was that she seemed so much more beautiful without soot all over her face. He could kick himself. Was that all he could think of? Could he think of nothing to say? What was she even doing here?

"You can put your sword away Aiden," said the girl. "I've come to help you."

Aiden frowned and took a step towards her, finally finding his wits again. "How do you know my name?"

She smiled and held up her hands. "Everyone in Torelia knows your name. You were the one chosen to go with the wizard to rescue the Eagle Riders. Plus, you saved my life once. You think I wouldn't find out who you were?"

"But who are you?" said Aiden, jabbing his sword at her.

"I don't remember seeing you in Torelia," said Iolair. "And I see a lot."

The girl seemed to pause a moment to gather herself. "No, you probably did not see me. The old woman I came with was quite ill and I spent much time with her."

Aiden frowned, wondering if it was the same old woman he had also rescued from the fire. "You still haven't told me who you are."

She looked up at him. "And I would rather not do so until that sword is pointed elsewhere."

Aiden did not move. Should he trust her? He glanced over his shoulder. "Iolair?" he said, questioning.

Iolair tilted her head and blinked once, slowly. "I don't think she's a threat."

Aiden lowered his sword but did not put it away.

"I'm Erin," she said, holding out a hand of greeting.

Aiden warily switched his sword to his left hand and moved around the fire to shake Erin's hand. Her hand was soft and light, but there was a firmness to her grip that sparked surprise in Aiden's eyes.

"I never had the chance to thank you," said Erin. "You saved my life."

Aiden pulled back his hand and sat down by the fire, putting the flames between them once more. He rested his sword across his knees. Erin twisted a lock of hair through her fingers, unbothered by his wariness.

"Can I ask you something?" said Erin.

Aiden nodded. Her hair sparked red in the light of the fire.

"Why did you come back for me?"

Aiden thought back to his conversation with King Brandr. Everyone had wanted to know why he had gone back for her, but he hardly even knew himself. He had told the King that he had gone back because no one else would, but it felt weird to say that to her. He shrugged, feeling suddenly very self-conscious. "I don't really know. I suppose I'd have regretted it if I hadn't even tried."

Erin stared openly at him, her blue eyes glistening. She had stopped twisting her hair and it now hung down over her shoulder, curling slightly. "Thank you," she said, her bravado gone.

Aiden watched her through the flames. She seemed small again and vulnerable, like she had in the burning building. What was she doing so far out in the forest? Had she really come to help? And how had she managed to find them?

Just then there was a rustle in the trees and Falkor entered the ring of firelight. The wood he had collected scattered and the wizard's sword was in his hand more quickly than Aiden could turn around. Nuin, the spear, blazed in his other hand. He advanced upon Erin, but the girl looked up at him undaunted. Aiden gripped the hilt of his sword, but he did not know whether to stand up and face her again.

"What are you doing here?" said Falkor angrily.

"I've come to help," said Erin.

"Well you can't," said Falkor. "It's not safe. Go back."

Not safe, Aiden thought. Falkor had cared nothing for his safety when he had chosen him for this mission. But he seemed to care about this girl. Did he know her? Maybe he had seen her in Torelia or knew her old lady?

"From what I hear this country's only hope is to find the Eagle Riders and I'm going to do my part, whether it's safe or not," said Erin.

"There are other ways to do your part back in Torelia," said Falkor. He must know her, thought Aiden, or else he would not have mentioned Torelia.

"Let the soldiers plan their war. Here I can be useful," she said.

Falkor stared at her and Aiden saw the muscles in his jaw tightening. He thought the wizard would send the rune smashing into her.

"If you won't let me come with you, I'll just follow along behind," Erin said.

"I'll take you back myself," said Falkor, "and make sure you don't follow us."

Erin smiled. "I don't think so. You can't afford to waste time in taking me back there."

Where did she find the courage to speak to the wizard like that, thought Aiden.

Falkor and Erin stared at each other with such intensity that Aiden dared not move. Finally, the wizard sheathed his sword in one fluid movement, letting the rune fizzle into darkness.

"It seems I have no choice then," said Falkor, through gritted teeth. "But you will do exactly what I say at all times. Understood?"

Erin nodded, a smile beaming across her face. Aiden stared at her in awe until she met his gaze and he quickly dropped his eyes. He slowly fitted his sword back into its scabbard, sensing her eyes watching him over the flames. When he eventually looked up again Erin was on her feet and moving towards her horse. Aiden let his shoulders slump. She was staying then and he was going to have to get used to her being around. The thought filled him with excitement and just a little bit of fear.

They settled into camp for the night. Erin unpacked her horse, while Iolair went out hunting, and Falkor divided up some food for a meal. It was just cold food, dried meat and cheese and some bread. Aiden doubted they would get a chance to cook anything hot on the whole journey. Not unless Iolair deigned to bring back a spare rabbit or two.

"I suppose you brought your own rations then Erin," Falkor called across.

She smiled back at him. "Of course, but it's all dried stuff. Nothing fresh. We should save it for later in the journey."

Falkor made an unimpressed sound and turned back to cutting the cheese before handing both Aiden and Erin their chunk. They all sat round the fire to eat, leaving plenty of space between each other. Aiden focused on his food, eating slowly, savouring each mouthful, but once he was finished he had no other distraction from the growing silence around them. He watched Erin out of the corner of his eye. It was so strange that she of all people would turn up in the middle of the forest, when he had not seen her at all since the day of the burning building.

Aiden broke the silence. "How did you come to be at Torelia?"

Erin chewed her mouthful and swallowed slowly. She drew her knees up to her chest and clasped her hands so that her face was half hidden. "I escaped the City before the attack, but my family were not so lucky." She she stared into the fire. "I don't want to talk about it."

Aiden bit his lip, wishing he had chosen something else to talk about. "My parents didn't make it out either," he said.

Iolair arrived back, swooping gracefully between the trees to join them, but she did not come too close to the fire. She hovered just behind Aiden's shoulder so that he had to shuffle round in order to see her. The firelight danced golden on her feathers.

"I don't know how any of you expect to see a thing after spending all evening staring into that fire," said Iolair.

Aiden paused, unsure if they were being rebuked or not. All the Eagles he had met so far had been very stern and serious. But Falkor laughed.

"We don't expect to," said Falkor. "It makes little difference to our pitiful night vision anyway."

Iolair blinked slowly. "Well these fires of yours are not something I plan to get used to. The moon and stars give more than enough light for the night."

Aiden smiled. Her voice was much gentler than Skaldar's or her father's and there was no hint of annoyance, only mild puzzlement. Maybe she was just as curious about them as he was about her.

"I'll take the first watch," said Falkor. "Iolair, you second, and Aiden third. Erin will have to earn a place in my trust before she is given a watch."

Iolair ruffled her feathers and, with one beat of her wings, lifted herself into the branches of a nearby tree. She settled into a comfortable position just outside of the ring of firelight, tucking her beak snugly under her wing. On the ground they tidied up the remains of their meal and Erin brought her bedroll over to the fire.

Aiden settled down into his blankets with his back to the fire, his face looking out into the darkened forest. He tried to ignore thoughts of those he had left behind and forget about the strange presence of Erin, sleeping in her bed on the far side of the fire. All that mattered now was to rest. He closed his eyes and drifted off to sleep.

23. A Council of War

Tristan watched Aiden disappear into the forest, then folded his arms and scuffed the ground absently with his foot. He took a deep breath and buried his sadness deep inside. He could not go with them. There was no point in moping over something he could not change. It was the right decision but his heart did not want to agree. He did not move, even as the rest of the crowd that had come to see Aiden, Falkor, and Iolair slowly dispersed. The clearing quietened and slowly he became aware of Branwyn and Andor speaking in low voices behind him.

"…should be going with him," said Andor, his voice sharp. And yet a slight tremor betrayed his fear.

"Don't be silly," Branwyn replied calmly and gently. Tristan's brow creased. What feelings was she really hiding beneath that quiet exterior? She continued. "We'd just get in the way."

"Then what are we supposed to do?" said Andor, his voice becoming desperate.

"Right now we just have to wait," she said.

Tristan tilted his head to watch them out of the corner of his eye. Branwyn tried to give Andor a hug, but he pushed her away. There was something in the stubborn frown on Andor's face that reminded Tristan decidedly of Aiden. He would need to keep an eye on him, especially if he shared Aiden's reckless spirit. Branwyn, on the other hand, calmly let him push her, although he thought he saw a glint of sadness in her blue eyes. His brows creased. They were just trying to put their family back together and it had been torn apart again.

"What good is waiting?" Andor shouted back at her, dropping an abrupt silence over the clearing. Eyes darted their way and Tristan stepped quickly to their side.

Andor frowned at his arrival. "If you've come to tell me there's nothing I can do, then just go away."

Tristan bit back a startled laugh at the fire behind the green eyes. "No, that's not what I've come to say."

The green eyes narrowed.

"If you want to do something then you've got to be ready to do it," said Tristan. "Only a fool attempts a mission he's unprepared for."

"Aiden wouldn't wait," said Andor.

"No, but he is a reckless fool at times," said Tristan with a smile. "And he gets away with it because he can use the runes better than most soldiers can use their sword." Tristan leaned closer. "Andor, you want to rescue your parents, but right now you lack the skills and the help. You have no choice but to wait for Aiden to return. What you can do is use this time. Use it to learn the skills you need. Practice the runes. Learn to fight. Learn how to survive in the wild."

As he spoke the anger drained from the boy's face and Tristan felt a little lighter. His words had spoken as much to himself as they had to Andor. Yes, he was waiting for the Eagle Riders to return, but that did not mean there was nothing to do.

Tristan glanced between Branwyn and Andor. "Come help me at the Feather Guard base. There's plenty to do and you could learn a lot from Rook and Signy. I might even teach you some weapon skills too."

"I'm not sure I'll be any use at that," said Branwyn quietly, dropping her eyes, "but it would be good to have something to do. To feel like I'm helping." She looked up at him then, through a stray strand of dark hair, and he saw there both her longing and her fear.

"You'll do better than you think," he replied with a smile, trying to reassure her. "Andor?"

The boy considered him and then nodded once.

They set off back towards the bridge and the path to the Feather Guard cabins. Tristan walked side by side with Branwyn, Andor leading a few paces ahead.

"Thank you," said Branwyn quietly, nodding towards Andor. "I wouldn't have known what to say to him. We had a plan and then Aiden left and I didn't know what to do anymore." She turned and looked at him, a smile lifting the corners of her brilliant blue eyes. "You've given us both hope."

Tristan felt his mouth gaping as he reached for words. The tiny twinkle in Branwyn's eyes told him she had noticed. He grinned back and pushed away his embarrassment. It was good to see her smile.

They stepped off the bridge and into the patchy sunlight of the cliff top. Tristan stopped and put a hand on her shoulder. "Aiden asked me to keep an eye out for you and I will."

Branwyn smiled shyly and looked at the ground. Tristan let his hand drop from her shoulder, the gesture feeling suddenly awkward. After a second they continued through the forest to the Feather Guard base, reaching the cabins to find Rook and another man standing at the foot of the spiral stair. Both looked up at their arrival.

"Tristan. A message for you," said Rook.

For a second Tristan's heart jumped. Could it be from his father? No, his rational mind caught up with him.

"You've been summoned to the council in the great cavern,"

said the messenger.

Tristan frowned.

"Allan asks that you report there immediately."

Tristan nodded. He was loathe to leave Branwyn and Andor just after he had promised to help them, but he could not ignore a summons from Allan. Tristan looked to Rook. "I've said Branwyn and Andor can help us out here. I'm sure you can find them something to do and show them the ropes while you're at it."

"With pleasure," said Rook, turning to ruffle Andor's hair while the boy ducked out of his reach.

"I'll be back as soon as I can," said Tristan to Branwyn, almost reaching out to pat her shoulder but thinking better of it.

She smiled back at him. "We'll be ok."

Tristan nodded. How was it that sometimes she appeared so small and sad and at other times, like now, she seemed to be brimming over with a strength he could not fathom? Reluctantly he dragged his eyes from her and followed the messenger down into the caves.

In the great cavern the messenger pointed Tristan to a smaller cave at the back. The guards on either side of the entranceway let him pass without challenge. Inside, the small cave was lit by the steady glow of fire runes carved into the walls. A long table took up most of the space and already six people sat around it. Tristan recognised Allan and Odmund and guessed that the others were some of the people who had escaped to Torelia from the City or nearby villages.

Tristan hesitated in the doorway, but at the far end of the table Allan stood and beckoned him in. "Take a seat Tristan." Tristan crossed the cave and took the empty chair next to Odmund.

"Let's begin," said Allan. "I have called you all here to form an emergency council of war. Our King has been captured. In times such as these leadership would fall to his chief advisors, but as you know Hakon has turned traitor, Arthur is missing, and Falkor has gone to find the Eagle Riders. The Princess also left this morning on an important mission to seek the aid of more wizards—a mission that has become even more pressing now that Falkor has gone. In the meantime we are all that remains of Teraan's leaders, though many of you may not have considered yourself as such before today. The Princess herself has asked me to form this council to act on her behalf until she returns."

Allan took in the whole room with his gaze. "This is an unconventional gathering, but let me explain who I have chosen and why and if you think there is anyone else who should be included, I will hear your suggestions. From the City I have chosen Bradan of the Palace Guard and Dorcas of the City Guard, the two highest ranking soldiers to have escaped here. Also Odmund, the swordmaster, and Tristan, now Captain of the Feather Guard and son of the Captain of the Eagle Riders. I hope he will speak for both the Feather Guard and the Eagle Riders." Tristan felt the eyes of the room on him as Allan spoke and with it the burden of responsibility. "Finally, I have invited Maddok, elder of Faraig, and Ester, elder of Darrogie, the two villages closest to here and where immediate reinforcements are most likely to come from."

Tristan looked round at the others at the table. Bradan was a tall man with thick arms and long hair tied back from his face. Tristan recognised him from the Palace, but he had not had many dealings with him before. There was a nondescript look about his face and Tristan wondered how he would cope with suddenly being thrust into leadership. Dorcas he did not know. She had grey flecked hair cropped close about her head and although she seemed small, she had a capable air about her and an intelligence in her eyes. Odmund was his usual stoic self, arms bared to the world, proudly wearing their multitude of scars. His presence gave Tristan comfort.

"You have chosen well," said Maddok, the old man sitting to

Tristan's left. His face was wrinkled, but there was a wisdom in his quiet voice. Around the table the others were nodding in agreement.

"I see one obvious absence," said Tristan.

"Who?" said Allan, eyebrows raised.

"There are Eagles here too," said Tristan. "It wouldn't be right for them to be left out."

Allan's brow creased ever so slightly. "Will you not speak for the Eagles?"

Tristan shook his head. "I speak for the Feather Guard and to some extent the Eagle Riders, but I cannot speak for the Great Eagles. It would not be... polite."

Allan folded his arms, thinking. "Speak to them then. Ask if one of them will join us at our next meeting."

Tristan nodded. It would have been better to send word to them now, but he sensed that Allan was not keen on having their presence and was eager to begin without delay.

"If everyone is happy," said Allan, "we shall get down to business. A search party has been sent out for the Eagle Riders and more wizards are being sought. What is our next priority?"

"Defence," said Bradan. "This place may be magically hidden, but it's only a matter of time before the Brathadair find us."

"Training too," said Odmund. "Right now we have men from the Torelian Guard, the Palace Guard, and the City Guard. They need to be able to fight as one cohesive army and not a rabble of soldiers. And if more come from Faraig and Darrogie there will be a whole new set of challenges to face."

"Our men may not be fighters," said Ester, "but they know how to work together."

Odmund inclined his head. "Nevertheless they will still need trained."

No one argued this point.

"Anything else?" Allan asked.

Tristan licked his lips, the beginning of an idea forming. They needed to know where the Brathadair were and what they were doing. And they needed to know in enough time to act upon it. But before he could speak Maddok spoke up.

"How are things in the City?" he asked. "We'll need someone to keep an eye on what the Brathadair are doing. There's no point in training when we don't know what we're training for or defending against."

"We have a small patrol stationed in secret in the City," said Allan. "They will keep us informed."

"Will that be enough?" said Ester.

"It is all we can afford," said Allan. "But they are not there to fight. They are there to spy."

The others around the table nodded. We need to keep watch on our own borders too, thought Tristan. A small patrol in the City could easily miss something. He opened his mouth to speak, but Dorcas was already talking.

"We need to set up a perimeter," said Dorcas. "And have more regular patrols in the forest. Then we'll have advance warning of anything that comes our way."

There was a lot of nodding around the table. Tristan pressed his hands together. That was the very idea he had been trying to put into words. Why could he not form his thoughts into useful practical suggestions? How did his father do it all the time?

The conversation moved from plan to plan as they discussed setting up a perimeter, adding extra patrols, creating sentry posts in the forest, and fortifying the alder wall. Really it ought to be done with magic, but they did not have enough people skilled with the runes and Tristan could think of no better way, so he kept the thought to himself. Talk moved to defensive strategies within the heart of Torelia, creating barricades and planning escape routes.

Tristan listened, but he felt detached. Every idea he had had was spoken before the words could reach his mouth. They were all going to think he was useless. It was no way to represent the Feather Guard, let alone the Eagle Riders. If his father was here he would be at the centre of the discussions, not sitting quietly in the background.

The talk droned on about barricades and tunnels, but Tristan could not help but think it would be easy for the Brathadair to block them in from both sides and kill them all. Unless they could not cross the river—that would leave an escape route from the caves. The idea began to grow and Tristan thought it over, ignoring the rest of the conversation as he did so. Then he spoke, not caring who he interrupted. It was about time he was given a chance to speak.

"We need to destroy the bridge."

Silence fell.

"Tristan we were just talking about which tunnels to barricade and which to leave open," said Allan. "Weren't you listening?"

Tristan shook off his words. "It almost doesn't matter. If our enemies take that bridge and cross the river we'll be trapped in these caves."

Allan folded his arms and gave a small sigh. "Then we'll hold the bridge."

Tristan bit the inside of his cheek. Allan spoke as if to reassure him, but Tristan sensed beneath it the patronising tone of one explaining something complex to a small child. Did Allan think he knew nothing of battle strategy?

"That won't be easy," said Bradan.

Tristan glanced at him in relief, his confidence growing once more. "We only have a small force," Bradan continued. "We can't fight a large battle on two fronts."

"I know," said Allan. "That is why we're barricading the tunnels. As we were just discussing."

"The Brathadair can break down a barricade," said Tristan. "But they can't rebuild a bridge. We should destroy it. Then we decide where the battle is fought."

"No," said Allan, his voice growing louder. "The Brathadair will come here to destroy Torelia. I won't do it for them."

"And if we're all dead, at least the bridge will survive to aid the Brathadair as they spread their evil further across the country," said Tristan, sarcasm turning his voice bitter.

"We are not destroying that bridge," Allan barked, slamming his fist onto the table top. "You speak as though the enemy was on our very doorstep Tristan. As though the history of this place means nothing. Torelia has never been found. There is no reason to think it will this time."

He saw now Allan's reluctance and for a moment he sympathised. What would it be like to be the first Captain to lose Torelia? Yet these were difficult times. Everything that had once been certain was being taken from them. Tristan had once believed that the Eagle Riders were invincible, now he was not so sure.

"A lot of things have happened recently that have never happened before," said Tristan quietly.

Allan stared him down. "Just because your Eagle Riders have failed you, it doesn't mean Torelia will too."

For a moment the room was deathly silent. Everyone looked at Tristan and he could see in their eyes their sympathy and their condescension. They did not see him as a fellow leader, not truly. No, they saw him as nothing more than the favoured son of the King's favourite Eagle Rider Captain. A relic of the heroes who had failed them. Tristan seethed inside, but he relaxed his shoulders and let out his anger. If his father had been here he would tell him this was not the time for arguments. Tristan would honour that. He would do the Eagle Riders proud in their absence.

When Tristan did not retaliate, Maddok quietly turned the conversation away from the bridge. They began to discuss training and numbers of soldiers and the best tactics for attack. Tristan leaned back in his chair. No one would meet his eye. Maddok and Ester descended into lengthly discussions as they tried to estimate how many from their villages would be willing to fight. Odmund droned on about the extra weapons and equipment they would need. Tristan's mind drifted. How did his father survive these meetings? Maybe if he spoke more his mind would wake up. But Allan's rebuke had cast him mute. All he could think about was getting back to the Feather Guard cabins and to people who did not think he was trying to be a hero, just because his father was an Eagle Rider.

"It's settled then," said Allan, jolting Tristan out of his thoughts. "Bradan, Dorcas, and I will start on fortifying Torelia. Odmund, you and Tristan can be in charge of training and equipment. We need a full inventory of all our weapons. Maddok and Ester you can return to your villages and see if there are any willing to join us. We shall meet again once you are back."

Tristan sighed with relief as the members of the council stood, chairs scraping across the floor. He flexed his shoulders. It was good to be on the move again. The hours of sitting had stiffened up all his muscles and his injured right leg was paining him.

On his way out of the cave Odmund fell into step beside him. "You shouldn't let Allan bully you into silence."

Tristan stopped and raised his eyebrows. "Didn't you hear him? Anything I said after that would have sounded childish and stupid."

"It wasn't a bad idea about the bridge," said Odmund. "Just badly explained."

"Why didn't you say something?" said Tristan, feeling betrayed.

"Allan doesn't respond well to conflict. It wouldn't have helped."

"It would have helped me," said Tristan.

Odmuned just smiled. "You're strong enough to take a hit. Next time just be more subtle with him. Now, to training. I'll arrange for things to begin tomorrow. In the meantime we should get started on assessing what weaponry we have."

Tristan nodded, trying to shake off the dregs of the meeting. "I'll see what we've got at the Feather Guard base and get it into fighting shape."

"Good," said Odmund. "I'll see you at the training ground tomorrow then."

They went their separate ways. Tristan hurried up the passageway to the forest above, glad to be out of the stuffy cave. With the clear air his energy returned and he jogged back to the cabins. The muscles in his legs, weakened after his injury, began to tug sharply as he ran, but it was a good pain.

Back at the cabins he found a hive of activity. Rook must have been hunting, for he was now showing Andor how to skin a rabbit. Signy was up in the tree, speaking to one of the Eagles and Branwyn had started a fire in the old fireplace and was cooking bannocks in a pan over the flames. Their slightly sweet aroma filtered across the clearing to him, making his stomach rumble.

Branwyn waved at him as he approached. Her cheeks were rosy from the fire. "You're just in time for lunch," she said.

Tristan sat down on the tree stump beside her.

"How was the meeting?" she asked, flipping the bannock in the pan with practised ease.

"Long," said Tristan.

She glanced at him, as if expecting more, but he did not feel like talking about it. She flipped the last bannock onto a cloth laid out by the fire.

"How was your morning?"

"Better than most mornings of the last few days," said Branwyn. "It almost felt normal, in a strange sort of way. It feels like years since I last baked bread. And it's been good to see Andor with a purpose again. He's been following Rook around all morning." She glanced fondly over at her cousin.

Tristan smiled at her. Without such a burden of worry she was beautiful. He wondered if anyone had ever told her that before.

A moment later the others joined them and Tristan flicked his eyes away from Branwyn's face. It was not the time for such thoughts. As she passed out the bannocks, the two Eagles took to the sky and disappeared above the trees. Tristan frowned. He had meant to speak to them as soon as he had got back, but he had become distracted.

"They're just going hunting," said Signy, catching his gaze. "I did offer them some of our rabbits, but they said they'd prefer to hunt their own."

Tristan shrugged. "Just someone remind me I need to speak to them when they get back."

"So your meeting?" said Rook. "What news?"

Tristan looked back at his fellow Feather Guards. "We've all got work to do this afternoon."

"Can I help?" said Andor.

Tristan smiled and nodded. "We need an inventory of all our weapons and equipment. And if it's not battle ready then it needs to be."

Rook waved it off and grinned at Andor. "No problem. With five of us it will be light work."

Branwyn leaned over to him. "I don't know anything about weapons," she whispered, a slight frown on her face.

Tristan shook his head. "Don't worry, you'll be fine. It's not as hard as it sounds."

They finished their lunch quickly and set to work. Rook set up a pulley from the main cabin, loaded the equipment and weapons onto it, and lowered it to the ground with a great clanking of metal. At the base of the tree Tristan and Signy began sorting them, teaching Branwyn and Andor as they did.

"Swords here, daggers here, spears here. Put any archery equipment over here," Tristan said. "If it's dirty or rusty then it needs cleaning and if it's chipped or cracked then we'll need to take it to the smith."

"What about this?" said Andor, holding up a long weapon that was part spear, part sword.

"That's a quarter-spear," said Tristan. "The Eagle Riders use it for fighting from the air. I don't know if it will be much use for anyone here, but we probably need all the weapons we can get. Start a new pile for them over there."

"So many names," said Branwyn, picking up two swords of different length.

Tristan laughed. "You don't really need to know the names. If it looks the same, then it probably is."

The piles of weapons grew quickly and soon Rook shouted down to say that the store was empty. They turned to cleaning next, wiping away cobwebs and dust with damp rags, and sharpening the blades with whetstones. Signy focused on the archery gear, assigning strings to bows and checking the fletching on arrows. Tristan sat with Branwyn and showed her how to sharpen the daggers with a whetstone. She was hesitant at first, but after he guided her through the movements she picked it up quickly.

They spent the rest of the afternoon getting all the weapons ready. Like Rook had said, it was a much smaller task than it would have been without Branwyn and Andor's help. And due to Rook and Signy's vigilance over the years, there was very little that was broken beyond repair. All in all, Tristan was pleased with their work.

As they finished up, Andor shyly fingered a sword before picking it up and weighing it gingerly in his hand.

"That one's a bit big for you Andor," Rook called over.

Tristan got to his feet. "Let's get the practice swords out for bit," he suggested. "I did promise I'd teach you."

Andor put the long sword down and ran over to join him.

"Come on Branwyn," said Andor, tugging at her arm. "You have to learn too."

She shook her head and stayed firmly on the ground. "I wouldn't be any good."

"Oh go on," said Tristan, extending a hand to her. "You don't know until you try."

She hesitated, then, grabbing his hand, she pulled herself up. "You might regret this."

Tristan laughed. "Never."

Rook reappeared with five practice swords and dropped them in a bundle on the ground.

"Count me out," Signy called over. "I want to finish fletching these arrows."

Branwyn frowned at Tristan. "How come Signy gets out of this?"

"Firstly, she has an important job to finish. And secondly, she knows how to defend herself," said Tristan.

"And how do you know that I don't?" said Branwyn.

Tristan moved quickly, snatching her wrist and pinning it behind her back, before hooking his ankle around hers and gently dropping her to the ground. "I know," he said.

She stared up at him with a startled expression on her face. He released her and a sudden uneasiness gripped his insides as he waited for her reaction. He suddenly realised that he cared a lot about what she thought of him.

"Ok, so maybe I don't know how to defend myself," said Branwyn, looking sheepishly at anywhere but his face.

"That's why I'm going to teach you," said Tristan, extending a hand to her.

She took it, shaking her head with a small smile.

Tristan and Rook began their teaching, starting with a few

basic moves. Andor took to it quickly and his fearlessness reminded Tristan of Aiden. Branwyn needed a lot more coaxing. She cowered behind each blow, even when Tristan swung his sword as gently as he could.

"Try not to be scared of it," said Tristan as she stumbled back from him again.

"It's only natural," said Branwyn, leaning on her sword with its point in the ground. "You are trying to hit me."

"How else will you learn how not to get hit?" Tristan countered. "Anyway I promise I won't hurt you. Trust me."

She pursed her lips, but raised her sword again, countering each of his swings with a clack.

"See. That's better. You can block stronger when you don't shy away from it."

She gave him a sheepish smile. "I did tell you I wouldn't be any good."

Tristan shook his head. "You're just not confident. Be fearless, like Andor."

Andor grinned and jumped over to poke her with his wooden sword.

"Hey," she cried, dancing away from him.

Andor chased her for a minute before Tristan jumped in and tackled the boy, wrestling him to the ground.

"I get a feeling that's training over," said Rook, spinning his sword in his hand before throwing it onto the pile.

Tristan lay on the ground panting and nodded. "I'm famished anyway."

They ate dinner together as the light faded around them. When the Eagles returned to roost in their eyries, Branwyn nodded up to them, reminding him that he needed to speak to them. The Eagles were taciturn, but Tristan sensed that they were pleased with the outcome of the council meeting and even more pleased to have been invited to the next. By the time he returned, the others had disappeared off to bed. He went to his room and flopped gratefully onto his blankets.

The next morning he awoke to the smell of fresh bread. Branwyn was up already, cooking at the little campfire in the clearing below the cabins. Rook sat beside her, sampling little bits while she futilely batted his hand away. Tristan joined them and Branwyn passed him a bowl of porridge with a slice of fresh bread.

"So Tristan gets the special treatment then?" said Rook, raising his eyebrows.

"You've had yours already," she retorted, but Tristan did not fail to notice the tiny blush in her cheeks.

"Go and make sure the others are up," he said to Rook. "We all need to be over at the training ground today. I'm helping Odmund with the training and you lot have a lot more weapons to sort through."

It was not long before they all finished breakfast and headed off through the forest to the clearing amidst the trees. Odmund was already there putting men and women through their paces. Upon Tristan's arrival he left them to it.

"How was yesterday's work?" said Odmund.

Tristan passed him the list he had drawn up. The swordmaster scanned it, nodding every now and again. He looked up. "It's a good start, but we're going to need more. A lot of that is Eagle Rider gear. It won't be much use for the kind of fighting I expect we'll get."

"I know," Tristan conceded. "Rook and Signy will get started on the weapon store here today, though from what they say the weapons here have not been kept in nearly as good condition as the kit at the Feather Guard base."

Odmund snorted a laugh. "Well they would say that."

Tristan gave a wry smile. He feared the Rook and Signy were right. It was an armoury built from discarded swords and the blunted blades used for practice.

The day passed quickly between training and assessing the guards to cleaning and sharpening weaponry. There was a buzz about the place that reminded Tristan of a festival if it had not been for the fact that they were preparing for war. In the afternoon, Odmund and Tristan found time to put Andor and Branwyn through their paces. Tristan saw some improvement with Branwyn, but too often she backed away from his swings rather than meeting them. Her strength was not the problem, for when she did clash with him he felt it. She just seemed afraid to take a hit or give a hit.

Their training was cut short by the arrival of a messenger from Allan, who pulled Tristan and Odmund aside.

"Maddok and Ester have returned," she panted. "From their faces I'd say it's not good news."

Tristan and Odmund followed the messenger quickly along the cliff top and over the bridge to the island in the middle of the river. The roar of the river was loud in Tristan's ears, but he was pleased to see that the two Eagles were able to join them. Then he caught sight of Maddok and Ester, deep sorrow etched into their faces. He remembered Ester as a lively woman, but now she seemed sunk into herself. Next to her, Maddok's face was no longer lined only with age but with worry too. Once all were assembled Allan nodded to Maddok to speak.

The old man heaved a great sigh. "We returned to our villages yesterday, but when I got back to Faraig the place was in turmoil. While I was gone the Brathadair had come with a dark wizard at their head. They told the village that the King had fallen and that they should join the Brathadair or die. Most were too scared and agreed to join them. A few called them traitors and they were killed on the spot. Many were killed, but many more stayed to join the wizard. Those who came here with me are the few who escaped, but we are mostly old folk and women and children."

Ester nodded slowly, tears glistening in her eyes. "The same happened in Darrogie this morning. One of my sons was killed."

Silence descended over the group. It was finally happening, Tristan thought. The Brathadair were coming to Torelia. They could not know for certain where it was, but they were closing in. It was only a matter of time.

24. Trust

"So how long will it take us to get to Cairn Ban?" Erin asked, shouting ahead to Falkor, whose horse led the way.

"Long enough," said Falkor, keeping his eyes ahead and his voice even. "There's still time for you to turn back."

Erin lifted her chin. "I'm not going back. So tell me, how many days?"

"Surely you took that into consideration before choosing to come," said Falkor, a challenge rising behind his words.

"Well I know roughly," said Erin. "Anyway, can't I be interested in our journey?"

"You could have been interested in it without having to come," Falkor replied sharply, swivelling on his horse.

Aiden found himself almost holding his breath as he watched from behind. He expected Erin to hunch down in her seat and fall silent, but she held Falkor's gaze, her reddish hair tangling around her head in the wind.

"Are you going to tell me how long or not?"

Falkor paused, gave her a hard stare. "It's probably three more days riding."

"Thank you," said Erin. "That's all you had to say in the first place."

Aiden bit back a smile. She had guts standing up to Falkor like that. The wizard turned forwards again and she glanced back at

Aiden, a sheepish grin on her face. Erin slowed her horse for Aiden to draw alongside.

"He's so frustrating," said Erin, loud enough that Falkor could probably hear her.

Aiden smiled. "I don't think it's easy to gain Falkor's trust."

"How did you manage it?" said Erin.

Aiden gave a laugh of disbelief. "I'm not sure that I have." Falkor never really told him anything, just ordered him about.

"But he brought you?" said Erin, screwing up her face in a puzzled expression.

Aiden shrugged. "I can use the runes I suppose." But was that all there was to it?

Erin raised her eyebrows. "And what about me? Do you trust me?"

Aiden looked down at the back of his horse's head. He certainly liked her and he had had no hesitation in rescuing her. But now that she was more than just a tear-stained face in his memory, did he trust her? "I don't know," he said truthfully. "I've really only just met you." It seemed unreal that she—the very one he had rescued from the burning building—was here now. She had a name, little else. There were too many questions that he wanted to ask her, but he did not know how.

Erin gave him a thoughtful look, nudging her horse forward. "I trust you," she called back over her shoulder.

Aiden's heart gave a tiny leap. He half wished now that he had told her he did trust her. Shaking his head, he shifted his gaze to the horizon. Of all the things to be worrying about now and he chose this. He almost felt guilty that he had barely thought about those left behind in Torelia. It seemed like the new day had cast a veil over his previous troubles. There was nothing to do now but the task at hand.

The wind danced around him, whispering of distant places,

blowing away thoughts of Andor and Branwyn. Across the moor the horses cut a thin path through the heather, while Iolair flew above them, her golden form a silhouette against the sun. Behind them the green line of the forest grew ever more distant, while the grey shadows of the mountains grew closer but not smaller. He was a long way from home.

Aiden shifted in his saddle, trying to ease his stiff muscles, unused to riding. His pony was a solid creature with a shaggy mane and though he was growing fond of the beast, he could not keep from looking up to the sky at Iolair. No matter how vast the horizon, his gaze was always drawn back to her. She floated effortlessly on the wind and it awoke in him a deep longing to be up there with her.

They continued until midday when Falkor called a halt. Aiden gratefully slipped from his horse's back and sank into the shade under the branches of a solitary tree. He took a long swig of water. Erin dismounted lightly and patted the neck of her horse. Iolair swooped down, landing gracefully beside them. The horses shied a little, but she merely ruffled her wings and blinked slowly in the sun. Falkor unbuckled one of his saddlebags and brought over some food to share out.

"How is the sky today?" Aiden said to the Eagle.

She turned her golden gaze on him. "The wind is fresh. The air is clear. It reminds me of home."

Aiden smiled. "What's it like to fly?"

Iolair clacked her beak. "That would be like asking you what it's like to walk."

"I suppose," said Aiden, looking down at his feet.

"What you really want to know is what it would be like for you to fly," said Iolair. "I'm afraid I can't answer that. For me, to fly is to be free. It would not be the same for you."

Aiden nodded and tried to keep the smile on his face. "I know.

But it doesn't stop me from wondering."

Iolair tilted her head gently. "It would probably be very cold for you."

Aiden laughed, but inside he felt a twinge of sadness. He wanted to be up there with her, but he knew he never could.

Just then Falkor broke into his thoughts. "It's important that we're ready for whatever we might find at Cairn Ban. Which means Aiden, you need to learn to fight."

"I can fight," said Aiden indignantly.

"And can you win?" Falkor added with a raised eyebrow.

Aiden opened his mouth to protest, but Falkor was already on his feet and unstrapping two long wooden staffs from the back of his horse. He sighed and put the rest of his food aside, trying to ignore the grin Erin hid behind her hand.

Falkor returned throwing one of the staffs to Aiden. He threw the other at Erin. "I don't know why you're laughing. You're fighting him."

Erin barely caught the staff. For a moment her expression was one of outrage and shock, then she set her jaw determinedly and got to her feet. She expertly tied her hair back into a braid as they moved out from the shade of the tree and onto the mossy grass. Iolair tilted her head, watching them with interest.

"Fight," said Falkor.

Aiden glanced momentarily at Erin. She was just a girl, not a warrior like Marsaili. Then Erin struck. Aiden blocked her, just. She was good, but he had been unprepared. Next time she would be on the defence. Aiden swung his staff at her, but she was ready and ducked it. Her staff whipped out and caught him full in the stomach, winding him. His knees jarred onto the ground. He stood up slowly, pretending he was hurt more than he was. Then he lunged. This time there was a satisfying thud as his stick collided with Erin's arm. She gasped but showed no other sign of pain. Then in a few swift moves Aiden found his staff flying from his grasp. Erin gave him a smug smile.

Heat rose in Aiden's cheeks. He was not going to let her beat him. He swung faster and harder, but every time he upped the pace she matched him. When she jabbed him in the side, for what felt like the tenth time, he made one final desperate effort to catch her. But Erin anticipated him. She struck upwards, jarring his whole arm as she knocked the staff from his grasp. Then she swiped low, catching the backs of his knees and toppling him unceremoniously to the ground. She pressed the tip of her staff down onto his chest.

"I thought you said you could fight," Erin said.

"I can fight," Aiden protested, but he let his arms flop out on either side of him and grinned. "I just can't fight as well as you... yet."

"We'll see," she replied, an amused smile on her face. She lifted her staff and reached down to give him a hand up.

"We should get moving again," said Falkor, his gaze on the horizon. "We've still got a lot of distance to cover today."

Aiden followed his gaze and thought he saw something moving along the ridge they had descended earlier that day.

"What is it?" said Aiden, pointing.

"Cu-Sidhe, maybe," said Falkor. He turned to look at Aiden. "Whatever it is we don't want it to catch us."

Aiden shivered and wiped the sweat from his forehead. He had always wanted to see one of the fierce dog-like creatures, but out here, in the wilds, it seemed suddenly less appealing. He took a swig of water and packed away the rest of his food, his appetite gone.

After the brief rest they moved steadily uphill, further into the foothills of the mountains, the only sound the clopping of the horses hooves over the soft ground. The evergreen expanse of the forest was just a smudge on the horizon behind them. A nippy wind whipped up around them and Aiden drew his cloak tighter across his shoulders. It felt like something was watching them. He glanced back, but he did not see any movement and he tried to put it out of his mind. He nudged his horse forwards, drawing alongside Erin, hoping that her company would distract him.

"Where'd you learn to fight like that?" Aiden asked her.

"Oh here and there," she said, smiling and shrugging. "The boys I knew growing up were always fighting and I didn't see why I should be left out just because I was a girl."

"You're good you know," said Aiden, wondering who all the boys she knew were.

"I know." She beamed back at him, loose strands of hair blowing across her face.

Aiden's mouth gaped as he searched for words.

"Where did *you* learn to fight like that?" she asked, innocently.

For a moment Aiden considered his answer. He frowned. "I'm not that bad."

Erin laughed. "Sorry, but you did get beaten by a girl."

Aiden scowled at her. "I've fought girls before."

"And did you win?" said Erin, her face suddenly serious.

Aiden hesitated. "No. But I was fighting Marsaili, one of the Princess' bodyguards."

Erin just laughed more.

"Hey," said Aiden. "You forget I saved your life."

She turned her merry blue eyes upon him. "Maybe at Cairn Ban I'll get the chance to return the favour." She laughed again and kicked her horse into a canter, throwing her arms out and letting her hair fly wildly behind her. Aiden frowned. How could she be so happy when all around them the world seemed to be falling into chaos?

That night they camped on the top of a ridge, looking down on a mountain loch that glowed eerily in the light of the moon. There was not enough wood for a fire, so they ate in the dark. Iolair left briefly to go hunting, her feathers gleaming softly in the night. Again Aiden felt a great longing to go with her and soar high above the world.

With no fire to sleep around, they laid out their bedrolls haphazardly.

"Aiden, you're first watch, Iolair second, and I'll take third," said Falkor.

"What about me?" said Erin, dropping her blankets in the midst of rolling them out.

"I still don't trust you," said Falkor.

Erin folded her arms stubbornly. "Why not?"

"Does it matter?" said Falkor. "I say you're not taking a watch. And I seem to remember the condition of you coming, was that you would obey my every order."

"Fine," said Erin, reaching back down to grab her blankets. She picked them up and moved further from Falkor, spreading them on the ground not far from where Aiden sat.

The camp settled down to sleep. Iolair tucked her head under her wing while the others wrapped themselves in their blankets. Aiden stayed sitting and gazed out into the darkness. It was a clear night and a multitude of stars twinkled above his head. Out here a second felt like a thousand hours and, at the same time, no time at all.

"Aiden, are you awake?" Erin whispered.

"I hope so. I'm on watch," Aiden replied, with a smile.

"Oh," she said.

Aiden glanced over at her.

"Do you think I made a mistake coming here?" she said.

Aiden frowned at her, wondering why she would ask him something like that. "I suppose it depends on why you came."

"To help you," Erin replied, surely and without hesitation. "And everyone else." It was hard to tell in the dark, but she seemed to be watching him intently. "I couldn't bear the waiting around any longer. I had to do something."

A wry smile crossed Aiden's lips. He knew the feeling well. He had fought against it himself many times over the last few weeks.

"Then it wasn't a mistake to come," said Aiden. "If you ask me, we need all the help we can get."

A small laugh escaped her lips. "I'm not sure Falkor would agree with you."

"What makes you say that?" said Aiden.

"He won't let me help."

"He let you come," said Aiden, glancing over at the sleeping wizard and wondering if he really was asleep. "He's probably just being difficult because he feels responsible for your safety."

"You really think so?" said Erin.

"Yes," said Aiden. "Anyway, it's me he really needs to worry about. I'm the one who can't fight."

Erin laughed quietly.

"Don't worry about it," said Aiden. "You can't change where you are now."

"No," said Erin, almost to herself. She rolled over onto her back and gazed up at the stars.

The rest of his watch passed slowly. Erin's breathing deepened as the moon rose into the sky. Aiden's eyelids began to droop. He rubbed his face and yawned.

A twig snapped.

Aiden sat up and squinted down at the mountain loch, gleaming in the moonlight. All was still. He lifted himself onto the balls of his feet. He wanted to stand and get a view over the heather, but something held him in a crouch. He could see nothing, but there was a tiny rustling, as if something crept through the heather towards them. He patted his hand over the ground, grasping for the hilt of his sword, all the while keeping his eyes up.

Something rushed at him from the side, leaping towards him. It was giant, wolf-like, all teeth and claws, fur spiked in a black silhouette against the moon. Aiden's fingers tightened around his sword, but it was too late. Suddenly a flash of gold came from above, a burst of air knocking him to the ground. Iolair screeched, wings fully spread, feathers splayed, claws tearing into the thing on the ground. It yowled and squirmed, snapping at her. But Iolair flapped out of reach and raked her talons once more through its fur. There was a yelp and a high pitched whine and the shadowy thing darted away into the heather. Iolair followed it a few paces, screeching into the night after it.

"What was that?"

Aiden jumped at Erin's voice directly behind him.

"Are you alright?" said Falkor.

Aiden turned, hoping they could not see the shakiness in his limbs. "I'm fine," he said, but Falkor's attention was fixed on Erin.

Iolair swooped back into camp and began wiping her claws on the ground. There was blood and fur caught in them.

"A Cu-Sidhe," said the Eagle. "Hoping for an easy meal no doubt. But I taught it a lesson. It should have known better than to attack with an Eagle present."

"Thank you," said Aiden, smiling at Iolair.

Falkor frowned. "We all need to be more vigilant. It must have been following us for a while."

Aiden rubbed his arms. So there had been something watching them today.

"We should start putting runic wards around our camp each night," said Falkor. "I'll cast some now and then we should all go back to sleep."

"Is it safe?" said Erin, pulling her blanket closer around her shoulders.

"If it comes back I will finish it," said Iolair. "You have nothing to fear."

They all settled back down, but even with Falkor's runic wards and Iolair keeping watch, it took Aiden some time before he finally drifted into sleep.

The next morning Falkor woke them early and they set off even before the sun was fully above the horizon. Their path led them through the heather down off the ridge. They rode in silence, in single file, with Falkor leading and Aiden bringing up the rear. Although it would take longer, they gave the mountain loch a wide berth. Falkor warned that it was Kelpie territory and Aiden's imagination ran wild, remembering all the old stories of water horses that dragged their unwitting victims to the bottom of their loch to drown. After last night's incident Aiden no longer felt confident in dismissing his fears. He kept looking back over his shoulder, expecting to see a black shape waiting to lure them back.

Only when the loch was some miles behind them did Aiden nudge his horse forwards and draw alongside Erin. She glanced sideways at him, twisting a strand of her horse's mane around her fingers. She wore her green cloak, the one that had first drawn Aiden's attention to her. The material rippled around her, making her fade in and out of view. Sometimes in the corner of his eye she seemed to disappear altogether. It was this cloak that had brought him here, thought Aiden. Without it he would never have followed her and been caught in the fire.

"Where did you get your cloak?" Aiden said.

She turned to him with a small, puzzled laugh. "This old thing?" she said, taking the edge of the cloak and holding it out to flap in the wind. Runes sparkled in the cloth.

Aiden moved closer, grabbing the cloth between his fingers. "Either you don't know it's worth or you are trying to hide it," he said. "My father is a cloakmaker. I know this is no ordinary cloak."

She gave a sideways smile and tugged the material out of his hand. "And I know it takes no ordinary person to see that this is not an ordinary cloak. How is it that you see the runes so easily?"

Aiden shrugged. "I just do."

"But who taught you? Someone must have taught you." She frowned at him.

Aiden shook his head. "I taught myself."

Erin raised her eyebrows. "Does Falkor know that?" she asked in a low voice.

"Yes," said Aiden. "Whether he chooses to believe it is up to him." Aiden stopped then at the wide-eyed look of disbelief on her face. "What? Don't you believe me?"

"I do," she said, smiling. "It's just funny that you're here because Falkor needs someone else who's good at magic and yet you must be the only person in the country who taught themselves. I'm surprised he trusts you."

Aiden could think of nothing to say. When he thought about it like that, it really did not make sense for him to be here. So why had Falkor brought him? Did the wizard really trust him? But he must or why else bring him? Aiden's thoughts ran in circles, so he pushed them away and turned back to Erin.

"You still haven't told me where you got the cloak from."

Erin turned, looking out across the horizon. "It was a present."

Aiden waited for her to explain further, but instead she fell silent. He frowned. Last night she had been so open with him, but now she was closed off again. He could not figure her out.

At midday they stopped again and Falkor got out the practice staffs. Aiden and Erin faced each other. For the first few thrusts and parries the wooden staffs clacked resonantly against each other. Aiden met each of her blows, but he knew that she was only warming up. The next swing cracked across his ribs and he bit back a gasp of pain. Erin smiled at him. Aiden gritted his teeth and lunged back at her, but she danced away and flicked out her arm, sending his staff sailing out of his hands.

"You need to anticipate what she's going to do," said Falkor.

Aiden gave a futile laugh. "That's easy for you to say. I'd like to see you fight her."

"Very well then," said Falkor. He held out his hand for the staff. Aiden passed it to him.

Erin raised her own staff in readiness. She seemed undaunted. Without warning they began to spar, thrusting and blocking, ducking and weaving, their feet constantly on the move, circling and circling. Their staffs were a blur of motion, swirling through the air. Aiden took an involuntary step back as their swings came closer to him. He marvelled at their grace and at their deadly precision. Then Falkor twisted his staff around Erin's, rapping her hard across the knuckles and ended the match with the point of his staff at her throat.

"I'll never be that good," said Aiden with a laugh.

Falkor raised an eyebrow at him. "I don't expect you to be. Not yet. That kind of skill doesn't come from a few days of rushed training."

Aiden folded his arms. "Well years of practice are not going to do me any good right now."

Iolair ruffled her wings. "Fight with magic," said the Eagle.

The beginnings of a smile formed on Aiden's face. Why had he not thought of that before? Now that he had, he could see the runes forming in his mind and how to use them along with the sword.

Falkor shook his head. "Fighting with magic is a complex skill that only a few ever master."

Aiden frowned. "I could do it. Surely magic, like sword fighting, is only instinct. But magic is an instinct I have."

Falkor was silent, his grey eyes sweeping over Aiden.

"I think he could do it," said Iolair.

Falkor glanced at the Eagle, shaking his head. "You might as well try. But don't overdo it, else you'll use up all your energy."

Aiden took up his staff again and faced Erin. His mind was racing. The runes and the moves had seemed so clear a minute ago, but now he did not know where to start. He shifted from foot to foot. It's just instinct, he thought, so don't think too much. The first rune came to mind: Fearn, the shield. He did not bother to draw it but held the mark in his mind and let its power flow through him. Erin was quick to attack, catching Aiden off guard, but her staff glanced harmlessly off an invisible barrier before Aiden had even raised his own staff in defence.

"That's cheating," she exclaimed.

Aiden grinned. "Since when have there been rules to cheat?"

Erin's look of indignation changed to one of determination. She attacked again and their staffs met with a crack. Aiden used the speed of Peith to dodge Erin's next swing and then put the strength of Dair into his own. Erin took a step back, disconcerted. They circled each other a few times, catching their breath.

"You never draw the runes," said Erin, "and yet clearly you're using them."

Aiden shrugged. "Maybe I don't need to."

Falkor frowned and narrowed his eyes, but Aiden ignored him. He was not going to let the wizard distract him. This time Aiden took the offensive using Nuin the spear to break through Erin's defences. But Erin sidestepped unexpectedly and whipped her staff into Aiden's side. Pain smacked across his ribs and in the following moment of confusion Erin hit him three more times. Aiden grimaced. While he had been focusing on other runes, Fearn, the shield, had slipped from his mind. He would have to work on that.

"That's enough for now," Falkor called, glancing over to the horizon. "I think it's time we were moving on again."

Aiden and Erin packed their staffs away and prepared to ride.

"You did better with the runes," Erin called over.

"Yes," said Falkor, "but when you lost control of the magic it all went wrong. Few people can fight well with magic and even fewer totally rely on it. Beware that your strength does not become your weakness."

Aiden nodded, silently accepting both compliments and warnings.

They rode hard for the rest of the day, following a stream across the moorlands. That night when they camped, they could see the edge of the moor disappearing into a new forest of great beech and oak trees. Falkor set the watches and although he still did not assign one to her, Erin stayed up with Aiden on his watch and they spoke quietly until it was time to wake Iolair.

The next day they left the moors behind and entered the forest, following a grassy path through oak and beech, the horses hooves rustling through the last of the winter's fallen leaves. The land became hillier and sometimes, through breaks in the trees Aiden saw back across the moors to how far they had come. Ahead of them, beyond the forest, mountain peaks rose into the sky like sleeping stone giants.

"Cairn Ban sits on the nearest slopes," said Falkor, his voice breaking through the silence that had gathered around them all morning. "By my reckoning we'll be there before nightfall."

"What will happen tomorrow?" said Aiden, suddenly remembering why they had come. So far he had thought only of the journey and nothing beyond.

"Until we know what we face, it is difficult to make plans," said Falkor. "But I expect we will have to sneak into the old fortress."

Aiden frowned.

"Don't you have any idea of what we're facing?" said Erin.

Falkor shook his head. "The Eagle Riders thought they were going to face a mounting Brathadair army, either that or the dark wizard himself. Either way, they came here and did not come back."

Aiden shuddered. "That must have taken someone quite powerful to stop them."

"Couldn't we sneak in tonight?" said Erin.

"No," said Falkor firmly. "Night is when dark magic works best. We will go in the day because light is our ally."

They walked through the afternoon, not stopping for training now that their destination was close. The mountains grew ever closer, the forest dense with bracken and the unfolding of new green leaves. Iolair flew low with them now, weaving in and out of the trees. She *kii-ed* quietly to herself sometimes and Aiden sensed that she longed to be above the forest. Yet they did not want to announce their presence and no one wanted Iolair to meet the same fate as the Eagle Riders.

Falkor's reckoning was correct and they were within sight of Cairn Ban before the day was done. It was a fortress, perched on top of a jutting crag, nigh on inaccessible. There was one long road winding up the mountainside, but even that Aiden struggled to see through the rocks. They made camp at the foot of the mountain, hiding themselves amongst some boulders and a scattering of trees. Iolair landed silently beside them.

"I do not like that place," said Iolair, gazing up at the fortress on the crag. "There is a shadow over it."

Falkor nodded. "It has been like that for over a hundred years, ever since Sorcier first took over the place. After he was defeated, the Kings of Teraan abandoned it. What else do your keen eyes see?"

Iolair glanced back up at the fortress. "It is strange," she said. "It is a ruin, deserted, empty. I see no signs of life. No people, no fires, no tracks, not even signs of a battle. I would say there was no one there but for the shadow over the place. You say it has been this way for many years, but my gut tells me that whatever evil was once there has not gone away."

"What about the Brathadair army?" Erin whispered.

"Maybe they've moved on," said Aiden.

"Or maybe there never was one," said Falkor, stroking his chin. "Maybe it was all a ruse to draw out the Eagle Riders. To make sure they all came."

"Are the Eagle Riders definitely there?" said Erin.

Falkor rubbed his chin again and spoke as if to himself. "They must be hidden inside. And we must go in blind."

"What's the plan then?" said Aiden.

"We enter the fortress," said Falkor. "We need to know if the Riders are there or not. Iolair, do you see anywhere where the Eagles might be being kept?"

The Eagle ruffled her feathers. "There aren't many entrances big enough for birds of their size. I could probably narrow it down to a few possible locations."

"Good," said Falkor. He turned back to Aiden. "There are two main ways into the fortress. The most obvious is the road which goes straight to the centre, but there is also a small mountain path that enters higher up the hill. Tomorrow I shall take the road with Iolair above to guide me to the places where the Eagles may be. Aiden, you will take the mountain path and sneak into the main fortress. Your mission will be to scout the buildings for signs of anything suspicious. If you encounter the enemy do not engage them unless absolutely necessary. Is that clear?"

Aiden nodded.

Erin cleared her throat and folded her arms. "You've not mentioned me in any of your plans."

Falkor gazed coolly at her. "That's because you're not coming."

"What?" Erin spluttered, advancing upon the wizard. "I came all this way to help you and now you won't let me."

"I never said I was going to," said Falkor. "And you promised to do as I said."

"No," said Erin, shaking her head. "If you were never going to let me help, then why did you let me come?"

"If you weren't here where I could keep an eye on you, then you would be somewhere else doing something reckless." A hard edge came into the wizard's voice. "You could be killed—very easily. I think the burning building proved that."

Erin flinched visibly at his words. Aiden felt a pang of sorrow for her.

"Maybe I don't care if I die," said Erin, glaring at him.

Falkor gazed back at her, unflinching. His grey eyes seemed to soften. "Well I do. So you're not going into that fortress. You will stay here until we return. And if we do not return you will ride back to Torelia and tell them that we are not coming back."

Aiden gulped. He was only now beginning to realise just how very alone they were.

"Do you understand?" said Falkor. He walked forward and gripped Erin by her shoulders.

She nodded once, reluctantly.

Falkor let her go, turning to Aiden. "Rest well tonight. At dawn we enter the fortress."

25. Searching for Courage

Branwyn stoked the ashes in the campfire, her arm heavy after the afternoon's sparring.

"Someone else can cook tonight Branwyn," said Signy. "Or we could all go down to the kitchens."

Branwyn shook her head. "It's ok. I like to cook." It was the one thing she was good at, the one thing she could do without someone else having to instruct her. And it reminded her of home.

She made stew from the rabbits Andor had caught that morning and dished it out into bowls. It was a quiet meal time. No one said it, but they were all wondering what kept Tristan so long. Branwyn's eyes flicked to his uneaten plate of food. Whenever she thought of him, a strange mixture of anticipation and fear bubbled inside her. She wished he would hurry back, but at the same time she was afraid of what news he would bring.

Next to her, Andor waved his hand about in the air in odd, jerky movements.

"What are you doing?" said Branwyn.

"Practicing runes," said Andor, without shifting his gaze, "but I can't remember how to draw Coll."

"I don't know," she replied. "I only know the names. Isn't that one for wisdom? Do you really think you'll need it?"

Andor stopped and turned to frown at her. "They're all important Branwyn. But I suppose I could come back to it."

He started again but with a different shape. This time the rune came to light. Andor smiled, throwing it in her face. Branwyn's hair whipped back in a sharp gust of wind.

"Eadha," said Andor, grinning.

"Hey," Branwyn protested. "Careful. What if you didn't have it under control?"

"I did, didn't I?" said Andor, the smile vanishing from his face.

"Yes," said Branwyn, with a pang of guilt. She should not scold him. It was good to see him focused on something positive, unlike the anxious thoughts that seemed to plague her own mind. "Just don't throw it in my face again, alright?"

"Alright," said Andor, the grin creeping back onto his face.

Darkness grew deeper around them. Andor continued to draw runes, creating flashes of light in the air. Across the fire, Rook and Signy sat playing an old battered board game. Branwyn wondered what game it was, but her mind was too full to contemplate joining them.

Some time later Tristan appeared through the trees, a lantern bobbing in his hand. His steps were heavy, his injured leg dragging as he approached the fire and slumped down into a seat. His eyes were dark and hooded by a frown. Andor dropped the rune he was casting, and Rook and Signy looked up, game forgotten. All eyes watched him expectantly. Branwyn almost did not want to know what had made his usually carefree face so lined with worry. He met their gazes but did not smile.

"The Brathadair are coming... here," Tristan said.

Silence met his remark. Panic clutched at Branwyn. She had been right to be afraid.

"But how do they know where we are?" said Rook in disbelief. "Torelia is a secret refuge. Very few know of its existence, let alone where to find it."

"All it takes is one traitor," said Signy.

Tristan held up his hands and shook his head. "Somehow they know or they've learned enough to know the right place to look. Whichever it is, it doesn't change the fact that the Brathadair army is moving steadily towards us. It will be here in a matter of days. Maybe less."

"I thought we were safe here?" Branwyn said, the words choking in her throat. Andor shuffled closer to her side and hooked his arm around hers.

Tristan's brow creased and she saw sadness and regret in his eyes as he looked at her. "I thought so too, but now it looks like we must fight."

"Can't we go somewhere else?" said Andor.

"We can't leave Torelia until the Princess returns from her mission," said Tristan. "And in truth we have few places left to run to."

Branwyn drew her knees up to her chest and tried to still the trembling in her limbs. Why could they not be left in peace?

"So tomorrow we prepare for battle," said Rook. It was not a question. Branwyn took a deep breath. The thought of battle terrified her. She glanced at Andor expecting to see fear in his eyes, instead, she saw bright and steely resolve. She tried to draw courage from him.

"Are the Eagles not back yet?" said Signy.

Tristan glanced up at the empty eyries. "They won't be back tonight," he said. "But they might be our only hope. They have gone to speak to the Fae clans living deep in the forest to the south. The Eagles think they will give us sanctuary."

"We have not had dealings with the Fae for many years," said Rook, frowning. "What makes you think they will heed us now?"

Tristan shrugged. "I don't know, but I trust the Eagles."

No one disputed that.

Rook and Signy said goodnight, and Branwyn urged Andor

to his bed, even though she did not think she could sleep herself. She sat up with Tristan while he ate and waited for him to tell her it was not true—that the Brathadair were not really coming—but the silence just stretched out around them. Tristan glanced at her occasionally and she thought he was going to speak, but he never did. Eventually Tristan stood and kicked earth over the fire, dousing the flames. She squinted up at him through the sudden darkness.

"It's late. You should get some rest," said Tristan, offering her a hand.

Slowly Branwyn reached out to take it. His strong hand grasped hers and pulled her to her feet.

"I'm sorry you're caught up in all this," said Tristan quietly. "You don't deserve it."

Branwyn gave a tiny nod. His words seemed to bring her fears alive. She felt shaky inside, like she might cry. She held herself together and climbed the spiral stair up to the cabins. In her room she lay down on her bed and stared at the ceiling. How was she to survive a battle? She could barely swing a practice sword. Tears threatened and she screwed up her eyes. She would not let this defeat her. Tomorrow she would learn to fight, no matter how much she hated it.

When morning came Branwyn felt stronger. All was not yet lost. The Eagles might return with news of the Fae or the Princess might return with wizards to fight alongside them. Or she even dared to hope that Aiden might come back with the Eagle Riders themselves. And she would learn to defend herself. There was still time. All was not yet lost, she told herself again.

Branwyn hurried along the cliff top to the training grounds with Rook, Signy, Andor, and Tristan. The clearing was already busy with soldiers drilling. The clang of swords filled the air. Weapons were being handed out and carted off to the north forest where the perimeter was being fortified. Branwyn set to work alongside Signy, attaching fletching to arrows and stacking them in bundles ready to be taken to the perimeter. Rook and Andor soon left for the north forest themselves. Branwyn almost shouted Andor back, but she stopped herself. She was afraid to let him out of her sight in case she did not see him again, but this was something she could not protect him from. And Rook would look after him like he always did. She was starting to rely on him to look out for Andor, to teach him the things she was unable to. Rook was a good man and she wondered what they had done to deserve such kindness from him.

Across the clearing she watched Tristan leading drills with Odmund. Sometimes he stood to the side and shouted instructions to the men, or sometimes he fought one-on-one with an opponent. She watched as closely as she could while still focusing on her work, trying to understand what he did to disarm the other man or to avoid being hit. His movements were so swift and precise. How did he do it? She flinched as Tristan's opponent landed a hit on him. He brushed it off and in two quick moves had disarmed the man. Branwyn gulped. She knew she would have to learn to take a hit and keep going. It was not going to be easy.

"Need a break?" said Signy, standing and flexing her fingers.

"Oh," said Branwyn, realising that she had completely abandoned the task at hand.

"Ever shot with a bow before?" Signy asked, picking one up from the pile next to her.

Branwyn shook her head. Signy passed the bow to her and gave her a string to go with it.

"Hook one end over the bottom," she explained. "Then wedge it under your foot and bend it until you can hook the other end."

Branwyn did as instructed and was surprised at how tough the wood was. It took some effort to bend it and then, even under all that pressure, it did not snap. Signy watched from a distance, offering no help. Branwyn scowled a bit at first, but when she finally managed to string the bow herself she was grateful that Signy had not interfered. She smiled to herself, realising that Signy was looking out for her, just as Rook was looking out for Andor. They took a bundle of arrows over to the targets set up between the trees.

"Take the bow in your hand and place an arrow on top," said Signy. She adjusted Branwyn's grip until she was happy. "Now hold the arrow in place and lift the bow to aim."

Branwyn lifted it, pulled back the string and frowned as the arrow dropped off to one side.

"Try again," said Signy, smiling.

Branwyn adjusted her stance until the arrow stayed pointed firmly at the target. She wanted to do well, if only to show Signy that her faith in her was not unfounded.

"Draw the string back to your face and sight down the arrow," said Signy.

Branwyn pulled back the string, her arms wobbling with the strain. Quickly she sighted the target and loosed her arrow. She laughed as it flew straight and embedded itself in the straw bag.

Signy clapped. "Are you sure you've never done this before?"

"I think that was beginner's luck," said Branwyn.

She loosed a few more arrows, all of which sailed past the target and into the trees behind. Signy gave her tips on how to keep her aim true and slowly but surely her arrows began to hit the target again. As she practiced an ache grew in her arms, but she did not want to stop. She had found her rhythm and her confidence grew with every arrow that hit the target. She was so focused that she almost forgot about the impending battle.

"You're a natural." Tristan's voice came suddenly from behind, making her jump.

Branwyn smiled shyly, hoping that the heat in her cheeks was not becoming visible.

"Ready to practice with another kind of weapon?" Tristan asked, holding up the dreaded practice sword.

Branwyn's smile faded, but she nodded. She held out the bow to Signy, but the Feather Guard shook her head.

"Keep it. It's yours now."

Branwyn slung it over her shoulder and followed Tristan back to the main training ground. He steered her out into the midst of the sparring. Despite the bow she carried proudly on her shoulder, Branwyn hunched into herself, her confidence already slipping. She flinched back from the flailing blades that swung far too close for comfort, but Tristan held her steady. He led her beyond the main clearing and further into the trees where they found a space away from the rest of the soldiers. Branwyn was glad there would be no witnesses to her failings. Tristan handed her the wooden sword, rolled up his shirt sleeves and faced her.

"Aren't you tired?" she asked him, carefully setting her bow aside.

He replied with a reproachful smile. "Stop stalling."

She pursed her lips and raised her sword, ready. He came at her quickly and she tried not to think too much as she used her sword to block his blows. She caught each swing but it jarred down her whole arm.

"Keep your arm straight and strong," said Tristan. "Trust that you are not going to get hit."

"I do," she said. But she knew it was Tristan she trusted not to hurt her, rather than any faith in her own skill.

Tristan increased the pace of his blows, not stopping until she missed one. He gave her only a moment to reorientate herself before starting again. She managed to keep pace for a time, but soon her arm was straining and her breath rasped in her throat. She missed a swing and Tristan's sword glanced off her side. Branwyn cried out, more from shock than pain. She clutched her side and backed away. She wanted to stop, but Tristan's sharp voice urged her on. "In battle you can't just stop if you get hit."

Scowling, she got back into position.

Tristan watched her intently. "What are you waiting for?" he asked, his voice stern, almost angry. "I just hit you, so hit me back."

Branwyn hesitated. This was what she hated about fighting. She did not want to hurt anyone and it rankled her that her survival now depended on doing just that.

Tristan seemed oblivious to her internal dilemmas. A frown creased his face. He was annoyed at her. "If your life is on the line, are you just going to stand there and let them take it?"

Branwyn sensed something in his voice that she had not picked up before. Something deeper than anger. Desperation? It was like he needed her to learn this as much as she needed to herself. He had promised Aiden he would protect her. Branwyn felt the panic arise in her throat again. If he wanted her to learn this badly, then he must truly believe that there was a chance she would find herself in the middle of a battle, with no one to protect her but herself.

"Come on," said Tristan, holding his arms wide.

She took a deep breath and swung at him. He batted her away easily.

"Keep going," Tristan urged.

She tried again and again, but every time he knocked her away, almost sending the wooden sword flying from her grasp. Now she was starting to feel angry. Why did he keep pushing her? He cared so much about keeping his promise to Aiden to keep her safe, that he did not care about what she felt.

"Learn from your mistakes," said Tristan. "Look for my weak spots."

This time she swung from a different angle, but it made no difference. He knocked her back. Before he could speak she sliced at his side, but he was ready. Her sword spun from her hand and landed on the ground with a thud. With an exasperated sigh, she bent to retrieve it.

"The reason you're getting nowhere is that you're not really trying to hit me," Tristan said, his voice strained. "You're trying to hit my sword. You're not going to incapacitate your enemy by doing that."

"Maybe I don't want to incapacitate anyone," she said. The words conjured up gruesome pictures in her mind.

"And if it's that or die?" he said. His face was stern and she could sense his desperation just below the surface.

Branwyn's chest felt tight. She was going to cry. Not now, she thought.

"Maybe this is easy for you," said Branwyn. "You've grown up amongst Eagle Riders and wizards and soldiers, but me... I'm a baker! I don't know how to fight. I don't even really want to know. All I want is to have my family back and go home." Silent tears streamed down her cheeks, but she no longer seemed to care. "You think this is helping? It's not. You're just making me more scared. I know you made a promise to Aiden... but don't you care about how I feel?" She took her wooden sword and threw it at his feet. "I'm done," she said, turning her back and walking away as quickly as she could.

Before she had taken more than a few steps his hand on her arm stopped her, roughly pulling her back to face him.

"How could you think that?" said Tristan, his eyes soft and sad.

Before she realised what was happening, he took her face in his hands and pressed his lips to hers. Branwyn took an involuntary step back, even as she felt a jolt of energy tingling from her head to her toes.

"What are you doing?" she said, the words slipping out.

Tristan shook his head slowly, a smile of disbelief on his face. "Do you really think the only reason I don't want you to die, is so that I don't have to break my promise to Aiden?"

Branwyn looked down at the ground, a flush of heat rising in her cheeks. It dawned on her then, suddenly, all his previous actions taking on new meaning. He did not want her to die, simply because he did not want her to die. He liked her. He liked her a lot.

"I didn't realise," she said, lifting her eyes back to look at him again. There was a flutter in her stomach, but she took a step back towards him. She had no idea what would happen, but he followed her lead and stepped towards her, coming closer, putting his arms around her. He pulled her close and she timidly put her hands round his waist. Tristan hesitated. When Branwyn did not pull away he leaned down and kissed her again.

Branwyn forgot about everything else. All she knew was his closeness, his arms wrapped around her like a shield. Her tears dried into sticky trails across her cheeks. She felt like she was floating and only Tristan's tight grip on her kept her feet on the ground. For a moment, Branwyn felt completely happy and completely safe. She wanted it to last forever. Then her mind seemed to catch up with her and she pulled her head back, feeling elated and at the same time a little awkward.

Tristan grinned down at her. "At least if I die in battle I'll have no regrets."

Branwyn stepped back from him. "Tristan, don't joke about that," she said, frowning deeply.

"I'm sorry," he said. "You know I don't find it easy either. I want my family back too and I wish as much as you do that we could avoid a battle."

Branwyn sighed. "I'm afraid."

Tristan pulled her into a hug, his strong arms once more wrapping around her. She leaned her head on his chest and wished that he would never let go. "Branwyn," he said gently. "I'm not going to let anything happen to you."

She held him tighter.

"It's alright to be afraid," Tristan said after a moment. "There can be no courage without fear. That's what my Dad told me a long time ago."

He smiled down at her and Branwyn found that she could not hold her frown for long. Then he grinned and reached down to the ground, picking up the wooden sword she had thrown at his feet.

"Another round?" said Tristan, holding her sword to her, hilt first. "Or have you had enough for today?"

Branwyn shook her head, wiped her eyes and took the sword.

They sparred for a while longer. Branwyn still got nowhere close to hitting Tristan, but it did not fill her with dread as it had before. She would not be alone. Tristan would look after her. As they practiced she caught his eye and could not help the smile that spread across her face. That was when he knocked her weapon from her hand.

"Don't get distracted," said Tristan, grinning.

But Branwyn could not help it. When he smiled like that she did not want to look anywhere else.

She tried to defend herself with bare hands, reaching to grab Tristan's practice sword and wrest it from his grasp. But he was too strong and pulled her in to grab her around the waist and swing her round.

"You two seem far too happy for the news I've got."

Branwyn froze and her cheeks blushed bright red. Rook watched them, eyebrows raised. How long had he been there? He seemed neither angry nor surprised.

"What's happened?" said Tristan, growing instantly serious, letting go of Branwyn but still standing close enough that their shoulders were brushing.

"The first Brathadair scouts have been spotted outside the perimeter wall," said Rook.

With a sickening lurch Branwyn remembered why she was

learning to fight. It was not a game, nor was it a way to spend time with Tristan. There really was a battle coming.

"Signy has taken Andor back to the cabins," said Rook. "You should go join them Branwyn."

She glanced at Tristan, unsure. The last thing she wanted was to leave him. Gently he took her hand.

"Go," he said. "I'll be back before morning."

Before morning? It was not even night yet. "Will you be fighting?" she asked anxiously.

"Hopefully not yet," Tristan replied. "But we need to make sure things are ready. You'll be fine."

Her hand slipped from his and he followed Rook away, back to the main clearing where Odmund and all the other soldiers would still be training. Branwyn found herself standing alone. Her thoughts were all over the place. One moment she worried about the battle, next she thought about Tristan and excitement bubbled inside her. Then she remembered where he was and her worry returned all over again. All the fears she thought Tristan had banished came rushing back, except worse, because now she had him to worry about too. And yet at the same time, she remembered the kiss and there was a skip in her heartbeat that no fear could ever cause.

26. Cairn Ban

The deserted fortress of Cairn Ban towered above Aiden in the grey light of dawn. He paused, his breath clouding in front of his face in the cold. After more than an hour's climbing, the light of the rising sun was finally streaming over the mountaintops, but the old fortress itself was still in shadow. The mountain path, a steep and narrow thread of a trail, twisted away amongst the scree below. Aiden glanced up. There was just one last steep scramble before the mountain met the hewn stone of the fortress walls.

The walls were grey stone, grey as the mountains themselves, and had been built so that they formed a seamless barrier with the rock face of the cliffs above. Crenellated battlements cut across the sky, but Aiden could see nothing of what awaited within. Silence lay heavy about him, only trails of wind whispered through the stones. The fortress brooded over the valley and Aiden shivered as he sensed the sinister presence Iolair had spoken of the night before.

Aiden looked up to the lightening sky. There was Iolair's outline wheeling above the battlements. She would have located the entrances by now and would be going to meet Falkor at the front gate. Their vague plan was beginning to play out, but once inside the fortress anything could happen. Would they really be able to help? Would the Eagle Riders even be there? Aiden frowned at the bare walls of his destination. Would he even find this door

Falkor had promised? And if he did would it even still open? It felt like this tiny mountain path had barely been trodden in the last hundred years.

Only one way to find out, Aiden thought. He lifted a foot and continued his climb.

A trickle of stones tumbled below him and Aiden froze. Had he loosened something while climbing or was there someone else down there? He crouched low and peered back down the path, sketching Ailm, the seer, and bringing the rune to his eye. For a moment the path seemed empty—this sinister presence was really playing on his nerves—but then he caught sight of a familiar green hood and breathed out in relief. He should have known that Erin would not bow easily to Falkor's plan. Her pointed silence this morning and deep frown as she stood stiffly, arms folded, had not spoken of one content at being left behind.

Aiden waited until she had climbed closer and then quietly called down, "I can see you."

Erin looked up at him, pulling her hood down, the glowing runes fading from its surface. "Took you long enough," she said, panting between words. She scrambled up the last bit of path and stopped at his side.

"If Falkor knew you were here..." said Aiden, raising his eyebrows and glancing towards the far off road, as if somehow the wizard could see them.

Erin cut him off, hands on hips. "I'm going to prove to Falkor that I'm just as capable and useful as you are. And don't bother arguing because I'm coming whether you like it or not."

Aiden paused, shaking his head in resignation. "Fine, but when we get back Falkor's wrath is on your head." He started back up the hill before he could worry about the wisdom of his decision. Erin's footsteps echoed his and he could imagine a smug smile playing across her lips.

It took them a few more minutes to reach the top of the path where a tiny ledge levelled out and allowed Aiden and Erin to stand and peer down the dizzying drop. The old walls of the fortress, built from solid stone blocks, jutted straight out of the mountainside forming sheer cliffs above and below. They must have been at least as tall as the abandoned tower back in Teraan City. Aiden placed his palm on the grey face of the wall, running his fingers along the crack between two stones. Despite almost one hundred years of abandonment they showed no signs of crumbling.

Aiden and Erin edged further along the ledge. They picked their way through tumbled stone, the silence pressing down upon them. Even the wind seemed to have stilled in the lee of the walls. In places rock falls had pulled away parts of the path and Aiden and Erin had to walk so close to the walls it was as if the fortress was trying to push them back down the mountainside. The only movement or noise was their own and yet it felt like they were being watched.

Further along the path they found the small doorway: a narrow archway cut into the rock between the natural cliff and the man made walls. A tumble of loose stones obscured the entranceway. Aiden hesitated, scanning the sheer cliffs and towering walls that cast the little archway into deep shadow. It would be an easy place to set a trap and they were about to walk straight into it.

"Do you think we can get through?" Erin whispered beside him, the sound of her voice making him jump.

Aiden glanced at her. "That's not what I'm worried about." He took a small step forward.

Erin reached out a hand to stop him. "You think it's a trap?"

"There's only one way to find out," Aiden whispered, with a shrug. "Wait here and keep watch. I'll check it out."

A slight frown creased Erin's brow, but she dropped her hand and let him go. Aiden turned back towards the door. His shoulders tensed, eyes straining upwards as he neared the enclosed rock-filled archway. He clambered up onto the stones, freezing momentarily as they shifted beneath his feet. But the crunching of stone was the only noise. Nothing else moved. No enemies jumped out to attack him. Aiden let out a long breath.

He reached the outer face of the archway. Scree filled it and he ducked his head so as not to hit the roof of the arch. Once inside, the loose stone sloped down until it came to rest against an old wooden door. The door was splintered and crooked, lighter patches filtering through from the other side. Had the Eagle Riders tried to come this way or had they just flown over the battlements?

Aiden climbed down to the door and pushed at it. Stones shifted under his feet as it scraped open. He winced and froze as the sound echoed around the archway. He hoped there was no one on the other side to hear. After long seconds of silence and stillness he pushed the door a little further. Stones trickled and then it jammed. Aiden kicked at it, but it would not budge. It would have to do.

He peeked through the gap to a tiny courtyard beyond, enclosed on all sides by tall grey walls and the mountain face. It was empty. More tumbled stone was piled up against the door on the other side. Had someone put it there on purpose, to stop people from using this entrance? Or maybe a hundred years of rockfalls had collected in this corner. Either way the door would not be moving any further. Luckily the gap was probably big enough to squeeze through.

Aiden turned to beckon Erin and jumped at the sight of her face peering down after him.

"What happened to keeping watch?" said Aiden.

"If there's anything to watch it's going to come through that door," said Erin.

"Well that's encouraging," Aiden murmured to himself, turning back to the door. He beckoned Erin after him, forming Peith, the thunderbolt in his other hand.

"We go quick," Aiden whispered.

Erin nodded.

Before he could let himself think, Aiden pushed through the gap in the door. Erin followed so closely she clipped his heels with her boots and they both stumbled into the grey courtyard. Then, almost as if they had triggered something, a great rumble sounded from behind them. They both froze and Erin clutched at Aiden's arm, her eyes wide.

After a moment, when it seemed clear that the noise had not brought any enemies upon them, Aiden carefully stepped back towards the door. The space where they had just climbed through was filled again by stone.

"It's blocked," he said, pushing against the old wood. It gave a little under his touch but was quickly followed by the crunching of more scree falling into the gap. "I don't think we'll get back out this way," Aiden whispered.

Erin nodded, face pale. Did she suddenly regret her decision to come? Or did she now realise just what it meant to come?

"Let's go," said Aiden. He licked dry lips, taking a step out of the shelter of the archway. Stone slabs paved the grey courtyard, moss and other small plants growing up through the cracks. A few rocks had tumbled beyond the doorway, but otherwise the courtyard was empty.

Erin followed, close enough that their arms were brushing. She kept one hand on the hilt of her sword. Aiden held Peith, the thunderbolt, bright in his hand and led the way across the courtyard. On the far side a short, steep flight of stairs led under the thick inner wall of the fortress and opened onto a bigger citadel where the castle and its buildings sat pale in the morning light.

All was silent and it scared Aiden far more than a horde of soldiers would have. His heart beat loudly in his ears as if it echoed around the empty citadel.

"Where to?" Erin whispered at his shoulder.

Aiden shrugged. "The plan was to get inside and look around."

"So we just pick a door?"

"Do you have any better ideas?" said Aiden, turning back to her.

Now Erin shrugged. "I just thought it might have been more obvious. I mean, shouldn't there be more signs of... of a battle or something?"

"You would think so..." Aiden rubbed his arms, goosebumps prickling under his sleeves. Something was not right here.

"If the Eagle Riders are prisoners here, where are the guards?" said Erin. She ran a hand over the pommel of her sword.

Aiden gazed about the citadel. Wind whispered through the bare stone. "Maybe they're not here anymore. Maybe they never came in the first place. Or maybe they were here and now..." No, he would not think it.

"Maybe they're dead," said Erin quietly.

Aiden's head whipped round sharply and he glared at her.

Erin held up her hands. "That's what you were going to say, wasn't it."

Aiden did not answer.

"We have to admit it's a possibility," said Erin.

"What could possibly kill ten Eagle Riders without a trace?" said Aiden.

Erin bit her lip. "There's only one way to find out." She glanced across to the castle.

Aiden clenched his fists. He could not believe it. The Eagle Riders could not be dead. What hope would they have then against the Brathadair? How would he tell Tristan?

"Let's go," said Erin, nudging him. "Let's get it over with."

Aiden nodded.

They darted across the open space and flattened themselves

against the walls of the nearest building. The stone was cold, but there was more to it than that. The cold felt alive, as if the sinister presence hid within it. Aiden gulped and kept moving, shuffling along until he came to a thick oaken door. It sat ajar. Whatever awaited them lay somewhere beyond.

Aiden tried to push away the deep unease that was growing in his mind. Erin gave the tiniest of nods. Her blue eyes were wide, her knuckles white as they gripped her sword, yet she did not hesitate nor turn back. Aiden drew strength from her courage and slipped ahead through the door.

Nothing happened. A single pale beam of light shone dimly in a dark and dusty entrance hall. Two passageways led away into different parts of the castle.

"I don't think we should split up," Erin whispered, a tremor in her voice.

"No, I don't think we should," Aiden agreed.

"Which way then?"

Aiden hesitated. Either way could lead them into danger, either way could ensnare them in the trap that had caught the Eagle Riders. And if this place had killed the Riders, what chance would they have? Aiden ran a hand through his hair, his fingers shaky. Erin watched him, waiting. The choice was his.

Aiden stepped forward, then stopped. Above their heads a silvery light began to glow, getting steadily brighter. At first it was just a haze, but it began to take shape, growing wings and a tail and a beak, becoming an Eagle. It floated above them, circling their heads. Flapping its wings, it flew across the hall and into the right hand passage leaving a faint trail of silver light behind it.

Wordlessly Aiden stepped after it.

Erin caught his arm. "Can we trust it? Maybe it's part of the trap."

Aiden frowned and shook his head. "I don't know how to

explain it, but everything about this place feels bad except for that Eagle."

Erin glanced up at the silver trail, her face creasing. She turned back to him. "If you trust it, I trust you."

"I do," said Aiden. It was just like the Silver Eagle of his dreams. He was meant to follow it then and he was meant to follow it now.

Aiden moved after the Silver Eagle into the gloom of the passageway. There was no light but the silver trail glowing eerily against the stone walls. Erin walked close to him in the darkness, her shoulder brushing against his, their footsteps echoing in the shadows. The Eagle led them along the passageway, down stairs, and through a great hall with its roof partly caved in. There were many doors to choose from, but the Eagle was always waiting for them. It led them on, further into the castle, up stairs and round corners until Aiden was not sure that he would know the way out again. Where was it taking them?

At last the Silver Eagle slowed and hovered before a door. Even as they approached, it went no further. Aiden frowned at Erin, but she only shrugged. He stepped towards the door. The Eagle glowed brighter until Aiden had to squint to look at it. Then, in a voice that was both everything and nothing, it spoke one word.

"Beware."

The Eagle faded away into the grey light, leaving a bright spot in Aiden's vision. He glanced back at Erin. Her face was taut, but she nodded. Aiden stepped up to the door. It was made of thick oak, but he sensed no magic in it as he pressed his palm to the wood. He pushed it gently and was surprised when it swung open easily at his touch. He peered into the room beyond and gasped.

"What do you see?" whispered Erin, trying to peer over his shoulder.

"The Riders," said Aiden, suddenly breathless.

Erin's eyes lit up and she tried to push past him. "Come on

then. Let's get them out."

"Wait," said Aiden, grabbing her round the waist and pulling her back.

Her eyes widened and she pushed him away sharply. "What are you doing?"

Aiden frowned. "There are no guards. Don't you find that strange?"

Erin threw up her hands. "What does it matter? The Riders are right there. We can get them out."

"If the Riders are here then why haven't we seen a single enemy? Aiden looked both ways along the corridor, but there was nothing to see in the shadows, nothing to hear in the silence. He bit his lip. He may not be able to see it, but he could sense it. It was too still, too quiet.

"This is our chance," Erin whispered. "That Eagle led us here. You said you trusted it."

Aiden pressed his lips together. "I do. And it told us to beware."

Erin folded her arms and sighed. "Then what do you want to do?"

"All I'm saying is that we go careful," said Aiden.

Erin quirked an eyebrow. "After you then."

Slowly, Aiden pushed the door open further and slipped into the room beyond. It was circular with a domed roof, a ring of slit windows high up the walls letting in streaks of grey light. Around the edges the Riders were trussed up against the walls, hanging limply from the heavy chains that bound their wrists and ankles. They had been stripped of their armour, boots, and cloaks, and the tattered remains of clothes that they wore barely hid the clotted blood of half-healed wounds. A few raised their heads and squinted at the movement Aiden had caused at the door. Others just stood, faces expressionless in helpless defiance.

"They're all here," Aiden whispered. Whatever enemy held

them captive had not yet seen fit to kill them.

Arthur was chained nearby and Aiden crept over to his side and touched his arm. The Captain was much diminished since Aiden had last seen him. He was smaller, hunched, and his face was pale and sunken, streaked with blood from a cut on his forehead. Yet the eyes that opened were bright and alert and Aiden's heart surged with hope.

"Aiden," said Arthur in wonder.

"We've come to rescue you," Aiden whispered. He ran his hand along the chains, runes flaring hot under his fingers. There was strong magic in these chains, making him squirm inside. He would have to break them somehow.

"We must be quick," Arthur said. "Dageny will know by now that you are here…"

"Who's…" Aiden began, but stopped as a sudden hollow fear clouded Arthur's eyes. Aiden jumped round, but it was only Erin coming through the door.

"Is that Serineth?" Arthur whispered. "Are you mad bringing her here? If Dageny catches her—"

"What?" said Aiden, frowning, confused. "You mean Erin?"

"Yes Erin, *Serineth*, Princess of Teraan."

"He doesn't know," came Erin's voice, as if from a long way off.

Aiden swung round and stared at her, his mouth dropping open. Serineth, the Princess of Teraan, was Erin. He somehow could not reconcile the two. Erin gazed back at him, her mouth moving as if she was going to speak but could not find the words.

Arthur interrupted. "So you just let him bring you, knowing the danger you'd be in."

"I came of my own accord," said Erin defiantly, turning her gaze to the Eagle Rider Captain. "I wanted to do something real for my country."

"Serineth, you're no use to your country if you're dead," Arthur said sharply.

"And unless we have Eagle Riders to fight against the Brathadair it won't matter whether I'm dead or alive." Her stark words echoed around the room. She turned to Aiden again, her eyes softening, pleading. "I was going to tell you."

"Yeah, when?" said Aiden with a bitter laugh. His words sounded feeble and foolish. He was an idiot for not having realised sooner. How long had she spent laughing at his ignorance? He had saved her life and yet even that had not been enough for her to trust him with the truth.

"There's no time for this now," said Arthur. "You've got to get her out of here before—"

"Before what?" came a new voice. Aiden whirled round as a man swept into the room, a black cloak billowing around him. A slow smile spread across his features and his green eyes glinted wickedly. He was flanked by a dozen or so hard-eyed men filing into the room behind him.

"Run!" Arthur yelled.

Aiden darted across the room, sensing Erin, a flash of red and green running beside him, but a sudden terror gripped him and his legs stumbled and shook beneath him. Uath, dread. Aiden fought against it, focusing his mind on the image of Dair and using its strength to keep his feet moving. But behind him Erin slumped heavily to the floor, hiding her head in her hands.

Aiden's concentration slipped and Dair vanished from his mind. The clutching fingers of Gort, the binder, wound their way around his ankles and up to his knees, pulling him to the ground. He struggled, trying to crawl to the door, but one of the men came and with a twist of his hand, tightened the grip of Gort around him. Aiden was pulled to his feet, the golden bands of light holding him still.

The man dragged Aiden back and stood him next to Erin in

front of the green-eyed man. Silent tears trickled from the corners of her eyes. Part of Aiden felt sorry for her, the other part still did not know what to think. How could she have deceived him like that? How could she have been so stupid as to come? How could she say that she had trusted him?

"I can't say I'm impressed by the rescue party." The sharp green eyes of the dark wizard gazed coolly at them.

Aiden clenched his jaw and glared.

"Leave them out of this Dageny," Arthur called across. "They're just a couple of young soldiers trying to be heroes."

Dageny folded his arms. "Nevertheless, they made it all the way here." Dageny stepped forward and lifted the hair out of Erin's face. "And you remind me of someone."

Erin flinched at his touch, but she looked at the floor and said nothing.

Then Dageny laughed. "Of course. You look just like your mother. Though the Princess herself was the last person I expected to come here." He smiled again. "My dear, you do realise you've just handed me your kingdom?"

A tear dripped from Erin's cheek to the floor. Fire rose in Aiden's throat until it felt like he could not breathe. Now the Brathadair would win and it was his fault. Why had Erin lied to him? Why had he let himself be fooled?

Dageny swept forward and grabbed Erin, spinning her to face the Riders. She cried out and cowered from him, but he wrapped an arm across her shoulders, the golden twines of Gort, the binder, flowing from his fingers and twisting around her neck. Erin froze and gulped. In Dageny's other hand Nuin, the spear, was held menacing and ready.

Dageny leaned in and whispered into her ear. "You should have died in that burning building, but this I think makes up for it. Wouldn't you agree? You see, these men and women, these Eagle

Riders, have spent weeks refusing me. Even despite my more… persuasive techniques. I wonder though, how much they value your life."

Erin opened her mouth to speak, but almost instantly Dageny tightened the ring of runes around her neck. Eyes wide, Erin clutched at her neck, but her fingers brushed ineffectually through the golden light. She struggled for air.

"Well Arthur?" said Dageny. "Are you and your Riders prepared to comply with my wishes now?"

"Nothing has changed," said Arthur.

Aiden strained his neck to see where Arthur was chained to the cavern wall, to see the expression on his face, but the runes held him in position. The Eagle Rider Captain trod a dangerous line. Erin's breath came in great shaky gasps and still she fingered the runes, unable to free herself from them.

"Don't play games," said Dageny. "We both know this is Princess Serineth. The real question is how much she has to suffer before you will help me."

The green-eyed man held Nuin, the spear, to Erin's neck, pressing it into the soft flesh under her chin. Although it seemed that only light touched her, a dark stain of blood blossomed and trickled down her neck. Erin bit her lip. Her whimper of panic echoed around the chamber.

Aiden struggled against his captor. He may be angry at Erin, but he did not want to see her suffer at the hands of this wizard. Yet he too was trapped in the runes and each movement he made only tightened the grip of Gort around his body.

"Well Arthur? Will you do as I ask?" said Dageny.

Arthur stayed silent but glanced around the room at the other Riders. There was a dark moment of hesitation and Aiden was not sure that they would concede to save Erin's life. But then Leif gave the tiniest of nods and then Maire and Mathias and the others and at last Arthur said, "We'll do it."

Instantly the rune faded from Dageny's hand, but the dark red stain on Erin's neck remained. In his bonds, Aiden's body quivered with fear and anger.

Dageny turned to his men and began issuing orders. "Take the Riders down to the cave. And bring the Eagles too. We need all of them." His gaze fell on Aiden, the green eyes flicking up and down him once, disdainfully. "Tie him up somewhere out of the way, but keep watch. I suspect it won't be long until Falkor comes skulking around."

Then Dageny whirled out of the door dragging Erin with him.

A black clad soldier pulled Aiden roughly to the edge of the room, tying him to the wall with a piece of rope and stripping him of his weapons. He stood a short distance away, fingers drumming the hilt of his sword, daring Aiden to try and escape. Around them chains clanked to the ground as the Riders were released and marched from the room.

Aiden struggled against the rope. How could the Riders so meekly obey their captors? Why didn't they fight back? Surely together they were more powerful than Dageny and his acolytes? But none of them made any attempt to fight. Had they given up? Was this the overwhelming shame of defeat? Anger rose within Aiden. There must be something they could do to stop Dageny.

Aiden's hands were tied but he brought Teine, fire, into his mind, willing the rune into the air in front of him. Sweat beaded on his forehead and the twines of Gort that bound him glowed brighter, stinging his skin. But Aiden pushed through and a flickering Teine floated before him. He let the rune drop onto the rope around his hands. It burst into a brief flame, searing his skin, but in a moment the tattered remains of the rope dropped to the ground.

"No you don't," said the guard, rushing towards him.

Gort's bindings gripped Aiden still, but he mustered his

will, his resolve, and summoned Nuin, the spear, prying its point between the golden bands that held him. There was a flash as the runes fought each other and then suddenly Gort grew slack around him. Aiden shook free of the runes, seeing them fall to the ground and extinguish like ashes from a fire. Then the force of the soldier slammed him into the wall. His head rang as it bounced off the stone. The guard wrestled him to the ground, reaching for one of the chains that had moments ago held an Eagle Rider. He clamped it down on Aiden's wrist.

"See how your runes like that," whispered the guard.

Aiden put out a hand, groping for the wall, for anything to catch himself before he fell. His knees buckled. There was a heaviness in the chains that seemed to drain him instantly of all energy and he sagged against the wall. He tried to bring a rune to mind, to break free, but the image of it seared the back of his eyes so that for a moment he was left almost blind. No wonder Dageny had managed to defeat the Eagle Riders. There was magic in these chains like nothing he had ever felt before. A magic beyond the runes. Wild magic.

27. The Battle for Torelia

Tristan waited, his feet cramping as he crouched at the base of a tree. His eyes strained, searching the forest for movement. All was still, silent. Too silent.

He let his gaze travel the northern perimeter. The line of alder trees swayed lightly in the breeze, creating both a physical and a magical boundary, the magic of Fearn in their branches hiding the wooden barricade that had been hastily constructed over the last few days. Men and women of the Torelian Guard were spread along the line, some like him, crouched in the undergrowth, others in platforms in the trees, arrows resting gently on bowstrings, ready to be drawn at the first signs of trouble.

A gust of wind rattled through the trees bringing with it the faint tramp of feet, the snap of twigs, and the dull clink of armour. It was an army on the move.

"They're not even trying to be quiet," Rook whispered, his voice little more than a breath on the wind.

Tristan frowned, unease twisting in his gut.

Branches rustled from behind as Odmund crept towards them through the undergrowth.

"The Brathadair are close," said the swordmaster. "They can't know our exact location, so there is hope yet that the magic of the boundary will shield us from them. Nobody engages unless we are seen."

Tristan nodded, though how long would the boundary really shield them? It was, after all, just a big circle of trees whose magic cast a veil of secrecy over the waterfall and the surrounding forest. But that secrecy was their greatest defence and as soon as the Brathadair broke through, it would be taken from them.

A few minutes later the first black shapes of men flickered into view between the trees. They marched nearer, yet remained beyond the boundary. Tristan raised a hand to steady his men. The Brathadair drew closer until he could see the ripple of their cloaks and the glint of dappled light on their armour. Then they stopped, just on the far side of the perimeter. One soldier stepped forward and crouched down, fingers brushing the ground, all the while his eyes casting around as if looking for something but unable to see it. Tristan held himself still, barely daring to breathe.

The soldier stood, taking the bow from his shoulder and drawing back an arrow in one smooth movement. The arrow shot up, sailing over the alder wall and sticking into the ground a few feet from where Tristan crouched. For a moment the world seemed to stand still. Nothing moved, not even the wind through the trees. Then the Brathadair soldier slung the bow back over his shoulder. Tristan slowly released the breath he had been holding. They had not been found.

Suddenly the arrow burst into flame, sending out a blast of white light in an ear-rattling explosion. Tristan was thrown to the ground, his ears ringing and bright spots filling his vision. Cries pierced the air and beside him a person writhed on the ground, flames tearing through their clothes.

A thunderous shout rose from the Brathadair army, rumbling through Tristan's chest. The soldier who had fired the arrow now raised his sword and pointed it at them. A line of archers formed amidst the trees, loosing a volley of arrows. They rained down, bursting into flame as they landed, exploding all around in flashes of bright light.

Tristan rolled and ducked, cowering behind a tree. He took a deep breath, his mind racing. Then his training came flooding back to him. "Archers," he yelled, and heard his call echoed along their lines. There was the creak of many bows and the Torelian volley let fly. Across the alder wall some of the enemy slumped to the ground, but even as they did, more emerged from the forest to fill their places.

The Brathadair surged, rushing forwards like a great beast, its jaws opening ever wider. The soldiers raised swords and axes above their heads like silver spines, black cloaks billowing around them. Tristan unsheathed his sword, gripping the hilt as if he would never let go. There was a crack as the first wave of the soldiers hit the barricades. They slowed, surprise flashing in their eyes. A fierce smile crossed Tristan's lips. The magic of the alder trees had at least done its work in hiding the barricade from sight.

The rhythmic thud of axes began, hacking away at the planks and logs that spanned the gaps in the boundary. Another volley of Torelian arrows rained down and the rhythm faltered. Sharp commands drifted across to Tristan on the wind. The Brathadair pulled back.

Tristan peered around the tree he was sheltering behind. "What are they doing?" he said to Rook.

"I don't know—" Rook began.

A great boom and crack of splintering branches split the air. The Brathadair lines parted as the top of a great pine began to sway. It tilted forwards and back and forwards again. For a moment it hung poised, straining towards Torelia. A soldier with an axe chopped at its base. With a sudden, rapid accumulation of speed the tree crashed down across the boundary, dragging alder trees with it. Dust billowed, splinters flew, planks snapped. The barricade was crushed.

The Brathadair regrouped, raising shields above their heads and surging once more towards the boundary. The Torelian archers fired, but this time the arrows bounced like hailstones off the shields and armour. Another volley came from the enemy and Tristan ducked back behind his tree.

"They're almost through," said Rook, dodging an arrow.

"Swords out," Tristan shouted, his call rippling along the defences.

Tristan clutched his own sword, ready. The rain of arrows stopped abruptly and a great roar came from the enemy lines. A swathe of men poured through the gap in the alder wall, swords up, shields high. Tristan's insides turned ice cold and for a second he could not breathe. His fingers clamped around his sword hilt. This was it: where it all began and, maybe, where it all would end.

Rook clapped him on the shoulder. "Good luck." Then he was gone, sword raised against their enemy.

Tristan jumped out from behind the tree. Instantly he was in the midst of the fray. Soldiers came at him and he parried and thrust and sliced his sword, blocking attacks from one direction and then almost immediately from the next. It felt like fire shot through his veins. Alongside him Rook battered down the enemy with his longsword.

Both ways along the boundary as far as the eye could see men and women fought hand to hand, steel on steel, trading life for death. Already bodies littered the ground. How many of them had truly believed in their cause and how many had just been forced to fight to save their families and their own lives?

Another wave of Brathadair swept through the trees. Tristan stumbled back, the press of men almost unbearable. How would they ever have enough soldiers to quell the seemingly endless flow of the enemy? A Brathadair lunged towards him, but before the soldier could strike an arrow knocked him down. Tristan glanced up and saw Signy firing down from one of the sentry posts in the trees.

"Signy, don't get trapped," Rook yelled up at her.

Even as he said it, Tristan was pushed back further. There was a distant crash as another tree fell. More black shapes of the enemy scurried through the alder wall and began to flank the battlefield. If the Torelians did not move quickly they would soon be cut off from the canyon and the rest of Torelia would be vulnerable.

The horn sounded. Two blasts. But it could not be. Two blasts meant the fight had already reached the canyon. How was that even possible? Unless this fight had only been a diversion, keeping the bulk of their forces occupied at the boundary while the Brathadair struck at the heart of Torelia. Tristan felt sick. Branwyn was back there.

"Tristan." Odmund's voice carried across the battlefield and Tristan spun away from his attacker to see the swordmaster a short distance away, blades locked with a Brathadair soldier. "Take your patrol back to the canyon."

Tristan barely managed to nod as a black figure jumped at him. "Rook, Signy, gather the patrol and with me," Tristan called. Then he sliced at the legs of the man attacking him and left him struggling on the ground, jumping over him as he pelted back towards the canyon.

He dodged between the trees, shoulders tensed, waiting for an arrow to hit him in the back at any second. The trees thinned and the rushing of the river carving its passage through the canyon grew louder. Yet there was another sound too—the clash of swords.

Tristan put on a burst of speed and emerged onto the cliff top. A group of Torelians valiantly defended the cliff path and the entrance to the caves. Brathadair surrounded them, pushing them further and further back. There was a scream as someone fell from the cliff. More of the enemy raced towards them along the top of the gorge, following the river upstream, swordsmen bringing ropes to abseil down the cliffs, while archers formed lines, sending arrows not just at the men guarding the caves but also across the river into the forest at the far side. A few of the trees caught fire, spots of flame licking along their branches.

Rook, Signy, and the rest of the patrol joined Tristan at the edge of the trees. A thought flashed through Tristan's mind—if someone had told the Brathadair that Torelia was on a river, then it would not have been difficult to find the river and follow it straight to them. Maybe that was how they had been found so easily. But there was no time to think about what that meant.

"We have to stop those men," said Tristan. Some of the Brathadair had already slipped past and were gathering further upstream, nearer the waterfall. They were tying ropes to the trees, preparing to abseil down the cliff and attack the defenders from behind.

"And the archers," said Signy. "If they keep spreading fire it will be difficult to escape on the far side."

"We charge them," said Rook.

With a gulp Tristan nodded. It was the quickest, if not the safest, way to stop them. They could not risk the Brathadair making it down the cliffs... or into the caves. What would happen to Branwyn? Rook and Signy raised their swords, as did the others who had followed them. Tristan pressed his mouth into a grim line and then led the way, flying out from the trees at the unsuspecting Brathadair.

The first few men spun in surprise, some half drawing arrows on strings, others raising their bows like staffs. Tristan's sword cracked through a wooden bow and the soldier fell at his feet. More Brathadair came pounding along the cliff top. Tristan raised his sword and met the thrust of another enemy, then with a quick circular movement he brought his sword round and stabbed the man. Desperation pushed him onwards and through the mass of soldiers. He ducked a swing that went over his head, knocking the man down as he passed. Another he met with a clash, but he pushed him away with a kick. A short sprint over open ground and then the satisfying chop as his sword sliced through the first rope. It snaked away over the cliff top. A woman from the Torelian Guard followed him and began chopping through the next ropes. Screams filtered up from the canyon as the Brathadair fell.

Tristan smiled at the women over their brief victory, but moments later his smile turned to horror as an arrow flew from behind him and stuck straight through her neck. She dropped dead instantly. Tristan gulped down bile, but there was no time to stop and mourn her. He had to keep fighting. Branwyn's face flashed into his mind and he could not bear the thought of her sharing that woman's fate. With a cry he rejoined the fray.

He fought as if nothing else mattered, pouring all of his frustration and anger along his sword. What right did the Brathadair have to take over the kingdom, to take his father from him, to endanger the ones he loved? He sliced down soldiers as they came, but always there were more. A knot of Torelians and Brathadair fought at the entrance to the cliff path, pushing one way and then the other. The battle seemed to stand on a knife edge, neither side quite able to gain the advantage.

"Signy," came an anguished cry.

Tristan's head jerked up and he looked towards the cliff edge, where Rook was swinging his longsword viciously. At his feet lay the slumped form of Signy, a slow trickle of blood staining the ground around her. They were surrounded and being slowly pushed back towards the cliff. Soon they would join those who had fallen from the cliffs to the river below.

Tristan fought his way through to them, turning to stand alongside Rook, the press of the Brathadair sudden and fierce. He swerved the cut of a blade, but the single step back sent pebbles crumbling from beneath his foot. His arms flailed as he tried to keep his balance.

Rook reached across and stabbed the man who had been about to finish him off. Tristan barely had time to catch his breath before the next attacker came. He lunged forward, aware that there was now nothing between him and the fall to the river. His attacker stumbled back. Tristan dug in his heels, bracing himself, but instead of returning his blows the man turned sharply around.

The air surged with a roar and there was a frenzy of movement from upriver. Another patrol of the Torelian Guard had arrived and were slicing through the Brathadair like a scythe through wheat. Allan stood at its centre, a bloodied sword in his hand. Tristan's opponent scrambled away and minutes later the last of the Brathadair were fleeing back into the forest.

"Good work," said Allan, coming over to clap Tristan on the shoulder. "Though I'm almost certain they will be back. And in greater numbers."

Tristan nodded. "They're trying to spread us thin before mounting a full attack."

"I'm giving the order to block the cliff path and the entrances to the caves on this side," said Allan. "You should take the rest of your men to the bridge. Hold off the Brathadair for as long as you can."

"We should evacuate the caves," said Tristan. "If the Brathadair break through then they will have us trapped."

Allan hesitated. "No. I won't be the one to lose Torelia."

"Allan," Tristan began, but the Captain of the Guard held up a hand to silence him.

"Odmund and his men are still defending the perimeter?"

Tristan nodded. "I presume so."

"Then we have time yet," said Allan. "If it seems that the bridge will be lost, then send word to start the evacuation."

Tristan bit back an angry retort, but his attention was suddenly drawn to Rook lifting the injured Signy from the ground. She slumped against him, her face covered in blood, matting in her blonde hair. Tristan rushed over.

"She lives yet," said Rook, his voice choked with a mixture of hope and pain.

"Get her down to the caves," said Allan. "Aniinna is down there. We'll seal the entrances behind you."

"Rook, wait," said Tristan, catching his arm.

Rook gave the briefest of smiles. "I'll make sure Branwyn and Andor are safe."

"Thank you," said Tristan. He turned away, burying the urge to follow Rook down to the caves. He wanted to see Branwyn with his own eyes and know that she was safe, but he held himself still. He had orders and they would not win this battle unless everyone did their part. Tristan turned his face resolutely upstream, towards the bridge. He would see that Branwyn was safe by not letting the battle get to her.

Tristan and the remaining soldiers followed the strip of ground between the forest and the gorge, going upriver past the waterfall. The sun, high in the sky, beat down on them and Tristan realised it must be past midday. A wave of weariness washed over him. He blinked a few times and forced himself into a jog. He had to keep moving before exhaustion took over.

Past the waterfall the bridge came into view. Such a narrow graceful arc across the torrent of water and yet so much depended on it. As they approached, the clash of swords and cries of men grew louder again. Brathadair were amassing at the edge of the forest, each wave of attack bringing them a little closer to the river and to the bridge. Odmund and his men, now much depleted, still fought hand to hand amongst the trees. Torelian archers lined the cliff top to the south of the river, while a reserve of men waited on the bridge itself, picking off any Brathadair who made it through. The Torelian lines held yet, but they were too few against too many. It was only a matter of time.

Suddenly a great cry rose from the forest and everyone turned to look. The Brathadair raised a broad golden runic shield above their heads and the few arrows that still fell on them glanced harmlessly off it. They began to push forward, knocking down any who stood in their path. Amidst the fray Tristan heard Odmund's voice yelling, "Retreat to the bridge."

The men on the bridge readied themselves, creating a corridor where the men who had been fighting could run through to safety while they fended off any Brathadair who tried to follow. Tristan and his patrol joined the lines, his sword once more a deadly weight in his hand. As the last of the Torelians ran across they closed the gap, standing on the bridge five men abreast against the enemy.

The force of the charge sent shockwaves through the defenders and Tristan staggered back even though he was not in the front line. After the initial hit, the press of men tightened around him as the Torelians began to push back. Tristan was pinned from all sides, barely able to move. His chest squeezed in the sudden panic of being trapped, but he swallowed down his fear and joined the others, adding his weight to the fray. Slowly he felt himself take a step forward. They were pushing the Brathadair back. Another step and suddenly the crush abated, men fell apart and as soon as there was room to swing a sword again the battle began.

Tristan found himself stuck in the middle of the bridge, surrounded by his own forces, unable to reach the enemy. He was jostled from side to side as soldiers clamoured to reach the fight. On every side he could hear heavy breaths, armour clinking, swords clashing, cries of pain and anger, and below it all the rush of the river thundering towards the waterfall. The air reeked of sweat and blood and Tristan could feel his own skin sticking to the inside of his armour. It was never-ending.

Then the rain of arrows returned and they had nowhere to hide. The Torelians raised their shields but there were too many gaps. Tristan's skin prickled as all around him deadly shafts began to land. The man in front of him was hit, slumping onto him, blood streaming from his neck. They were all going to be slaughtered.

"Take out those archers," someone next to him screamed. "Or we're not going to win this battle."

From the island behind him Torelian archers began to loose arrows.

Tristan turned and recognised Bradan. His face was plastered with sweat and splatters of blood. Tristan wondered if his own face looked like that. "They're not over the river yet," said Tristan, trying to convince himself as much as the other man.

Bradan staggered under the force of an arrow on his shield. The barbed tip tore through the round metal plate. He laughed. "No they're not, but it won't be long. Especially since we've left them a nice sturdy bridge to use. You were right—we should have destroyed it before they even got here."

"No use trying to change the past now," said Tristan. "We'll just have to make sure we can hold it." He ducked as another arrow passed by his head, almost close enough to feel the feathers brush his ear. The soldier to his right was knocked into the water, the river sweeping him under the bridge and out over the waterfall.

"Pull back to the island," a voice yelled.

Tristan was carried by the wave of men, desperate to escape the rain of arrows. The Brathadair surged forward. Tristan stumbled onto the island in the centre of the river.

"Hold," the voice called again.

Tristan recognised it now as Odmund and saw the swordmaster standing by the edge of the bridge ready to meet the enemy. Tristan turned himself around and gripped his sword. He caught sight of

Rook's red-bearded face on the far side of the island. When had he returned? Had he seen Branwyn? But there was no time to reach him and ask.

They met the enemy with a cry and a clash of blades. Now the Torelians had the space to move and it was the Brathadair trapped in the confines of the bridge. Tristan's steel met steel and he sliced and cut and parried at whoever came at him. With a kick he sent one man tumbling backwards into the river where the churning water took him. But no matter how hard he fought the Brathadair kept coming. The next soldier ducked his swing and surged past him. Before he could go after him, another man was there. The battle began to spread across the island. Torelian archers from the far shore let loose another volley of arrows, but still they bounced harmlessly off the runic shield. We need an Eagle Rider, thought Tristan.

A flash of light sped through the air, coming from the trees behind the Brathadair. It hit their runic shield, crumbling it into tiny flecks of dust. A cheer rose from the Torelian shore. Tristan looked instinctively to the sky, but it was empty, not an Eagle in sight. Who then?

On the far shore stood two women with long dark hair, almost identical in appearance. With a twist of her hand one of them drew another rune and sent it flying towards the Brathadair. Soldiers scattered, half pulling back to face this new threat. The two women drew more runes in unison, trails of light flying from their fingers. They shot them at the Brathadair.

Then, feet pounding along the riverbank after them, ran two familiar figures.

Marsaili and Niamh.

The sisters rushed at the Brathadair, scything down any who got in their way. Marsaili swung her sword, swiping low, slicing high. She ducked a Brathadair sword, elbowing her attacker in the face. Niamh was close behind. Soldiers converged on her but she spun, step, strike, step, strike, until nothing but carnage littered the ground at her feet.

The Torelians rallied, their archers once more firing upon the enemy. The Brathadair faltered as a whole wave of men fell to the deadly shafts. Runes shot at them from the side in quick succession and many whirled in confusion. On the island the Torelians regrouped, men and women once more fighting their way onto the bridge.

A shout sounded from the Brathadair shore and those still surviving on the bridge made a sudden dash back to the forest. The Torelians swept forwards. Marsaili and Niamh gave chase to the edge of the trees, roaring their defiance, swords raised above their heads. An arrow shot from the forest at Marsaili, but she sidestepped and laughed, flicking her long braid over her shoulder. Tristan cheered with the rest of the Torelians.

On the island Tristan stuck the point of his sword into the ground and leant on it, breathing heavily but feeling oddly elated. He straightened as the sisters crossed the bridge towards him.

"Marsaili, Niamh," Tristan called.

"Tristan," they greeted him, clasping his arm warmly.

"You decided to join us then," said Tristan.

"Sorry we're late," said Niamh.

Marsaili wiped a hand across her brow, smearing blood across her forehead. Tristan doubted it was her own.

"We met some Brathadair in the woods on our way in," said Marsaili. "They were no match for us and our new friends." She nodded over to the side.

Tristan's gaze followed hers to the two dark haired women making their way towards them on the island.

"Freya and Anya Thronsdottir," said Niamh. "Wizards," she added, grinning.

416

"You found them then," said Tristan, feeling hopeful again. He turned suddenly to look at Marsaili and Niamh. "What about the Princess? She didn't get hurt in this fight of yours?"

"Serineth?" said Niamh. "Isn't she here?"

"No," said Tristan. "She went with you to find the wizards."

Marsaili shook her head slowly and looked at the ground. "The Princess went after Falkor the day we all left."

"What?" said Tristan.

"Haven't they come back?" said Niamh.

Tristan shook his head. The sisters glanced at each other, their faces turning pale, lines creasing around their eyes. Fear rose in Tristan's throat. In all the time he had known them Marsaili and Niamh had never been fazed by anything. At least they never let it show.

"How did the Princess even manage to go after Falkor?" said Tristan.

The sisters glanced at each other again. "We helped her," said Niamh eventually.

"What were you thinking?" said Tristan, his eyes growing wide.

"She's the Princess," said Marsaili defiantly. "We don't control her actions, we just keep her safe."

"And how do you do that when you don't even know where she is?"

"She's more capable than you know," said Niamh.

"We might not know where she is," said Marsaili. "But neither does our enemy. That makes her safe."

Tristan raised his eyebrows, unconvinced. "You do realise that if Torelia is lost then we will have to flee, Princess or not. And if she comes back to find the Brathadair occupying Torelia what will happen to her then?"

Marsaili fell silent.

"Maybe it won't come to that, now that we have wizards again," said Niamh.

But just then, as if mocking them, the warning horns sounded again. Tristan whipped his head around to see the Brathadair, regrouped and re-emerging from the trees.

Odmund's voice cut through the air and the Torelian lines reformed, blocking the way across the river. Marsaili and Niamh pushed their way to the front while the wizards, Freya and Anya, took up positions on the island, one on each side of the bridge. The Brathadair charged, holding their shields up ahead of them, swords and spears poking through the gaps. A volley of Torelian arrows clattered harmlessly off them. Runes sparked and a few fell, but the army kept moving. The Torelians raised their shields. There was a crunch as the two sides met.

The battle began again, both sides vying for the small strip of bridge. The fighting continued late into the afternoon. With the two wizard's help they managed to keep the Brathadair at bay, but the Torelians were tiring and their hold on the bridge was slipping. Though they frequently swapped places, so that no man was continuously at the front line, more and more soldiers retreated with small injuries—signs of carelessness. Tristan too had taken his turn in the melee and received a slash across the arm that cut through his leather wrist guard. It stung fiercely as Rook wrapped a rough bandage around it.

Tristan prepared himself to rejoin the fray, but before he could move an arrow pierced the ground at his feet. His head jerked up and he saw, with dismay, enemy reinforcements arriving on the far shore. Another arrow dropped and he jumped back. To his left someone screamed. Then another cry as the hail of arrows increased. At the same time the Brathadair on the bridge renewed their efforts, hacking into the defenders with a frenzied energy. Tristan cast about wildly.

"Freya," he called. "Is there nothing we can do?"

The wizard, sword drawn, knocked down her opponent with a kick before answering. "I cannot draw the runes fast enough to protect us all and certainly not while fighting."

An Eagle Rider could do it, thought Tristan. But the Eagle Riders were not here.

Bradan grabbed Tristan's arm. "We're being slaughtered out here." They ducked as more arrows came flying down. "We have to pull back."

Tristan cast about wildly for Odmund and saw the swordmaster on the far side of the island felling the Brathadair with each swing.

"Odmund," Tristan yelled.

The swordmaster finished off the man he had been fighting and looked about. More arrows fell, Torelians and Brathadair alike crying out as they were hit. Soldiers dragged their injured comrades from the battleground, only to be hit themselves by the next volley. Odmund quickly stepped back, but even he was hit by an arrow in the arm. Without a sound he broke off the shaft, leaving only a short spiked stump, and swapped his sword to his other hand.

"Fall back," Odmund yelled. "Fall back to the trees."

The cry was carried through the ranks and the Torelians began slowly to give ground, carrying the wounded with them as they left the island and the bridge to Brathadair control. Tristan sped across the bridge, turning to fight as soon as his feet touched the shore. The Brathadair pursued them relentlessly, cutting down many as they ran. Tristan blocked and ducked and thrust his sword, his every sense fizzing. Desperation fuelled him. He could not let the Brathadair any further. He had to make time for Branwyn to escape the caves.

"Wizards, the bridge," came Odmund's clear voice.

Flashes of light sped from Freya and Anya's hands, bursting into flame and thunder as they hit the bridge. Stone cracked and began tumbling into the rushing waters below. Some of the Brathadair jumped the gap to the shore. More runes flew and this time a whole chunk of the bridge dropped into the water. Brathadair fell with it into the river only to be washed away. The rest of the bridge held for a few minutes more before it began to crumble under the weight of men. At last it toppled and the gap between the island and the riverbank became too great to jump.

Tristan's throat felt thick. How long had those stones spanned the river? He was glad Allan was not here to see its end.

Fighting on the shore continued until the last of the Brathadair were taken down. Arrows still sailed over the river towards them, but most fell short, doing little damage.

A brief cheer ran through the Torelian troops, though it was as much for relief as for victory. Tristan sighed. It was only half a victory. It would not take long for the Brathadair to find another way across the river. But just as he thought they might have some respite, a messenger came running through the trees. The woman stopped, catching her breath as the soldiers gathered around her. Tristan took his place next to Odmund and saw that Bradan and Dorcas were both among those who had survived the bridge. For a second he panicked, but then Rook turned his face towards the messenger too.

She spoke. "A second army has arrived."

"What?" Gasps sounded all around. Someone stifled a cry. Another dropped to their knees. Tristan licked his lips, his mouth suddenly dry.

"They're climbing down the cliffs. They're almost in the caves."

"Who's still in the caves?" said Odmund.

"Everyone," said the messenger.

Tristan's heart turned ice cold. Branwyn.

He ran from the gathering, following the river downstream and past the thunder of the waterfall. He stopped and looked down to the gorge. Ropes dropped down the far cliff, black shapes pouring down. Many more awaited at the top. Tristan clenched his fists and grimaced. He had no doubt that Torelia was lost, but he could not give up. Not until Branwyn and the others were safely out of the caves.

28. Mountain and Sky

Aiden hung from the chains that held him, his strength draining away. The last shuffling footsteps of the Eagle Riders faded. The remaining soldier at the door twirled Aiden's sword and smirked. Aiden dropped his head. They had failed. He had failed. He could barely move— he could not even bring a rune to mind without it burning the back of his eyes. The Eagle Riders were gone, defeated, and Erin, Serineth, the idiot girl, had handed herself straight to the enemy. Aiden screwed up his eyes. If only he had known, he could have stopped her. If only she had trusted him.

A tiny thud broke the silence. Aiden opened his eyes and saw the guard slumped on the floor. A figure stepped over—a figure with a brown coat, sandy hair, and cunning grey eyes.

"Falkor." The word escaped his mouth in a whisper.

"I see you did not heed my advice," came the cold reply.

Aiden strained forward. "Falkor you have to be quick. Dageny has Erin. He's making the Eagle Riders do some magic. I don't know what."

"Dageny," Falkor whispered in horror, his face contorting. Aiden had never seen such emotion on the wizard's face. "How did he get Erin?"

"She followed me up the mountain," said Aiden.

"And you let her come," said Falkor, his voice hardening.

"She came of her own doing," Aiden said. "You can't blame me for not stopping her when no one told me who she was."

Falkor's eyes narrowed. "And yet still Dageny has her." He turned away from Aiden.

"There was nothing I could have done," Aiden whispered.

"Except not bring her," said Falkor sharply. "You may not have known who she was, but you did know I had forbidden her from coming. How can I trust you when you never do as you're told? How do I know you're not Brathadair?"

Aiden snorted a laugh. "If I was Brathadair I wouldn't be chained to the wall! If I was Brathadair I wouldn't have told you about Hakon's plan in the first place! Maybe if you had trusted me more we wouldn't be in this mess now."

Falkor turned slowly and Aiden flinched, expecting Suil, the prophet to rip the truth from him. But Falkor stayed his hand, pressing his lips together.

Aiden sighed, then his brows creased together. "How did Dageny even recognise her? I didn't and I've lived in Teraan City my whole life."

Falkor's cold eyes surveyed him. "Dageny once trained as a wizard in the Palace. But he did not make the cut."

Aiden's mouth dropped open. "Then you've known about him all this time."

"No," said Falkor, glaring at him. "Dageny died years ago." He clenched his fists. "Or so I thought."

"Then what's going on here?" said Aiden, desperately. "Are we facing Dageny or Sorcier?"

Falkor rubbed his forehead. "Both… I think."

"What!" said Aiden.

"If Dageny is here, if he has all the Eagle Riders and the means to make them do what he wants, then there's only one thing he's trying to do." Falkor paused. "He's going to make them use the feather key to release Sorcier."

Aiden gulped. "Will it work?"

Falkor looked at the ground and sighed. "We have to assume it will."

Aiden felt cold inside. "Can you stop him?"

Falkor fixed his grey eyes upon Aiden. "Not alone."

"Are you going to let me out then?" said Aiden.

Falkor stared at him. He turned to the door. Aiden's mouth dropped open. The wizard was going to leave him. Then Falkor stooped and ripped something from the belt of the fallen soldier. He returned and slotted the key in the lock of Aiden's chains. A breath escaped Aiden's lips.

Falkor raised an eyebrow. "I may not trust you, but that doesn't make us enemies."

The chains clanked to the floor and Aiden rubbed his wrists. Lightness returned to his body in a wave that made him feel like he was floating. He closed his eyes. The images of the runes came readily to mind.

"What magic was that?" Aiden asked. "It made the runes impossible."

A brief frown crossed Falkor's face. "I don't know. Whatever it is, it veils this whole place. It causes havoc with the runes. You should be careful—only use them in dire need."

Aiden nodded. It explained the emptiness, the sinister presence, the shadow only seen in the corner of the eye.

"Come on," said Falkor. "No time to lose."

Aiden snatched up his sword from the fallen guard and followed Falkor into the corridor beyond. It led them further on, further into the castle, through echoing halls and dark passages. It was so empty and silent that Aiden could almost believe that they had never found the Eagle Riders. It was like the fortress itself wanted them to forget why they had come.

They continued, at last reaching the top of a staircase that petered away into darkness. Falkor led the way, descending, down and down, stair after stair, until the the blackness around became so deep that Aiden realised they were entering into the mountain itself. Hewn stone walls hemmed them in, ancient torches still in their brackets, waiting to be lit, and smooth steps going ever down.

Abruptly they stopped. The steps levelled out and the tunnel widened for a few paces before the arched opening of a cave. Falkor held up a hand. Metal scraped over stone. An Eagle let out a heart-rending cry. Both Falkor and Aiden jumped forward.

Beyond the arched entrance lay a great stone hall, its walls carved from the heart of the mountain. Stalactites and stalagmites, some joined into pillars, formed a circle around the centre of the cave, a faint unnatural light emanating from within. Interspersed between these ragged stone columns were the Eagles, wings pinned to their sides by heavy chains. Kael tried to beat his wings, tossing his head from side to side as a black clad soldier looped his chains over one of the stalagmites. His feathers were in disarray and in places clumps appeared to be missing entirely.

Within the pillars the Riders formed a circle, each one on their knees with a Brathadair Guard hovering over them. Dageny stood in their midst, Gort, the binder, in one hand still hooked around Erin's neck. He handed something to Arthur. It looked like a feather, but it glinted of metal and runelight.

Arthur took the feather and touched it to Kael's beak. Then he passed it on to Leif. But in the passing something strange happened. A light flashed, making Aiden's eyes glance away. When he next looked, both Arthur and Leif held identical feathers. Leif touched the feather to Jormandar's beak and then passed it on, the same thing happening until each Rider held a metal feather in their hands.

The room fell silent. The Eagles shifted on their feet and Aiden imagined they would have been flexing their wings had the chains not held them down. Across the circle the Riders glanced at one another.

"Get on with it," said Dageny, squeezing Erin so that a stifled cry escaped her lips.

Halvard began, taking his feather and pushing it point downwards straight into the rock at his feet. The pillar at his back, next to his Eagle Kanook, began to shine with hundreds of runes. One by one they lit up and then popped out of existence. Across the circle Svana took her feather and began to push it into another space in the rock. On the pillar behind her more runes flashed and then faded. Goosebumps rose on Aiden's arms. He was both awed by the power of the moment and afraid of what was to come.

Without a word Falkor stepped forward into the light of the cave, leaving Aiden alone in the shadows of the entrance. One of Dageny's black clad soldiers charged at him, a jagged short sword in his hand. Falkor dived to the side as Peith, the thunderbolt, came flying towards him. Then blades clashed in a flashing of steel. Falkor twisted his sword and thrust Nuin, the spear, into the man's chest. He slumped to the ground as another soldier leapt forward, but Falkor spun and sliced him across the stomach. The wizard took the last few steps to the inner circle of pillars, the Eagles making way for him to pass.

A scream rent the air.

Dageny pressed a knife to Erin's neck and already blood slowly dripped down onto her clothes. On the ground Arthur crouched poised, the last metal feather in his hand. There was no good outcome. It was Erin's life against whatever evil the Brathadair hoped to unleash. Arthur made his decision and pushed down on his feather. The rock swallowed it. The last of the runes on the pillar began to light up and then fade into black.

"Dageny," said Falkor, his voice hard and cold.

The dark wizard turned slowly, green eyes glinting. "You're too late Falkor," he said. "The prison can't be closed again."

"Sorcier's dead," said Falkor.

Dageny smiled. "You thought me dead all these years and yet here I am."

"Let her go," said Falkor, nodding to Erin without taking his eyes from the other wizard.

Dageny laughed. "The show's not over yet."

The last rune popped out of existence. Aiden froze. Time seemed to slow. Silence stretched across the room. Everyone waited and watched the place where the last feather had disappeared into the rock.

Nothing happened.

Then a great crack resounded through the cave. A fissure appeared in the centre of the stone floor, spidering out to the cracks where the feathers had disappeared. A blast of air whipped through the room, knocking Aiden back against the wall and sending all those in the circle staggering. Dageny tumbled backwards, Erin flying from his grasp, the golden bands of Gort, the binder, fading from around her neck. She drew in a deep gasping breath.

Aiden scrambled forward. In the circle the Riders clambered to their feet, wrestling free from the soldiers that had once stood over them. The Eagles flexed their wings, snapping and shaking free of their chains. Whatever magic had held them had been broken by the opening of the tomb.

Snatching up the scattered weapons dropped by the men Falkor had killed, Aiden rushed to the inner circle. An odd tingle passed through his body as he ran between the pillars, but he shook it off. Two Eagles flanked him, snapping beaks at a Brathadair soldier who tried to slice him. Mathias and Halvard quickly took the weapons from Aiden and finished off the last of the Brathadair guards who had stood over them in the circle.

Aiden whirled around to see Erin on her hands and knees in

the middle of the circle, watching with a terrified expression as the cracks in the rock around her began to widen. Behind her Dageny rose to his feet and reached out a hand to grab her once more. Yet before he could a rune flashed and burnt against his skin. The dark wizard drew back and lifted his head sharply with a black glare.

"Falkor," he spat.

Aiden took his chance and darted forward, grabbing Erin's arm and pulling her away from the widening crack in the rock. The Eagle Riders surrounded them and together they began moving out from the circle of pillars. Free now from the weight of the dark magic the Riders were changed. Colour flushed their cheeks and hands grasped swords with a steady strength. The Eagles followed them, hopping between the pillars, wings flapping, clacking beaks or swiping claws at any of the remaining soldiers who dared to come too close.

Within the circle of pillars light suddenly flashed. All heads turned to see Falkor and Dageny circling each other. Neither held any weapons, but their hands glowed like embers of fire. Falkor flicked his wrist sending a rune flying. Dageny ducked and almost instantly sent another flying back. Spheres of runelight glowed around the two wizards, sparks flying as runes hit and bounced away. A great shudder ran through the cavern and shards of stone fell from the roof, crashing and splintering across the floor.

"We need to go now," said Arthur.

"What about Falkor?" Aiden yelled.

Runes flashed again and sparks flew. The light blazed, silhouetting the pillars and between them the black shapes of Brathadair soldiers recovering and regaining their feet. From the doorway a new patrol arrived. Mathias, Sigurd, and Johann broke away to attack.

"Falkor can take care of himself," said Leif. "We need to get Serineth away."

"We'll fly her out," Mathias called, knocking back one of the soldiers with his foot and pointing to an exit at the far end of the cavern. Aiden could only assume it led out through the cliff somewhere.

"That's not going to work," said Kael, spreading out his wings.

Aiden swallowed at the devastation he saw. There were gaps in Kael's feathers so that he could see the skin and bone beneath.

"Dageny had our flight feathers cut," said Jormandar. "It will be a hard enough task flying ourselves out. We can't carry anyone."

"I think Petrana's wing may even be broken," said Anca, a tremor in her voice.

Arthur's eyes flicked between his Riders and Eagles and the oncoming forces. More Brathadair appeared from the far end of the cavern, blocking the Eagles' exit through the cliffs.

"We split up," said Arthur. "Mathias, take Anca, Johann, and Halvard. Go with the Eagles to the cliff gate. Make sure they get out then get yourselves out. The rest of you, with me. We get the Princess out. Now go."

Kael gave a great screech and spread his wings, propelling himself through the line of advancing soldiers. Sudden chaos erupted. Men were knocked in all directions as the Eagles moved as one. Some ducked and rolled aside, weapons flashing. A sharp aquiline cry ripped through the air. Mathias and the others ran after them, shooting runes back at the soldiers.

"Come on," said Arthur, pushing Aiden in the other direction, back towards the stairs. Aiden's feet moved almost of their own accord. At the doorway he paused once to look back. He heard Dageny's cry, sending men after them. There was a flash as one of Falkor's runes exploded in the dark wizard's face, stumbling him backwards. And then Aiden was on the stairs, legs burning as he forced himself upwards as fast as he could go.

A weight tugged on his hand and he realised that Erin still held on to him. Aiden's mind flashed back to the first time he had met her. They had been climbing up a stair of a different sort then, but they had still been running for their lives. That was before she had lied to him. Before she had put them all in danger. Aiden pulled his hand free of her grasp, not looking back to see the expression on her face.

At the top of the stairs they burst into the corridor, panting. Aiden's breath rasped in and out, burning the back of his throat. Shouts echoed along the passageway and Arthur pointed in the other direction, ushering everyone past before running himself. The castle flashed by, the echoing shouts growing louder, definitely behind them. Erin tripped and crashed to the ground. Sigurd picked her up again, barely lessening his stride.

They approached a junction and at last Aiden recognised where they were. He could almost see the faint trail of the Silver Eagle hanging in the air. The right hand passage was where he and Erin had entered that morning. It led back to the mountain path. The other way he did not know, but it must lead towards the main entrance. The shape of an idea began forming in his mind. He slowed and stopped even as the others followed Leif into the left hand passage.

Erin tugged his arm as she went by. "Come on."

Aiden shook his head. "They're going to catch us if we don't do something."

Erin stopped now too. "What are you saying?" she said, her blue eyes widening. Black bruises ringed her neck where Gort had strangled her.

"Aiden there's no time for this," Arthur called back along the passageway.

"I'm going the other way," said Aiden, stepping back. "At least some of soldiers will follow me. You'll have a better chance."

"No," said Maire, stopping. "We'll block this passage behind us.

They won't be able to follow." Even as she spoke she drew runes, priming them to bring the roof down after them.

"They know this place better than we do," said Aiden. "And right now they know exactly where we're headed. We've got to make them doubt that or else they'll just wait for us at the main gate."

"He's got a point," said Sigurd.

The Riders were silent, all now at a standstill. Finally Arthur nodded. "Alright, do it. But block the passage too."

Erin grabbed Aiden's hand. "Aiden, no. You'll get caught. The mountain path is blocked, there's no way out."

Aiden pulled his hand free of her grasp. How could she care about him now when all she had done was lie to him? "I'll find a way," said Aiden, a hard edge creeping into his voice.

"Serineth now," said Arthur.

Erin hesitated and for a moment Aiden thought she was going to refuse, but then Svana grabbed her arm and pulled her on. Aiden darted into the other passage, the walls rumbling as Maire brought the roof down behind them. There was no changing his mind now.

He ran a few steps along and then waited, forcing himself to stop even though every instinct in his body urged him to run. He could only draw the soldiers away if they saw him. The thunder of running feet grew louder. The first soldier appeared, shouting something unintelligible. Aiden ducked as Peith smashed into the wall above his head, leaving a crumbling hole in the stonework. Now it was time to run.

Aiden dashed along the corridor, air rushing in and out of his lungs. Ahead a door loomed and he burst out into the citadel, squinting and slowing in the sudden rush of sunlight. He cast about wildly for a way out. There—a twisting stair to the battlements where the fortress climbed higher onto the crag.

The door behind him banged open and an endless stream of

Dageny's soldiers seemed to pour out. Aiden ducked his head and ran, his feet pounding across the cold stone. He drew Fearn, the shield, flinching into himself as runes sparked and bounced off it. He took the stair, two steps at once, legs burning. Another courtyard and then another stair took him further onto the crag. The final battlements lay ahead, unmoving, sheer cliffs dropping away below them on either side. A cold wind swirled around him. He started for the stair at the far side, hoping it would lead him back down into the fortress, to a way out, but suddenly there was a man there, sword drawn. Aiden swivelled, but already more soldiers were emerging from behind him.

There was no way out.

Aiden ran on to the edge of the crag, to the stone parapet that bounded this final courtyard. He hardly slowed as he ran headlong into the solid stone. His fingers grazed along the rough rock. Within seconds the soldiers were behind him, forming a tight circle, swords pointed towards him. Aiden's hands shook as he turned to face them.

"Give up," said the leader. "You're trapped."

Aiden glared back defiantly, but his heart stuttered at the sight of another figure walking calmly and purposefully across the courtyard towards them. Fear spiked his chest and his defiance drained away. It was Dageny.

The dark wizard pushed through the ring of soldiers, his voice sharp as he shouted, "After the Riders."

The men backed away, turning and running back to the fortress. Aiden gulped. If Dageny was here then… then what had become of Falkor? Was he dead? Aiden's eyes snapped to the dark wizard advancing upon him.

"You have nowhere else to run," said Dageny, reaching the parapet and peering over the cliff. "That is unless you'd like to jump? But no. I think you love life too much." Dageny gave him an amused smile.

Aiden took a step back. From the corner of his eye he glanced over the parapet. The thought of falling from such a place set his head reeling. The runes came to mind and he wondered if he could take Dageny by surprise and get past him. Hands behind his back, he drew Peith, throwing it straight into the dark wizard's face. But Dageny raised his hand instantly and the rune clashed with something and bounced back at him. Aiden ducked but was knocked back against the parapet.

"I've heard a lot about you," said Dageny, slowing lowering his hand. "You're good, but you've much more to learn. I think Falkor has been slacking in his teaching."

"Falkor didn't teach me anything," said Aiden, trying to hide his fear behind brave words. "No one did. So you have no idea what I'm capable of."

"No?" said Dageny, raising one eyebrow. "Nevertheless, I'll give you the same choice I have given everyone." The wizard smiled. "Join me or die."

A gut-wrenching fear twisted Aiden's stomach. He had faced death before, but never like this. There had always been a way to fight, a way to live. This time to survive he would have to give up and betray all those that he loved.

"You could learn from me," said Dageny, his voice smooth, enticing. "You could learn from the dark master, Sorcier himself. You could become great. It's more than you'll ever be offered by the Eagle Riders or their King."

Thoughts raced through Aiden's mind. They had all lied to him. Erin had hidden who she was, but then so had everyone else. He had uncovered the plot, but no one had truly believed him. They had thrown him out. They did not trust him. What allegiance did he owe any of them?

But then he thought of his parents, captured by the Brathadair, and of Branwyn and Andor trusting him to do what was right. He would not betray them.

Just then something silver caught his eye. It was the Silver Eagle, hovering in the air above the courtyard. The Eagle spoke in a voice that was both everything and nothing. "Don't be afraid Aiden. There is a way to safety."

Aiden's eyes flicked nervously between wizard and Eagle. Dageny frowned at Aiden and glanced in the direction of the Eagle, but he did not seem to be able to see it. The wizard's frown deepened and he began to advance again, as if he knew something was afoot. Aiden shifted nervously but kept his attention focused on the Silver Eagle.

"Follow me," said the Eagle. Then it flew over Aiden's head and out beyond the cliff.

Aiden kept his eyes fixed on the silvery bird and before he realised what he was doing, he scrambled up onto the stony parapet and teetered on the edge.

Dageny's eyes flashed angrily at that small movement of defiance. "I see you have chosen death," he said.

In that moment Aiden's fear almost overcame him. He looked down to the valley floor, so distant and small. Then he forced his eyes back to the silver outline of the Eagle.

"Follow me Aiden," said the Eagle. "Don't be afraid. I offer you life."

"It makes no difference to me whether you die by my hand or by the fall," said Dageny. "Either way I win."

"Maybe not," said Aiden. A smile crept across his face and though his fears still swirled around him, a courage more than just his own batted them away. His toes flexed against the solid stone beneath his feet, his heartbeat echoing in his ears. A cool wind brushed his cheek. Ahead the Silver Eagle floated, waiting for him, and he felt comfort in its presence. Dageny suddenly darted forward, arms reaching to grab Aiden, but he was too late.

Aiden jumped.

The wind rushed through him and stole his breath away. He spread his arms wide, feeling more alive than he ever had before. And then in a sickening moment he realised he had lost sight of the Silver Eagle and was free-falling to his death.

29. Into the Forest

Branwyn heard the rumble even as she sat in the great cavern behind the waterfall. The paths to the north were now sealed. She glanced nervously to the other side, imagining Brathadair racing down towards them, trapping them in a tomb of stone and water. Her muscles grew tighter and tighter, but she took in a breath and let it out slowly. She was safe. Tristan would not let them get to her. Branwyn closed her eyes, remembering the tight hug he had given her that morning, the quick kiss and the whispered words, *I won't let any harm come to you...*

"Branwyn," Andor shook her arm.

Branwyn opened her eyes. Andor pointed to the north tunnel where a trickle of people emerged into the cavern. They came in twos or threes, many leaning heavily on their companions. Wounded from the battle. She saw the blood now, could almost taste its metallic scent in the air. Branwyn gulped. It was really happening. There really was a battle raging just outside.

Andor jumped to his feet and ran over towards the people. Branwyn frowned after him and then felt her feet start to move of their own accord. It could not be, she thought. But it was. Rook walked towards them, Signy draped over his arms.

"What happened?" said Branwyn as she reached him. Her eyes widened, her mouth dropped open in disbelief. It could not be Signy she looked at. Signy was always so full of life.

"Stab wound I think," said Rook. "Before she got knocked out."

Branwyn glanced from the matted blood in Signy's hair to Rook's face. His words were even, matter-of-fact, but his face could not disguise his worry.

"Over here," said Branwyn, leading him to where she had seen the healer Anniina setting up earlier. There were rows of blankets set out over the stone floor, some already occupied by men and women with bandaged limbs or heads. At the sight of Signy, Anniina dropped the herbs she was mixing at a nearby table and rushed over.

"Lay her here," she said.

Rook gently lowered Signy to the ground.

"Bring me water and rags," Anniina said to Branwyn.

Branwyn froze, so surprised to be asked anything. Where would she even find those things?

"By the table," said Anniina sharply, flicking her grey hair over her shoulder before leaning down to sweep Signy's bloodied hair from her face. "Quick girl."

Branwyn darted over and found wooden buckets already filled with water. On the table sat a pile of clean rags. She grabbed a few and hurried back to the healer with the bucket in tow, splashing her ankles as she walked. Anniina barely acknowledged her other than to take the rags from her hand. Branwyn watched as she began by washing Signy's face, drawing runes as she went. A few moments later Signy coughed and her eyes flickered.

"Good, good," the healer muttered to herself. "Now bring me bandages and herbs," she said, her voice turning sharp again. Branwyn was on her way within seconds, grabbing what she needed from the table and hurrying back. This time when she returned, Anniina pulled her down onto her knees next to her. "Let's see your bandaging skills then."

"Me?" said Branwyn, unconsciously pulling back.

"This is only the beginning," said the healer. "If we want to save all these people then I'm going to need help."

Branwyn's mouth opened and closed. She had thought she would spend the entirety of the battle just waiting and listening but maybe... maybe there was something *she* could do. A way she could be helpful. "Alright," she said, rolling up her sleeves. "Show me what to do."

Anniina gently lifted Signy's head and directed Branwyn on how to bandage it. It was a long gash above her eye and already it was starting to bleed again. Anniina crushed up some of the herbs and pressed them into the wound before Branwyn covered it with the cloth. They shifted onto Signy's other wounds. Once they peeled away layers of clothing it was clear that Signy had not been stabbed but rather sliced across her midriff. It was a deep and nasty cut and even in her unconscious state Signy's body jerked as they cleaned and bandaged it.

Anniina turned to Rook. "It's the best I can do for now."

Rook nodded, his eyes grim. "Thank you. Now I must get back to the battle."

Branwyn caught his arm. "Tristan?" she said.

Rook gave her a small smile. "I saw him not long ago. He's fine."

The relief brought a smile to her face and for a moment she felt the knot in her stomach loosening.

"Branwyn," said Rook, his voice turning more serious. "There is only one way out of here now. If any Brathadair come down the cliff or if you hear that the bridge is lost then you need to get yourselves out. Go up to the cabins or hide in the woods. Just don't let yourselves get trapped down here."

Branwyn licked her lips, her mouth suddenly dry. She nodded and felt her fear returning.

"Girl," came the sharp voice. "More water."

Branwyn turned instinctively at the command, grabbing the

bucket of water and rushing after the healer. She glanced over her shoulder, but Rook was already gone. Even before being asked she went back to the table for more bandages. Then knelt with Anniina beside the next casualty.

"I can help too," said Andor, kneeling across from them.

"Carry the water then boy," said the healer, not even glancing up from her patient.

Andor frowned. "I mean I can draw runes."

This brought up the healer's head. "Show me Beith."

Andor flexed his fingers and drew the rune. It shone bright and unwavering in his hand. Branwyn smiled for him. It was the best she had seen him do yet.

"Now put it here," said Anniina, pointing to a smaller cut on the wounded soldier in front of them.

Andor cast the rune, his face poised with concentration. The rune soaked into the wound and although Branwyn saw no obvious change, the healer's eyebrows lifted. "Good," she said, her voice lilting with pleasant surprise. "Now draw with me."

Together they cleaned and dressed the man's wounds, Anniina and Andor casting the runes while Branwyn assisted with the herbs and bandages. As soon as they finished Anniina led them to the next patient. She worked her way systematically through the casualties, always going first to those with the most severe injuries. Branwyn and Andor assisted her, quickly learning what to do as they repeated it over and over again. The more they worked the more Anniina trusted them and soon they were left to treat the less serious patients without her watchful eye.

The injured came in waves as they were brought off the battlefield. Branwyn scurried around doing what she could for them. She barely had a chance to stop or think or breathe. Moments of calm came sporadically, but these moments only gave a chance to go around again and tighten up a bandage, add another rune, or offer a drink of water.

Branwyn saw more blood that afternoon than she had in her entire life. The smell of it clung to her hands and when she looked down at herself there were spots of red splattered over her clothes. Once, not so long ago, that would have bothered her. She wondered briefly what had happened to the girl she had once been. Then Anniina called her back to the present.

A young soldier was brought to them, blood dripping down his arm, his eyes rolling wildly in his head. Branwyn ran over with the water. She clapped a hand over her mouth, almost dropping the bucket. Anniina lifted the man's arm and his hand hung down at the most unnatural angle. Anniina turned to Branwyn, fixing her with her clear gaze. "Fetch the knife and hold it in the fire for at least a minute before you come back."

Branwyn nodded, her mind completely detached from her body as she walked over to the table and picked up the knife. She tried not to think about what it was for as she held the blade over the flames of the fire. But no matter how much she tried, she could not wipe the image of him from her mind. With a horrible lurch she realised that in her head the soldier's face had become Tristan's. She snatched up the knife and ran back. A sigh escaped her lips when she saw that it was not Tristan, but that did not relieve her. Tristan could just as easily be injured, except maybe he was still up there with no one to carry him down to the healer.

Branwyn looked away as Anniina did what needed to be done. The young man did not cry out and when she looked back she saw Andor holding runes steady above the stump of his arm. Sudden guilt pinched her chest for her lack of courage. Andor was the one who should be scared, not her. She pulled herself back together and moved with Anniina and Andor around the rest of the wounded.

Gradually the wave of casualties lessened and Branwyn found a moment of quiet. She regretted it, almost, for it brought back all the things that the busyness had kept away. Her fingers were raw from the constant wet then dry, her feet ached from standing on them so long, the blood that caked her was not her own, and the rumble in her belly reminded her she had not eaten since first thing that morning. And with all that came the fear and the worry. What was happening up there? Where were Tristan and Rook? Were they still alive?

Branwyn wandered back to where the wounded lay and crouched next to a soldier who had recently had an arrow pulled from his leg. He looked at her gruffly, but she swallowed and spoke anyway.

"What was happening up there?"

The soldier glared at her, but when she did not move his expression softened. "It's not pretty," he said.

"Are we winning?" said Branwyn.

The soldier shrugged. "Hard to say. The main fight was at the bridge when I left. The Princess's guards, Marsaili and Niamh, have returned though with two wizards."

"There's a chance then?" said Branwyn, feeling suddenly hopeful.

The soldier gave a laugh, which quickly became a cough. Branwyn fetched him some water. "Don't get your hopes up," he said, handing her back the cup. "They have bought us time and that is all."

Branwyn stood and walked away, holding tightly to the cup to hide her trembling hands. She had not dared to ask about Tristan or Rook for fear of what she might hear. Now she wished she knew.

A rumble shook the cavern and Branwyn stumbled on her feet. Dead silence filled the space and all eyes looked upwards and out. A runner pounded down the tunnel from the south.

"Where's Allan?" he called, his words echoing off the stone.

"Allan's outside," someone said.

But at that same moment Allan strode into the cavern from

through the waterfall, a group of soldiers around him. Allan gave a few sharp gestures and the soldiers broke away rapidly, one running to the barricaded tunnels to the north, another further into the caves to the kitchens, and the last sprinting through the cavern and up the southern tunnel. The runner hastened to Allan's side and they spoke quietly for a minute. Allan's face grew grim.

Branwyn rushed over to Anniina and Andor. "What's happening?" she whispered, with a growing dread.

Anniina shook her head and Andor frowned. Branwyn glanced about wildly.

"I think that rumble came from the bridge," said Andor quietly.

Rook's words came back to her. *There's only one way out now… Don't let yourselves get trapped.*

A call to attention rang around the cavern. The Torelian Guard assembled by the waterfall. The villagers from Faraig and Darrogie began to spill through from the other caves until the great cavern was filled with people. Allan climbed onto a high step.

"The bridge has been destroyed," he said, his voice stilted. "As we speak Brathadair are climbing down the cliffs."

A murmur ran around the cave.

A grimace spasmed across Allan's face. "It has been decided to abandon Torelia. We evacuate now to the southern forest."

The cave erupted into noise. People swarmed towards the southern tunnel. Soldiers shouted, ordering them into a line.

"Help me get the wounded to their feet," said Anniina.

Branwyn and Andor rushed to where Signy lay. Together they took an arm each and lifted her onto their shoulders. Signy moaned and winced. "What?" she croaked, eyes flickering open.

"Signy, it's Branwyn," said Branwyn, beginning to drag her forwards. "The Brathadair are almost upon us. We need to move you out of here."

Signy's eyes blinked fully open and she made some effort to

plant her feet more firmly on the ground. "Help the others," she said. "I can walk myself."

Branwyn frowned, unsure, but she loosened her grip on Signy's waist. The Feather Guard took a few steps before collapsing onto her knees.

"Don't be silly," said Andor, grabbing her arm again and lifting her partly off the ground. Branwyn rushed to help him.

"No," said Signy. "Just give me a minute. Help the others first."

Reluctantly Branwyn nodded and took Andor by the arm, leading him to another soldier. They helped him to his feet and passed him his sword, then he managed to hobble over to the line of people exiting the cave. Others were not so able and they had to lift and half carry them to the arms of villagers who pulled them on into the tunnel. They ran back and forth many times, but slowly the cave began to empty. Only the soldiers remained, barring the way through the waterfall. No sound came from through the waters, but occasional flashes of movement told Branwyn that the battle was very close indeed. She pushed the thought from her mind, turning back to those who needed her help.

At last there were only two of the wounded left. "Take Signy and get yourselves out," said Anniina, draping the arm of another soldier around her shoulders and heading up the tunnel ahead of them.

Together Branwyn and Andor half carried Signy towards the tunnel that led up to the southern forest. They hurried up as fast as they could, stumbling more than once when Signy lost her footing. The tunnel grew dark and Branwyn realised that no torches were lit. There was no time to stop though. A short distance behind she heard the clang of steel, which meant only one thing. The battle had reached the caves. How many of those brave men and women, who had stayed to hold off the enemy, would never make it up the tunnel to safety?

Branwyn pushed them on, sweat soaking through her back. They broke out of the tunnel into the fading evening light. A short stretch of cliff path lay before them. Branwyn slowed, the sudden drop at her side making her head spin. She glanced down at the churning waters of the river below. On the far side streaks of ropes dangled down the cliffs, men swarming down them like ants. She bit back a scream and pulled Signy further up the path.

At the top Branwyn halted. She looked around for Anniina, or anyone, but she could not tell where the others had gone. People moved about amidst the trees, but there was no sign of the guards who had led the evacuation. The air was filled with smoke, fire crackling along the branches of trees. What should she do now? Where should they go?

"To the cabins," Signy croaked, weakly lifting her hand.

Branwyn glanced at her pale face, hidden partly under bandages. If Signy could find the strength, thought Branwyn, then so could she.

They moved and it was just in time, for an arrow pierced the ground where they had been standing moments before. They dashed into the trees, Signy crying out as the sudden movement jarred her wounds. The woods seemed blacker than they ever had before, acrid smoke cutting their throats, the trees wisping and cracking like charcoal as they ran past.

They reached the clearing where the cabins of the Feather Guard stood and stopped. A tear welled in the corner of Branwyn's eye and dripped down her face. The cabins were destroyed. In places, blackened timbers still clung to the trees, but most had collapsed to lie scattered amidst the ashes of their campfire. Even the great oak that had held the cabin for so many years, had been burnt to its core by the fire.

At Branwyn's side Signy fell to her knees. The Feather Guard reached out and took a handful of ashes, letting them run through her fingers. Was there nothing the Brathadair would not destroy?

"We can't stay here," came Signy's voice.

Where then, thought Branwyn. There was nowhere else to go, except deeper into the forest.

Suddenly Branwyn heard a rustling in the trees. She looked up and at first saw no one. Then out of the half-light a figure emerged. He was dressed in the greens and browns of the forest and wore a ruff of silver fur around his shoulders. A graceful bow and quiver of arrows were slung over one shoulder and a curved knife hung from his belt. Branwyn would have thought him a woodsman if not for his pale, pale eyes. She glanced around, searching in vain for a weapon of any kind, but there was nothing.

A sharp cry came from above and the silhouette of an Eagle descended upon them. A flush of hope spread through Branwyn's entire body. The Eagle swooped down, landing next to the strange man. Then more people seemed to appear amongst the trees, all with the same pale eyes.

"I am Hotah Ahote, chief of the Ahote clan," said the first man with the silver fur.

"You're Fae," said Signy, grabbing Branwyn's arm and pulling herself back to her feet.

Hotah Ahote inclined his head. "We have heard your call for help."

Branwyn glanced from the Fae to the Eagle. The Eagles had done it. They had found the Fae and persuaded them to help. "You'll help us win the battle," Branwyn blurted out.

The chief gave a tiny shake of his head. "No. We are not here to fight. The Eagles have told us of your plight and we are willing to offer you sanctuary."

"The Brathadair are already in the caves," said Branwyn.

"Fear not young one," said the Eagle. "We will hold them off so you can escape."

Branwyn glanced back towards the river, torn. "And those at the bridge?"

"We will help them escape," Hotah Ahote repeated. "Now gather those you can from this forest and we will begin the journey away."

Branwyn's brow creased. Help had come and yet still it could not abate her fear. Where was Tristan? "Keep close," she whispered to Andor, the thought of loosing him too almost bringing tears to her eyes. They moved into the trees, calling out to those who had come up from the caves. They spread the word quickly and began to lead people back to the charred remains of the cabins.

Branwyn cast her eyes around, scrutinising every face in the hope that she would find Tristan. Yet she recognised no one. The first group began to leave, following one of the Fae into the forest. Signy, leaning heavily on the shoulder of another injured soldier, called back to her.

"Come with us Branwyn."

Branwyn bit the inside of her cheek and shook her head. "I can help here still." She would not leave until she knew he was safe.

She took a few steps in the opposite direction, back towards the canyon. Andor tugged on her arm. "Don't be a fool Bran. He can take care of himself."

Branwyn paused. Men and women from the battle were starting to join them. They barely stopped as they ran by, except to shout warnings and point them away from the river.

"What's happening?" she cried to no one in particular.

"The bridge is taken," one called.

"The caves are lost," another shouted.

"Run!" said a third.

Branwyn stood frozen. "Tristan!" she screamed. Please let him have escaped. Please let him not have gone down to the caves to find her. The thought of leaving him behind was almost too much to bear.

"Branwyn! We have to go!" Andor shouted. He pointed through the trees and Branwyn saw that it was no longer just Torelians running towards them.

She looked back at Andor and realised she had been a fool. She should have left long before. She grabbed Andor's hand and started running, following the Torelians and the Fae as they hurtled into the forest. If only she could have found him. But like Andor said, Tristan could take care of himself much better than she could look after herself.

Something caught the corner of her eye and she turned just in time to duck the sword flying at her head. Andor's hand slipped from hers. There was a thunk as the sword lodged into the tree behind her. She darted away but heard the splinter as the Brathadair soldier dislodged his blade and stepped after her. She tried to scream, but nothing came out. What a fool she had been.

Branwyn ran, her only thought now to escape. The man kept coming, his long strides easily covering the distance between them. Branwyn tripped and thumped into the ground, her breath shooting from her lungs. She rolled over, just as the sword hit the ground beside her. The man raised his arm to swing again. She scrambled to her feet even as her mind told her it would not be enough. Her back tensed, ready for the inevitable blow.

There was a crack and a golden light flashed in the corners of her eyes. She turned and staggered backwards in time to see the fading glow of runes. Aiden, she thought, but it was Andor who stepped out in a fury of flashing sword and battered back the Brathadair soldier before he could attack her again.

"Andor," she cried, as another soldier jumped out from between the trees. Andor blocked him, but he was not quick enough. A patch of red blossomed through his ripped sleeve and his sword dropped to the ground. Branwyn reached out and grabbed it, bringing it up before the soldier could attack again. She parried one jarring blow and then another and then the sword was knocked from her hand. She cowered. This was it.

But the killing strike never came.

Branwyn opened her eyes. A new figure had appeared, slicing down the Brathadair soldiers. Her heart jumped, but she did not dare think it. Then he turned and she saw his face. She sighed with relief.

Tristan rushed to her side, pulling her to her feet in one strong movement. "Are you ok?" he said.

Branwyn flung her arms around him and found that she could not hold back her tears any longer. Tristan stroked one hand through her hair, gently prising her arms away.

"We have to go," he said, tilting her head so that she had to look him in the eye.

Branwyn sniffed and nodded, wiping the tears from her eyes. It was going to be ok. Tristan pulled Andor to his feet and then took her hand, leading her away from the battle and deeper into the forest. It was as if courage flowed from him into her. Her breathing began to settle and her legs found their strength. She gripped his hand more tightly and did not look back. Torelia was lost and their only hope now was to follow the Fae deep into the forest.

30. Wings

The wind whipped at Aiden's face as the jagged grey of the mountains rushed by. He flailed hopelessly through the air, the panic overwhelming him. What had he done? He was going to die. He screwed up his eyes and time seemed to flow endlessly around him. Why had he listened to that ghostly bird? How did he even know it had been real? He had dreamed of it often enough before—maybe it was all just a figment of his own imagination.

His thoughts turned to Andor and to Branwyn. He had promised them he would come back. The thought of them waiting for a return that would never happen sent a spike of pain through his heart. Who would help them rescue his parents and aunt and uncle? It was his fault they were caught in the first place. He should never have gone to work in the Palace. He should never have let himself be swayed by dreams of adventure and Eagle Riders. Those dreams had cost him all he had. If only he could speak to his family one last time. Just to say he was sorry.

Someone screamed and for a moment Aiden thought he had lost control of his voice. Then the scream came again, swirling around him on the wind. Aiden's eyes snapped open. The scream was not his. He looked down and saw the treetops racing to meet him. Something flitted past the corner of his vision. The Silver Eagle come to offer one last piece of useless advice. He turned his head, but the shape was not silver. It was golden and it was solid.

452

Iolair.

Aiden's body collided with her soft feathers and he buried his face into them. The wind died away as Iolair swept back up into the air. He caught sight of the ground, almost close enough to touch. The tip of Iolair's wing brushed the branches of a tree. A jagged rock face raced towards them. Iolair's muscles bunched and a few wingbeats later they were up and away, the ground dwindling below.

Aiden's breath came in great heaving gulps and he lay there, gripping tightly to the feathers, moving with the strong rise and fall of Iolair's wings underneath him. He laughed out loud, a great rolling laugh that brought tears to his eyes. He buried his face into Iolair's feathers again. He was not dead. The Silver Eagle truly had led him to safety. Iolair had saved him.

The air around Aiden grew colder and he lifted his head, the wind whipping through him. Iolair's wingbeats slowed and they soared now, high above the mountains, the fortress of Cairn Ban tiny below. A smile twitched at the corners of his mouth and he sat back, gazing up at the endless blue that surrounded him.

"Hold on," Iolair cried, beating her wings so that they sped higher into the sky.

Aiden leaned in and grabbed the place where her wings met her back. Iolair flew high until the air grew thin and the wind cut at Aiden from all sides, stealing the breath from his mouth. He looked down and saw that the world had become indistinct. The mountain peaks were just grey smudges below. Aiden wished he could stay up there forever.

Suddenly Iolair tucked her wings to her sides and they began plummeting again towards the earth. A cry of surprise tore from Aiden's lips and he clutched desperately at her feathers.

"You could have warned me," Aiden shouted.

"That would have been no fun," said Iolair, clacking her beak in what he assumed was laughter. Then she tucked her wings closer to her sides and they began hurtling even faster.

Adrenaline shot through his body and Aiden found himself laughing too. His joy at being alive outweighed any fear. He flattened himself to Iolair's back, gripping her feathers until his knuckles went white. The wind raced over them and the mountains rose up to meet them, growing bigger and closer every second. They dipped below the peaks and the rocks flew by so quickly all he could see was a grey blur. He let loose a joyous sound. Then as suddenly as she had dropped Iolair spread her wings and they were gliding through the air above the forest.

"How do you like to fly?" said Iolair, tilting her head back so she could see him.

Aiden's eyes streamed from the wind. He leaned down closer to Iolair's head. "I can't feel my fingers or my nose," he said, smiling. "But this must be what freedom feels like."

Iolair blinked at him. "Maybe I was wrong. Maybe it is the same for both of us."

Aiden took a deep breath and looked back up into the sky. He caught a glimpse of silver, and there, flying just above them, was the Silver Eagle. Aiden smiled and slowly nodded his head. "Thank you," he whispered.

The Silver Eagle bent its wings and flew around them in a wide circle, leaving a shimmering trail behind. Who are you, thought Aiden. The Silver Eagle circled back. *Who are you?* it seemed to say.

Aiden smiled and shook his head. Don't tell me then, he thought.

The Silver Eagle circled once more and then angled away, flying further into the mountains. Aiden watched as it went, silver fading into the clouds. The wind blew back to him and on its breath he thought he heard two words.

Eagle Rider.

Acknowledgements

The inspiration for this book came from a verse in the Bible in Isaiah 40 v 31: *"But those who trust in the LORD will find new strength. They will soar high on wings like eagles. They will run and not grow weary. They will walk and not faint."* It has taken over 8 years from the very first draft of "Eagle Rider" to the completed "Eagle's Guard". There have been many moments over those years when I have had to trust in the Lord, but each time He has given me new strength. Without God this book would never have been finished—so thank you God!

Thank you to my family for the continual encouragement over the years. Thank you Mum and Dad for seeing me through the highs and lows, for always supporting me, even when following the dream was not the most logical decision, and for never doubting that I could do it!

Thank you Iain for being the best illustrator and advisor I could ever have wished for and for the amazing art that has helped this book come alive. Thank you for designing the runes, thinking up the title, and for all those hours talking through plot points until we got them just right. Eagle's Guard is as much your achievement as it is mine!

Thank you Steve for that out of the blue email you sent me one day, asking if I wanted to publish my book. I will forever be grateful for this opportunity and I hope it is the start of many books to come. Thank you for showing such enthusiasm for the world of the Eagle Riders and for putting so much time and effort into helping me make it the book it is today. I have learnt so much about writing during this process and I know the book has benefitted hugely from your input. I hope you have enjoyed the journey as much as I have!

Thank you to all the test readers, both friends and anonymous, who read an earlier draft of the book and gave me very useful feedback. Your comments helped to shape the final draft and many of your thoughts will continue with me into the next book.

Thank you to all those people who have encouraged me, advised me, listened to me and inspired me over the years. You may have no idea, but even the tiniest word of encouragement stays with me for a long time and helps me to keep writing and writing better.

Fiona, Michelle, Eilidh—you three were there right at the beginning and I'm so glad to finally be able to share this finished book with you. Thanks for sticking with me all those years!

Amy—thank you for all your encouragement over the years and for being so excited about the book. Knowing there was someone out there who wanted to read Eagle's Guard made me so much more excited to write it!

Geoff—thank you for reading and re-reading the book so eagerly and for all your creative feedback and technical advice. Your sheer enthusiasm has been such an encouragement!

Alex—thank you for that summer when you texted me almost every day to keep me motivated. Who knows where this book would have ended up without you!

Mairi—thank you for listening to my rants and sharing in my triumphs, and always believing I was capable of writing a good book!

Louise, Sophia, Tamara—thank you for taking me on holidays, and for not laughing at the idea I might one day publish a book!

My Scripture Union family—if you've been on camp with me then that's you—thank you so much for being the most supportive, creative, inspiring, talented, loving and encouraging team I could ever wish to be part of. You have all inspired me to keep trusting in God and to keep writing!

About the Author

Lindsey Stirling was born in Ayrshire and grew up in the Highlands of Scotland with her Mum and Dad, brother Iain, Skye the cat, and a dog called Spark. Her childhood was spent reading lots of books, climbing mountains, and exploring ruined castles. She studied Archaeology and Celtic Studies at the University of Aberdeen and graduated with an MSc degree in Archaeology of the North in 2014. She now works as an archaeologist in the Highlands and regularly makes use of archaeology, Scottish and Scandinavian folklore, and the Bible to inspire her writing. She still enjoys reading lots of books, climbing mountains, and exploring ruined castles, along with the new family dog Broc.

Be the first to hear about the next book in the Eagle Rider Saga by signing up to Lindsey's mailing list at www.lindseystirling.uk. You will also receive exclusive artwork and regular updates from Lindsey.